Books by Li

INVERTED FRONTIER

BOOK 3
NEEDLE

LINDA NAGATA

Mythic Island Press LLC
Kula, Hawaii

This is a work of fiction. All the characters and events portrayed in this
novel are fictitious or are used fictitiously.

Needle

Copyright © 2022 by Linda Nagata

First edition: July 2022

ISBN 978-1-937197-40-7

Cover art copyright © 2022 by Sarah Anne Langton

Mythic Island Press LLC
P.O. Box 1293
Kula, HI 96790-1293
MythicIslandPress.com

NEEDLE

REMEMBRANCE

"DO YOU RECOGNIZE it?" Lezuri asked.

Pinched between thumb and forefinger, he held up a slender needle for Urban to see. Ultra-thin and a full twelve centimeters long, the needle's silvery surface sliced light into sprays of rainbow glints.

"No," Urban answered, tense, wary, wondering where this was going.

"But you can guess."

"Is it like that needle you used to penetrate the hull of my ship?"

"Yes, except this one won't activate. It won't grow spontaneously. It doesn't have that capability, but everything else is there. Everything I know. All of it folded into a quantum-scale matrix."

Lezuri offered the needle to Urban. "Take it. It won't harm you. It's a gift, from me to you. All my knowledge yours—if you can work out how to access it. If you can do that, then I am wrong, and you are ready to go to Tanjiri."

CHAPTER ONE

LEZURI'S NEEDLE HAD remained a mystery for well over a century—a mystery that more than ever, Urban was anxious to solve.

He sat cross-legged at the low table in the front room of the cottage he shared with Clemantine. Holding the needle gently between thumb and forefinger, he turned it back and forth, admiring the way it refracted light.

The needle felt cold, yet when he passed it through a column of steam rising from the brewing teapot, no condensation appeared on it. Other than the slight friction coefficient of its surface—a structural convenience that allowed him to hold on to it—Lezuri's needle had never demonstrated any willingness to interact with the world.

Soft footsteps on the garden path outside the cottage served as an auditory alert—not that Urban needed one. With his expanded senses he had watched Vytet approach.

He reminded himself to look up as Vytet came in. It was important to make eye contact. A smile and a nod of welcome would assure his guest that he was present within this avatar and paying attention—which of course, in some way, he always was.

Vytet paused in the doorway, tall and willowy as ever, her gender lately indistinct. A delicate, feminine face, almost childish—but with the slim, hard, youthful body of a teenage boy. She wore only a long, patterned skirt, leaving her smooth hairless chest bare.

Vytet eyed the needle.

"That thing," she said, coming inside. "Do you still need it?"

His gaze returned to the needle's refracted rainbow glints. "Not so much the knowledge it contains. Still, it's a puzzle I'd like to solve."

"A puzzle Lezuri left for you . . . how to get it to open." She sat down across from him. "So strange that we never found the solution, somewhere in the memory of the silver."

"Sooth."

"Though of course Lezuri's ancient consciousness resided within the Rock, separate from the silver of Verilotus, and perhaps not within its memory."

Urban held the needle out to her. She took it cautiously. Stroked it. Turned it over and squinted at it while Urban poured the tea.

"I want you to work out how to open it," he told her.

A soft, skeptical chuckle as Vytet laid the needle in a padded case, lying open on the table.

"I *have* looked into it. You know that. And I've concluded this physics, like the physics of the Blade, is beyond us, that our minds are not designed to comprehend such things."

Urban sipped his tea, savoring an awareness of the silver within him. His connection to the silver of Verilotus and the vast living memory it contained had faded to nothing as *Dragon* departed that system—sixty-four years ago now. Yet some portion of silver remained tangled in his mind, tempting him, always, to immerse himself within its trove of memory—a personal memory of all he'd done and discovered since the silver had augmented his senses.

"Our minds are adaptable, Vytet."

"Yours more than mine."

She said this because she'd rejected a permanent entanglement with the silver. She'd lived with it during the years they'd spent at Verilotus, but in the end she'd discarded her planetary avatar, explaining, *I'm losing myself in obsession, endlessly chasing the chains of memory the silver contains.*

Vytet had not been alone in that decision. Among those who had continued the voyage, all but Urban had made that same choice.

Still, for all her life, Vytet had trained her mind to see the world in new ways, and in her mind—her brilliant, adaptive mind—she walked paths that Urban had never been able to follow, either as himself or as one of his highly specialized Apparatchiks.

He needed Vytet to reconsider the puzzle of the needle.

Setting his cup down with a soft tap, he said, "There must be another way to approach the problem, one we haven't considered yet. Lezuri created that needle here, aboard *Dragon*. If he can do it, *we* can do it. And if you crack this puzzle, my guess is we'll be one step closer to cracking the physics of the Blade."

This last argument did not win her interest as he'd hoped. Instead, she drew back, lips pursed in wariness, eyes narrowed, and her youthful brow drawn down in a worried scowl.

"Why would you want to bring that knowledge back into the world, Urban? A knowledge like that . . . it would let you tear apart worlds."

He did not allow his gaze to waver. Nothing of fear could be heard in his tone as he asked her in a gentle voice, "We need to know, don't we? We're bound for Tanjiri. An entity exists there— Lezuri believed it anyway—and the evidence suggests he's right."

Tanjiri had been a cordoned star of the Hallowed Vasties, cloaked in a swarm of orbiting objects so abundant they'd hidden the star's light. But the cordons had disintegrated all across the Hallowed Vasties. At Tanjiri, as everywhere, starlight shone through.

Nearly two millennia had passed since then—and much of Tanjiri's cordon was simply gone. The Apparatchik known as the Astronomer had mapped a wide, chaotic belt of scattered debris shepherded by rare, broken megastructures. Those remnant ruins constituted only a small fraction of the former cordon. Urban interpreted the missing mass as evidence of brutal warfare. And yet somehow a living world had survived through it all—through the creation of the cordon and its cataclysmic collapse.

Designated Tanjiri-2 in the Master Star Catalog, the planet continued to orbit as it always had, within the star's habitable zone. But in the millennia since the star catalog had been compiled, Tanjiri-2 had acquired a large moon, Tanjiri-2b, miraculously blue-green and alive like its partner, and rotating independently. If it had been a natural moon, formed in the planet's distant past, it would have long since become tidally locked, with one face always turned toward its primary. But Tanjiri-2b enjoyed its own complex cycle of day, night, and a twilight bathed in the varying blue-green glow of the planet.

Something had created that moon.

Thinking about it, a shiver prickled Urban's skin.

Did Vytet see it? *Maybe so.* Her scowled deepened. She eyed him with a mistrustful gaze.

"Are you saying you've changed your mind?" she asked. "That you won't go to Tanjiri unless you possess this knowledge?"

"That's not what I'm saying."

Even so, Lezuri's remembered warning haunted him: *You are not ready to encounter what exists there.*

Did that remain true? Despite all he'd learned at Verilotus?

He did not speak of such doubts aloud. Instead, he assured Vytet, "We *are* going, but I want your help with this, because I want to be as ready as we can be."

CHAPTER TWO

A DULL INTELLIGENCE, obeying a scheduled command, roused Clemantine from cold sleep. Her rekindled consciousness checked first
on the status of the ship, confirming the only significant change to
be *Dragon*'s position as the courser continued to slowly decelerate,
drawing ever closer to Tanjiri.

She dressed in a sleeveless lavender tunic and knee-length olive
tights, then left the warren, transiting to the gee deck. There, she strolled
the empty path that wound among the little parks and the cottages, listening to birdsong while longing for the sound of human voices.

The personnel map reported only Pasha, Vytet, and Urban present, though they were nowhere about.

Nearly all of the ship's company had chosen to spend the last
decades of the passage to Tanjiri in cold sleep. Yet despite their
prolonged absence, the gee deck showed no sign of neglect. Every
cottage and every garden appeared pristine, kept that way by automated maintenance systems.

Bees hummed, leaves rustled faintly at the touch of a gentle
breeze, a hummingbird's wings buzzed unseen somewhere near
by—and Clemantine found herself wondering if it wouldn't have
been wiser to eschew perfection and allow the gardens to overgrow
and the cottages to become stained with moss and time . . . to
acknowledge the absence of those who ought to live there. As it
was, despite the passage of years, the perfection of the deck suggested a recent abandonment, as if everyone had only just been
spirited away—and wasn't that an unsettling thought, one that cast
doubt on the reliability of memory.

Still, time *had* passed since the ship's company had last been together. And the deck had changed, subtly, slowly. Trees had thickened or been replaced. The composition of species had been rebalanced, tiny primates introduced, along with darting damselflies, and the colorful, shimmering hummingbirds that were her own design.

The gee deck's web of life had grown ever more complex, while the potential hazards of Tanjiri drew ever closer.

She reached the side path to her own cottage. Strolled to the open doorway.

Inside, Urban sat cross-legged at the low table, shirtless, eyes closed, deep in meditation . . . or not there at all. An abandoned avatar, a lean living statue with sparks of *ha* glinting in the palms of his upturned hands as they rested in his lap. He used to leave his avatar in the bedroom, feigning sleep, but more and more often in recent years he neglected to put himself away.

On the table, a pot of tea gone cold.

She said, "I'm back."

He already knew that, of course. A DI set to monitor activity within the cold sleep chambers would have noted her waking and alerted his ghost on the high bridge or his ghost in the library—multiple instantiations of the same mind, continuously trading memories. And through his expanded senses, he would have perceived her presence as she approached the cottage.

Yet he had not risen to meet her, instead waiting for her to speak, allowing her words to be the key that wakened him. Awareness arrived on his face in the form of a sly smile. His eyes opened, to look up at her with that warm teasing gaze she knew so well.

"I've been waiting for you," he said, soft and low. "I've missed you and I want you to stay with me this time. We're almost there— and soon now, things will start to change."

Over the years since Verilotus, Clemantine had established a pattern: one hundred days in cold sleep with her ghost dormant in the archive, and then a hundred days of existence on the gee deck while her ghost served a shift on the high bridge.

That would change now.

"I'm not going anywhere," she assured him as she sat across the table from him on a pale-green pillow. "Even with our deceleration"—she felt it as a slight, unpleasant pressure—"in a hundred days we'll be among the outer band of megastructures."

A subtle shift in his gaze together with a slight lowering of his chin alerted her. "You're worried," she said, surprised.

"Of course I'm worried. We still have no answer to the question of why no other people, no other entity, ever visited Verilotus."

"That again?" Hadn't they talked this subject dry?

"The Blade is a beacon," he insisted. "If there still are other entities on the scale of Lezuri, they should have investigated. It would have been an easy venture. It's taken us just sixty-four years to make the crossing to Tanjiri. Yet we never found any sign or record in the silver that anyone or anything had visited that system, not until we arrived."

Sooth. It was an important question, but they did not have data to answer it. Urban knew that and still he could not leave it alone. Discussion of the topic had the feeling of ritual as Clemantine commenced to reiterate possibilities. She started with the simplest. "Maybe no one else exists."

Lezuri and his partner goddess had tried to kill each other off. A similar enmity, more successful in its execution, could explain the silence.

Urban dismissed the suggestion with a shake of his head. "No. The answer has to be more complex. Besides, we know there's some kind of presence at Tanjiri. That celestial city is alive."

"But is it inhabited? Or is it like Silk?"

Clemantine's memory reached back millennia. The city they'd inhabited at Deception Well, the city where Urban had been born, had existed long before their people came to take it over. Clemantine remembered the day they'd arrived, remembered watching the feeds from the hundreds of camera bees that had been sent in ahead of human scouts. The city had been very much alive, overgrown with forest and home to birds and insects, a well-balanced ecosystem. But all those people who had built the city and who had lived there . . . every one of them had been dead and gone.

Not a memory she cared to explore any further. So without waiting for a response, she pushed on to the next phase of the discussion. "But if there still is an entity at Tanjiri—"

"Lezuri believed there was."

"Yes. Maybe it's just not interested in anything outside its own system."

"But the *Blade*," he countered, making no effort to hide the longing in his voice.

She cocked her head. "Don't assume your desires are shared by others. *You* are obsessed with the Blade. But this entity, if it exists, surely already understands the physics behind the Blade. It created a world, Urban. A huge, living moon. It had to have used something analogous to the Blade to do that."

His brow furrowed and a distracted look came over his face, a sure sign that his intellect had turned elsewhere. "Or maybe," he mused, "it knows about Verilotus's sentient missiles."

Clemantine's heart rate spiked at mention of the missiles. They were Lezuri's creation. A trio of them had pursued the outrider, *Artemis*, consuming it in a blossom of white light, obliterating what she had feared, at the time, to be Urban's last ghost. A psychic scar that still had not healed.

"*Sooth*," she whispered. The sentient missiles *were* a fearsome deterrent, operating through their own bizarre and incomprehensible physics. "It could be that all such entities avoid each other for fear of mutual destruction." Then she smiled. "And yet here we are, come to disturb such a being."

He smiled too and spoke jokingly though it was true. "It's just we have a lot of questions to ask."

"So we do." But with Lezuri still haunting her thoughts, she added, "Let's pray it doesn't prove to be a mad god too."

CHAPTER THREE

THROUGHOUT THE YEARS the fleet had lingered at Verilotus, Pasha had divided herself to make twice the use of her time.

In her physical avatar she'd explored the world, most often venturing on her own, but at times seeking out her closest friends among the ship's company: Tarnya, Alkimbra, Clemantine. She had even spent long stretches in Riffan's chatty company. The man could make friends with anyone! By taking advantage of his social skills, she'd met and talked with a fascinating array of people from all around the great circle of Verilotus. But none had known anything of the physics that permitted the existence of their ring-shaped world and the vastly larger ring-shaped Blade that surrounded it.

So Pasha had dedicated a ghost-self to that mystery, puzzling over it in the company of Vytet and Naresh, along with three of the Apparatchiks: the Engineer, the Mathematician, and the Astronomer. It had been a heroic effort, yet they'd gotten nowhere. And when the fleet finally departed Verilotus, they had put the question aside.

"To be revisited later," Pasha murmured to herself. She stood alone in the front room of her cottage, eyeing the generative wall, presently modulated as a display screen. Onscreen, and running by default, was a short video loop.

The sequence began with the Blade, imaged by a probe as it approached the anomaly's crisp white non-surface—a featureless boundary, with no visible detail or texture, though at this point the probe had been only a hundred kilometers away.

That distance shrank rapidly. As the probe closed in, the Blade filled the screen, still with no hint of detail within its white glow.

Then, for a fraction of a second, the display went dark, marking the moment when the signal from the descending probe had ceased.

The video shifted. It pulled back in time, back to the viewpoint of a second probe, sent to monitor the first. As before, a smooth white glow filled the display, but now the descending probe could be seen against that glow, appearing as a simple dark spot, visible for several seconds . . . then gone. In the moment of its disappearance, the Blade brightened instantaneously as if the probe's mass had been converted into harmless white light.

Pasha knew from other, more distant observations, each calibrated to account for light-speed delays, that the entire vast circumference of the Blade, more than two million kilometers, had brightened in the same instant and held that glow for several days before slowly fading.

She did not have a theory to account for this behavior. Just a gut feeling, a guess, that the Blade was no physical thing. She suspected it to be a seam, a vein, a crack in reality opening onto another universe where the laws of physics had little in common with the universe she knew. She longed to understand it, to at least grasp the basic concept of it, but she was no closer to that now, sixty-four years after the fleet departed Verilotus, than she'd been when the probe descended.

It still rankled that she'd been kept from the Cauldron, that place of alien dimensions discovered by Urban. How she'd longed to study the Blade from that perspective! What might she have learned there? What might she have discovered? But she'd never been allowed the chance.

A gentle voice spoke from the open doorway. "Obsessing over old questions again, are you?"

So unexpected was this visit that it sped her heart and made her flinch. "Vytet," she gasped, turning to regard the tall, willowy figure of the ship's lead engineer. "I didn't notice you there. Come in, come in."

Vytet stepped past the threshold and gestured at the display. "This makes an appropriate backdrop to my futile mission. Urban has asked me to look again into the puzzle of the needle."

Pasha scowled. "Why? What's changed? We spent years on that. Even Naresh agrees, without some other evidence, some breakthrough discovery, our studies long ago reached a dead end."

Vytet took a seat on the couch. She leaned back, stretching her long legs out in front of her while regarding Pasha with a thoughtful gaze. "I told Urban the physics is beyond us. That our minds are not designed to comprehend such things."

Pasha's eyes narrowed, but she resisted the impulse to argue. Vytet had made this claim before, and though Pasha could never condone such a limiting belief, she saw no point in debating the matter yet again. So she only asked, "And what did he say to that?"

"He told me, *our minds are adaptable*—and that got me thinking."

"Uh oh." A little smile of anticipation. Taking a seat in a cushioned armchair, Pasha leaned forward, elbows on her knees, eager to hear what Vytet meant to do.

"I have always tried to be adaptable," Vytet went on. "To see the world from different perspectives, and to be seen from different perspectives."

Pasha nodded, acknowledging Vytet's ever-changing physical manifestations.

"But I have always desired to remain, at my core, as myself. My human self. And I'm not willing to change that."

Pasha said nothing, waiting patiently while Vytet circled in on what she had come to say.

"There are many ways of adapting," Vytet mused. "Before Urban returned to Deception Well, when he was alone on this ship, he adapted by creating specialized versions of himself."

"The Apparatchiks!" Pasha said in a burst of excitement, her mind leaping ahead. "You could do the same thing. Create an independent version of yourself. Give it the problem and then let it adapt, let it change into whatever mode is necessary to comprehend a solution."

"I've never looked into how Urban created the Apparatchiks," Vytet admitted.

"I have." Pasha's hand squeezed into a fist as if to catch the knowledge and hold it. "They began as ghosts, standard copies of himself that he then modified to serve the purposes he intended for them."

Vytet raised an eyebrow. "Then you know how to do it? How to modify and reshape a personality? You can help me with it?"

Pasha leaned back in her chair, thinking. "I know the means by which it was done . . . though I've never tried it, or tested the process."

"Of course not."

"Or even looked at it in detail."

"I understand. It would be an experiment."

Pasha nodded as a shiver prickled her skin—fear and anticipation tangled together. She met Vytet's gaze. "Consider this. If the goal is to create an alien mind, one that can comprehend what we cannot, then your Apparatchik will need to be free to re-design itself and adapt as it sees fit."

"Taking the journey that I am unwilling to take myself," Vytet murmured. "That could be dangerous."

"Yes." The unknown always presented a risk.

Vytet's eyes sparkled. "Even so, it's a way forward. A new mind would open new vistas."

"Agreed." Pasha too felt the allure of the project, but more than Vytet, she knew there would be costs. "Urban won't like it," she warned. "He'll resent the presence of an artificial being not under his direct control. He'll resent it more, if I'm involved."

"Hmm." Vytet looked thoughtful, as if she needed a few extra seconds to parse the meaning behind these words. Evidently she reached some benign conclusion, because she shrugged. "You did what you had to do to evict Lezuri from *Dragon*. I didn't like it at the time, but it was necessary. Urban surely must have come to accept that."

A cool, cynical smile. Pasha knew it went deeper than that. Yes, she and Clemantine had done what Urban had not dared to do.

They had burned and blasted *Dragon*'s body, risking the life of the ship to drive Lezuri out—and in doing so, they'd proven Urban wrong. That had the effect of leaving all his future decisions open to question. Worse, in his eyes, during his long absence Clementine had brought Pasha onto the high bridge, where she had learned to pilot the courser. Pasha still undertook that task each time her shift came around. She insisted on it.

"He has never accepted my presence on the high bridge," she told Vytet. "He tries to hide his resentment, but it's there all the same. If he could get away with it, I think he would have the high bridge to himself again, with not even Clementine beside him."

Vytet's brow furrowed. "I never sensed such friction. Are you sure you're not seeing trouble where it doesn't exist?"

"Oh, very sure. I feel the 'friction' every time I meet him on the high bridge. He doesn't make his resentment explicit. But in that place, it's hard to hide anything."

"Hmm . . ."

Vytet sounded doubtful. She *looked* doubtful, and that sparked Pasha's ire. "I'm not making this up. I'm not imagining it."

"No, I'm not suggesting you are. But given that you believe he is trying to hide his resentment, I think it's on you to strive not to see it. And for me, I will not allow any such irrational feelings to dictate what I can and cannot do. Urban has asked me to crack the puzzle of the needle. He will have to accept my need to walk this new path—and my need for you to walk with me."

Again, Pasha narrowed her eyes, but she nodded. "Just don't expect the path to be smooth," she warned.

CHAPTER FOUR

MONSTERS, CLEMANTINE REFLECTED, *have a way of sneaking up out of the dark.*

In this version, Clemantine existed as a ghost alone on the high bridge of the courser, *Griffin*—a specialized persona, edited to endure. Cold, stern, ever alert, and unforgiving, she held the ship's semi-sentient philosopher cells under her tight command.

Those cells functioned together as *Griffin's* composite mind. The ship itself was a bio-mechanical weapon—one devised by an ancient alien intelligence known as the Chenzeme. Those old murderers had endowed the cells with an instinctive drive to despise and destroy any lifeform alien to their killing ships.

Over the years, Clemantine had worked to ease the hateful nature of *Griffin's* hull cells so that her ceaseless immersion within their alien conversations had become more bearable. But she had only diluted their basic nature. The cell field remained ready to take on any defensive action that might be required to protect the fleet. She made sure of that.

Because monsters have a way of sneaking up out of the dark.

This time, she shared the thought with the cell field. The bridge translated it into something the Chenzeme cells could understand, introducing it to the field at a hundred thousand points of contact. Individual cells adjacent to those points instantly assented to the thought—it was a reminder of what their deepest instinct warned them to be true—and they passed it on to the cells around them. Those cells echoed it in turn. Within microseconds, the field reached consensus.

An automated response followed as cadres of cells performed standard readiness tasks: test and confirm the health of the propulsion reef, ensure sufficient quantities of chemical fuel for the navigational jets, execute diagnostic tests of the gamma-ray gun, survey the positions of every vessel within the fleet—and re-scan the Near Vicinity in an endless hunt for those monsters ever-suspected of hiding in the dark.

The constant flow of data among the hull cells expanded to a torrent. The ship's senses sharpened. Clementine rode those senses, sharing the cells' cold confidence as they inventoried the fleet:

Running in staggered array ahead of *Griffin* were the four surviving outriders—*Khonsu*, *Lam Lha*, *Pytheas*, and *Elepaio*.

Two sentient missiles escorted that vanguard—a gift of Verilotus.

And accompanying *Griffin*, though separated by a gulf of thirty-five thousand kilometers, *Dragon* and all the precious lives that courser carried.

The fleet slowly bled off velocity as it prepared to enter Tanjiri System—a long-drawn-out deceleration to ensure no damage to *Dragon*'s rotating gee deck.

Theirs was no stealth approach. They came to Tanjiri openly, the two coursers' luminous hull cells revealing both ships to anyone bothering to scan the void. Urban meant their visibility to be interpreted as a statement of good will, but it might just as well be seen as bravado, a declaration of untouchability: *We have no need to hide!*

Clementine had wanted to take *Griffin* in first, far ahead of the fleet, to probe for dangers among the broken megastructures and in the vicinity of the living worlds. But Urban had not agreed.

"*Griffin* is a weapon," he'd argued. "An alien weapon. Sending it in first would be construed as a threat, a warning."

"*Dragon* is a greater weapon."

"Yes it is, but it differs from *Griffin* in the most critical way. *Dragon* carries human life. Tanjiri was a human settlement. Whatever exists there now is human, or human descended. We'll need to prove we're human too—and that we're not looking for a fight."

Clemantine did not share *that* thought with the hull cells, knowing they would rebel against it. Given their Chenzeme nature, they always looked to fight.

A faint sensation, generated by the lateral lines of *Griffin*'s gravitational sensor, seized her attention. A sure indication that something had shifted in the Near Vicinity.

Something dangerous?

She scanned her surroundings once again.

Nothing visible. Not yet.

Urban's voice came to her from across the void, carried by a precisely targeted communications laser: *You sensed it?*

Yes.

Maybe an alignment of megastructures, drawn together by their mutual gravity.

An explanation so benign it triggered a flash of Chenzeme temper across her ghost mind. Clemantine had long ago come to share the paranoia of the philosopher cells. In a cold voice, she countered Urban's suggestion with a more likely explanation. *They've noticed us at last. Turn all telescopes toward the belt of ruins. We need to see what's stirring there.*

CHAPTER FIVE

ONCE, IRKED BY the Apparatchik known as the Bio-mechanic, Pasha had wondered how such a corrosive personality could come to be. This question led her to another: How had Urban created the Apparatchiks? Her incessant curiosity demanded an answer, so she had embarked on a foray into the library to find out.

She had begun by looking at *Dragon*'s history. As recorded in the library, it began in the hours after Urban had taken control of the Chenzeme vessel. Frantic, overlapping log entries testified to the tumult of those early days. Then, abruptly, the log expanded, branched, and grew organized. That shift marked the point when the Scholar had taken on management of *Dragon*'s information resources.

With that date and time in mind, Pasha had initiated a new search.

Dragon's library was far older than Urban's conquest of the ship. When he'd seized the courser, he'd brought with him a copy of *Null Boundary*'s library, and that library contained copies of libraries from other ships and from worlds now lost.

Pasha had searched that vast resource, hunting for files or applications that had been opened or modified in the hours before the Scholar began his work. And eventually she had turned up an obscure utility, very old. Its creation date lay some thirty-six hundred years prior to the capture of *Dragon*, but its log recorded that it had been used six times during those early days. Its function: to modify the persona of a ghost.

———

Vytet scowled, wrestling with a brew of skepticism and rising anger as she studied what was purportedly a text-based model of her persona—line after complex line. The thousands of lines presently displayed on a huge virtual screen were only a minuscule fraction of the whole. Each line allegedly described some aspect of her. As if what she was could be dissected and dissociated into discrete modules, coded in colors that shifted as her focus shifted to highlight associated traits.

She saw on display there the doubt, the uncertainty, the flagging confidence in her own abilities that she'd wrestled with and struggled to suppress throughout her life. Also there, her deep pride, rising from the certainty that she had been endowed with an intellectual brilliance that allowed her, and her alone, to see past the horizons of others and gaze more deeply than anyone else into the workings of reality. Even as a ghost, she flushed to see these vanities and deep inner conflicts, these *flaws*, written out in antique verbiage.

Worse than this was the sight of her passion to engage in a fluidity of form and gender—the very core of her emotional existence—written out and crudely described as a wild freedom, an inner exploration, a denial of typical boundaries, a revulsion at being narrowly defined . . .

Narrowly defined, just as this utility sought to define her.

She loathed everything she saw on that screen. Almost unbearable knowing that Pasha was there beside her, reading the text that claimed to model exactly who Vytet was.

They stood together in a private chamber of the library, locked away from the sight—and the oversight—of any other member of the ship's company. Thanks be given to the Unknown God for that. Vytet did not want anyone else to ever see this offensive documentation of her inner life.

She snuck a sidelong glance at Pasha, dreading her judgment. But Pasha wasn't even looking at the screen anymore. She had turned aside and opened a new, smaller window. It floated at an angle in front of her. Her hand hovered above it, fingers moving occasionally to scroll or select.

"This is so very interesting," she said in a quiet, transfixed voice as if thinking aloud. "There's no direct coding required. The utility uses pre-sets, allowing a selection of desired traits to be added to the personality matrix. If existing traits conflict with that, the utility highlights them, asking permission to delete. And it allows the intensity of the new traits to be adjusted, as well as the intensity of the old."

She turned to Vytet, her green eyes somehow both bright with curiosity and stern as steel. "Come see. This is your project. Your Apparatchik. You're the one who needs to define it."

Vytet worked with the utility, selecting from the list of pre-set traits, slowly defining her Apparatchik. Each addition required subtractions and adjustments among other traits. It was no simple process. She very soon recognized that the utility had been created by an inspired genius who must have spent decades, if not centuries, studying the structure and conflicts of human personalities.

At rare intervals, Pasha offered advice. "Look here," she said, early in the process. "This pre-set for dissociation. You can allow it your knowledge, while withholding some percentage of your personal memories."

"Is that a good idea?" Vytet asked. "Knowledge without context?"

"Consider it as knowledge without prejudice, allowing the Apparatchik a fresh start, a fresh outlook."

And later, "I think this Apparatchik should begin as a simple creature, with its intellect closely focused on the problem you want it to solve—"

Vytet broke in, alarmed. "No, its primary value must be the safety of the fleet."

"Yes, of course. But let it construct its own personality in the way it perceives as best to solve the problem. It doesn't need to be a full-fledged humanistic personality. It's not as if you mean to keep it around, like Urban's Apparatchiks . . . right? Once the problem is solved—or if it proves unsolvable—you can delete it."

Delete it?

Until that moment, Vytet had been focused solely on the challenge of creating a properly specialized Apparatchik. Only now did she consider the closing moves of such an experiment, and a simulated chill caused her ghost to shiver.

Not so long ago, she had ended another experiment by deleting an entity under her control. She had dis-assembled and recycled the substance of that version of herself that had become endowed with silver. Despite all the sexual and surface changes she'd made over the years, Vytet still cherished her physical continuity—to an irrational degree. Ordering the destruction of that older version of herself had been one of the hardest things she'd ever done.

Could she do it again?

"*Yes,*" she said quietly. "You're right, of course. The Apparatchik will likely become some alien thing that we'll need to delete when the experiment is done."

Vytet continued to shape the Apparatchik. Even though the goal was to create a relatively simple being—childlike and questioning—every decision, every deletion and addition to the menu of its abilities, felt critical. She carefully considered each one, consulting with Pasha and weighing the warnings generated by the utility— warnings that now came with every amendment she made.

: Variation within the selected configuration exceeds recommended parameters. Restore core identity modules to ensure subservience to the primary form.

Subservience was not her goal. The nature of the experiment demanded that Vytet push past the warnings, and past a growing sense of guilt as well, which was why she felt a rush of relief when a window unexpectedly opened within the chamber's wall. They had been discovered! And now someone else would either validate or condemn what she was doing. *Good.* She needed another's judgment. She welcomed it.

But it was only the Bio-mechanic, confined within his frameless window. Her shoulders sagged in disappointment.

The Bio-mechanic had come dressed, as always, in a dark green bodysuit that blended with a restless background suggestive of living cell tissue. Though based on Urban, he'd diverged over the centuries of his existence, both in appearance and personality. He had long limbs, a lean face, hair in tight coils that floated with no pretense of gravity, and a suspicious, short-tempered nature. Gazing past Vytet, he studied the evolving configuration with an ominous scowl.

"Why?" he asked, turning within his window, his angry gaze seeking an answer, first from Vytet and then from Pasha.

Standing with hands on her hips, Pasha returned his scowl. "How did you get in here?" she demanded. "This is a private chamber."

"So it is. My own lost copy plotted a revolution with you from within just such a chamber."

Vytet had not been part of that revolution, but she recognized the parallel and a simulated flush of embarrassed heat warmed her ghost cheeks. "We're not plotting a revolution."

"No. You're creating a new being."

"A new Apparatchik."

"As I said."

Vytet considered this. The Bio-mechanic was an Apparatchik, existing only as a ghost. But in her present form she was a ghost too, an electronic entity within the ship's library. Was there any meaningful difference between her and him?

"You have done it wrong," he informed her. "You've edited away your own core beliefs when you should have enhanced them. That's why you're getting the warnings."

"We know why we're getting the warnings," Pasha said.

Vytet nodded. She gestured at the display. "I *want* my Apparatchik to think differently, to be independent, to know what I know, but not to be constrained by my conclusions. It must doubt and test and question the math and physics I implicitly believe. My goal is to endow it with a mind more flexible than my own."

"You have given it that freedom?" the Bio-mechanic asked. He looked appalled. "How will you ensure its loyalty to you? To the ship? To the ship's company? You do understand that it will grow, and adapt, and change?"

Vytet's ghost, mimicking the physiology of her living avatar, simulated a guilty tension, an embarrassed heat.

"This Apparatchik is not like you," she explained. "I have made it a simple persona, dedicated to a single task, and I do not mean for it to exist indefinitely. It is a disposable asset. A tool to be used for a short time only."

His lip curled. "You say that now."

"I mean it."

A soft, scoffing hiss. He turned his gaze to the display of personality traits. And to Vytet's dismay, the screen shifted. A new set of clauses appeared in the Apparatchik's evolving definition.

"What is that?" she demanded. "What have you done?"

The Bio-mechanic returned his cold gaze to her. "I do not trust this creation of yours. So I have given myself special access to it. I will watch over it, and when it becomes a threat, I will eliminate it."

"That's not up to you," Pasha argued. "It's Vytet who will decide—"

"No," Vytet interrupted. "It's all right."

She thought she ought to be angry at the Bio-mechanic's peremptory interference. Instead she felt relieved. After all, didn't a project as unique as this one demand an element of outside oversight?

Not that there was a choice.

She turned to Pasha. "Let's review the configuration. I think it's nearly done."

Awareness winked on. A disorienting plunge into existence. And a new mind asked its first question: *What is this?*

The answer came easily: Paradise.

A sense of wonder filled this newborn mind as it perceived the concept of the Universe and its own deep knowledge of the processes that had allowed the astounding creation of which it was a part.

But a question remained, a question that nagged and stung and insisted on solution. A question embodied in the memory of a gleaming incorruptible needle: *How can such an impossible thing be possible?*

To solve that puzzle was the very reason for existence.

For my existence. I was made for this . . .

She recognized herself then as a discrete being, a virtual entity, an electronic ghost endowed with knowledge but devoid of a past. Nothing more, really, than an intellectual system designed for the singular purpose of discovering and decrypting the hidden mechanism that would allow her to understand and open the needle.

"I am the Cryptologist," she whispered.

Her simulated eyes opened. Her gaze lifted. She perceived her surroundings with dual senses: visually, as the simulation of a little enclosed chamber, and on a deeper level, as the electronic information structure that defined that chamber.

In the same way, she perceived the three entities sharing the chamber with her. The scope of her embedded knowledge allowed her to recognize each one of them. There was the Bio-mechanic, an artificial being like herself. Pasha Andern, an exobiologist and engineer who had helped to design her newly aware mind. And Vytet Vahn-Renzani.

Curiosity sparked as the Cryptologist studied Vytet. "I was once you," she realized. "But no longer."

CHAPTER SIX

ALL THROUGHOUT THE crossing, the Astronomer had dedicated two of the fleet's telescopes to watch Tanjiri, while the other scopes continued the standard survey of the Near Vicinity.

But now, at Urban's request, the Astronomer turned every lens toward Tanjiri's belt of ruins. Working in concert, the telescopes recorded simultaneous images of specific coordinates. The data comprising those images was then sent to *Dragon*, where a Dull Intelligence combined the separate observations into a highly detailed view of a small section of the belt. All these instances were then tiled together to create a composite image—a huge, three-dimensional map displayed within a dark chamber of the library. The map depicted a vast territory encompassing thousands of widely scattered objects, all moving through long orbits.

Clemantine strolled among them. As her gaze passed over each object, a tag bearing a numerical designation loomed into view. Most of the tags were blue, indicating known objects, mapped during earlier observations. Only a few tags were red, marking objects that had not been mapped before.

Most of the debris tumbling within the belt ranged from dust grains to objects a few hundred meters in their longest dimension. Some few were several kilometers. And then there were the rare megastructures, hundreds of kilometers in length, sharp-edged and slowly rotating. To Clemantine, they looked like fragments left behind from the shattering of hollow worlds. Some still vented icy clouds of water vapor and atmospheric gasses.

So far, the map depicted results only from an initial survey. That survey was already being repeated, with the DI instructed to compare each incoming instance with the original image, checking for unpredicted or anomalous motion that would distinguish an object subject to powered movement from those passively orbiting within the complex gravitational forces of the belt.

So far, no hint had emerged as to what lay behind the gravitational anomaly.

Clemantine stepped outside the map. "Zoom out," she instructed, turning to regard it as a whole. "Show all tags for newly identified objects."

The attendant DI obeyed. The map shrank, while a hundred or so tags appeared, too tiny to be immediately legible, all marking objects so small they appeared as pinpricks, if she could make them out at all.

A familiar, stern voice spoke through her atrium. *Don't assume the threat is tied to a novel object. Danger could easily lie with one long since mapped and known, but active now.*

Clemantine smiled, pleased at this rare contact from her dark twin. *Sooth*, she answered. *Though we don't know there is a threat.*

Wiser to presume it. Perhaps a gamma-ray weapon moving into position?

Perhaps. But there will always be risk in any attempted contact. That's well known, and accepted.

The risk should be mine, her twin's cold voice insisted.

That argument again. If Clemantine had had air in her ghost lungs, she would have sighed. *You know my mind better than anyone—because I've shared it with you. You know I agree with the consensus, that our best chance at peaceful contact is to present a human face.*

And I am no longer capable of that?

Clemantine resisted the natural urge to speak false comfort. No point in it, given that her memory of this conversation would soon be passed in full to her dark twin. *Just so. We both know it's true.*

The reply came in a grudging monosyllable, *Sooth.* But then, after a moment, she added, *Though I'm better prepared than he is.*

So you're worried about Urban too.

Clemantine had wondered if her concern was misplaced. She knew now it was not.

You noted it first, her twin said. *He's become hesitant, unsure of himself. You've considered that on some level he doesn't really want to go to Tanjiri.*

I've wondered about that, yes, Clemantine conceded. *But now I think that's wrong. It's not that he doesn't want to go. It's that, for all the strength of this fleet, he still feels vulnerable. That's the root of his obsession with the Blade.*

That knowledge would certainly be good to have.

Of course you would think so.

A cold chuckle, but no argument.

Command is shared, Clemantine concluded. *We'll decide together what risks to take.*

She returned her attention to the map, its display still filtered to show only newly discovered objects. None had been flagged as particularly interesting. All were "new" only because they were so small and dark that past surveys had missed them, or else they'd been hidden behind other objects.

"Return to full display," she instructed the attendant DI.

The boundaries of the belt of ruins ranged from between 780 million to 1.4 billion kilometers from the central star; objects within the belt required up to twenty years to complete a single orbit. Rare collisions had been observed, influenced by both chance and the megastructures' gravitational effects, but so far, all relative motion appeared to be passive in nature, unpowered objects orbiting in a slow celestial dance.

"Redisplay the map in infrared," she instructed.

If any of the objects emitted any heat above ambient, that would stand out within the infrared portion of the spectrum. But shifting the spectrum only plunged the chamber into darkness. Nothing remained for Clemantine to focus her gaze on. The belt—this closest portion of it anyway—appeared cold and utterly lifeless.

"Restore."

Only in the inner system did life advertise its presence. The Tanjiri Trinity—planet, moon, and celestial city—traveled together in a stable orbit around the star. Yet no radio communications had ever been detected from them, or from the belt.

She crossed her arms, thinking about that.

After a few seconds, she decided, "It's time."

She left the library, and ghosted to the high bridge.

CHAPTER SEVEN

URBAN'S GHOST STOOD watch alone on the high bridge, immersed in the senses of the ship and linked to the pensive chatter of *Dragon*'s hull cells as the field strove to understand the gravitational anomaly. Hypothetical scenarios were proposed, discussed, evaluated, rated for likelihood—and a potential response lined up should the scenario prove true.

Every scenario led to the same conclusion: <*kill it*>

Chenzeme instinct, forever reflecting a simple worldview.

Urban would block that instinct when the time came, but for now he allowed the cells to freely speculate, valuing the insight and the deep experience of the field's composite mind.

But nothing came without cost. The wary unease within the cell field magnified his own tension—or maybe his tension had infected the field as Lezuri's warning re-echoed in his thoughts: *You are not ready to encounter what exists at Tanjiri.*

Urban had insisted, *I want to see it anyway.*

That had not changed, but proximity had brought a full, visceral recognition of all he risked. One wrong decision in the next few hours could very well end the existence of the fleet.

A moment of startled surprise—quickly suppressed—as Clemantine joined him, her ghost in intimate proximity with his own among the branchings of the high bridge.

Pasha's not here**, she observed. **Did you chase her away?

Resentment rose in him—*suppress that!*—as he answered obliquely, ***We're so close now. I need to be here.***

Her amusement, cold and glassy, spilled out across the cell

field—and his resentment surged again. *Dragon* was his avatar. It *was* him. He'd inhabited the high bridge alone for more than a millennium. When Clemantine had first joined him there it had been a shock for her, but also for him. He had traded isolation for entanglement. On the high bridge, every subtle shift of her emotions—and of his—stood revealed.

She wanted him to share that same intimacy with Pasha, and he had tried, only to have his resentment leak out among the hull cells, disturbing them with the puzzle of his alien emotions.

The cell field is on edge, she observed.

The cells see danger everywhere.

They're not wrong. The anomaly could be explained by a gamma-ray weapon moving into position.

You've been talking to her.

The other Clemantine, her counterpart on *Griffin*, had made the same suggestion, framed in the same words, with the same cool note in her voice. The similarity only fed Urban's worry.

Suppress that!

The two were not the same.

This Clemantine, *his* Clemantine, shared her memories with the other, but it was a gift, not an exchange. To endure her unceasing immersion in the hateful chatter of *Griffin*'s hull cells, that other Clemantine had transformed herself into a cold, ruthless being, dedicated only to the protection of the fleet—and wisely, she had refused to directly share what she'd become. For that, she had Urban's gratitude. And over the years, she'd earned his trust. But he did not love that Clemantine.

Still, the two versions often talked to one another.

Do not become her, he thought in a silent plea.

Aloud, he explained, *I've instructed the Pilot to direct each vessel in the fleet to undertake random minor course changes. We're still far enough out that we make a poor target.*

Still with that cool, purposeful note in her voice, she said, *Even so, it's time. We're close enough now. We need to announce our presence. Only a stalking predator approaches in silence.*

His tension spiked at this proposal, spilling over into the cell field, intensifying the anxiety of ongoing conversations even as he argued against her claim. *It's not like that. We're not approaching in stealth. We haven't hidden ourselves. If anyone is watching, they've seen the glow of our hull and of Griffin's. They know we're coming.*

Sooth. But what are we? An utterly strange, alien warship. So it must appear. If they have seen us, if they know we're coming, that's all the more reason to send the message and reassure them by letting them know we're human. At the least, it might make them hesitate to strike.

The message she spoke of had been recorded years before, a greeting repeated in the three languages known to have been used in Tanjiri System.

I think it's too soon, he said, despising his own doubt. *We're not ready yet. As we get closer, we'll learn more. Maybe pick up weak radio signals.*

No, she insisted. *It is time. Send the message. Set it to repeat. Whether we get an answer or not, it'll help define what to expect in this system.*

The message went out as a radio signal, repeating every few minutes for the span of an hour. The signal would require roughly sixty-one minutes to reach the outer periphery of the belt of ruins, and far longer to reach the celestial city, now on the far side of the star. A reply could not be expected before twice the time, and no reply would come at all unless there existed an antenna system capable of receiving what would by then be a very weak radio hail.

In twenty-four hours—the ancient measure of a day on Earth and so an acknowledgment of a shared past—he would begin again.

Two hours passed. Then four. Then a full day. Then two days— and no reply came.

In the bedroom of the cottage he shared with Clemantine, Urban's avatar—his precious, irreplaceable, silver-augmented avatar—lay as if asleep.

But he was not asleep. He lay listening to the concerns of the machine minds that controlled the fleet's two sentient missiles. Jubilee had given the missiles to him as he'd prepared to leave

Verilotus. When he had questioned the wisdom of accepting such a dangerous gift, she had assured him, *You need never use them. But if sometime, somewhere, some mad god should threaten your existence, you will have at the least this chance to make a defense.*

Through the silver, Jubilee had introduced him to the missiles' machine minds, and through the silver, he continued to share their mindspace, and to control them. They possessed simple, identical personalities: alert, analytical, and utterly patient, as machine minds should be. He had not given them names, designating them only as missile one and missile two.

They had reached out to him to share an interesting finding. They possessed no language that he could sense, communicating instead by raw thought, so that he knew what they knew.

They had sensed the presence of faint knots of force scattered all throughout the belt of ruins—anomalies undefined within the physics he knew. He guessed these forces indicated dimensional intrusions. The missiles interpreted the phenomena as evidence of the presence of entities much like themselves.

Urban drew slow, deep breaths, an exercise to keep his fear at bay.

Lezuri had insisted he was not ready to encounter what existed at Tanjiri. In his heart, he knew that to be true.

CHAPTER EIGHT

SET LOOSE WITHIN the library, the Cryptologist made it her first task to review every study ever made of the enigmatic needle. It didn't matter that she'd inherited knowledge of all these studies from Vytet. Human memory was imperfect. Vytet may have overlooked or forgotten or misinterpreted some critical datum, or failed to perceive a logical connection. Therefore, in the quest to decrypt the puzzle of the needle, a review was the necessary first step. The Cryptologist happily embraced the task, eager to pursue the question so deeply encoded in her nature.

But other questions tweaked her curiosity too. Why had Vytet given her knowledge but no memory of life? Why did some entities choose to exist within physical avatars? Was the Blade that had been observed at Verilotus an object or a boundary?

So many peripheral puzzles! So many fascinating questions awaiting answers. But she did not allow herself to be distracted. She pursued her review to completion. And she found no new insights. Vytet had been thorough in her study of the needle and she had not worked alone. Naresh, Pasha, the Engineer, even the Bio-mechanic—that brooding entity whose invisible presence accompanied her own formless existence, observing her every action, her every decision—all of them had turned their considerable intellect to the needle. And they'd exhausted every avenue of research. The Cryptologist found herself with no new leads, with nothing, beyond her own deep desire to crack the needle open.

There must be a solution!

A cold chuckle intruded on her thoughts, the sound of it injected into the matrix of her existence. Next, a voice she recognized as belonging to the Bio-mechanic said, "It's a cruel thing they've done, to imbue you with an obsession to solve an unsolvable task."

Cruel? She did not think so.

There must be a solution, she insisted. Not in audible words as his had been, but as a thought, since he had just demonstrated his access to her internal dialog. *The needle was created here, on the ship. It was offered as an intellectual test. There* is *a solution.*

"I applaud your confidence. I shared it once, though I learned better. Tell me, what is your next step?"

There are peripheral mysteries endowed with physics as strange as the needle. The Blade, for one, though that is distant now and difficult to study. There is this substance called silver and the entanglement it allows. And also, the sentient missiles.

"You have no access to those," he said.

She noted a peculiar sharp tension suddenly present in his voice and wondered at it, but she did not let it divert her. She wanted to discuss the missiles.

They are so interesting. Don't you agree? Both in the mystery of their propulsion and in their greedy blossoming. You have seen the video record of it. As if another universe has opened its white maw to bite off and consume a portion of this one.

"I had not thought of it in such *poetic* terms," he admitted.

This pleased the Cryptologist. Vytet had designed her to think original thoughts and already she felt herself fulfilling that function—still, she was no closer to her goal.

She returned her attention to her studies, focusing this time on all that was known about the missiles. Most remained at Verilotus under the control of the woman, Jubilee, a strange hybrid entity who—

No.

The Cryptologist caught herself. She pulled back, resisting the allure of peripheral questions, consciously realigning her curiosity with the quest.

Knowing the Bio-mechanic continuously shadowed her, she thought, *Two sentient missiles accompany the fleet, yet I find no research on them. Has no one ever studied them?*

"Why question me when you know the answer?"

They belong to Urban.

"Yes. Only one mind may control them, and only through the entanglement of silver."

Jubilee gave them to Urban.

"She gave their loyalty to Urban," the Bio-mechanic corrected. "The missiles are sentient. They desire to serve a higher mind. These two that accompany the fleet now serve Urban."

I would like to talk to them.

That cold chuckle again. "They don't belong to you, and you have no means to communicate with them, given the only way to do it is through the silver."

Only through the silver . . . ?

Within her own deep well of inherited knowledge, the Cryptologist found the answer to this half-formed question. *Ah, I understand. The silver is a physical information system. I cannot access it as I am.*

"You cannot access it at all. It is beyond you."

In this moment, that is true.

The Cryptologist now faced several questions. To pursue answers to each, she sought to replicate, but discovered the library allowed her only a single instance.

How irritating!

There would be no simultaneous solutions. But there were many ways forward.

First, the basics: A physical information system required a physical avatar to use it. A moment's thought revealed to her that she had no real knowledge of how to create such an avatar. However, there *was* a utility. She reviewed its documentation.

"You cannot use that," the Bio-mechanic informed her.

You are wrong. This is a well-designed utility. I understand how to employ it.

"You are an Apparatchik," the Bio-mechanic said. "You exist within this library, and only here."

The Cryptologist examined the code that defined her—and found no such restriction. *Again, you are mistaken.* She had been endowed with a task and she would do what was needed to solve it . . . so long as she did not endanger the ship or the ship's company. That was her restriction.

Hmm . . .

The utility required a template. Vytet had many such templates in the archive, one for every time she'd modified her avatar. The Cryptologist could just re-use one. That would be simple enough.

She chose the most recent.

But then she paused, weighing every parameter of the project against the injunction to bring no harm to the ship's company. And she realized she could do better. Vytet's avatar was extravagant in its height. A smaller form would draw significantly fewer resources from the ship's limited supply, and that would reduce the (already minor) risk of a future shortage that might (theoretically) endanger the ship's company. She acted at once, instructing the utility to decrease the planned height of the avatar. It did so, automatically rebalancing all other dimensions.

Has it never occurred to you to do this? she asked the Bio-mechanic.

"No, never," he answered.

She noted a bitter tone in his voice.

You are a strange entity, she observed.

"Not a distinguishing characteristic, given my present company. Consider this: even if you successfully inhabit this avatar, it will not give you access to the silver. None of the ship's company who rejected the silver has been re-infected with it here aboard the ship. And none of the ship-born have been touched by it either."

The ship-born . . . ?

Ah, yes.

She recalled that four members of the ship's company had left the fleet, choosing to remain behind at Verilotus. Three had been replaced with the ship-born—individuals all newly conceived.

"The silver can only be acquired on Verilotus," the Bio-mechanic concluded.

I see that as a premature conclusion, the Cryptologist replied.

She perused the catalog of all of Vytet's past configurations, admiring her progenitor's affection for a rainbow of existences. And wouldn't it be better to re-use one of these past designs, rather than duplicating Vytet's current form? *Yes.* She did not want to be mistaken for her progenitor.

After a brief search, she settled on a youthful female aspect with pale skin, light-blue eyes, and short black hair. Pretty and non-threatening—traits that should prove useful should she find herself among the ship's company.

She set the avatar to growing. Then, shifting focus, she began a review of all that was known of the silver.

CHAPTER NINE

STILL NO REPLY from the radio hail.

But the Astronomer's successive surveys of the belt of ruins had turned up an interesting anomaly: a tiny object that moved in defiance of any simple orbital path.

When the Astronomer recorded his discovery in the ship's log, numerous DIs took note. They sent out alerts, rousing dormant members of the ship's company. Moments later, ghosts began to gather in the library.

The architecture of a ghost muted emotions and still Urban sensed excitement and tension in the growing crowd around him. He'd been among the first to manifest in the library, alongside Clementine, Vytet, and Pasha. Others winked into existence as they emerged from dormancy: Tarnya, Kona, Shoran, Naresh . . .

They stood together on the smooth plane of the library's unbounded floor, facing two highly magnified images of the object that had captured the Astronomer's attention.

The first image showed only a chip of darkness, visible at the liminal edge of a background megastructure, where a sparse vapor of expelled gases scattered distant Tanjiri's light. That chip had not been visible in any earlier survey.

The second image showed the object as it appeared in the infrared spectrum. Because of the widely separated positions of the observing telescopes, the images they produced could be combined to create a three-dimensional extrapolation of the object's shape. It looked very much like an outrider—thin and elongated, a cylindrical form narrowing to a point at the near end—visible because it was slightly warmer than the standard cold temperatures of objects in the belt.

Riffan popped into existence, a delighted smile on his face. He pushed past Vyet and squeezed Urban's shoulder in greeting. "So we've woken something, at last!" he exclaimed as he turned to the image in wide-eyed wonder.

Urban envied his enthusiasm. He wished he shared it. His own ghost-self suffered a simulated knot in its belly as Clemantine's cautionary words returned to him: *Only a predator approaches in silence.*

"Not much detail in these images," Naresh observed in his usual calm, clinical tone.

"Perhaps that's because it *lacks* detail," Pasha suggested. "It could be that its surface is smooth and uninterrupted by any complex geometry."

"Certainly a possibility," the physicist allowed. "Even likely. Time will tell."

"Without knowing its size, we can't gauge its distance from us," Vyet mused. "And we'll need more observations to determine the direction of its movement."

"It's silent," Urban reminded them. "It hasn't answered our hail. That concerns me."

In truth, he was more than concerned. He felt haunted. The object's silence had dredged up a very old memory. Long ago, he'd been told a story of the first time a human ship sighted a Chenzeme courser. Never before had an alien intelligence been encountered. The crew had been fired up with a sense of wonder. *It seemed a miracle, dreadful and awesome.* But the courser had remained distant, and made no reply to their radioed greetings.

After a time, the crew had observed a flash of heat on the courser's hull that induced a brief blurring of its image. Later, it was understood the alien vessel had emitted a cloud of bioactive dust, but no one grasped that at the time. The dust eventually encountered their ship, infecting it with a self-replicating plague.

The story of that encounter had been told to Urban by the sole survivor.

"We need to know more," he said urgently. "How far away it is, how fast it's moving. I'm initiating a radar scan."

"That could be taken as an aggressive action," Kona warned. "We don't want to look like we're trying to acquire a target."

Urban met this with a slight smile that probably didn't hide his impatience. He and his father remained stubbornly alike in appearance. So much so, that he sometimes suspected the old man of taking the contrary position just to delineate the differences between them.

"It needs to be done," he insisted.

"I think so too," Clemantine said. "But let's announce our intentions first. A new radio message. Let it know we're about to do the scan."

Urban nodded. "Agreed. I want you to take care of it. Compose the message, and send it."

Send the message if you like, a cold, familiar voice said, audible to everyone gathered there. The other Clemantine, speaking from across the void. *I'll do the scan. If the vessel objects, let it target* Griffin.

Urban looked into the eyes of the local version. Clemantine nodded her assent. And Kona added, "It's the logical strategy."

Griffin was their insurance. Though the smaller courser carried a copy of the library and archival copies of every member of the ship's company, *Dragon* remained their home. If need demanded it, *Griffin* would always be the ship they chose to sacrifice. The other Clemantine knew that. She wanted it that way.

"All right, then," Urban agreed. "Tarnya?"

"Yes?" she asked, her brows raised in question. Tarnya was good with people, a natural politician. She tended to speak for the ship's company in these limited discussions.

"I'd like you to see to it that everyone's awake. Encounters like this are the reason we're here. No one should be sleeping through it. And Riffan . . ."

Riffan turned to him, bright eyed. "Yes? What can I do?"

"Make sure everyone updates their archival copies across the fleet, in case the next few hours turn out to be our last."

CHAPTER TEN

JOLLY HUACHO EMERGED from cold sleep into a state of quiet terror. Wide-eyed, he took in the sight of the softly luminous wall-weed that cradled him. The cocooned bodies of three anonymous others, dead-still among the weed's long tendrils, shared the little zero-gravity chamber with him.

No. Not zero-gravity. His body had weight; he was hanging against the wall-weed. That meant *Dragon* was accelerating. Or decelerating? He tried to work it out, but his fear-haunted mind rejected the question. Closing his eyes, he strove to soothe himself, whispering, "*Don't panic, don't panic, don't panic.*"

Oh, how he hated cold sleep! And the irrational fear it induced, that he would never wake up again. Even so, he had retreated to the sanctuary of cold sleep over and over again, ever since leaving Verilotus. Skipping through the years, still fleeing the loneliness he'd hoped to leave behind on his birth world.

No regrets.

He mouthed the words. He did not regret his decision to join this company of Dragoneers—that's how he thought of them. He would not allow himself to regret it.

As his mind quieted, he envisioned his mother, his sister Jubilee, all his other siblings, and the vast open skies of Verilotus. He missed them all. But he would not be with his family even if he'd said no to Urban's invitation. Because he would have gone wayfaring. He would be wandering even now around the vast circle of the world, growing old and bitter as he searched for a lover who surely did not exist.

For all the strangeness of his fate, this—an open-ended future of radical possibility—remained the better choice. Exhaling tension in a long soft sigh, he embraced yet again the reality of his present existence, one in which anything could happen.

Calmer now, he looked around again and saw the other cocoons dissolving, the white gelatinous matter flowing away in threads, returning to the generative walls to be stored for future use. So he was not waking alone, at a scheduled time he had set.

That meant something interesting had happened, and Urban was summoning everyone to awareness. Jolly had left instructions with his DI that in such circumstances it should bring him to wakefulness faster than the optimal timeline. He did not want anyone, even his closest friends, to witness the momentary panic that always accompanied his revival.

The dissolving cocoons revealed faces. He recognized Sayuri, Zariah, and Abby—all ship-born, but adults now. Adults at his last waking. A flush warmed his cheeks at a memory of intimacy.

He wiped away remnant gel from his own cold-sleep cocoon as clothing budded off the wall beside him. Hurrying now, he pulled on the knee-length shorts that had become his customary wear, and a sleeveless form-fitting shirt.

The ship-born had begun to stir, rolling over in the wall-weed, eyes open but unfocused, doubtlessly questing for information on when and why they'd been awakened. This reminded Jolly to query his DI. The response came back at once: *An unknown vessel has been sighted. We are attempting to establish contact.*

Ohhh . . .

So this was it. Very soon they would encounter the god at Tanjiri and they would live or die at its discretion.

"We'll live," he said in whispered syllables barely audible even to his own ears, "and we'll see great things."

Without waiting for the three ship-born to fully waken, he kicked free of the wall-weed, dropped to the floor, and left, pushing his way through the chamber's gel door.

———

The Cryptologist discovered that facts about the silver were scarce, though observations were abundant. With the exception of the ship-born, who had not existed at the time, everyone among the ship's company had experienced the silver during their years on Verilotus. Significantly, all but two had rejected the augmentation when the time came to depart that world.

One of those two was Urban, the ship's master. And then there was the Verilotus native Urban had brought aboard—Jolly Huacho, who had been born to the silver.

Surely this Jolly Huacho would know best how to manipulate the silver and transfer it, avatar to avatar . . . yet he'd left scant records in the library. Where then did he store his personal history? And why had no one interviewed him?

I will interview him.

She sought for his ghost in the library, but he was not there. So she shifted to a different matrix, entering for the first time her physical avatar. It lay cocooned within the ship's tissue when she woke within it.

The hyper-reality of this new existence shocked her. Too much input. Too many senses. She felt her mind drowning while her body lay trapped, blinded and weighty with a physicality she'd never experienced before.

So she fled, sending her ghost back to the library and yet . . . *she* remained. This mind within the flesh. "How can I go back?" she whispered into the little airspace allowed within her cocoon.

A copy of her ghost returned to her from the library. *No, go back,* she thought. Too late. Its mind blended with hers, became trapped with her. She tried again, generating a new ghost and sending it to its freedom—and still she remained. No longer an electronic entity, but an artifact of this flesh, generated by it, existing because of it. Trapped.

The cocoon opened, spilling her into a little chamber, empty but for herself and waving tendrils of wall-weed. Again, a ghost came to her from the library. *Stay away!* she thought. *One of us at least should be free.*

A voice answered, speaking within her mind, *One of us is free.*

"You," she whispered, recognizing her own former self, her core self, her ghost, extant within the library. How she longed to be that ghost again, and not this version, encumbered with the rapid rhythmic pounding of a frightened heart.

Calm down, her ghost-self chided. *Deep breaths. Embrace the existence. There must be compensations.*

"I hope so." Soft words formed of whispery air. A fascinating action, this speaking of words. Her chest rose and fell, leading her to consider the working of her lungs, and from there, the beating of her heart, the hunger of her belly, the churning of her thoughts.

Cool air brushed her bare skin, a pleasant sensation counteracting the heat of a frightened flush. So yes . . . perhaps there *were* compensations.

It was not yet mid-morning, ship's time, when Jolly left the warren and entered onto the gee-deck. The simulated sky suggested mixed weather: bright-blue overhead but with a distant buildup of gray clouds that implied rain to come.

Not that it ever really rains here.

Jolly missed rain, along with the unpredictability of wind and lightning storms. He missed mountains too, and the sight of the silver rising in deep twilight to gleam beneath the stars.

He had been so excited, triumphant and awed in those first years aboard *Dragon*. But as time passed, all the miraculous new discoveries he'd made came to feel ordinary. Artificial night followed artificial day in an endless chain and little changed except the ship-born, gradually growing up.

Jolly had spent much of their youth in cold sleep, aware on some level that he was waiting for them to catch up to his age, which he guessed to be mid-twenties. It was hard to keep track. Everyone else was so much older! And he'd done it. The ship-born had become his peers, though in recent decades they'd mostly slept too.

But now, at last, *Dragon* had made the crossing . . .

He hurried on with rising excitement down the short, curved path to the pavilion. Already he could hear voices in quiet conversation. He followed the sound to the amphitheater, with its four curved tiers of seats sheltered beneath a vine-covered pergola. It surprised him to find the seats all empty.

Only three people had arrived ahead of him: Clemantine and Vytet, standing beside the dais, and Urban, who sat cross-legged on it, watching Jolly with a half-smile.

"You ready for some action?" Urban asked him.

A question that left Jolly breathless with the imminence of change. "We're here, then?"

"We are, and it looks like something here knows it."

"We're waiting on the radar return," Clemantine explained. "We're guessing it'll be several minutes, at least."

The sound of footsteps and excited voices warned that more Dragoneers had emerged from the warren and would soon reach the amphitheater.

For no reason Jolly could see, Urban suddenly stood up, looking alarmed. "*It's too soon,*" he murmured, turning to the display screen at the back of the dais.

Jolly followed his gaze. At first, he thought the screen was just blank and black, but then he realized there was a vague shape in the darkness.

"By the Unknown God," Clemantine whispered.

"What?" Jolly asked. "Is that it?"

"Yes," Vytet said as she too studied the screen. "That's it, and it's far closer to us than we ever suspected."

Fabric walls deployed around the amphitheater, rolling down from the frame of the pergola while the canopy shifted to black. Soft, shuffling noises and nervous whispers in the rows behind Jolly testified to the presence of all sixty-six members of the ship's company.

His early arrival had earned him a seat in front, between Kona and Pasha. He leaned forward, studying the image of the local vessel on the display screen, though really, there wasn't much to see.

Griffin's powerful radar had yielded only faint echoes, enough to reveal the vessel's position and its size—just forty meters from bow to stern.

"Smaller than an outrider," Vytet observed from her post on the dais.

Urban stood beside the low stage. "Too small to carry a meaningful amount of chemical reactant, and too slender to house a propulsion reef or a nuclear reactor."

From her seat at the end of the front row, Clemantine spoke in clipped syllables. "We've seen this before, haven't we?"

Jolly shifted anxiously. What was she implying?

Kona offered an explanation, his low voice rising easily over a soft tumult of whispers. "The dimensions are familiar, aren't they? It's reminiscent of our own sentient missiles."

No, Jolly thought, gripping the armrests of his chair. *It can't be over this soon. It can't.*

He looked to Urban for some sign, some reason to doubt Kona's conclusion. If only he could see a flash of white teeth, that familiar rogue's grin, he would be reassured. But Urban stood motionless in the dark.

"We don't yet know its trajectory," Vytet pointed out. "Or its rate of acceleration, if any."

A voice spoke from a seat behind Jolly. He recognized it as belonging to Naresh, the physicist. "That will come soon. We need to plan our response now. Do we attempt further communication? Or do we destroy this solitary weapon while there is time?"

"We haven't come here to start a war," Urban said.

A rustle of movement caused Jolly to turn. He saw Naresh standing two rows back. "I'm not suggesting that. But we have a right to defend ourselves."

"We have not been attacked," Vytet pointed out, her voice pitched to soothe. "Stand by . . . the Astronomer has enough data now. He has calculated the object's trajectory."

The display shifted. The vague image of the local vessel winked out, replaced by a schematic map of the fleet. In the vanguard, the four outriders, with the sentient missiles a distant escort. *Griffin* came next. *Dragon* trailed behind.

With the map established, the point of view raced away. The tags that marked the fleet retreated to one side of the screen, congealing together so it became impossible to distinguish them. And then, finally, on the opposite side of the screen, another tag appeared. This one marked the position of the local vessel. A curving line linked it to the fleet.

"The good news," Vytet announced, speaking over a fresh tide of murmurs. "The object is not accelerating."

Clemantine stood up. "But it's definitely coming to meet us."

Jolly felt Pasha stir beside him. "Might that be a good thing?" she asked, sounding tentative, as if still building a theory in her head. Then she too stood up, turning to face the rows of seats. "Assume for a moment it *is* like our missiles. The fleet is too widely separated for one such vessel to be effective against us. It seems to me more likely that it's an emissary, rather than an assault force—"

"If so, why hasn't it responded to our radio hail?" Naresh asked.

Jolly spoke. He didn't really mean to. He'd never before tendered a comment in any gathering of the ship's company. What did he know, that they did not? They, who had lived for centuries. Yet he found himself speaking aloud: "What if it's a scout, tasked with discovering what we *really* are?"

A soft little laugh from Pasha, and heat rushed into his cheeks. But she was not scoffing. "I think that could be right," she said. "What are we anyway, but something utterly alien? Though we've made the claim, we've offered no real evidence of our human origin. Why should we be believed?"

Urban spoke then, a quiet tension in his voice as he said, "Look closer at the map. It's clear now, *Dragon* is the target."

Onscreen, the point of view slowly zoomed in on the fleet, while the dashed line extrapolating the local vessel's trajectory remained visible. Jolly saw that the line bypassed the outriders and *Griffin*, to converge on *Dragon* in just two days' time.

"We are the source of the radio hail," Clemantine said in explanation.

Suddenly everyone was talking, debating with their neighbors what should be done, or standing up to project their opinions over the rising noise. The lights came up. Vytet strode to the center of the dais and, raising both hands, she called for quiet.

The chaos of voices calmed as Urban stepped up beside her. "We need to minimize any perceived threat we might present to this system," he said. "So I'm sending *Griffin* away. *Lam Lha*, *Elepaio*, and the missiles too. They'll veer off, bypass this system. But *Dragon* will continue to advance, because *Dragon* is the target."

That rogue smile, at last. It gave Jolly courage despite the implication of his words.

"After that, we take on the task Jolly has set for us—to convince this scout ship we are who we say we are—and I think I know how to do that."

The Cryptologist lingered in the warren, flexing her fingers, her toes, her facial muscles. She blinked her eyes, and stretched—exercises that bound her mind closer to this new body. She herself had no memory of a prior physical existence, but the body knew how to move. It had retained Vytet's knowledge of balance and motion. The Cryptologist found that if she didn't think too deeply about *how* to move, only that she wanted to move, a well-honed brain-body connection made it happen.

A fascinating process, really. Her initial shock had passed, yielding to wonder at the complexity of this new existence.

Advancing cautiously at first, but faster with practice, she made her way through the warren. She saw no one else, and the open chambers she passed were all empty.

Through her atrium, she messaged her ghost in the library. *Am I able to ascertain the physical location of Jolly Huacho?*

The ghost answered, *I am. He is presently in the amphitheater, with the ship's company.*

Having inherited from Vytet an understanding of the geography of the ship, the Cryptologist asked no further questions. She hurried from the warren, transitioning to the gee deck, and then following the short path to the amphitheater.

"Let me go with you," Jolly pleaded.

He had rushed after Urban as the gathering broke up, catching him just a few steps outside the pavilion, a hand on his arm to secure his attention while Clemantine looked on with an amused half-smile.

Jolly always felt short, standing beside them. But that was all right. He wasn't a kid anymore. He looked Urban in the eye and insisted, "I want to do this. I've been a passenger since I got here. But finally, this is something I can do."

Urban intended to lead a small party outside the ship. They would go dressed in skin suits and tethered for safety, and they would reveal themselves to the local vessel—a first step toward confirming their human identity.

Clemantine tried to discourage him. "You've never been outside the ship before and this is not a good time to run the experiment. You have no idea what it's like to sense the void all around you. You don't know how you'll react."

"No, I'll be okay." He returned his focus to Urban. "You know I can handle it. I've been through the silver. *We've* been through it."

Urban's lips turned in a slight, crooked smile. "*Sooth.* You can come. Get yourself a skin suit, and get the Engineer to tutor you on the protocols for going outside. You've got time. I'm going to wait a few more hours. Let the gap close. Make sure we're close enough for the local vessel to see us when we show it who we are."

Something behind Jolly caught Urban's attention. His gaze shifted. His dark brows knit in a scowl. Clemantine looked too. Her eyes widened.

Jolly turned around—and saw a smiling woman approaching on the path from the warren. Like him, she wore shorts and a sleeveless shirt, and she stood no taller than he did. He found her pretty, with her light-blue eyes and delicate features. Yet the sight of her brought a chill because she was no Dragoneer. He had no idea who she was.

Her gaze met his. She smiled as if she knew him. A pretty smile that made him want to trust her despite a strong instinct to the contrary. When she was only a few steps away, she said, "I am here to interview you, Jolly Huacho. I desire to know everything you know about the history, effect, and operation of the silver."

Jolly turned to Urban, hoping for insight on what was going on, but Urban was elsewhere, his avatar frozen in a narrow-eyed glare fixed on the pretty woman. A moment later his lips twitched. He turned and stalked back to the amphitheater. "Vytet!" he shouted. "We need to talk."

Clemantine looked undecided if she should follow or not, while the woman continued to smile at Jolly. A smile too fixed to be real, but it drew him in all the same.

"You still carry the silver, don't you?" she asked. "Show it to me."

He did. He raised a hand, revealing the bright silvery sparks of the *ha*, dancing across his palm and between his fingers.

CHAPTER ELEVEN

"EXPLAIN," URBAN COMMANDED, his furious gaze scanning his crew of Apparatchiks, each one contained within his own frameless window. Urban had abandoned his physical avatar, manifesting in the library. "Explain to me what that thing is doing on my ship."

The Bio-mechanic cocked an eyebrow and answered in slow, self-satisfied words. "You asked Vytet to try again to solve the puzzle of the needle. This is her solution, to approach the problem from a fresh point of view. It's daring, don't you think, to create an Apparatchik stripped of one's own core beliefs?"

"Is that how this entity was made?" the Scholar asked, clearly intrigued. "Is it then still an Apparatchik?"

"Never mind *that*," Urban growled, in no mood for philosophy. He glared at the Bio-mechanic. Of all the Apparatchiks, this one had worked most closely with the Chenzeme elements of the ship and over the centuries his persona had taken on aspects of Chenzeme attitudes. He'd become cold, distant, disdainful, and deeply competitive. And he'd learned to keep secrets.

"Why didn't you tell me?" Urban demanded.

"You would have stopped the experiment."

"*You* should have stopped it. That thing has manifested. How is that even possible?"

"Ah. In truth, it proved quite easy."

"So you *were* part of it?"

"Just an observer. I have taken it as my duty to monitor all the Cryptologist's activities to ensure she brings no harm to the fleet."

"The Cryptologist?"

"A name she took for herself, given her core task is to decrypt the puzzle of the needle."

The Engineer asked, "What progress has she made?"

The Bio-mechanic turned to him. "None at all, though she *is* a determined thing."

With a growl of disgust, Urban abandoned the conversation. Shifting back into his avatar, he checked the personnel map. It showed Vytet still inside the amphitheater. He turned to go back in, and as he did, he caught Clemantine's outraged gaze.

It's an Apparatchik of Vytet, he told her.

Shock stole her voice. She could only mouth a single syllable. *What?*

He nodded and stalked inside. "Vytet! We need to talk."

Vytet stood beside the dais, engaged in conversation with Pasha and Naresh. All three looked around as Urban crowded into their circle.

"You created an Apparatchik," he accused. "One that doesn't share your core beliefs. An independent entity."

Pasha reacted first, lowering her chin and crossing her arms—signaling she'd been part of it.

Naresh, by contrast, turned to Vytet in astonishment. "You didn't?"

Vytet read Urban's anger and reacted to it, speaking in a softly soothing voice as she affirmed, "It's true, I did. You asked me to try again to solve the problem of the needle. I saw this as the best way—and you made no objection."

"How could I?" he demanded. "I didn't know."

"But the Bio-mechanic knew. He was there. I assumed he would inform you."

"He decided not to, knowing I would have stopped the experiment."

"*Ah.*" She shrugged. "Well then, I apologize. But there's no need to be so upset. The Apparatchik is a tool, designed to address a specific problem. And when that task is done—solved or dead-ended—I mean to delete it."

"No, Vytet. You can't just delete it."

"Why not? It's just a ghost."

He gritted his teeth. Could she really not know? "It's not just a ghost. She's here. She's outside."

Vytet cocked her head. "Explain?"

He half turned. "Look there. The woman talking to Jolly. That's her."

"No."

"Yes."

"*Oh shit*," Pasha whispered. "The Bio-mechanic said he would watch the Apparatchik—"

I have been watching her, the Bio-mechanic interrupted through their atriums. *She is an ambitious 'tool,' closely focused on the task you have given her. Why should I interfere? She has not yet placed the fleet in danger.*

"It's a dangerous precedent," Urban answered, each syllable weighted with anger. "She is an artificial personality. She shouldn't be able to manifest on her own like that. She shouldn't want to."

Ah, the Bio-mechanic said with a soft chuckle. *You're worried I will emulate her.*

"Do you mean to?" Urban asked him.

I confess to some curiosity, but I have found, as you've just confirmed, that it's not within the spectrum of my permitted actions.

"Don't try it," Urban warned. "I need you as you are."

Oh look, the Bio-mechanic said. *Jolly is attempting to infect Vytet's new tool with silver.*

Urban looked again, and saw Jolly with his palm raised, pressed against the palm of the Cryptologist.

The two were not alone.

The trio of ship-born youths had discovered the stranger. They crowded around with looks of amazement while Clemantine watched with wary eyes.

"Jolly, don't!" Urban shouted. A plea, a command, uttered aloud but cast through his atrium too. He bounded out of the amphitheater, fired by the fear that this creation of Vytet's would soon gain even more power.

Jolly responded, yanking his hand away, breaking the connection with the Cryptologist. But that initial moment of shock transformed to resentment when he looked up at Urban. "There's no harm in it, Urban. You know it won't work." Jolly's gaze cut to Clemantine, then back again. "I only wanted to prove that to her. I can't wake the *ha* if there's no *ha* within her to waken."

Clemantine nodded her agreement. "You know it's a harmless exercise. That's why I let him do it."

One of the ship-born spoke up then—Sayuri, a girl of restless nature whose bold dark eyes seemed always to be evaluating those around her, seeking some amusing weakness. "If only it *could* work," she said.

Like her cohort, Sayuri had perhaps twenty years of experiential age. All three ship-born had grown from infancy in the first two decades of the crossing, and then entered cold sleep, waking only annually after that, along with a majority of the ship's company.

"I would love to experience the silver," she told Urban. Then she cast a coy smile at Jolly. "He's tried to share it with me a hundred times, in a hundred ways. But nothing works." She gestured at the Cryptologist. "This strange creature insisted she must try it anyway."

Abby, another of the ship-born—quieter and more thoughtful than Sayuri—asked Urban, "Did you know she claims to be an Apparatchik of Vytet?"

"So I've heard," Urban answered as he studied the problematic woman.

"But that's impossible, isn't it?" asked Zariah, the last of the trio.

Sayuri rolled her eyes. "Isn't she here, bro? So it's not impossible." Her gaze shifted to Urban. "And you don't want her here, do you? But she's a real person now and you can't just get rid of her."

"That is the key point," Clemantine said as Vytet, Pasha, and Naresh joined them, gathering around this new being.

Vytet's downturned mouth connoted regret, ambivalence, uncertainty. Pasha, by contrast, eyed the Apparatchik unselfconsciously, her green eyes ablaze with horrified fascination.

For her part, the Cryptologist had been closely following this discussion, eyeing each speaker in turn. Now she said, "This avatar has opened new possibilities in my studies. I will keep it, though I will maintain a minimal impact on the ship's resources so as not to endanger the fleet." She turned to Jolly. "I have many questions, so I will interview you now."

Pasha held out a hand. "Slow down. I want to know—"

But Jolly cut her out of the conversation. Shooting Urban a guarded look, he asked, "Are you okay with that?"

Vytet said, "I created her to solve the puzzle of the needle. If you want her to succeed, then give her what she wants."

Urban glared, rigid with anger, but what could he do? *Nothing.* Sayuri had correctly summarized the situation. The Cryptologist was undeniably real, alive, a unique being, and as such she was endowed with rights like anyone else. No way now to roll back her existence. He had no choice but to accept it.

In a voice low and gruff, he told Jolly, "Go ahead. Answer her questions."

"I still want to go with you," Jolly said.

"Go where?" Sayuri asked, anxious and eager—but neither Jolly nor Urban answered her.

Urban told Jolly, "I'll message you when it's time."

Then he left, signaling Vytet and Clemantine to follow. Pasha came too, casting backward glances at the Cryptologist. Urban did not look back, but he watched with his expanded senses as Jolly and the Cryptologist set off the opposite way around the winding path.

In a quiet corner on the other side of the pavilion he halted. In a low, urgent voice he told the three, "This must never happen again. No more artificial entities, electronic or physical. Vytet, you'll inform the ship's company. You'll let them know this was a misunderstanding. And I'll see to it that restrictions are added to the library."

He did not mean for this to be a discussion, so he turned to go. But Vytet couldn't leave it alone.

"What do you mean to do with her?" she asked.

"There's nothing I can do!"

"I didn't mean for this to happen, Urban. I planned all along to delete the Apparatchik. I never imagined—"

"That's just it! We intend them as tools, but they're complex evolving systems, independent, and never entirely predictable. I created the Apparatchiks because I was alone. I had no choice. And they've changed over time. You've seen it. Especially the Biomechanic. Can you predict how this new one will evolve?"

Vytet's mouth turned down in worry. Clemantine saw it too. "There's something more, isn't there?" she asked.

"The Cryptologist will do nothing that could endanger the fleet," Vytet assured them. "That's a core value."

Sarcasm edged Urban's words. "Yeah? Well, that's nice."

Vytet closed her eyes a moment. Then she caught Pasha's gaze. Receiving a nod of encouragement, she let out a slow breath and spoke the disturbing truth. "I needed to ensure the Apparatchik was independent, that it would think differently from me. So I pushed past the warnings and eliminated most of its core identity modules."

Clemantine leaned forward, her voice low. "You're saying it's not you. Not really even a version of you."

"Yes, exactly. It needed to be a different persona. To think in a different way."

Urban's hand clenched into a fist, fingernails biting into his palm. "Damn it, Vytet!" He shifted his wrath to Pasha. "And you let her do this."

"Don't blame Pasha," Vytet countered. "*You* wanted this. You wanted it because Lezuri is still haunting you, still manipulating you, still infecting you with doubt and fear. If you need to solve the needle to get past that, this is the only path I know to take."

CHAPTER TWELVE

THE CRYPTOLOGIST IS *a very strange person.*

That was Jolly's impression after answering what felt like a thousand questions about growing up on Verilotus, his adventures there, on what it had felt like to manipulate the silver, and on what he'd seen when he visited the core of his ring-shaped home world. She'd even asked if she could take tissue samples, to replicate studies done long ago.

A strange person, but intriguing too.

Sensing at the start that the interview would go long, Jolly had invited the Cryptologist to relocate to his cottage. The ship-born trio had not needed an invitation. They had come along too. He didn't mind. They were his friends and sometime-lovers. But Sayuri and Zariah had soon grown bored with the Cryptologist's incessant questioning, and had drifted away. Abby had stayed until a game of flying fox started up, and then she'd left too.

Now Jolly had the sofa to himself. He lay staring up and out through an open window, watching a troop of small green birds known as mejiro bouncing between a rain tree's pink blossoms.

The Cryptologist surprised him with her next question. "Has your silver augmentation suppressed your natural curiosity?"

Jolly turned his head, quirked an eyebrow. "Why ask that?"

The Cryptologist sat cross-legged on a large square pillow, her hands resting palms-down against her thighs. She had not moved her hands since she'd sat down two hours ago. It was as if she'd forgotten she had hands, or that they were not really part of her. More like tools that she had put away for the time being.

She used her facial expression in the same way. For all the time they'd talked, she had watched him with an intent gaze, her eyes bright with an unwavering curiosity, never exhibiting a hint of confusion, distraction, boredom, or embarrassment. It was unsettling to hold someone's attention for so long, and yet he found it alluring too.

He had studied her in turn, trying to see something of Vytet in her mannerisms, her posture, in the shape of her face—a pretty face, with wide blue eyes and a smooth, pale complexion, framed by a thick mass of smooth black hair. She was supposed to be based on Vytet, but he could not see it, or maybe he did not want to see it. He wanted to think of her as an original person. Of course Vytet had shown many different faces to the world. So he'd been told.

In answer to his question, the Cryptologist said, "You have stated that you rarely engage with the silver."

"Right. It's all too far away now." At Verilotus, he'd learned to transit the silver, and to use it to find those friends and loved ones with whom he'd shared the *ha*. But all connection to his home world had long ago faded from his sensorium. "It's only Urban I can sense now."

"Yes. You explained this limitation. You also stated that you carry within you an extensive information resource compiled during your years on Verilotus, especially during that phase when you were lost within the silver, and afterward, when you learned to control it. Why do you not engage with this resource? It is as if you stand at the door of a library but refuse to go in. Natural curiosity should lead you to enter and explore—but perhaps the silver itself discourages this?"

Jolly's cheeks warmed with an embarrassed flush. "I don't think that's it." His gaze shifted again to the tree outside, only to find the birds had moved on. "I just don't like it." He tapped his head. "What's in here isn't much compared to Verilotus. But it *feels* overwhelming. Like I could get lost again. You know that's why Vytet gave up the silver, right? It's why they all did. You don't think Vytet is lacking in curiosity, do you?"

"I do not, but I recognize that Vytet's curiosity is tempered and limited by fear."

Turning his head again to regard her, he met that same alert expression. "And does fear limit *your* curiosity?"

She answered brightly, "No. I have not yet met that boundary."

"But you can *be* afraid?" he asked with some anxiety.

"Oh yes. The module exists. I fear many things, such as violating social norms, causing nerve pain within this avatar, or inadvertently taking an action that would endanger the fleet. But I do not fear to ask questions."

Jolly laughed softly. "That is certainly true."

The Cryptologist stood up suddenly, still with that alert gaze, still with her palms pressed against her thighs, but now she smiled. "I observe you are tired of questions." She performed a slight bow. "I will leave you now so that you may recover."

"Wait." Jolly sat up. "Where will you go?"

"I will place this avatar in cold sleep until it is needed again."

Jolly found he didn't want her to go. "But everyone's awake," he said. "You should stay too. I'm hungry. Aren't you? We could get something to eat and you could ask questions of some of the others."

"You want me to stay." She sounded puzzled.

A fresh flush stung his cheeks. "Sure. I'm curious about you."

"Why?"

"Well, because you're someone new . . . and very different from anyone else I've ever met."

"Different how?"

He ducked his gaze as his cheeks brightened with yet more heat. He said the first thing that came to mind. "You ask unexpected questions. I like that." He looked up again, and though he felt embarrassed, he knew she was not. So he dared to speak the truth. "You're a strange person, and I'm strange enough to find that intriguing."

"I am strange? In what context?"

"A social context. In your mannerisms, your interests."

"Ah. That is likely a result of the eccentric selection of modules defining my personality."

"Why don't you have a name?" Jolly asked her.

"A name?"

"Something besides the Cryptologist."

"That is my name. It's the name I gave myself."

"Oh. I'm sorry."

She cocked her head, but he waved away her unspoken question. "Let's go to the dining court," he suggested. "And—"

He broke off as an alert reached his atrium. Urban calling. He accepted the link.

Do you still want to go outside?

Yes!

Then meet in the warren. We're getting ready now.

Right after that, Urban issued a general alert, speaking to every Dragoneer: *Dragon will be easing off its deceleration, beginning now. We'll be coasting for the next hour or so.*

Jolly scrambled to his feet. "I'm sorry," he told the Cryptologist. "Something's come up. I can't go to the dining court after all. But maybe we can meet later?"

She studied him, her eyes narrowed in thought. "Yes. Presuming no hostile intervention from the approaching vessel, it should be possible for us to meet later."

Jolly grinned. He couldn't help it. "We'll be all right," he assured her. Then he darted out the door.

Alone on the high bridge, Urban listened to Clemantine's cold twin argue against his dictate that she should leave the system—leave and let *Dragon* confront the local vessel.

My duty, my purpose, is to protect the fleet. The first risk in any encounter should be mine.

And in a different situation that would be true, Urban conceded. *But here, now, the local vessel has picked out Dragon. We are the target, and that makes you our refuge. So go. Go now, while there is only one potential weapon in play.*

There must be more, she mused. *There has to be.*

He knew there were more. His sentient missiles had sensed thousands of dimensional intrusions scattered throughout the ruins. But all he said was, *It would be illogical to assume this is the only one.*

Eventually, he persuaded her, and *Griffin* veered off, accelerating swiftly as it moved deeper into interstellar space, accompanied by the missiles and two outriders. If things went wrong—if this venture to Tanjiri ended badly, perhaps with his avatar consumed in a blister of inter-dimensional white light—the missiles would be lost too, because he had no means to replicate the silver within any future avatar, and without the silver, he would vanish from the missiles' mindspace. And then? They would coast through all time, waiting with machine patience for instructions that would never come.

At least then he would be free of any temptation to ever use the hellish devices . . . a thought that triggered a pulse of grim humor.

A submind shared these speculations with his avatar. The merging memories induced a cynical half-smile. *Don't give up on me yet,* he thought—and sent a submind back.

He had changed into a pale gold skin suit in preparation for the imminent venture to the hull. With *Dragon* coasting, the warren had become a zero-gravity environment. Urban drifted in the main passage, hood-down, following the progress of the local vessel as he waited for his team to assemble.

Periodic radar pulses proved Pasha right in her early suggestion that the vessel's hull was smooth and featureless, just like his sentient missiles. Very soon, the local vessel would sweep past *Pytheas* and *Khonsu*, drawing closer to *Dragon* than either outrider.

Shoran joined him first. "At last, something to do," she said with an eager grin. She and Clemantine were of a kind, two powerful women, tall and strongly built. At Deception Well, Shoran had been a planetary guide. She lived for adventure. Today she wore a light-green skin suit, with her long silver hair bound tight in a coiled braid.

Clemantine and Pasha came next. They arrived together, but not companionably. Clemantine, in a softly glowing silver skin suit, looked irked, her lips pressed together in a tight line. Pasha wore light blue, a pastel color that set off the flustered blush in her pale cheeks. Urban guessed they'd been discussing the Cryptologist.

"Are we ready?" Shoran asked eagerly, seeming oblivious to the tension.

"One more," Clementine told her.

Many others had wanted to go, Riffan among them. "Next time," Urban had promised him. He'd limited their number because this venture was an experiment, and potentially risky. He had never visited *Dragon*'s hull before. No one had. And he had no idea how the local vessel would react to their presence outside the ship.

"Who are we waiting for?" Pasha asked, looking irritated at the delay.

"He's here now," Urban said.

He had watched Jolly with his extended senses as the kid rushed from the gee deck and transitioned to the warren. Now Jolly appeared at the end of the tunnel, breathless and flustered and still dressed in his day-to-day clothes as Urban had known he would be.

Heat suffused Jolly's cheeks as he shot down the tunnel to join the team. "I know I'm late. I'm sorry."

Despite the absence of any simulated gravity, he suffered the weight of Urban's annoyed gaze.

"You're supposed to be wearing a skin suit," Pasha scolded him.

"I know." He didn't need to be reminded that his participation in this expedition was an indulgence, a privilege he hadn't earned. He was well aware of that. "I didn't realize you meant to go this soon," he told Urban. "And the Cryptologist's interview ran long. I still need to generate a skin suit." Of course he'd never done that before and he had no idea how to do it.

"I've done it for you," Urban said as a shapeless, writhing, lime-green fabric drifted free of the wall-weed, startling Jolly so that he shied away.

"Is that it? How do I put it on?"

"It will put itself on you," Clementine explained with a cool, amused smile. "It's keyed to you. It knows who you are. You just need to get your clothes off first."

"Oh."Jolly glanced around. Should he duck into an open chamber to change?

Then he caught sight of Urban's narrowed eyes, the quirk of his lips into that familiar rogue's smile. He couldn't tell if Urban was angry or amused—not that he liked either option.

"It's called a skin suit because it fits against your skin," Urban said. "It's the only way you can wear it."

"All right."

Clothing was customary among *Dragon's* people—*of course it was!*—even so, no one ever seemed bothered by moments of nudity . . . except Jolly. Where he'd grown up on Verilotus, the unclothed body was only ever seen by a lover.

But Verilotus lay far behind, and Jolly had worked hard to adapt to new ways. He resolved not to hide. But he did turn his back. A compromise. Quickly, he peeled off his clothes, leaving them to drift. The touch of the warren's cool air against his skin induced a shiver. Then something touched his back. Something warm and soft. He grabbed at the glowing wall-weed to turn himself around and as he did, the green fabric of the skin suit enfolded him, wrapping his arms, his legs, his torso. Thin gloves formed around his hands. Then the suit contracted just a little, until it lay snug against the lean muscles of his slender frame. Only his head remained exposed.

A voice spoke in his atrium—warm, feminine, caring. *Safety checklist complete. No detriments detected. I am fully functional, with energy reserves at one hundred percent.*

"Are you the skin suit?" Jolly asked aloud as he experimentally flexed his arms and stretched his legs.

Affirmative.

He could see that tiny scales composed the fabric of the skin suit. The scales shifted configuration as he moved.

"Really, is this all?" he asked no one in particular. "This will keep me alive?"

"It'll give you a chance to survive," Urban said casually. And then, in a sterner tone, "You were supposed to acquaint yourself with how to survive outside."

Another flush of heat in his cheeks. "I shouldn't have stayed so long with the Cryptologist," he admitted. "But she's an interesting person. I think you'd like her."

"She's not a person," Urban said. "She's an Apparatchik. An intelligent program working to solve a specific task."

Clementine spoke cautiously, "I don't think we've worked out *what* she is."

And Shoran said, "I want to meet her."

"But she *is* a person," Jolly insisted. "Just because she's different, that doesn't make her less." He remembered the day he'd met Urban, and how strange, how almost inhuman Urban had seemed. Jolly's experience in the world had expanded since then, so that despite the oddities of her mannerisms, the Cryptologist felt more familiar, more human to him, than Urban had on that first day. "She's curious and bold and full of enthusiasm," he declared. "And she's fun to talk to, even if she is a little strange."

"And she's pretty," Shoran added with a wink and a smile.

Jolly ducked his chin, suddenly shy, but he couldn't help grinning as he agreed, "She *is*."

A low hiss from Urban.

And then Pasha spoke, sounding contrite. "I helped design her, Jolly. And Urban is right. She's nothing like a natural person and she should never have been allowed to manifest. That was my mistake. Don't let yourself get entangled with her, because it's not going to last."

Jolly opened his mouth to argue, but Urban spoke first. "Let's get going. Let's get this done."

They rode out to the hull, packed together in an oblong transit pod. The pod moved slowly, pushing through bio-mechanical tissue and sliding among Chenzeme computational strata. Urban listened, as Shoran and Clementine used the time to advise Jolly on what to expect when they emerged.

"It's overwhelming," Shoran warned him. "Especially the first time. You're going to feel dizzy, disoriented, vulnerable. Just accept it, and try not to worry. Know that your suit will take care of you. And you'll be tethered, so you can't get lost."

"Just make sure you don't touch the hull cells," Clemantine added.

"But the hull cells are everywhere . . . aren't they?" Jolly asked.

"We won't be standing on the hull," Urban said, his tone sterner than he'd intended.

"Oh. Okay."

Jolly was naïve. He'd been awake only a few years aboard *Dragon* and though he'd learned a lot, he still didn't grasp the complexities of this new-to-him world, or the inherent dangers it presented, and he had only a shallow understanding of the cultural philosophy they must follow if they hoped to hold on to their humanity. Deception Well had survived as a human-centric culture only because its people had forcefully rejected the destabilizing presence of artificial beings. The ship-born understood that. Unlike Jolly, they'd grown up in this milieu. In some sense, Jolly was the alien here—and that frustrated Urban, because he loved the kid like a little brother and wanted the best for him. Nothing good was going to come of his fascination with the Cryptologist. That Jolly could feel easy in the company of such a creature troubled Urban to his core.

Even so, he gentled his voice and explained, "*Dragon* is no longer decelerating, so we'll be able to safely drift a couple of meters above the cell field."

The local vessel would have noticed their velocity had stabilized. Urban imagined it watching, waiting to see what came next.

He told Jolly, "When we emerge from the hull, we'll be easily visible against the background of the cell field."

"Easily visible targets," Shoran joked.

No one laughed.

Jolly had hardly been aware of the transit pod's movement, but he noticed when it stopped. He sensed a slight jerk, and the faint white noise of its passage gave way to silence.

"Are we there?" he asked.

"Yes," Urban said. "I'm opening a space between the hull cells."

Jolly assumed it was that version of Urban on the high bridge who created the opening.

Motion drew his eye. He glanced at Shoran and saw that she had her hood up and sealed. Past white reflections, he could see her face through her transparent visor.

He reached to pull up his own hood, but Shoran stopped him with a touch. Through his atrium, she said, *Don't try to do it manually. Tell your suit to seal up.*

Jolly nodded, too aware of his racing heart and a slick of sweat on his skin that his suit had not yet absorbed. He blinked to activate his atrium's display. Then he found and focused on the suit icon. *I'm ready. Seal up, okay?*

Stand by, the suit answered in its pleasant feminine voice.

Jolly sucked in a deep breath and held it as the fabric of the hood slithered over his head and across his face, sealing at his neck. He felt a faint pressure against his closed eyelids, and when he tried to open them, he could not. But a moment later, the pressure eased. He blinked his eyes, and found himself looking out from behind his own transparent visor, while a soft current of cool air brushed his lips.

You okay, Jolly? Urban asked.

Yes.

He hoped it was true.

If your suit tells you to do something, do it. Understand?

Yes.

His heart beat harder. A glance around showed him that everyone was sealed up now. Abruptly, his suit stiffened. He tensed, feeling trapped. But when he tried, he found he could move, although with a slight resistance now.

Beyond Urban, the pod's wall opened, retracting in a swiftly widening circle—and Urban moved out into the darkness beyond. Clemantine followed, and as she did, a gleaming white snake emerged from the periphery of the opening, moving swiftly to meet her, locking on to the belly of her suit.

Go ahead, Jolly, Shoran said, gesturing at him. *The tether is automatic. Move toward the egress and you'll be hooked up.*

Jolly nodded, forgetting to answer verbally. He let go a long, slow breath. Then, with his jaw set, he dug his gloved fingers into the pod's soft wall and gently pushed, sending himself gliding slowly to the threshold. As Shoran had promised, a tether emerged to meet him. He felt it nudge against his belly. And then he was outside, with the light of the pod behind him and an explosion of stars ahead. He sucked in a sharp breath, awed and astonished and strangely jubilant as he beheld the vastness around him.

Then he reached the end of his tether. A gentle tug on his belly turned him around. The tether had firmed up, gone stiff. It did not allow him to bounce back. His gaze followed it to *Dragon's* brilliantly luminous hull.

The courser had been dark, its philosopher cells dormant during the years at Verilotus. Only after they'd left had Urban wakened the cell field. Now, against that glare, the egress appeared as a dark circle. He watched Shoran emerge from it, the light-green glow of her skin suit mostly washed out. Pasha came next, her skin suit vaguely blue.

Jolly turned around, locating Urban and Clemantine. They floated at the end of their tethers, two points on a circle that the team would form around the egress.

Next, he let his gaze explore the vast glowing hull. They had emerged halfway along *Dragon's* monstrous length. Dizziness seized him as his terrestrially evolved brain strove to define a sense of up and down. For a fractured moment, he felt himself floating above a curving plain, and then his perspective shifted and he felt on the verge of plunging down a cliff face. Instinct caused his limbs to flail, his hands to grasp for the tether.

No.

You're not falling.

A deep breath. A soft laugh. And a nod of acknowledgment to ancient ancestors, eons past, who had survived to produce more offspring because a quick instinctive grasping gesture had prevented a fatal fall from a tree or a cliff. But that archaic instinct had become a hindrance in the world he lived in now.

*Jolly? Urban asked again. **You okay?*

*Yes! he answered, hearing the ecstatic enthusiasm in his own voice. **This is amazing!*

He looked next inward toward the belt of ruins. He was in the shadow of the ship, hidden from Tanjiri's fierce glare. But other objects, crescent-shaped and tiny with distance, caught and reflected the star's light. Jolly counted two, three, four, *six* mega-structures—broken fragments of the swarming architecture that had once enveloped the star. There were more, of course. Many of the bright points he took for stars might actually be debris left over from the cataclysm that had broken the cordon.

Where is the local vessel? he wondered aloud.

Out there ahead of us, Shoran answered. *Your suit can show you, but it's too small, too dark, and still too distant to see.*

Jolly's suit produced a green pinpoint on his visor, whispering to him that this was the vessel's location. He sighed, disappointed. *So we can't see it, but we're hoping it's watching us with a telescope?*

We can see it, Urban corrected. *Just not with our eyes.*

They stayed outside for a full hour, watching the stars and the slow, slow parade of distant ruins. Jolly had cleared his visor of the green pinpoint, but he kept looking toward the place it had marked, hoping to be the first to see . . . *something.* Some reaction to their human presence here on the edge of Tanjiri System.

But Urban—fortified with extended senses that enabled him to perceive the light gathered by the fleet's telescopes even as he gazed through human eyes—saw it first.

It's changing, he announced in an astonished voice.

Jolly looked again—and then he saw it too. Where the green pinpoint had been, there now gleamed a faint mote of white light.

From his post on the high bridge, Urban watched as the hull of the local vessel began to glow in a familiar wavelength. Memories surfaced; he had seen such a transformation before. A nervous quiver passed among the philosopher cells, a rising uneasiness that told him the cells remembered too.

Long ago, in the hours before he'd taken *Dragon* for his own, he had watched a huge, ring-shaped alien artifact slowly take on the shape of a Chenzeme courser, with newly synthesized philosopher cells gleaming on its hull. That metamorphosis had been undertaken to persuade *Dragon* that it and the artifact were akin. But the ruse had failed—and *Dragon*'s philosopher cells remembered that too.

<*wrongness*>, the cells suggested.

<*false chenzeme*>

<*revulsion*>

An especially aggressive cell lineage demanded: <*kill it*>

– *negate that* – Urban commanded, his argument flooding the cell field from the hundred thousand links he commanded.

– *it is weak / we are strong / watch observe learn* –

The scale of his argument overwhelmed the philosopher cells. Their innate killing lust quieted, replaced by cold watchfulness and a soft repeated declaration:

<*it is weak / we are strong*>

Clemantine's ghost joined him on the high bridge, and then Pasha too, the three of them tangled up together, immersed in one another's emotions—anxiety, curiosity, wonder, impatience, *fear*.

*It's changing, Pasha said, awe in her voice. *It's becoming like us, a Chenzeme vessel.

*It's not, Urban countered. *It's a chameleon ship. It's only reflecting our appearance . . . imitation as a first step to rapport and communication—or anyway, I hope so.

*Or it could know what we are, Clemantine suggested. *It may have encountered Chenzeme vessels before.

*I don't think so. Watch its hull cells. What is it saying?

Chenzeme ships communicated with one another through a symphonic display of light generated by their hull cells, in pulses too rapid for the human eye to discern.

*Oh, I see, Pasha said. *It's just noise, isn't it? Random noise. And our philosopher cells know it. They're challenging it.

*False Chenzeme, Clemantine added in a soft, menacing voice.

*It's a chameleon ship, Urban repeated. *It doesn't know anything about the Chenzeme. Maybe we're still alive because it wants to learn.

Clemantine said, *If it's only curiosity keeping us alive, I hope it has a lot more questions.

CHAPTER THIRTEEN

THE CRYPTOLOGIST SAT cross-legged on a lawn strewn with fallen pink blossoms, studying the thin, glassy needle as it lay within its open case, admiring the way light reflected and refracted against its surface. A beautiful artifact, truly, given into her care by Vytet.

She had sought out Vytet when a new scheme occurred to her, one that required her progenitor's cooperation. But Vytet had not wanted to talk. She had stood in the doorway of her cottage, refusing to admit the Cryptologist. She'd said, "I know you want to interview people, but you have no need to interview me. You know what I know."

"I know what you know," the Cryptologist agreed, hoping that an open, earnest gaze would soothe the anxiety displayed by Vytet. "Yet I lack your memories and therefore I do not know the context of your knowledge. This could be easily remedied. Since I am derived from you—"

"Derived from me, yes," Vytet interrupted. "But very different from me. Intentionally so."

"This is true. Still, it might be possible to share your memory."

"No."

A stern denial that both puzzled and troubled the Cryptologist. Perhaps Vytet thought her request frivolous? She tried to explain. "By sharing your memory, I'll share the experience of the silver— the better to understand it."

"No. Unraveling the silver is not your task." Vytet's focus shifted, as with some inner thought. "Wait here." She withdrew into her cottage, the gel door closing behind her. A minute later she returned, with a slender little case in her hand. Opening it, she revealed the needle.

Such a pretty thing.

"Take it," Vytet ordered. "Your task, your only task, is to solve the puzzle of how to open this needle. That is the purpose of your existence."

The Cryptologist knew this to be true. "Yet this puzzle can be approached from many directions, so that insight into one mystery might reveal a clue to another."

"Doubtful. In any case, you will have to find some other way forward. I have already given you most of myself. But my memories, my inner thoughts and conflicts, those belong only to me."

Vytet had withdrawn again behind her cottage door and the Cryptologist had retreated, needing to think on the encounter. As she walked the gee deck, she'd found herself drawn to this pocket park. It soothed her to sit on the grass in this hidden corner where pink rain tree blossoms slowly spun down around her.

She felt confused by Vytet's sharp rejection and cold bearing . . . her manner so different from the pleasant interactions she'd enjoyed with Jolly. Other people the Cryptologist had sought to interview had been wary—cool, uneasy, reluctant—but not hostile.

That was it, she decided, sliding a finger slowly along the needle's nearly frictionless surface. Vytet had been hostile.

Another puzzle to solve.

Jolly's gentle voice interrupted these frustrated thoughts. "Hey, there you are."

She looked up at him, saw his smile, and experienced a startling rush of pleasure. "Hello, Jolly."

His eyes widened as he noticed the needle in its open case. He dropped to his knees and leaned in to get a better look. "Is that it?" he asked in a whispery voice. Given his proximity, she couldn't help but notice the pleasant scent of his body and the smooth curve of his shoulder as it joined his neck.

"It's pretty, isn't it?" she said.

"It is. Have you learned anything about it?"

"I am still learning all that is known about it, and all that is

known of the silver too, and those interesting missiles, and the
Blade at Verilotus. Do they share the same physics? That is a question that needs an answer."

Jolly sat down with her on the blossom-strewn grass, arms resting on his bent knees, his eyes bright with excitement. "I got to go
outside the ship," he told her. "I saw the local vessel, the chameleon ship, with my own eyes. Just a spot of light, but it's close now.
Urban says it may be like our missiles. If so, you might learn something of their physics once we're friends with the people here."

"*Are* there people here?"

"I don't know. But doesn't it make sense to think that someone
here—or some *thing*—is curious about us, and has sent the chameleon ship to discover who and what we are? And if it's really
like our missiles, maybe it's controlled in the same way."

"Through silver?" she asked, intrigued by this idea.

He looked thoughtful. But after a moment he shook his head.
"No, that can't be right. I mean, if there was silver here, the Astronomer would have seen its glow, either among the megastructures
or on the nightside of the planet."

The Cryptologist did not agree. "Jolly, you are thinking of Verilotus. But Verilotus was a damaged world, flooded with silver."

He cocked his head. "You're suggesting there might be silver
here, but we can't see it?"

"*You* suggested that," she reminded him.

"Oh, *right*. You mean if the chameleon ship really is analogous
to our missiles."

"Can you sense the presence of our missiles?" she asked him,
wanting to follow this line of thought a little farther.

"Well, no. Only Urban is linked to them, and before that he
could sense them only from within the Cauldron."

The Cauldron!

Such a pity she had not existed in those years when the Dragoneers had lingered on Verilotus. If she'd been alive then, she would
have been augmented with silver, and she could have tried to visit
the Cauldron's tortured dimensions just as Urban had done. But
that avenue of research now lay far out of reach.

She looked down at the needle, admiring again the way it caught the light so prettily. "Perhaps there is something like the Cauldron here. Perhaps there is someone within this hypothetical space, watching us, trying to speak to us . . . and wondering that we don't listen?"

"*Oh*," Jolly said again, this time with soft urgency. He stood up suddenly. "We need to tell Urban."

The Cryptologist closed the needle's case and stood up too. "But can't *you* seek for such a connection?" she asked, recalling that Vytet's hostility had only echoed Urban's.

"I'm not very good at things like that," Jolly answered. "And anyway, Urban needs to know."

Through periodic radar pulses, Urban tracked the progress of the chameleon ship. *Dragon* had resumed its gradual deceleration while the local vessel, in a shockingly swift sequence of maneuvers, had reversed its momentum and tempered its velocity such that, in a few more hours, giant *Dragon* and the system's tiny defender would be running parallel, less than a kilometer apart.

And what would happen then? Urban wished he knew.

An alert reached him. Someone drawing near to his avatar. He extended his senses outward from his post on the high bridge and saw Jolly, with the Cryptologist beside him, stepping onto the path leading to Clemantine's cottage.

Urban's viewpoint shifted. He stretched and blinked, rising into wakefulness within his avatar. His gaze took in the sunny bedroom, and then he was up, striding into the front room to meet Jolly just as the cottage door opened to let him in.

"What's wrong?" Urban asked, reading the worry on his face.

The Cryptologist hesitated, lingering on the threshold—an interesting display of reserve for a creature who had shown no hint of hesitation just a few hours ago.

Jolly asked, "Would you know it, if the local vessel tried to talk to you, in the way you talk to our sentient missiles?"

Urban endured a flush of anxiety as he took in the full implication of Jolly's question. *Was* it possible? He looked at the Cryptologist, suspecting the question had originated with her.

"You might as well come in," he told her.

Jolly stood watching him, reading his face. "You *do* think it's possible."

"I don't know."

His missiles had sensed the presence of what they believed to be entities like themselves—many such entities, all around the belt. A well-armed system. But they had not reported communications with such beings or suggested the presence of silver here.

Urban looked around the room. With a silent command he sent the little tea table down into the floor. Plush carpet filled the footprint of its pedestal. He sat cross-legged on the carpet, hands cupped lightly against his thighs. "I'm going to look. You can stay here if you want to, but it might be a while."

"I'll stay."

Jolly moved to the couch. The Cryptologist sat beside him, her shoulder touching his, suggesting a personal intimacy that unsettled Urban. But he'd already made his opinion clear. It was Jolly's choice now.

Urban closed his eyes.

His awareness of the silver was similar to the proprioceptive sense by which his brain tracked the movement and position of his limbs, in that the awareness was always present, though not always perceived at a conscious level. He drew on that awareness now, descending into it—into the silver within him and the mindspace he shared with the missiles.

The missiles had gone away with *Griffin*, away from Tanjiri, into the dreadful emptiness of interstellar space. Already they were a billion kilometers distant yet still part of him, and all felt normal in that first moment of connection. The twin machine minds worked together as always with a quiet, analytical patience, reassuring in its familiarity and somehow soothing.

But that state ceased a moment after his arrival when another presence surfaced within the mindspace, filling it instantaneously and then bursting it open. Urban had no time to retreat or resist as his mind plunged into the depths of an ocean of silver, *alien* silver, similar but not the same as the silver he'd brought from Verilotus.

The presence remained with him, huge as an ocean-dwelling leviathan out of the most ancient mythologies, permeable as the ocean itself. Urban felt himself surrounded by it, embedded within it. Lost within the leviathan's vastness, he felt himself reduced to a fragile spark of awareness, nothing more than that—but nothing less, either. Still clinging to bright existence within the liquid presence.

A wordless urging, aimed not at him, but at the missiles. A sense that at last this was their time to release all restraint and blossom in the annihilating white light that was their destiny.

No.

In that space, Urban's objection resonated as faintly as the sound of a pebble dropped into an ocean and yet it had an effect, an apparent effect, as if time froze all around him, while his mind remained free to advance moment by moment into the future. He sensed the missiles, locked on the cusp of obedience, caught on the verge of an eager and exultant seppuku.

The missiles were far from *Griffin*. Far away from anything. Their deaths would cause no harm—but he needed those missiles or he might need them in some future space, some future time, if a future was allowed to him. But not here. *Not here!* Benign intention spilled from him. *We are only curious. We only seek to know.*

He thought in words but the leviathan did not. It touched his mind instead and he felt his awareness expand as if a submind had dropped in, bringing a sense of memory—but not his memory. This memory belonged to another, one who had watched the missiles, waiting to discover what sort of mind controlled them.

Urban understood then that his humanity had saved him.

In this memory, he heard the fleet's radio hail boldly proclaiming their human status, and he saw himself with Clemantine, Jolly, Pasha, and Shoran, adrift outside the ship—token proof of what they were.

But not proof enough. The leviathan had remained wary. If it had detected an alien mind linked to the missiles, a Chenzeme mind that had used a knowledge of humans as camouflage, *Dragon*'s existence would have ceased.

Time unlocked around Urban, sliding backward until the missiles forgot their ecstatic desire and the leviathan vanished from his stunned perception. The missiles continued on, accompanying *Griffin* ever deeper into the interstellar medium, their machine minds restored to a quiet, untroubled state.

Urban put into words a wordless knowledge: *We've been granted a reprieve.* They would be allowed to live. And he would be allowed to keep the missiles so long as he kept them far away.

Sooth. Never here.

He retreated. With a shudder he opened his eyes, aware that less than a minute had passed since he'd closed them. He felt the slow thunderous rhythm of his heart. A sheen of sweat lay cold against his skin. Lezuri had insisted he was not ready to encounter the entity that existed at Tanjiri . . . *but he had just met it!*

He had met it, and he had survived.

Jolly recognized his return to awareness. Sliding off the sofa, he knelt in front of Urban, his youthful face tight in concern. "Something happened, didn't it?" he asked. "You saw something. There really was something out there."

Urban nodded, stunned by what he'd sensed, what he'd been granted: a kind of permission to proceed.

Only now, as he went over it in his mind, did he recognize what he'd missed in the moment. Woven throughout the leviathan's wordless communication had been a sense of curiosity, intense and utterly human.

The Cryptologist stood silent and forgotten in a corner of the room, listening intently as Urban shared the details of his experience with Jolly, and with Clemantine too. Clemantine had returned to her home, breathless and already aware that something crucial had happened.

Crucial indeed! Tanjiri system possessed its own version of silver, and within that silver, a vastened entity. One that understood the nature of the silver so deeply it had reached out to Urban's sentient missiles, brushing aside their resistance to its will. No longer was Urban the only master of those weapons, though that in itself hardly mattered, not to the Cryptologist.

NEEDLE   83

Urban had communicated with the entity. *That* was what mattered. But he had needed the silver to do it and she would not be
able to replicate his feat until she somehow acquired the silver for
herself.

Frustration welled within her. She felt sure this entity could
explain to her the puzzle of the needle and all the uncanny physics
behind it—but only if she could communicate with it.

More people arrived at the cottage, insisting to Urban that he
tell his story again, and in full. The Cryptologist did not need to
hear it again. She slipped out of the cottage and returned to the
warren. Sealing herself within a small chamber, she lay cradled
amid darkened wall-weed while her agile mind strove to discover
some new path forward.

CHAPTER FOURTEEN

THE HIGH BRIDGE felt crowded and close and imbued with a shared tension that leached into the cell field. Urban longed to be alone there, to adopt the emotionless attitude of the aspect he called the Sentinel, and to simply watch as *Dragon* fell sunward with the silent chameleon ship now alongside, just over a kilometer away.

But Clemantine and Pasha wanted to be there too. Like him they wanted to be present and in position to react if reaction was required—though there was danger in that. The three of them often disagreed.

There should be only one of us here, Urban said. *One mind. One decision. And no fatal delay while we try to reach consensus.*

Clemantine answered this with knife-edged irritation. *Let it be. There is no quick decision to be made. There is no scenario under which we use our weapon—not if we want to continue. The chameleon ship could drop dust and we'd have no recourse but to accept it—unless you want to retreat?*

Stop, he growled.

Right. Then we'll continue as we are.

No, Pasha said. *I don't think we will. Look at the radar returns. The chameleon ship is pulling away.*

Urban looked, and saw that she was right. The chameleon ship had stayed alongside for just over two hours, mimicking *Dragon*'s rate of deceleration. But its trajectory had changed. Now the gap between them was growing.

Why?

Had they earned the leviathan's trust? Or had it lost all interest in them?

Was there to be no more communication?

And why had it not simply spoken to them, answering their hail in radio frequencies?

The three of them discussed these questions and more as the chameleon ship continued to withdraw. Minutes slipped past, then hours, and it became clear the little ship was not returning to its point of origin within the belt of ruins. Instead, it had taken up a tangential course that would return it to the belt at a point far ahead along the rough circle of orbiting debris.

"I want to follow it," Urban declared a day later. He had called a gathering of the ship's company. Now he stood on the dais, gazing out at the crowded amphitheater: four rows of seats, with sixty-four anxious, eager faces looking back at him. Only one person looked guarded and unhappy: the Cryptologist. She stood alone in the dark of a back corner, her gaze alert and wary and fixed on him.

"I want consensus to follow it," Urban went on. "As you know, I've already sent *Pytheas* after it, but I think we are meant to follow it too."

Clemantine stood beside him. She crossed her arms in a determined pose and said, "I concur. The vessel could have gone dark and withdrawn directly into the belt of ruins. Instead, it's maintained its luminous chameleon skin—an easy beacon for us to track. And we are in no hurry to reach the center of the system, are we? We have time. All the time we need and more. So let's follow, and see what it has to show us."

Motion drew Urban's gaze back to the Cryptologist. She had raised her hand, her mouth half open as if she meant to speak. But she was not alone in that. Several people stood up, Riffan among them, popping up from the back row.

"I say yes!" he declared. "I think it's a splendid plan. From Urban's brief encounter we know we're welcome here . . . more or less welcome . . . well, not forbidden anyway, supposing we come without the worst of our armaments. And I would hate to offend our host by declining what may be an act of hospitality."

Pasha had also risen to speak. She stood by her customary seat at the center of the front row, half-turned to listen to Riffan. Urban caught the slight shake of her head, the shift of her gaze upward as if beseeching the heavens for patience—a fleeting contempt unreflected in her strong, confident voice. "And if Riffan is wrong, if we are not meant to follow or if there is something farther along that might be construed as a threat, *Pytheas* will meet it first and give us warning. I too, say we should go."

"I disagree!"

The entire ship's company turned to look for the source of this unfamiliar voice—and discovered the Cryptologist in her dark corner. Urban's eyes narrowed. Did she have the right to speak here? Whether or not she did, she spoke on.

"The ruins are dead remnants. They will still be dead a hundred years from now. The interesting part of this system is the Tanjiri Trinity—planet, moon, celestial city, all orbiting together and all alive. The moon, the most compelling. Lezuri existed within computational strata housed inside a moonlike object called the Rock—"

Naresh took offense at this. He interrupted her, jumping to his feet with the energy of his objection. Targeting the Cryptologist with an accusatory finger, he said, "You are about to suggest the Rock and this massive, living moon are analogous. They are *not*. The Rock was a small object compared to Tanjiri-2b. And the shell inhabited by the so-called goddess of Verilotus was smaller still."

"Both were remnants," Urban reminded him. "We have no concept of their original size."

The physicist's sharp gaze shifted to Urban on the dais. "Nothing in the history of Verilotus suggests there ever were two large, living moons."

Alhimbra, the historian, answered this, though he did not bother to stand, just raised a hand and waved off Naresh's objection, saying, "They were likely dark moons."

Naresh squandered a few seconds glaring at Alhimbra, a silent interval that the Cryptologist seized on to speak again, quiet but determined. "Logic suggests the entity is there, within Tanjiri-2b, along with the answers I seek. That is where this ship should go."

Vytet answered this, resentment in her voice. "We will go there, *after* we've learned more about the composition of the outer system." Her gaze took in the ship's company. "The belt is not just dead remnants. The chameleon ship has proven that. I'm confident it will show us more as we follow it around the ring. And the more we learn now, the better prepared we'll be to approach the inner system."

Naresh too spoke in favor of following the local vessel. Then Shoran added her agreement, and after that—though an hour of discussion followed—consensus was never in doubt.

For many years, Vytet had been comfortable within a body of mixed gender, neither man nor woman, but with aspects of both. Many times in her life that form had given her such a sense of freedom. It was as if, by provoking the question of what she was, she could liberate herself from the tedious default answers implied by every social interaction, every tryst, every history she read, or drama she watched.

I am what I am.

But at other times, especially if she felt uneasy or uncertain or at fault for her role in an action gone wrong, she would take on a fully gendered aspect, wearing it like an armored shell that sealed away doubt and vulnerability.

The Cryptologist's physical existence had shaken Vytet. It had forced her to confront and question cultural values that she had assented to long ago. For all the millions of directions that evolution might have taken them in, the people of Deception Well had chosen to remain human, and to preserve in form, and much in function, the aspect of their ancestors. Theirs was a deliberately humanist culture, and to preserve it they had long ago rejected the creation of true artificial intelligences, or of artificial beings.

Inadvertently, unintentionally, and yet unarguably, Vytet had broken that most basic stricture. Worse, it was a stricture she believed in, and supported fully. To be sure, this ancestral existence came with limitations. She would never be able to comprehend the Universe as Lezuri must have at his peak. Even so, she cherished her humanity and drew a deep satisfaction from living within this familiar strata of existence.

But what human society—even their attenuated society aboard *Dragon*—could endure the destabilizing influence of artificial beings existing on a sliding scale somewhere between an intelligent tool and a fully realized person?

The Cryptologist, in its physical existence, constituted the greatest mistake Vytet had ever made. And it was a mistake that could not be undone. An intelligent being, once brought into existence, had rights, with the right to exist first among them.

No. What was done was done and Vytet would have to live with it . . . but not as she was. To recover her confidence and reject her own crushing self-loathing required a shift in who she was, *what* she was. She needed a different physical aspect, one with the ability to re-process fact and recast complicity so that she could once again function effectively despite what she'd done.

So as the days passed and *Dragon* coasted slowly around the belt of ruins, Vytet shifted, returning to an old, familiar form. Her soft, androgynous facial features grew more prominent: a stern brow ridge, thick eyebrows, a strong chin. Lean muscle added mass, while facial and body hair, and an Adam's apple, added definition. Vytet's voice deepened, and the presence of fully male genitalia became a pleasant distraction.

At his core, Vytet remained Vytet. A shift of gender and form did not erase history, memory, or responsibility. Nor did it bestow a bonus of confidence or intelligence. But morphology mattered.

As his body's feedback loops shifted, Vytet's thought patterns evolved too. Regret lingered, though not for the act of creating the Cryptologist. He saw that as a bold and clever sally at a solution, and he took some pride in it. The mistake, as the Bio-mechanic had pointed out at the time, was made when he'd deleted too many of those modules that contained his own core beliefs. By doing so, he had thought to give the Cryptologist an independent mind. His regret was that he'd succeeded.

But now that it was done, might it ultimately prove worthwhile? *Perhaps.* It might be that having crossed this forbidden bridge, some great discovery now lay within reach.

CHAPTER FIFTEEN

URBAN RESOLVED TO keep *Dragon* at a cautious distance. So as *Pytheas* and the chameleon ship progressed together around the belt of ruins, the courser trailed ever farther behind.

Pytheas kept watch, cataloging every object visible to its telescope and relaying the data back to *Dragon*. The Astronomer added these observations to the map of Tanjiri System.

Dragon contributed too. The courser's radar picked out rare dark shapes that neither *Pytheas* nor *Khonsu* had been able to observe. The faint echoes received from these stealthy objects replicated exactly the size and shape of the chameleon ship.

Urban could not prove the objects were dimensional missiles, but he believed they were. He interpreted them as guardians, stationed throughout the belt, there to protect the life of the inner system from any outside threat. They remained quiescent as *Dragon* passed. Urban made sure they had no cause to stir. He remained on the high bridge, day after day, monitoring the philosopher cells and stifling any hint of rash action.

One active missile was enough.

No. Better to think of it as one active pilot ship.

The chameleon ship could have easily returned to its original post among the ruins, but it had not. It could have gone dark again. Instead, its slender hull continued to glow in imitation of *Dragon*'s philosopher cells. Given the existence of its many quiescent counterparts, the behavior of this particular vessel and its continued visibility enforced the theory that it *was* a pilot ship, and that *Dragon* was meant to follow.

Seventy-seven days passed in this way, with the ships moving gradually inward, ever closer to the orbits of the outermost megastructures. Those orbits were long, requiring over twenty years to complete a full circuit around Tanjiri. By contrast, at the belt's inner edge, a full orbit required only twelve years.

More than three hundred twenty million kilometers separated the inner and outer bands of the belt—a vast area, and not confined to the plane of the ecliptic. So although the megastructures loomed large, they did not come close to filling the emptiness of the outer system. So far, *Dragon* had not gotten anywhere close to one—but that would soon change.

A massive structure lay ahead of them, the largest on this side of the star. It was an elongated object, its long axis vertical to the plane of the ecliptic. Radar revealed its near side to be mostly smooth and slightly curved, though scars and pock marks suggested it had suffered collision damage. Certainly, it was only a fragment of a once far-greater structure that had been torn apart by some unimaginable force, leaving this gigantic remnant. To Urban, it suggested a shattered fragment of eggshell, torn in three parts, though not quite separated.

The fracture lines revealed interior layers subdivided into rectangular cells, each measuring a hundred kilometers by ten, with the depth undetermined. Radar returns suggested irregularities within the cells. Perhaps drifts of frozen gases?

Accompanying the megastructure were many small glittering objects—probably debris, dragged along in the grip of its gravitational field.

In the Master Star Catalog, the megastructure had been tagged as Tanjiri-17, but the ship's company referred to it as D-1, short for Destination One, because if *Pytheas* continued on its present course, pacing the chameleon ship, the pair would intercept D-1 sometime in the next several days.

What little mass *Pytheas* could spare was being used to assemble scout-bots to explore the structure. The bots would assay and analyze the hidden details of the ruin, and hunt for signs of life, and for historical records too. A library, maybe?

Urban believed they would find something there other than cold dead ruins—why else would the chameleon ship have lured them this way?

The Cryptologist occupied a tiny chamber in the warren. She retreated there whenever she required sleep or, as now, when her mood darkened with a strange and senseless desire for time alone. Drifting amid the softly glowing wall-weed, she held the needle in its open case, glaring at its pretty rainbow glints.

She had studied the needle for all the eighty-six days of her existence, yet its composition and its mechanism remained maddening puzzles. Eighty-six days of effort. Eighty-six days during which she had exhausted every avenue of research she could think of, with nothing gained beyond an anecdotal understanding of the silver, and a historical knowledge of speculative, evidence-free theories of alternate physics. The latter she judged to be pure balderdash—a word she'd discovered during her research and had since found repeatedly useful.

Now, in the dim, silent isolation of the chamber, she went over what little she knew of the needle, of the silver, of the Blade, and the sentient missiles, hoping desperately to recognize some hint, some association she'd overlooked before, some bit of knowledge that could open a new path forward.

Into this milieu of frustration there arrived a message from Jolly. *Wake up*, it said.

She answered, *I am not asleep.*

Good, because you need to come to the amphitheater. Things are finally happening.

The Cryptologist queried her ghost in the library about what things exactly. An answer came in the form of a submind, bearing memories: *Pytheas*, echoing the actions of the local vessel, had undertaken a slight shift in course. The pair would soon pass inside D-1's orbit, approaching the megastructure on its sunlit side.

That side had been hidden all throughout their long approach, because although the megastructure rotated, it did so slowly, pirouetting on its long axis only once every 679 days. In the most recent images received from *Pytheas*, an intriguing glint of sunlight could be seen, refracting through some unknown substance just visible on the megastructure's jagged horizon. The extent of the illuminated substance slightly exceeded three hundred twelve kilometers—a tiny portion of the structure but significant because nothing like it had been observed before.

*Come on, Jolly insisted. *Come to the amphitheater. We'll sit together, and see the new images as they come in.

Had Jolly been present, the Cryptologist would have met this suggestion with a socially appropriate dismissive roll of her eyes. Instead, she said what he must already know. *All images are available within the library.

*Yes. But discussion will happen in the amphitheater. Everyone will be here, and who knows what you might learn? Something to inspire a new approach to the puzzle of the needle, maybe.

This time the Cryptologist did roll her eyes. *That is extremely unlikely.

*But not impossible.

Well, he was right. Technically anyway. The possibility could not be ruled out.

The Cryptologist found she had reached a state of such acute frustration that even this slight chance of inspiration, of minor enlightenment, tempted her.

*Meet me, Jolly insisted. *I'm saving you a seat.

It was true too, that she found Jolly's presence a pleasant distraction, and that she enjoyed his attention. She made it a habit every day to walk the gee deck's winding path for hours at a time, and every day Jolly would eventually come to find her, insisting they share a meal at his cottage or at the dining court. He would declare, "It isn't good for you to be alone and just thinking all the time."

He took her to play flying fox, a strange game without real purpose and yet physically exhilarating. Or they would sit together, listening to songs and music performed by members of the ship's company.

The Cryptologist valued these performances, as they often had the effect of easing the rigid tension of her mind, allowing her to explore creative thoughtways. While listening to the music and not really thinking about anything, she would sometimes discover previously hidden links amid the tangle of knowledge crowding both her organic and her ghost minds.

So perhaps Jolly was right. Perhaps, like the music, the discussion of the images would inspire new thoughts, and ultimately, new pathways of research.

All right, she conceded. *I'm coming.*

Pasha arrived at the amphitheater, hurrying to claim a seat at the center of the front row as the ship's company wandered in with all the usual sounds of shuffling steps and murmured conversation. She found Jolly there ahead of her, separated from Shoran by two empty seats. He looked up at her with an apologetic smile and, indicating the seat immediately beside him, he said, "I'm saving this for the Cryptologist."

"Ah."

Raised eyebrows and a teasing smile from Shoran; Pasha returned an annoyed scowl, all too aware of a flush of heat in her cheeks. The passage of time had not eased her discomfiture. She still rued the existence of the Apparatchik, and her part in creating it. Curiosity and hubris had gotten the better of her. She'd believed she could control the outcome of the experiment, and given that belief, the prospect of a breakthrough in their understanding of the exotic physics of the needle had been irresistible. And if there had been such a breakthrough, she might have forgiven herself. But the experiment had proved a failure. The Cryptologist had learned nothing new—and no one knew quite what to make of the strange new entity left over from the fiasco.

Well, no one but Jolly, who remained fascinated by it all. Oh, and Shoran too, who found Pasha's disgrace quite entertaining.

"Regrets?" Shoran teased as Pasha took the unclaimed seat beside her.

"You know it."

Riffan, Tarnya, Bituin—all approached the remaining empty seat in turn, but Jolly warded them off, holding out for the Cryptologist.

She came at last, walking into the amphitheater with her distinctively deliberate, almost mechanical gait. A cute little smile for Jolly, but was it real? *Unlikely.* The Cryptologist had been given only a limited emotional range, closely focused on solving the puzzle of the needle. She had probably assessed Jolly as a useful ally in that quest, and subsequently deduced the value of reflecting his obvious affection.

The Cryptologist paused, taking in Pasha's presence. "You are studying me as you always do," she observed, her voice flat and her face unreadable.

Again, Pasha felt her cheeks warm—a stupid reaction that sparked a flash of anger. "Yes," she answered coolly. "I think now it was cruel of us to burden you with an unsolvable task."

"I do not agree. While any curious mind will eventually meet a question for which no solution can be found, it is far too soon to declare my task unsolvable." She sat down, staring straight ahead, palms resting against her thighs as she continued to speak. "I have often experienced an intense joy in my pursuit, though I have little to show for it. Isn't that odd?"

The heat in Pasha's cheeks intensified until it stung and prickled, because she recognized herself in the Cryptologist's words. She too well knew the joy of being locked into the obsessive pursuit of a difficult question, of seeking a solution past frustration, past exhaustion, and the exhilaration that came at even the tiniest hint of progress. That drive to problem solving constituted Pasha's emotional core, just as it did with the Cryptologist. It was the reason she had helped Vytet create this Apparatchik.

Now the unforeseen consequence of that ill-conceived action sat musing beside her, speaking gentle words that provoked Pasha to confront herself and her own motivations anew. What other unintended consequences would follow?

The question evaporated amid a sudden quieting in the amphitheater. Looking up, Pasha saw that Vytet had taken the dais. She eyed this new version of him—tall and thin as ever, but now with a handsome and fully realized masculine aspect.

The shift from the feminine had been a gradual metamorphosis, unfolding over many days. Vytet now looked out at the ship's company through dark eyes deeply set within chiseled features. A short bristle of brown hair sprouted from his scalp, a longer, lusher growth formed a neat beard, and lean well-developed muscles appeared in contour beneath a clinging long-sleeved shirt.

Pasha's quick temper sparked again at the sight of him. What a damned annoying change . . . one she found all too distracting. *Focus!*

In a warm masculine voice that projected easily throughout the little amphitheater, Vytet said, "It's been 575 years since a majority of you made a very personal decision to leave Deception Well. More recently, Jolly Huacho made a similar decision to leave all that he knew behind. Only the ship-born have been given no choice." This last, said with a teasing smile, drew a chuckle from the gathered company.

"We want to go home!" Sayuri called out to additional laughter.

"Go on then," Clemantine retorted from where she sat with Urban in the back row. "It's just a short walk down the path."

Vytet allowed a few moments for laughter to subside. Then he spoke again. "*Pytheas* is closing in on D-1. In just a few more minutes we'll begin to see, for the first time, the other side of this immense megastructure. As we wait, I want to remind you that we are here because long ago we made the decision to dedicate our lives to exploration and discovery, and to satisfy our need to know and understand the history of our species, our rise and fall, and—I dare to hope—our rise again.

"Verilotus stands apart—an artificial world unaffected by the fall of the Hallowed Vasties, where people much like us, those of the ancestral form, have long enjoyed a home.

"Tanjiri will be different. This was once a cordoned system, the first we have visited. We know that something astonishing happened to the people here, and elsewhere across the Hallowed Vasties. The civilization that once existed here underwent a meta-

morphosis, enduring a brief era of massive growth on a scale we
cannot comprehend, facilitated by technologies we have not begun
to understand. In that time, the material resources of this system
were reconstituted into orbital structures so plentiful that Tanjiri's
light was hidden within their swarming shadows.

"What existed then? Lezuri hinted it was not human, and it's
possible nothing of humanity survives here. That would be a bitter disappointment, at least to me. But Tanjiri does not hold all
our hope. There are many more star systems left for us to explore.
What we find here—or what we don't find—will not, *cannot*,
define this voyage."

From behind Pasha there arose murmurs of agreement:

"Hear, hear."

"Just so."

"Well said."

A few even responded with brief, enthusiastic applause. Pasha
just pressed her lips together and looked away. As an exobiologist
she remained forever puzzled by this focus on the possibility of
human life, when thousands of other species had existed here too.
She hoped to discover an array of lifeforms, the descendants of
tenacious survivors, evolved in form and intellect to thrive among
the sparse ruins.

A fresh thought struck her then. A new perspective that induced
her to reconsider the creature sitting in the seat beside her. Though
the Cryptologist was not a product of the Hallowed Vasties, she
was a descendant of tenacious survivors.

Our descendant.

Pasha settled back in her seat with an embarrassed half-smile.
It was good to be reminded that interesting discoveries could be
made even close to home.

Vytet stepped to the side of the dais. Pasha tracked him with
a covetous gaze until the display screen lit up with video from
distant *Pytheas*.

Eleven million kilometers now separated *Dragon* from the outrider, a huge distance, incurring a light-speed delay of thirty-seven
seconds, one way.

But while *Dragon* trailed far behind, in recent days *Pytheas* had closed the gap with the chameleon ship. Now, only three kilometers separated them, and both vessels were swiftly dumping velocity at a pace that put them on target to rendezvous with D-1.

Onscreen, the chameleon ship appeared as a slender, gleaming dart—but that wasn't what caused Pasha to sit up straight and catch her breath in surprise.

Urban leaned forward in his seat at the end of the back row, gazing at the display screen, transfixed, certain he'd seen nothing like this before and yet . . . a sense of familiarity struck his mind, as if the sight had breathed life into some faded second-hand memory. Had someone once described to him a similar expanse of vacuum-adapted life?

He glanced at Clemantine, seated beside him, but found no hint of shared recognition on her face as she studied the display.

Turning again to the video, he scrutinized it in more detail. What had first appeared as a light-refracting band on D-1's distant horizon could now be clearly seen as the edge of a vacuum-adapted forest, the trees that composed it all of a kind. Or perhaps they were all one tree? For the many slender trunks together supported a graceful tangle of branching limbs that grew into one another, a shared system, with every trunk and every limb a deep-black, light-absorbing negative space.

Even so—even though D-1's slow rotation had carried the forest's edge beyond the terminator line and into night—the forest was not dark, because these trees made their own light. Pendulous bouquets of glowing, coin-shaped leaves grew among the branches, their soft white light reflected and multiplied by the pale, glassy substrate that formed the forest floor.

"It's beautiful," Riffan declared, from one seat over, wonder in his voice.

"*Sooth,*" Urban breathed, still sorting through the deepest strata of his memories, trying to recall where he had heard of such a forest before.

Pasha spoke from her seat in the front row. "This is a Sumerious

forest," she announced in a tone that suggested she did not sub-
scribe to any sense of wonder. Instead, she sounded puzzled, even
slightly offended—an exobiologist disappointed with the familiar.
"It's an ancient aesthetic, dating from the Commonwealth era,
before the expansion. Never very practical, and here, this far from
the sun, it's well outside its proper ecological zone."

"And yet the forest appears to be thriving," Clemantine
observed. "Even expanding. The trees on the perimeter are smaller,
aren't they? As if the forest is gradually spreading, colonizing the
surface of the megastructure."

"Possibly," Pasha conceded. "But the process must be achingly
slow, given the attenuated intensity of sunlight."

"Art takes its own time," Naresh observed. "And I suspect this
design was meant more as art than as a practical means to harvest
solar energy."

Pasha raised a dismissive hand without turning around. "Who
knows? The real question is, why is it here?"

Speculative answers were proposed and discussed in a general
blur of conversation until *Pytheas* crossed the megastructure's
orbit. Then a gasp of collective wonder erupted as D-1's sunlit side
finally came into view.

D-1 rotated so slowly that all throughout their long approach,
they had seen only the clean eggshell curve of what looked to be
the outer wall of the original structure. Now, for the first time,
they saw the sunlit face—and it appeared utterly different, cross-
hatched with an immense grid of the gigantic cells they'd seen
previously along D-1's fractured edges.

Those cells—rectangular, a hundred kilometers by ten—now
lay in full view, filling a vast escarpment for as far as the camera
could see. Shallow scallops, spanning multiple cells, contoured the
face of the escarpment. And here and there, from cell walls in the
deepest scallops, jagged peninsulas, kilometers long, extended into
the void.

The vacuum forest grew between the cells and also within them
on walls partly in sunlight, and partly in hard-edged shadow.
Glowing leaf clusters lightened the shadowed areas, but in sun-

light no leaves could be seen. Urban guessed they'd retracted or furled up so as not to interfere in the absorption of sunlight by the tangle of branches. He could not yet see how deep into the cells the forest extended.

It did not extend very far across the escarpment, covering several thousand square kilometers, no more. Beyond the forest's edge, there was only the grid of the cell walls, softened by irregular flows of pale colors reflecting the attenuated gleam of Tanjiri's distant light.

"These cells," Clemantine said, low-voiced. "They must have once been the interior of the structure, protected behind smooth walls."

Urban could not imagine the cataclysm that had sliced D-1 wide open.

Riffan stirred, stood up, and spoke above the tangle of murmured conversation. "I am still thinking about Pasha's question," he announced. "I think it is the right question to ask. Why is the forest here, and only here? We've seen nothing like it on any other megastructure. And why is it just in this one small area? If it's an old system running wild, surely there has been time since the cataclysm to colonize the entire megastructure?"

The Cryptologist stood up in the first row and turned to him. "I think it is correct to conclude the forest is not of great age. Working from historical records, I have calculated a range of potential growth rates for a forest of this type, the rate being dependent on both the intensity of solar energy received and the substrate. At the most, this forest is no more than six centuries old."

As she spoke, more of D-1's towering face came into view, along with two drifting objects hanging like broken moons above the empty cells beyond the forest.

Exclamations and murmurs of consternation erupted, and Urban rose to his feet. He recognized the two objects as the partial remains of what had once been the bow and middle sections of an ancient great ship. Each piece had been ripped open, its layers exposed down to the core chamber. A shiver of dread shot up his spine as he recalled the wrecked ships that had orbited the Rock.

One of the engineers noticed the parallel too: "That wreck looks like it was unzipped by explosives laid on the inside—deliberately scuttled, like the ships at the Rock."

"It can't be the same," Urban said. "D-1 is no outpost lost between stars, and the entity in this system is not broken and marooned."

"A different situation, but the same result," Naresh mused.

Someone, probably Tarnya, spoke from across the amphitheater. "This is what the chameleon ship wanted us to see. A warning, maybe, letting us know of some terrible event—and maybe that danger still lingers?"

"Maybe there are war bots in the ruins," Abby suggested. "Rogue defensive systems."

"That wouldn't explain why the wreck was ruptured from the inside," Clemantine said.

"Never mind that wreck!" Jolly called out from the front row. "Look at the chameleon ship. It's changing again. It's losing its Chenzeme glow."

The kid was right. The local vessel could still be seen at the side of the screen, much larger now, much closer—and much darker. Within seconds, its luminosity faded altogether. It took on a deep dark non-reflective surface and disappeared from sight, at least within the range of visible light.

Soon after that, *Pytheas* reported the chameleon ship's deceleration had ceased. It now coasted in a passive orbit, just a hundred meters from the tip of a large peninsula that extended two and a half kilometers from the towering main face.

Pytheas too ceased to decelerate, settling in to a stable gravitational pocket three kilometers out from the peninsula.

Urban issued instructions to launch scout-bots: one pair to explore the wreck, another to investigate the forested peninsula. He assigned an additional, solitary scout-bot to the chameleon ship, specifying that it should be launched at a slow, cautious, non-threatening velocity. Once launched, the scout-bot had no way to adjust its glide path, so the vessel could easily resist contact simply by moving a few meters—but it was worth a try.

Thirty-seven seconds elapsed before *Pytheas* received these instructions. Another thirty-seven seconds, until they were acknowledged. Soon after that, the scout-bots began to stream their observations as they approached their different targets.

Scout-bots 1 and 2 had been assigned to the wreck. They would reach their target first.

CHAPTER SIXTEEN

VYTET POSTED VIDEO from scout-bot 2 as it coasted toward the exposed interior of the shipwreck's middle section. From her seat in the back row, Clemantine looked on with a sense of foreboding. Some ancient horror had happened here. She mentally prepared herself for the likely discovery of bodies, all frozen beyond any chance of recovery, brain tissue shredded by rending knives of ice.

As scout-bot 2 approached the wreck, dim light, reflected from the sunward face of D-1, revealed concentric layers. On the outside, the hull itself, with frozen insulation beneath that, and then yawning black voids that were probably shuttle or cargo halls. Deeper still, a suggestion of a geometric grid that had to be a mausoleum of cold-sleep drawers on the hibernation deck. Near the core of the wreck, a layer of armored walls protected what had once been the ship's computational tissue. And then came the core chamber itself.

Scout-bot 1 moved against this backdrop. It had been launched first, its silvery ovoid shape a glowing mote against the dim terrain of the exposed core chamber. Just before contact, its four thin, jointed limbs extended to cushion its impact. It secured its position using the reactive surfaces of its footpads.

Several seconds later, scout-bot 2 made its own successful landing, this time on the hibernation deck.

The two scout-bots began their task of mapping and analyzing the wreck. A buzz of competing conversations filled the amphitheater as people discussed and debated the unexpected findings.

First and most obvious, despite the scale of destruction—and despite Clemantine's expectations—the bots located no bodies. Not in the warren or the halls or the tunnels. And every cold-sleep drawer was open and empty.

The large halls observed on approach proved to be cargo halls, all of them unexpectedly barren. There was no hangar. If there had been a landing vessel, it must have been in another section of the ship.

Clemantine stood to speak, her voice projecting over the crowd noise, which quickly quieted. "We can't tell yet what happened here. It's possible this ship was empty, carrying neither passengers nor cargo. But if there were passengers? Surely they survived . . . roused from cold sleep in time to strip the hulk of its cargo."

Riffan looked up from the seat beside her. "I want to believe that. Maybe they were taken off by another ship."

Tarnya said, "With all the resources here, they might have had time to *grow* another ship."

Naresh stood from his seat in the third row. "But why scuttle this one? It was definitely scuttled. Quite deliberately blown open from the inside. Though I don't believe that's what killed the ship. Vytet, can we have another look at the remains of the ship's computational tissue?"

The display shifted to show a dense stack of carbonized and crumpled layers. "This is what's left of the ship's mind and of its library," Naresh said. "It has been burned. Set on fire *before* the hull was torn apart and the interior exposed to vacuum. Chemical analysis puts the date of the fire at significantly less than a millennia ago. Perhaps only five or six hundred years."

Shoran stood, silver hair framing a doubtful frown. "Perhaps the ship arranged its own death, then? Empty, alone, stripped of hope and human contact . . ."

"By the Unknown God," Clemantine whispered, shaken by the suggestion. In a louder voice, she said, "I hope that's not it. Because it implies this ship wandered centuries and found no one—and that we'll find no one, no matter how many stars we visit here in the Hallowed Vasties."

This drew a low murmur of dismay. But then Vytet spoke again, assuring them, "Many possibilities remain. Let's look now at scout-bot 3."

Like Clemantine, Vytet had been unsettled by Shoran's suggestion. It seemed all too logical, too likely. It helped him to remember that Tanjiri System was not dead. Sunward, there was the Trinity, and even here among the ruins, the Sumerious forest thrived.

With a silent command, he banished the image of the dead ship, replacing it with a video of the chameleon ship, relayed from scout-bot 3 as it glided ever closer. Vytet did not expect the bot to reach its target. Instinct told him something would happen to prevent it. Perhaps the bot would be obliterated by a fractional second of laser fire. Or maybe a short kick of acceleration would push the chameleon ship out of the bot's path. Or, if the bot actually contacted the chameleon ship, a legion of disassemblers might erupt from the hull to swarm it, and take it apart molecule by molecule.

But Vytet's instinct proved wrong. The chameleon ship displayed no reaction as the bot approached and then touched down. Its feet immediately analyzed the smooth hull and found it to be composed of minute diamond scales, so well fitted that the boundaries between them could be distinguished only on a molecular scale.

Naresh remarked, "Those scales are likely a thin skin, with all the interesting structures sealed within."

"It would be interesting to try to crack it open," one of the engineers mused.

A suggestion that drew a harsh laugh from Kona. "Interesting in some ironic sense? Interesting to watch as the missile triggers, consuming D-1—and *Pytheas* too—in a dimensional intrusion?"

"I said it would be *interesting*," the engineer insisted. "Of course an experiment like that should be carried out on one of our own missiles."

The bot required only a few minutes to map the vessel's entire surface. It found no features at all. If there had ever been lenses, antennas, molecular sensors, or external propulsion, all of it had since been hidden within the diamond-hard outer shell.

Urban had held his breath when the scout-bot touched down on the chameleon ship. He felt stupidly disappointed when nothing at all happened. But he shook it off and shifted his attention to the last pair of scout-bots as Vytet changed the display.

Scout-bots 4 and 5 had been launched toward the forest. Vytet split the screen, displaying their videos simultaneously as D-1's microgravity gently accelerated them on their approach to the peninsula. As Urban watched, a lacy tangle of black tree limbs grew in detail, layer upon branching layer of them.

Scattered among the limbs were white leaf clusters, though the leaves were mostly furled, rolled up tight so that each cluster looked like a sparse bouquet of thorns. Here and there between the branches, white glints could be seen, suggesting an icy substrate at the level of the forest's floor.

The two bots reached the treetops, arriving a hundred meters apart. Each extended a long supple leg, grasping an outer branch. The branches proved to be lightly textured, allowing for a secure grip, and the bots easily arrested their descent.

Moments later, an initial analysis arrived: the outer surfaces of the black tree branches were safely inert, with no chemical or nanotechnological defense.

Despite the hundred meters separating the bots, their video feeds appeared almost identical. Only a close study of the branching pattern of the tree limbs allowed Urban to distinguish between them. The point of view rotated through a 360-degree scan— and in every direction the forest appeared the same. Black tree branches, scattered leaf clusters, and nothing else. No hint of any other lifeform, down to the molecular scale.

Next, the angle of view turned to the scaffolding of branches below them. Tanjiri's light defined the shapes of the branches and cast complex shadows among them, while highlighting the white gleam of leaf clusters. There was beauty to this forest, and yet everywhere was the same. No variety. No diversity. A suffocating monoculture. As his initial excitement faded, Urban felt repelled by it, and disappointed too. He had hoped for more.

Over the next few minutes the two scout-bots worked their way down through the trees, finding plenty of room to maneuver between the layered branches. In the deeper parts of the forest, some of the leaf clusters had unfurled, their coin-shaped leaves casting a soft white glow. But for whose benefit?

For no one's.

The forest was a relic. Naresh had described it as art. Its value lay in its delicate beauty, not in its contribution to a nonexistent ecosystem.

Scout-bot 4 reached the floor first. Its array of cameras revealed a host of slim black trunks growing a meter or more apart and rooted in an irregular substrate that looked like a rubble of white glass. Analysis showed it to be nearly identical in composition to the foundational layers of typical computational strata.

With its initial observations complete, the bot set off to explore the peninsula, moving slowly toward the main face of D-1. On the way, it passed stacked sheets made of the same glassy material that comprised the rubble. Though these formations varied from a few centimeters to several meters high, all had irregularly broken faces, with visible layers like sedimentary rock. Trees grew from the sides of the stacks and from their upper surfaces. And all throughout, threaded among the rubble and oozing from between the white glass sheets, were flows and crystals of glinting multicolored ice.

Urban guessed this substrate might be only meters deep on the peninsula. But *Pytheas* had earlier observed drifts of "ice" within the gigantic cells where the forest had not yet encroached—and those might well be tens of meters deep, or more. If, as it appeared, the forest fed on this material, gradually converting it to tree tissue and new trees, there was surely enough of the resource to support millennia of growth.

For the next few minutes, the murmur of subdued conversations filled the amphitheater. Urban listened as Clemantine and

Riffan traded observations. He remained silent, though he sympathized with the undercurrent of disappointment in their voices.

Then, as scout-bot 4 approached the base of the peninsula, its behavior abruptly changed. Its legs collapsed, so that its ovoid body dropped down against the glassy sheen of the forest floor.

At first, Urban thought it had malfunctioned, that some heretofore undetected nanotech had corrupted it. Then the video recentered, tilting upward a few degrees. There, obscured by the thin cover of the black branches, Urban saw something moving. Moving swiftly. The bot had dropped low to try to stay out of sight, but the gambit had failed. Whatever it was, it was closing on the bot with impressive speed.

Urban leaned forward, struggling to make it out. He thought he saw long, shiny black limbs, like one of the trees come to life, but that was absurd. A second elapsed, and another. A rushing tsunami of motion filled the screen. And then the video went blank.

Signal lost.

CHAPTER SEVENTEEN

CHAOS ERUPTED IN the amphitheater. People shouted. They rose to their feet. Urban could no longer see the display screen—not its blank half, nor the undisturbed feed from scout-bot 5. So he shifted the source of his visual input. Instead of seeing through his eyes, he utilized his atrium to review video recorded by *Pytheas*—but the outrider had captured nothing of the attack. The bots had ventured too deep within the trees for its cameras to track them.

Urban's fist clenched as he thought about those long, thin, spidery black limbs he'd glimpsed in the scout-bot's last moments . . . like a tree come to life.

He needed more data! Better observations. So he issued an order to scout-bot 5: *Climb, as fast as possible, back to the top of the canopy.*

Of course, the attack on the bot had occurred thirty-seven seconds before Urban observed it, and another thirty-seven seconds would need to pass before this latest order was received. Scout-bot 5 might already be gone, knocked out of service like its companion.

But then, less than two seconds later, the bot ceased its orderly exploration. Using its thin agile legs, it propelled itself rapidly upward through the weave of tree limbs. From the incoming data stream, Urban sussed that *Pytheas* had analyzed the situation and reached the same conclusion as him—that the bot should relocate to the canopy, where the outrider's cameras would have a clear view of its fate.

The data stream also carried the news that D-1's radio silence had ended. A local signal had been detected. But it was encrypted and unintelligible.

Urban immersed himself in scout-bot 5's surroundings—a spherical view stitched together from the bot's multiple cameras. Again, he saw distant movement among the branches. Something approaching, this time in flashes of color—vermilion and bright blue.

Clemantine caught her breath. Her hand gripped his. In a voice trembling with emotion she said, "They are people, Urban."

Are they?

He could not tell. Not yet.

His extended senses picked up her outgoing command, an order to *Pytheas* to bleat out a radio signal across multiple channels, in multiple languages, declaring that the bots intended no harm.

The thirty-seven seconds of transmission time might as well be an eternity.

Scout-bot 5 emerged from the forest, popping into the view of *Pytheas*'s cameras. It clambered across the treetops, back toward the tip of the peninsula, moving at a moderate speed—a ploy to lure its pursuers into the open. Through its cameras, Urban looked down into the depths of the forest. And for the first time he clearly saw the scout-bot's pursuers.

His breath caught. His heart pounded. Clemantine's grip on his hand tightened painfully, her breathing ragged as she repeated, "They are people, Urban. People like Nikko."

Shock stole the strength from his voice. He could conjure only a whisper when he replied to her, "And like Deneb."

Two names they had not spoken in centuries.

Long-sequestered emotions surfaced. His chest shuddered. A deep ache ignited behind his eyes. He squeezed his eyes shut—he wasn't using them anyway—while he continued to watch these strangers through the video that fed into his atrium.

Three of them. Moving rapidly upward through the trees, swiftly closing in on the scout-bot.

Clemantine put her strong arm around his shoulders.

"No," he whispered. "I'm all right."

Or if not all right just yet, he soon would be. A long-dormant routine wakened within his atrium. Already he felt the soothing effect of chemicals released to dull the sharp edge of ancient grief.

Nikko and Deneb had been part of the Null Boundary expedition. Fifteen hundred years ago now. Deneb had been his lover, the mother of his children, and maybe she still was both of those things, somewhere light-years away, but *he* had left her—this version of him—while another version had stayed.

Let it go!

He forced himself back to the present and saw that the bot was moving faster now, fleeing across the treetops, keeping just ahead of its pursuers, matching their pace. They followed within the cover of the trees, all graceful motion as they leaped and twisted and dove between the black branches. Like Deneb and Nikko, they were not people of ancestral form. They did not require skin suits, because their bodies were modified and adapted to tolerate vacuum.

Urban could not yet make out every detail, but he knew that instead of vulnerable human skin, their integument would be made of minute, ceramic-hard scales—a smooth, hairless shell to ensure the integrity of soft inner tissues. Their fingers and toes would be scaled too, each digit long and flexible enough to securely grip the branching trees.

Whenever they looked up, the scout-bot captured images of their faces. Urban glimpsed normal human eyes shielded behind an outer crystal lens, while below the eyes, a thick, living veil formed a seal across the nose, mouth, and ears. That veil was a membrane—he knew it as a *kisheer*—its function, to swiftly and efficiently convert the carbon dioxide of exhalations into usable oxygen.

Also like Nikko and Deneb, these people wore no actual clothing, though decorative membranes, shell-like under vacuum, protected and concealed their anal and genital zones. They did wear thigh holsters that held some kind of bulky tool. Maybe a hand-held laser used for slicing or welding . . . or for cutting down trespassing scout-bots.

They also wore headbands around their smooth craniums.

Of the trio, two were clearly masculine, one with bright blue scales, the other vermilion. The woman matched the men in size, her scales a mix of charcoal-black and silver patterned in complex spots like those of the ancient cat called a leopard. Her long limbs must have been the ones he glimpsed just before the loss of signal from scout-bot 4.

Now she led the others.

As swift and sure as any predator, she burst from the treetops as if she meant to launch herself into the void. But at the last possible moment, she used the prehensile toes of her left foot to grab hold of one of the topmost branches, arresting her momentum. Her long lean figure now floated in plain sight just above the trees, with the device from her thigh holster gripped in her hands. She aimed that device at scout-bot 5, just fifteen meters away.

At that same moment, Clemantine's order finally reached *Pytheas* and the ship began to bleat its message of peace.

The woman flinched—Urban saw this clearly—but her gaze did not shift. Half a second later, the bot's signal ceased, plunging him into darkness.

He shifted the source of his atrium's visual display.

Now he watched the woman through one of *Pytheas*'s cameras, the perspective foreshortened by distance but crisp and clear as she dropped back down into the cover of the trees.

What had happened here to make these people so fearful, so hostile, that they would strike out without hesitation, without asking questions—when surely they had never seen anything quite like the scout-bots before?

"I'm going out there to talk to them," Clemantine announced in a low determined voice. "This is a misunderstanding and we need to get past it."

Even as she spoke, Urban felt through his extended senses the swift passage of her ghost as it departed *Dragon*'s data gate. A copy of the Scholar followed after her.

He hissed out a long breath past gritted teeth, then nodded a belated consent. Clemantine would be better at this task than him.

Still, it would require thirty-seven seconds for her ghost to reach *Pytheas*—while it took only a few seconds for his anger to boil up, the heat of it stripping away his lingering shock.

"Why didn't we ever consider this possibility?" he demanded, barely registering the furious clamor that had taken over the amphitheater. "We should have *expected* to find such people here. It's only logical. We should have at least talked about it."

"How could we know?" Clemantine countered. "We had no evidence that people of any kind were here. No radio signals, no active nanotech, no sign of mechanical devices—"

"There was the forest."

"*Sooth*," she conceded. "There was that."

Urban could not see her. He only heard her voice, his visual sense still filled with the video from *Pytheas*. Flashes of color just beneath the treetops revealed the trio in motion again, advancing rapidly toward the tip of the peninsula.

"I don't understand why they still use this ancient form," Clemantine mused. "How is it that it's gone unchanged after millennia?"

"Why should they change?" Urban retorted. "We didn't."

"It's different with us. We chose to keep the ancestral form. They chose a path of change. Why did they cease to follow that path?"

Riffan spoke to this in fascination, in wonder, oblivious to the rising tension between Urban and Clemantine. "This *is* an early form," he said. "I've seen it in the histories. And what a wonderful design it is! Look how fast they move, how gracefully. Perhaps they have not changed because this design already serves them so well."

Sooth. It was a wonderful design. And Deneb had been so beautiful and so perfectly adapted to move between the inner spaces of *Null Boundary* and the airless ecosystems they'd found at the end of their journey.

Again, he chided himself, *Let it go!*

He drew a deep breath, then exhaled, striving to push all such memories away. In another couple of minutes, the trio would reach the end of the peninsula. One hundred meters beyond the tip of that fang-like protrusion the chameleon ship floated, stealthed and invisible even in sunlight.

"They must have seen the chameleon ship before it shifted," he said, thinking aloud. "Now that they've killed two bots, it's going to be their next target."

They might be aware of *Pytheas* too, though the outrider lay much farther out.

"I'll get there before they can threaten the chameleon ship," Clemantine assured him.

"But isn't it strange that they attacked the bots?" Riffan asked. "Why would they do that, unless they're accustomed to conflict? Unless they expected to be attacked?"

"They must have an enemy somewhere," Clemantine agreed. "But who? And what? And where?"

Urban scowled. His lip curled in contempt. "You know what's most likely. They've split into factions and they're killing each other—creatively—so that every unknown must be treated as a threat."

This theory, this potential situation, disgusted him. He had spent centuries crossing the void, and for what? Not to squander time on the petty squabbles of a petty people.

In a troubled voice, Riffan argued against this conclusion. "It can't be that simple. It's so easy to kill, to destroy, that a true factional war always ends within minutes. But by the evidence of that great ship, these people have been here centuries."

"And don't forget that the chameleon ship led us here," Clemantine reminded them. "We were meant to find these people."

Urban did not want to be convinced. "We have our own purpose."

Their little bubble of argument was only one of many as the amphitheater buzzed with voices debating different theories. Then Vytet called out, demanding a return to organized discussion. Argument gave way to a general rustling as people resumed their seats.

Urban looked outward again at the display screen, one half following the progress of the trio, the other exhibiting bullet

points derived from a library entry on a star system known as
Ju-Sakura.

"The Scholar has identified the phenotype of these people,"
Vytet explained. "Their likely origin is the Ju-Sakura system."

The phenotype had been common there, before the rise of the
Hallowed Vasties. But as in so many other settled systems, Ju-
Sakura's light had disappeared for a time behind a cordon, until
there, as everywhere, the cordon failed. Nothing was known of
Ju-Sakura as it currently existed.

"The form is older than Ju-Sakura," Clemantine said, projecting her voice to address the whole gathering. "It originated in Sol
System, if that matters—though given our estimated date for the
great ship's destruction, it's likely these people came here as late-
era refugees."

"I think this is correct!" the Cryptologist declared. She stood
up from her front-row seat and turned to face the gathering. Eyes
wide with excitement, she proclaimed, "I think it's likely these
people *are* refugees, that they were marooned here by the destruction of their great ship, and that they've been here for approximately six centuries."

"That is the age you've calculated for the forest," Vytet said. "It's
also within the range estimated for the death of the great ship."

"Yes, exactly. Nothing like this forest has been observed on any
other structure, strongly suggesting that these people initiated its
growth and—"

Clemantine's voice interrupted her—but not Clemantine as she
sat beside Urban. This was the voice of her ghost aboard *Pytheas*,
speaking by radio to the inhabitants of the forest.

*Greetings to you. We are strangers from a far star, passing through,
wanting nothing but to meet you, and to hear your history.*

A brief pause, and then she spoke again, or seemed to. In actu-
ality, the Scholar synthesized her voice, repeating her greeting,
first in the primary language of Tanjiri, and then in the dominant
tongue of Ju-Sakura.

The effect was immediate. Still within the cover of the trees, the
three presumed-Sakurans halted their sprint just short of the pen-

insula's end. For several seconds they clustered together, gesturing to one another with rapid hand movements while the local radio transmission continued, still unintelligible.

No reply came to Clemantine's greeting.

After a minute's silence, Clemantine replayed her words. The three Sakurans ceased their hand movements, remaining perfectly still until the message finished. Then the vermilion-colored man made a sharp gesture, as if to cut off discussion.

Leaving the others, he moved cautiously into the open. From the treetops, he gazed toward the local vessel, though it must have appeared to him as nothing more than a slim black void laid across a background of brilliant stars. He held up his hand, his palm turned toward the craft in the traditional gesture requesting peace. Perhaps he did not realize that just below him, the woman had her weapon aimed at the little ship.

CHAPTER EIGHTEEN

CLEMANTINE'S GHOST HAD instantiated in a simulated chamber within *Pytheas*'s library. The Scholar stood beside her.

Like all the Apparatchiks, the Scholar had begun as a ghost of Urban and still resembled him. But the Apparatchiks had diverged through time, the Scholar more so than any other. He had assumed an older aspect, sharp featured, with smooth, long hair that he wore tied behind his neck, its violet-gray color echoing the color of his eyes. Like his manner, his clothing was formal: a long, loose, dark-blue tunic embroidered with silver threads, and voluminous trousers in a matching color.

Clemantine required him for his skill with languages. She had studied the language once commonly spoken within Tanjiri System, hoping to be prepared should they discover survivors. But the Scholar felt these survivors were likely refugees from Ju-Sakura, and who could have predicted that?

Scout-bot 3, from its position on the chameleon ship, provided a crisp, clear view of the dark-shelled woman as she aimed her laser across the narrow gulf.

Who could have predicted these would be a violent people, unashamed to turn their weapons against a vessel that had offered them no harm?

With its array of cameras, the bot detected a coin of red light on the chameleon ship's hull. The little light swept left and right, up and down—a swift survey to reveal the ship's size and its distance. No kill shot followed. The woman lowered her weapon. She looked up at Vermilion and gestured in a series of complex hand signals.

Was this really how they communicated?

Vermilion nodded to her. Drifting above the forest, holding on only by the toes of one foot, he turned to look again across the hundred-meter gulf separating him from the chameleon ship.

Despite the clarity of the image, Clemantine could not read his facial expression, hidden as it was behind his kisheer, and behind the now darkly tinted lenses that protected his eyes. But as he crossed his arms, she read contempt in his stiff posture. A moment later, *Pytheas* received a new radio transmission, one that resolved into a male voice, low and combative, speaking Ju-Sakura's ancient tongue. So the Scholar had guessed right. He translated now, mimicking the man's voice and capturing its bitter tone.

"Why lie?" the Sakuran asked. "Why come to us now, with lies? We have not forgotten who you are or how you marooned us here. So do not insult us with lies. Speak the truth. Say outright that you have come at last to finish us. Volo warned you would."

As this speech ended, the Scholar's violet-gray eyes met Clemantine's. She saw her own wariness mirrored in his gaze.

In his customary voice, he told her, "I believe 'Volo' to be a name."

She nodded. Probably, Volo was the name of a person, though it could as easily be the name of a predictive program, a religious text, a machine intelligence, a post-human entity—or something other.

The Scholar added, "It seems the wrecked great ship *was* deliberately sabotaged, as we have theorized."

"Yes." And clearly the wreck and its history still defined these people. Her first task, then, was to establish her true identity.

"Let's try again," she told the Scholar.

He nodded, and then watched her closely as she explained, "We are not who you imagine. We are not those who did this to you."

The Scholar's lips did not move and Clemantine did not hear her translated voice, but the Sakuran did.

"No?" he barked out in challenge. "But you are their children's children."

"*No.* We are not them. We are strangers to you, and to this system. We don't know of whom you speak or what happened to you. So far, we know very little of this system. We have only just come here from a far star. We meant no offense when we sent the scout-bots ahead of us to explore the forest. We did not know anyone lived here. But now that we do know, we ask your permission to approach your home and visit you face to face. We have come a long way. And for a long time we did not know if we would find any survivors among the star systems caught up in the cataclysm that swept this region. Now that we have found you, we hope there will be peace and friendship between us."

"Fine words, but contradicted by the evidence. We have seen this vessel of yours before. We have observed it many times when you sent it to spy on us. And you speak as one of us, still with the accent of Ju-Sakura. If you have truly come seeking peace, then first admit the truth of your dark history."

Clemantine gritted her ghost teeth, frustrated at the error she had made. The Scholar's translation was too skilled. She should have instructed him to leave a stranger's accent in her simulated voice—but it was too late now.

She forged on. To counter her accuser, she mirrored him, reflecting a hint of his suspicion as she spoke in a sterner voice.

"The truth is, I do not yet speak your language. It's a simulated voice you're hearing, a translation provided by an electronic intelligence. By your appearance, we guessed Ju-Sakura to be your origin. We strove to imitate the spoken language of that system, even though our data is millennia old. It's strange to me that after such a span of time you still speak with the same ancient accent."

She left it at that, and awaited a response, all the while eyeing the three Sakurans. The woman had holstered her laser. She and her blue-scaled companion remained within the trees, watching Vermilion as he moved his hand through a lightning-fast series of gestures. But Vermilion did not seem to be gesturing at the other two. His gaze remained fixed on the chameleon ship.

"Can you read anything of these hand signs?" Clemantine asked the Scholar.

"No. They do not match any of the signaling languages in the library. But note the headband he wears."

"Yes, it looks like camera lenses are embedded in it—but why? Why not use his atrium to capture what he sees?"

"Ah, he speaks," the Scholar said. Then he shifted his voice, threading it with cold suspicion as he again imitated the Sakuran. "And what of your vessel? What is the clever explanation you have for that?"

Clemantine's lip curled in irritation, though she understood the strategy. Casting his people as victims, Vermilion strove to play on the guilt of the supposed oppressors—a desperate ploy that suggested he had no other defense.

But she was no enemy, just an outsider rightfully offended at his words. Let him understand that, and understand too that while she would meet him as an equal, she would not beg for his friendship.

"That vessel you are looking at?" she asked him. "It's not ours, and we know it's not yours. We've seen many others like it. They belong to someone, or something, within this system. Someone we would like to get to know. This particular ship met us. It led our scout ship here. We have to believe it meant for us to find you. Why?"

At this, Vermilion signed frantically, his fingers curling, stabbing, and flashing in front of the lenses on his headband in a ferocity of communication at odds with the uncertain tone of his spoken voice as he sought confirmation. "I don't know if I've understood you right. You say they led you here?"

Clemantine drew a hand across her throat, to stop the Scholar translating. "Who is actually speaking?" she asked him. "I had thought it was Vermilion, but if so, he's carrying on two very different conversations at once."

"Shall I inquire?" the Scholar asked.

"Yes. Translate this." In a cold, suspicious voice she demanded to know, "Who am I speaking to?"

Only after Vermilion executed several sharp gestures did the speaker respond. He said, "My name is Taddeus Li Kubba." The aggression had gone from his voice. He sounded even more uncertain now, worried maybe, that he'd played this encounter all wrong. "And your name?"

"My name is Clemantine. Is that you, Taddeus Li Kubba, there at the edge of the forest?"

Now the Scholar worked a puzzled note into his translation. "Clemantine. Maybe I have misunderstood your question? That is Aurelius Shenen, outside the trees. Okinowa Laikun and Kev Atatashi are with him. I am speaking to you from within our people's warren. It is, of course, impossible to speak aloud when outside. Or is this different for you?"

The Scholar raised an eyebrow. "Interesting." He gestured at his mouth and nose. "And certainly true, given their physiology."

True in a way. The kisheer did not just cover the lower half of the face, it entered the mouth and nose, making it impossible to speak directly. But their atriums would allow them to generate speech without involving the airways . . .

Clemantine cocked her head. "Are you suggesting they don't have atriums?" It was an outlandish idea.

The Scholar shrugged. "This seems to be what Taddeus Li Kubba is suggesting, and it would explain why they use a sign language."

Yes, it would. But what strange beliefs did these people hold, that would lead them to forego an atrium?

"Here is an interesting detail," the Scholar said as he posted magnified profile images of all three Sakurans. "Note this feature." An arrow appeared on the image of Aurelius, pointing to a blurred white line that ran from his headband to the upper edge of his kisheer, just above where his ear would be. "Perhaps this line is an external link between the headband and a listening device." Arrows popped up on the other two profiles. "The feature is common to all three individuals."

Bizarre, if true.

"Are you still there, Clemantine?" Taddeus Li Kubba inquired. "I'm here."

"Will you tell me *where* you are?" he asked almost plaintively.

"We know you are close. There is no light-speed delay, but we have not seen another vessel."

It wasn't surprising that they hadn't noticed *Pytheas*. The outrider was dark and distant, and they had surely been distracted by the chameleon ship. Though it was dark now, it had been illuminated as it approached.

"I'm going to show them *Pytheas*," Clemantine decided.

"They might still have defensive capabilities," the Scholar cautioned.

"I don't think so. But even if so, they're starting to believe us—and *Pytheas* is proof that we truly are strangers to any conflict here."

She ordered *Pytheas* to generate a display of hull lights. Moments later, the outrider lit up with rainbow lines that ran the length of its hull and defined its shape.

"Do you see it now?" Clemantine asked Taddeus Li Kubba. "That is our scout ship. It is a robotic scout ship, lying 3.1 kilometers off your position. We are not physically present there. I speak to you now as an electronic entity."

No more hand signs from Aurelius. He had gone still, staring across the gulf at *Pytheas*'s pretty display.

Taddeus spoke cautiously, "You have another ship, then? A great ship?"

"Yes."

"Where?"

"We are at some distance. A slow approach."

"You will come though?" A question asked with quiet desperation.

"Would we be welcome if we did?"

"*Yes!* I beg you, forgive my rough beginning. We *are* from Ju-Sakura. Our ancestors left there thousands of years ago—an incredible span of time, mostly lost to cold sleep. We were mistaken in you. I promise now you will find a warm welcome here—though not, I think, in the inner system."

"Those you despise, is that where they reside?"

He hesitated, and it was as if the carrier wave that connected them hummed with fear and doubt. When he spoke again, he did not answer her question, saying instead, "Please come. When you are here, face to face, we will tell you of our history and answer all your questions."

The Scholar eyed Clemantine. In his own voice, he said, "My guess is that information is the only thing these people have to trade. They will withhold their history, hoping to lure you in."

CHAPTER NINETEEN

WHEN TADDEUS LI Kubba's invitation was heard in *Dragon*'s amphitheater, it induced cheers and a round of applause—though not from Urban.

Turning to Clemantine, he said, "I don't like this."

She arched an eyebrow. "I agree there's little to like about these people. They're fearful, suspicious, violent, and defensive . . . but then so were we, that time a strange starship brought outsiders to Deception Well."

Urban slid down in his seat. He'd been a child during that incident, but he had no problem remembering it. "That was different. And it wasn't *all* strangers on that ship. We had to defend ourselves."

"Agreed. But these Sakurans thought they knew us too—as a familiar enemy. Given that, was their first reaction really so different from our own?"

He had to concede that it was not.

"We can get past this," Clemantine insisted. "We can get to a better place. And there's so much we can learn from them. They may have witnessed the rise of the Hallowed Vasties—or the end of it all."

"Sooth. You're right. I know."

Centuries had passed since Urban had conceived this expedition, but his goals remained the same. He had resolved to journey from the edge of human civilization to its source, exploring an inverted frontier of broken civilizations and transformed worlds, piecing together the history of what had happened in the

Hallowed Vasties—and standing witness to what was happening now.

These people were part of that.

"All right," he said, standing up. "This is where we begin."

He walked down to the front of the amphitheater. Vytet watched him, and moved aside as he stepped onto the dais. An expectant silence settled over the gathering.

Urban scanned the faces and caught the questioning eyes of Naresh, Shoran's eager gaze, Jolly in his excitement, the Cryptologist looking doubtful, Kona's measured stare, and Pasha, bright-eyed with ever-present mistrust.

He said, "For reasons I have not yet grasped, the entity at the heart of this system showed us the way to these Sakurans. We never would have found them on our own—and maybe that would have been better. There is a dark history here and I don't trust it."

He raised a palm to silence an onslaught of objections. "Even so, I recognize there is much to learn here—these Sakurans might be the only human settlement surviving in this system. And there's a lot we can offer them. So this is what I propose. Instead of continuing to follow *Pytheas*, I will take *Dragon* slowly sunward. But we'll select a small team to visit these people. They'll take the lander, spend a day, or a few hours—long enough to understand the situation and the history. Then we reassess."

Tarnya stood. "We need to do more than that. These people are clearly refugees, trapped here by the sabotage of their great ship and in need of our help. They don't even have atriums!"

Shoran said, "The entity must know of their plight. Why hasn't *it* helped them?"

"I wonder if they know of the entity?" the Cryptologist asked, her eyes narrowed in pitiless speculation. "They would be of some value if they do."

Kona's booming voice silenced the spreading commentary. "I agree with the proposed strategy. An advance team should be able to quickly assess the situation, gather answers to our questions, and determine the aid we might render, if aid is needed. But I don't see that much can be gained by lingering here. Our focus in this system lies sunward."

Jolly leaned forward in his front-row seat. His eyes sought Urban's. "I want to go," he said. "I want to be part of the advance team of Dragoneers."

Urban froze, stunned at this request, every fiber of his being resisting the proposal. Send Jolly out among an unknown and evidently desperate people? *No*. It wasn't worth the risk.

Like Urban, Jolly remained endowed with silver. If lost, this version of him, this avatar, could not be replaced as it was, but only in a version that lacked the silver.

But Urban said nothing, just looked away. He would talk to Jolly later, alone.

Riffan popped up from his seat in the back row. "You're not planning this as another one-way expedition, are you? The, uh, *Dragoneers* who go will be able to use the lander to return home, right?"

Urban cracked a cynical smile. He and Riffan had together made a one-way expedition to the Rock, where they'd found Lezuri. Riffan still wrestled with guilt over the unknown fate of his lost avatar. "Termination is always an option," he told Riffan. "But if the encounter goes well, the lander will return all Dragoneers to *Dragon*."

"Very good!" Riffan said with a pleased smile. "In that case, I also volunteer."

Many others spoke up then, eager voices volunteering to go: Shoran, Clemantine, Alhimbra, Mikael, Tarnya . . . half the ship's company—even the Cryptologist.

"I don't think more than five should go," Kona said.

Urban agreed. He looked across the rows. Caught Clemantine's gaze. *You truly want to go?*

A smile, a nod.

Once more he addressed the gathering. "Clemantine will lead the advance team. She'll decide who goes."

But as he stepped down from the dais, he added privately, *I don't want Jolly to go.*

And you? she asked as she strode down to meet him. *You don't want to go?*

A slight shake of his head. His current avatar was irreplaceable too and he did not want to risk it. Not for this. Not when greater possibilities lay ahead.

With a shrug, Clemantine took over the dais. "Those of you interested in a place on this advance team, send me your names. There is no one here who is not qualified to go. So I'll leave it to the Mathematician to select four at random from the volunteers."

Urban moved to the side of the amphitheater. On the display screen, the ongoing video slid to one side, making room for a list of names: thirty-one in all, with Jolly's name at the top.

Leave Jolly out of it, he urged Clemantine. *Make your selections within the range of two to thirty-one.*

That's not fair, she countered. *He volunteered, and he can take the chance with everyone else.*

He's not like everyone else.

Even so, you don't get to make the choice for him.

Urban gritted his teeth, quietly furious. But she had made up her mind. He'd given her the authority, and further argument would get him nowhere.

"The Mathematician will now make the first selection," Clemantine said.

Urban looked at the list of names. Tension knotted around his heart. Then the tension broke as Riffan's name lit up. Urban laughed aloud—while the company groaned and objections erupted:

"Riffan always gets picked!"

"Riffan always goes first!"

"He went to the Rock."

"He was first at Verilotus!"

"Riffan has always been lucky," Clemantine agreed. "*Next.*"

Shoran's name highlighted this time. She whooped, while a deep sigh washed across the company.

"And the third team member," Clemantine said.

Abby's name stood out.

"No!" someone shouted. Urban craned his neck, identifying

Zahn-Mei, one of Abby's parents. "Abby is too young. No experience."

Urban bristled. While it was true Abby had just twenty or so years of life experience, that didn't mean she was too young. Urban had been just a little older that first time he'd left Deception Well. But he didn't say anything. He didn't need to. Because Abby was standing up, facing her mother with an angry glare.

The two of them looked a lot alike. Abby had Zahn-Mei's deep blue eyes and shining black hair, but unlike her mother, her hair was long and loose and she always dressed in shades of gray and violet.

"None of us have ever experienced this situation before," Abby said. "And Clemantine said we're all qualified. I put my name in, I was selected, and now I'm going."

It was the boldest speech Urban had ever heard from her.

"Please select the final team member," Clemantine instructed the Mathematician.

Jolly's name lit up. The kid whooped louder than Shoran, while Abby laughed in delight. "We get to go together!"

Urban leaned forward, grimacing in disbelief, on the verge of calling out in protest like Zahn-Mei—but he caught himself. Jolly wanted this, and with Abby going, no amount of persuasion would change his mind. Probably, it would only trigger resentment. And anyway, it would be hypocritical to object. Like anyone else, Jolly had a right to make his own stupid decisions. God knows Urban had made plenty in his lifetime.

CHAPTER TWENTY

JOLLY HAD BEEN inside the landing ship, *Argo*, only once before. The little vessel had been made to ferry people from *Dragon* to Verilotus and back again—though it had made that round trip only twice. *Argo* could carry only half the ship's company at a time, and it had required an enormous quantity of fuel to climb free of Verilotus's gravity well, even when empty. Every outward-bound passenger would have increased the fuel requirement.

So in the end, only he and Urban, with their silver-augmented avatars, had boarded *Argo* for the last flight out. All the other Dragoneers had discarded their planetary avatars and left Verilotus as ghosts.

Now Jolly looked around *Argo*'s cabin in stunned surprise. The lander did not look at all like he remembered. Before, the interior had been packed with nine small chambers, stacked three high in a U-shaped configuration, each chamber just big enough to hold four people as they hibernated within cold-sleep cocoons.

Jolly remembered how his heart had raced as he'd crawled into one of the chambers, Urban crawling in behind him, telling him not to be afraid. He had no memory of the lift-off or the slow journey to *Dragon*, because he'd been in cold sleep for all that time.

In the landing ship's new configuration, there were only two cold-sleep chambers, stacked one atop the other at the back of the cabin, there in case of accident or some unexpected circumstance. They could bide in cold sleep for years if needed.

Not that they would need to. Jolly refused to believe that.

Five acceleration couches crowded the remaining space: one

seat behind another on either side of a narrow aisle, and one in front.

For only the second time in his life, Jolly wore a skin suit, one with the same lime-green color as when he'd gone outside. Maybe it was the same suit, he didn't know. It had emerged from the generative wall in his cottage as he prepared to leave, and he'd put it on.

He liked wearing it. It made movement effortless. Assisted by the suit, he bounded first up the aisle, seizing the single forward seat as his own. *Argo* had no windows, but all of its interior walls now functioned as display screens, revealing what lay outside. For now, all that could be seen was the white shell of *Argo*'s hangar pod. But once the lander was underway, he would have the most amazing view.

"Hey," Abby objected from behind him. "Why do you get that seat?"

Jolly looked around at her with a grin. "Because I move faster than you?"

"Asshole."

He laughed, glad Abby was coming along, but sorry the Cryptologist wasn't part of the team as well. She had wanted to be. She'd wanted it badly enough that she'd asked him to give up his seat.

"There is no chance of that happening," he'd told her. "I want this. I've done almost nothing since I joined this expedition. I need this."

"But I have a more adept mind than yours. I am in a position to learn more."

"Maybe so, but you're only interested in learning what these people know of the entity."

"Not true! I am also interested in a close inspection of the megastructure itself, as this might yield insight into the means of its creation, and that in turn might offer a clue to the puzzle of how to open the needle."

"So let the scout-bots do your research for you. *I'm* interested in the people. I want to meet them, talk to them, see for myself who they are and how they live. And I'm not going to give you my seat."

Now he looked past Abby, to see Shoran coming next up the aisle, with Riffan behind her, both bright-eyed and smiling.

"We are *so* lucky to be here," Shoran said as she slid into the seat across from Abby.

"I hope we're lucky enough to feel lucky tomorrow!" Riffan joked.

Clemantine boarded last, looking solemn. "Last chance to change your mind," she announced.

This drew a chorus of enthusiastic denials that induced in her a quirk of a smile. "All right, then. Let's do this thing."

Jolly braced, half-expecting her to kick him out of the front seat. She took the last empty seat instead. With a smile of triumph, he turned to face forward. As he did, gel straps oozed out of the seat, securing him in place.

Argo was ready to go.

"Initiating launch sequence," the ship announced, its voice that of a Dull Intelligence trained to pilot the lander.

"Into the unknown!" Shoran crowed.

"That is *not* something to cheer," Clemantine countered.

Still, it was true. In his ongoing conversations with Clemantine, Taddeus Li Kubba had made clear his people's feelings about the scout-bots: "We have no experience of such synthetic beings. We find them disturbing, uncanny, and we do not want them wandering among us, monitoring our lives."

So the surviving scout-bots had been kept far from the forested peninsula—a fact that delighted Jolly. There might have been nothing left to discover if the bots had been allowed to freely explore. Instead, the landing team would be the first outsiders to ever visit the Sakurans—and none of them knew what they would find.

Jolly felt movement: the little ship rotating within its pod. Then, in front of him, in front of *Argo*, the hangar split open. The two halves pulled away, revealing stars beyond. A slight bump, as *Argo*, still attached to *Dragon*, rode outward on a platform. The cell field blazed around them, vast and bright.

"This is going to be the roughest part of the ride," Clemantine warned.

Argo spoke again in its soothing voice, "Detaching, *now*."

Jolly imagined *Argo* releasing its docking hooks. Then he felt a second, stronger bump as *Argo* separated from *Dragon*, and also from *Dragon*'s ongoing deceleration. Within the grip of the gel straps, he felt suddenly weightless, while outside, the vast, luminous bulk of the courser raced past so quickly his eyes could not focus on the pattern of the hull cells. In mere seconds, *Dragon* was gone, and *Argo* floated alone amid a sea of stars.

Jolly turned his head to look for the courser and saw it receding, still decelerating, while *Argo* retained a slightly higher launch velocity. "*Wow*," he breathed.

"*Jol-ting*," Abby agreed.

Shoran laughed in delight, Riffan looked around wide-eyed and grinning, and even Clemantine had a smile. But then Jolly looked ahead again. He looked for their destination, D-1, but he saw only the uncountable, unreachable swarming pinpoints of millions of incomprehensibly distant stars.

It hit him then, how far from anywhere he was, and what a precarious position all of them were in. He leaned forward, reaching out with a gloved hand to touch the display screen in front of him, assuring himself it was still there, with the thin barrier of little *Argo*'s hull behind it . . . all that lay between him and infinity. If something went wrong, what could they do?

"Stand by for *Argo* to re-orient," the DI warned.

The lanes and clusters and scattered points of fierce unwavering starlight flowed in dizzying migration. Part of the display darkened, shading a cruel glare. *Tanjiri*, Jolly realized. The local sun. From this far orbit, just a swollen point of brilliant light.

So far from anywhere.

Jolly gripped the sides of his chair, aware of his heart, beating too quickly, and the trembling quality of his breath.

"Where is it?" he whispered, anxious to sight an island, any island, in this void. "Where is D-1?"

The stars ceased their migration. In the ensuing stillness, his eyes picked out a tiny, half-lit crescent. "*Oh*," he breathed.

"You see it now?" Clemantine asked.

"I do."

Clemantine had carefully prepared the landing party. They'd met several times, discussing the many potential hazards and complications they might encounter, and they'd created a simple ruleset for how to behave and stay safe. Even so, at the end of it, Clemantine had warned them, "Be ready, because for all our planning, we're still going in blind—and anything could happen."

Jolly understood that if the worst happened, he would die. Abby too. All of them. It didn't matter if they had superior Makers. Makers couldn't save them from a swift and deliberate act of malice.

Clemantine had said, "If we find ourselves in a bad situation, unable to extricate, we may need to terminate. Riffan's done it before."

Riffan had responded to this in a strained voice. "Ah, yes. My visit to the Rock."

Shoran, buoyed by her ever-present confidence, had winked and insisted, "We'll be fine, because this time there is no Lezuri."

"Commencing acceleration," the DI announced.

A gentle pressure pushed Jolly back, deep into his seat. No point in worrying. So he forced a smile. "This is going to be amazing," he said softly.

"Hey," Abby responded with a little tremor in her voice. "It already is."

During the long transit to D-1, Clemantine listened, again, to the concerns of her dark twin.

I don't like this at all, the other Clemantine complained. *We know far too little about these Sakurans to trust in their good will.*

They need us, Clemantine answered. *For now, I'm trusting in that.*

Griffin, coasting in the interstellar void, was so far away now that it would be many minutes before her words were received, and many minutes more before she heard her dark twin's reply. Truly, a slow discussion.

Her mind wandered, thinking of Taddeus Li Kubba and how, in every subsequent conversation she'd had with him, he'd clung stubbornly to that initial promise—that the Sakurans would reveal their history and answer all questions, but only when they met their visitors face to face.

Possibly, they still doubted the reality of Clemantine's claims. More likely, they feared *Dragon* would pass them by if they confessed too soon to some shameful truth behind the scuttling of their great ship.

Still, as Clemantine pressed them for information, they'd finally alluded to an event in their past: *A tragic incident that left our ancestors stranded here . . . and here we remain. As a people we've survived, but we've lost too many along the way.*

"Incident' is an interesting word, Clemantine mused, after reminding her dark twin of that vague revelation.

After a long delay, there came cold agreement. *Sooth. A small fanatical faction may have scuttled the ship, or it may have been done by consensus of the ship's company. Either way, the shockwave of that event will have shaped the culture of these people. Be wary of its ongoing reverberations.*

I mean to, Clemantine replied.

In the face of continued questioning, Taddeus Li Kubba had repeatedly pleaded for patience: *You are a greater people. We acknowledge that. We are at your mercy. But please, let us show you who we are—who we are now. Then, I swear, we will answer all your questions.*

There had been only one fact he'd freely confirmed: All of the founding generation and their immediate successors had long ago succumbed. *They lost their lives making a home for us here. We owe them everything.*

Clemantine sensed that despite that gift of life, D-1 made a poor home. She told her other self, *I'll be wary. But I suspect that what these people care most about is simply surviving one more day. And what they fear most, now that we've come, is that we might judge them harshly—and pass them by.*

I hope you're right. I despise this secrecy of theirs, though I do admire the way they've exploited our insatiable curiosity.

Jolly had slept for a few hours, but he was awake now, gazing in wonder at the view screens surrounding him. *Argo* had crossed the gulf and reached D-1. Now the little landing vessel skimmed the megastructure's broken face, so close, the great open cells hung like an impossible ceiling above them—a vast, frozen expanse where nothing moved except the tiny dark spot of *Argo*'s racing shadow.

Jolly watched the shadow cross great drifts of multicolored ice frozen to the cell walls, and he watched it vanish when it chanced to pass against a cell's deep, lightless back corner.

The ship spoke, "Commencing final deceleration in five, four, three, two, one."

Argo's engines reversed, leaving Jolly hanging against his straps as the lander rapidly shed velocity. Each giant cell they passed rolled by at an ever-slowing rate. He could see the glimmer of the forest ahead as it refracted sunlight, though it still looked very far away, and only slowly, slowly drawing closer.

He could not imagine what it had been like to live within this great structure when it was intact and part of the cordon encircling Tanjiri. He reminded himself that each cell passing overhead comprised a thousand square kilometers, bigger than the City of Glass had been at Verilotus.

But what had been contained within these cells? All they held now were ice flows and empty space. He saw no interior structures.

He wondered too why each cell looked almost exactly like every other, differing only in the detail of its icy holdings. Had the cells always been exactly like one another?

The thought of it—of being trapped within an artificial world divided into geometrically precise blocks, each identical to the other so that no matter how far a wayfarer wandered, there would never be anything new to see—that thought knotted his stomach and fed a sense of claustrophobia altogether new to him.

He shook his head, shook off his imaginings, and returned to the present. It felt to him as if they were rising toward a vast ceiling made of endlessly repeating tiles. So close now, Jolly could see what looked like shear marks scoured into the top of the cell walls.

What had caused that? What kind of weapon could have torn D-1 open?

In truth, he didn't want to know. He didn't want anyone to know. Looking at the face of that great structure he found himself desperately hoping that all knowledge of such forces had been forever lost in the cataclysm that had consumed Tanjiri's cordon. And for the first time, he questioned the wisdom of opening the needle. Might there be more knowledge contained within it, than it was right for anyone to know?

CHAPTER TWENTY-ONE

RIFFAN KNEW BETTER than to argue with Clemantine when her decisions involved the safety of the mission. But when she declared that *Argo* would approach no closer than three kilometers to the forested face of D-1, he could not completely resist the temptation.

"I hope the Sakurans don't interpret our hesitancy as mistrust," he mused aloud as he helped Shoran to distribute the bright-white go-packs that had been stashed in the emergency cold-sleep chambers.

"Of course they will interpret it as mistrust," Shoran answered with a laugh. "That's the point."

Clemantine loomed over Shoran's shoulder, an eyebrow arched, her gaze stern. "Exactly that. They have not earned our trust. Their secrecy has garnered *mistrust* instead and I want them to know it. If they hope to gain anything from us, they will be on their best behavior and answer every question we ask."

"Ah," Riffan said. "Right . . . but this is not going to be a meeting of peers, not if it turns out the Sakurans truly need our assistance. And we don't want to earn their resentment . . . do we?"

Clemantine shrugged. "We're here on their terms. It's up to them, how they receive us."

"Hard, but fair," Shoran said.

And wasn't that Clemantine's way?

You *are the idiot who trusts too much*, Riffan reminded himself. He'd proven that with Lezuri—a remembrance that brought an embarrassed flush to his cheeks.

"All right," he acknowledged. "I understand."

Discussion over, he turned to claim his go-pack.

The acceleration couches had been folded into the floor, leaving plenty of room to gear up in the bulky packs, all freshly assembled for this expedition.

The go-packs were an old design, but one Urban had used before. Looking at them, Riffan thought they resembled a flattened version of the shell of that creature called a tortoise, with hexagonal scales on the back and a soft, shallow cradle in the front. He backed into his, just as he'd done during a practice session before they'd departed *Dragon*. The cradle's soft white tissue flowed around him. It formed a support for his head while sealing across his shoulders, his chest, his hips, locking him in. He felt secure in its gentle grip. Through his atrium, he listened to a brief handshake conversation between the pack and his skin suit as the two DIs confirmed a successful integration.

Only then did he look around at the others. All of them had now melded into their own flat tortoise shells. Abby looked uneasy. Jolly too. Shoran, of course, was grinning, while Clemantine inspected each of them with a somber gaze.

"All right," she said. "We exit one at a time. I'll go first. Remember the rules."

The ruleset was simple: be polite, ask before touching anything, go nowhere alone, and make no promises.

That last one, Riffan reflected, would be the challenge. It would be so easy to promise knowledge and resources. But Clemantine wanted to understand these people—how they had come to be here and what they might do—before giving anything away.

He ordered his hood up, then approached the membrane that served as a lock. Clemantine was there ahead of him. Using handholds, she pulled herself into the dense black gel and disappeared. Riffan followed. The membrane sensed the pressure of his body and yielded to it, while denying the steady suck of vacuum. He transited easily, emerging into the void on the other side.

The go-pack knew what to do. Riffan felt a brief kick of acceleration as galleries of micro-nozzles fired, sending him soaring away from *Argo* and toward D-1's seemingly infinite face.

At first, he perceived that face as vertical and the forested peninsula as a horizontal projection reaching out to meet him.

But on an instinctive level, this made no sense to his brain—and his perspective shifted. D-1 became a vast plain and the peninsula transformed into a spike-shaped mountain, impossibly tall and narrow. Worse, the peninsula/mountain arose from the edge of a wide, forested ridge. A sheer ridge that plummeted downward for kilometers into darkness. And Riffan was plunging face down into it.

His stomach knotted. His brain tried to seize. He silently chided himself, *No, no, no you don't. You don't panic.*

Sucking in a sharp breath, he willed himself to keep looking, to make sense of where he was, of the incredible scale of this artificial world. But he could not. He broke out in a cold sweat, trembling within his suit.

Get a grip on yourself, idiot!

Only then did he notice Clemantine, eighty or ninety meters below him. Fixing his gaze on her, he concentrated on her crisp white shape as he strove to get his racing heart to slow.

Hard to find calm though, when he felt himself in the grip of D-1's microgravity. The go-pack had given him only a brief push, but D-1's pull was steady—and cumulative. He fell ever faster. The summit of the peninsula/mountain loomed on his right—and then he plummeted past it, hurtling toward the abyss below. And again he verged on panic. His fists clenched, his toes curled: ancient instinct urging him to grab at nonexistent branches. His heart pounded in his ears.

"Umm," he whispered to the go-pack past a dust-dry throat. "Perhaps we should slow down?"

The pack replied cheerily, "Deceleration scheduled to begin in five, four, three, two, one."

Micro-nozzles along the sides of the pack swiveled forward, ejecting visible streams of condensing propellant. His velocity slowed. His orientation rotated. He drifted down slowly now, feet-first. But the abyss still lay below him. And gravity's light touch still strove to pull him, body and mind, into that lifeless depth—until his go-pack cheerfully countered it. "Commencing horizontal acceleration."

More micro-nozzles fired, sending him soaring away from the abyss and over the lower forest surrounding the base of the mountain. He looked down at a tangle of black tree limbs less than a meter beneath his feet.

The Sakurans had radio-tagged a meeting point in the forest. The go-pack carried him to it. He had lost sight of Clemantine, but as he began to descend among the trees, he saw below him the white gleam of her go-pack and a flash of silver from her luminous skin suit, already deep within the maze of branches.

Seconds later, his foot brushed against something, the sensation of it communicated to him by the inner surface of his suit. Startled, he looked to see what it was—a cluster of leaves, furled now against the daylight that bathed the top of the forest.

Don't touch anything, his conscience chided him.

Well, he would do his best.

The go-pack continued to control his descent, firing its micro-nozzles in complex patterns, steering him gently between the branches. The urge to reach out and touch those branches was strong. He longed to discover by tactile sense more of their constitution. But rules were rules. He kept his arms crossed on his chest, his hands tucked away and his feet together, to resist temptation.

But even without touching the branches, Riffan could see they were not smooth and glassy like crystal, but matte black and finely textured.

He passed more furled leaf clusters.

A glance up showed the roof of the forest now some nine meters overhead. Jolly, in his lime-green suit and white pack, had just reached the top of the trees.

Riffan continued to descend past branches now striped in shadow. Here and there, a few leaves had unfurled, casting a pretty white light. As he went deeper, shadows accumulated, but so did the glowing leaf clusters. Together they cast the forest in an ever-more complex mosaic of light.

Twenty-two meters below the top of the canopy, his feet finally touched down on glassy white rubble. Immediately, he slipped. Out of instinct, he flailed and grabbed a branch to stop his fall. Technically a violation of the rules, but then Clemantine had her gloved hand wrapped around a branch too. Call it a necessary exception.

They had come to rest at the edge of an open area, roughly circular. For a span of some fifteen meters, no tree trunks sprouted from the slippery substrate, though an abundance of branches formed a lacy roof overhead. Waiting near the center of the clearing, around the open maw of a broad black pit, were the Sakurans. A crowd of them, thirty or more, women and men, a few children too. Their long toes clung to ground-level grips. Their long fingers held on to one another.

Riffan recognized among them the three who had pursued the scout-bots: Kev Atatashi with his bright-blue hue, Okinowa Laikun with the complex charcoal and silver pattern of her scales, and in front of all the others the tall man they'd first called Vermilion, though they knew him now as Aurelius.

As Riffan studied the Sakurans, they studied him in turn. He found their faces unreadable behind their kisheers, the glint of their eyes lost behind crystal lenses. He found too, something eerie in their stillness, and in the silence that pervaded this meeting.

He longed to break the silence, to speak a greeting on a radio channel already agreed upon. He wished Clemantine would speak. He said so on the team channel: *Won't you greet them?*

    When our team has assembled.

Jolly dropped down from the canopy.

    Be careful, Riffan warned him. *It's slippery. Catch hold of a branch.*

Jolly shot a glance at Clemantine, then did as Riffan said. His eyes went wide as he felt his feet slip, but he held himself up with a tight grip.

Abby came next in her lavender skin suit, and finally Shoran, wearing light green.

Dressed as they were in their scaled skin suits, the five of them were not all that different in appearance from the Sakurans, at least if one was willing to overlook stubby graceless fingers and feet that appeared toeless within the suit, and open expressions of wonder and fear clearly visible past their transparent visors.

We must look very strange to them, Riffan thought.

With her team now on the ground, Clemantine let go of the branch she'd been holding and rode her go-pack forward, one hand raised, palm out in greeting.

Aurelius moved to meet her. He too raised a hand, and then extended it. Clemantine clasped it, and they spun together in a slow circle.

Taddeus Li Kubba must still be inside the warren, because his voice spoke over the shared radio channel. A DI translated, mimicking him. "Greetings. We are honored to meet you and we are grateful for your presence here, and for your trust. Please, leave your transportation packs—you won't need them—and come with us into our home, where we may talk freely and show you who we are."

CHAPTER TWENTY-TWO

FROM THE LIBRARY, and also from within the little chamber in the warren where her avatar rested, the Cryptologist monitored every thread of information generated by the advance team. She did not do so in real time, but worked instead from behind a slight delay. This allowed her to shift among raw data streams, absorbing each at an accelerated speed.

From the perspective of a scout-bot she explored the forest in a region distant from the peninsula, where no Sakurans had been observed. The trees in that area exhibited an interesting difference from those on the peninsula. At irregular intervals along their winding, intersecting branches, they sprouted solitary cylindrical growths, suggestive of fruiting bodies. Most of these were as black as the tree branches, ranging in size from tiny nubs at the end of a short glassy stem, to a hefty fifty centimeters in length. *Exactly* fifty centimeters. Most interesting, those few fruiting bodies that achieved that finished length—none were longer—flushed with color. A bright, eye-catching orange. The only color within the black and white forest.

Intrigued by this discovery, the Cryptologist plunged into the library's vast collection, hunting down records of similar forests—but none described such fruiting bodies. She longed to cut one open. Surely the interior composition would reveal its purpose? But the scout-bots did not have the ability to do that . . . and anyway, such a line of research could not possibly aid her quest.

With this thought in mind, she shifted her attention from the forest to the substrate on which it grew—ancient computational strata that had been wrenched, twisted, heaved, and shattered, presumably by the violent apocalypse that had ripped D-1 apart. Stacked sheets of it, looking like white glass, could be seen wherever the uneven terrain had been thrust upward or forced down, while smooth-edged rubble filled the hollows between the trees. Organic elements, along with metals and metalloids, combined within the strata in a complex crystalline array. More organic molecules, as well as volatiles, remained locked within the ubiquitous flows of ice.

Within the time machine that was her mind, the Cryptologist fared back through the centuries to the era before the forest, when there must have been only rubble, white strata, and drifts of multi-colored ice. And farther back? Back before D-1's apocalypse—what then? What had existed, before all was shattered? What . . . except that glassy strata, each sheet intact and distinct from the next: layers upon layers of computational surfaces nourished by a cold flow of nutrients.

No evidence remained of anything else.

The Cryptologist visualized D-1 as a thinking machine. Perhaps even the body of a god? She had studied the testimony of Lezuri, who claimed to have arisen from the mass consciousness of a vast virtual world. Was that what had existed here? A world shattered and lost in the great struggle toward dominance that Lezuri had described . . .

All these thoughts led her to an intriguing possibility:

Might there still be coherent data frozen in these sheets?

She sent this question to the Engineer. An answer came almost at once: *Given the highly distributed nature of data storage in known computational strata, coherence is unlikely. But a sample-return mission is underway and we will eventually be able to examine the strata in close detail.*

Good enough.

She shifted her attention to video collected from a different source: Jolly's atrium as he dropped down through a deep shaft amid a crowd of colorful Sakurans. They surrounded him, their headbands emitting soft white light, just enough to show the way and to illuminate layer after layer of collapsed computational strata forming the shaft's scalloped and uneven walls.

The Sakurans used wall grips to control their speed, or they gripped one another. Jolly's head turned as he looked for his companions past the tangle of Sakuran bodies. There, a flash of lavender that was Abby in her skin suit. A glint of silver that might have been Clemantine, or it might have been one of the Sakurans. A burst of light green as Shoran emerged from the scrum with a grin and a question for Jolly: *You doing okay?*

Sure, he answered in high excitement.

He glanced upward. Looking through his eyes, the Cryptologist saw Riffan, his amber skin suit lit by the glow of Aurelius's headlamp.

The vermilion-colored Sakuran was the last of their group. The Cryptologist looked beyond him, past the top of the shaft to the tangle of branches that roofed the clearing. The forest's soft white light illuminated the tethered go-packs, anchored together at the mouth of the shaft, there to serve as a communications relay.

Positioning data tracked the party's descent: twenty, twenty-five, thirty meters below the surface.

Jolly looked around again—and the Cryptologist caught her breath at what she saw. The composition of the pit wall had abruptly shifted. No longer icy white strata, it now looked to be composed of some brushed silver metal, forming a perfectly circular bore five meters across.

The Cryptologist reached out with her hand, desperately desiring a sample—but then the wall became ice again, and Jolly's focus returned to the Sakurans around him.

He was falling faster now, dropping past them.

Forty-five meters below the surface, his restless gaze shot down to take in a well-lit floor not much more than ten meters distant. His gaze jerked to the right, where he saw long black fingers wrapped around the lime-green sleeve of his skin suit. Looking up, he met the gaze of the woman with the laser, the one who had destroyed the forest scout-bots. The Cryptologist remembered her name: Okinowa Laikun. She held onto Jolly's arm, slowing his plunge. Together, they landed gently on a floor of rough ice, fifty-six meters beneath the mouth of the pit.

Jolly bounced lightly, as if taking the measure of the micro-gravity. Shoran dropped down beside him. He turned to her and enthused, *This is amazing!*

Shoran's eyes crinkled as many more Sakurans dropped to the ground around her. *Enjoy it, but stay alert too.*

Okinowa Laikun stepped past them—tall and lean, moving with the grace and coiled tension of a stalking cat. Jolly's gaze followed her to a softly gleaming white circle set into the ice of the wall. She looked back at Jolly with bright blue eyes, visible now past their protective lenses. Crooking her fingers, she indicated he should follow. Then she leaned into the gleaming circle, disappearing into it. *A gel membrane!* Like the one serving as an airlock aboard the lander.

Jolly didn't hesitate. He plunged ahead, following Okinowa Laikun into the membrane. For several seconds as he pushed through its thick tissue, he saw only an unfocused white glow. In that time, the Cryptologist switched feeds, first to observe from Riffan's point of view as he drifted down beside Aurelius, and then to Clemantine, who had just landed.

The Cryptologist lingered in Clemantine's view, watching her withdraw two identical objects from her waist-pack—oval, silvery, eight centimeters on their major diameter, and studded with glinting camera lenses.

Ah, a pair of quiescent scout-bots.

The bots' long wiry legs had retracted into short dangles.

Clemantine handed one of the bots to Abby. *Take this through with you*, she said, her voice audible on the shared channel. *We'll activate it on the other side.*

Abby glanced around nervously. *What if they don't like it?*

I'll apologize. But we need the analysis. Now go. I'll be right behind you.

Abby nodded, and followed a peach-hued Sakuran toward the membrane, with Clemantine right behind her.

The Cryptologist shifted back to Jolly's point of view, finding him in a dim, narrow space between two glowing membranes. A glance behind showed Shoran emerging from one. Jolly pushed ahead, entering the other. Again, nothing to see but a soft white blur for the seconds he took to pass through it. Then a burst of light. Light in abundance—light *and* air—as he broke through to the other side. The data stream generated by his skin suit reported a breathable atmosphere and a lot of it, though the air was cold, well below freezing.

Abby, you need to see this! Jolly crowed.

I'm coming! Oh, there's a second membrane.

I know. Just come through it.

I'm here, Shoran said. *And it is amazing.*

Amazing?

No, not really, the Cryptologist thought. Interesting, yes. Definitely not amazing.

Jolly stood gazing at a long chamber, at least a hundred meters in length. It didn't run straight, so the Cryptologist could not yet see all the way to its end. The floor was brushed metal. So was the distant ceiling, eighty or ninety meters overhead. But the walls on either side were made of ice—scalloped, gleaming, multicolored—not geometrically precise. They faced each other across a gap of no more than ten meters and sometimes less—a space that felt crushingly narrow only because the ceiling rose so high.

Bright passages perforated the ice walls. Not just at ground-level, but also on the equivalent of second and third stories. Far down the chamber, an ice bridge vaulted the gap. And the light? It came from an abundance of glowing leaves like those in the forest, except here they grew in dense clusters from slender black trunks that did not branch but instead snaked up the ice walls and around the mouths of the passages.

At least a hundred Sakurans—probably more—had come to greet or to gawk at the visitors. They stood back from the gel membrane, but packed the chamber beyond, with more emerging from the side passages or approaching from deeper within the tunnel. The fine scales of their integuments ranged across many colors: pale pink, gleaming gray, a bold bronze, a pure black, and shades of brown, blue, teal, and rusty red. Most individuals were all of one hue, but some showed an even mix: blue scales alternating with teal, or red scales with brown. But the Cryptologist saw no others with the bold patterning of Okinowa Laikun.

All of them in their many colors had bright eyes open to the cold air, and beautiful, expressive human faces. They looked at Jolly with wonder, and with joy.

The Cryptologist counted five—no, six children of different ages scattered among them. Easy to spot because they jumped high in the microgravity to see over the heads of their elders, only slowly drifting back down. Every child carried what looked like a tablet. They held up the familiar devices, as if to show them to Jolly.

He chuckled softly, with joy, with amusement. Then he turned, looking back to see some of the Sakurans from the welcoming party emerging from the gel. Their thick membranous kisheers rippled with motion, undulating down, to settle on their shoulders like short capes, leaving their faces revealed—and leaving them free to smile and to speak, both of which they did, though the Cryptologist could not understand them. The outer lenses that had protected their eyes retracted too, compressing into thin, glassy ridges bracketing their eyes.

A flash of lavender behind the tall Sakurans hinted that Abby had come through—and then the Sakurans around her cried out in alarm. They recoiled, revealing a scout-bot stalking among them on its long, thin, articulated legs.

Oh no, Abby said on the team channel, sounding quite frightened herself. *I released it too early, didn't I?*

It's all right, Clemantine said. *We need it to analyze the environment and determine if it's compatible with our Makers.*

The bot tried approaching individual Sakurans, but each in turn backed away until one—a rather short male at the front of the gathering with an integument of deep-blue—held his ground. As the bot approached him, he crouched to meet it, as if to examine it, eye to eye. The scout-bot raised a spidery limb, reaching out to him. Shocked gasps mingled with cries of protest as the Sakuran mirrored the gesture, touching his outstretched finger to the sensory pad at the end of the bot's proffered limb—an action that allowed the device to collect a sample of his biome.

He nodded and stood up again, smiling, the tiny scales of his face sliding past one another, overlapping to allow a fluidity of expression. He looked first at Jolly, and then beyond him, speaking in a now-familiar voice. Translated, he said, "I am Taddeus Li Kubba. And you are welcome here. We're grateful you've come."

Warm words, though his restless gaze revealed an inner tension. The Cryptologist longed to know what lay hidden in his people's unspoken history. Some hint of the entity? She hoped so. Or perhaps a clue to the great forces that had shaped the megastructures.

The scout-bot's report arrived. The Cryptologist scanned it and scowled, puzzled by what it didn't show. The bot had detected no defensive Makers—no engineered nanotech at all—in the air or on the surfaces it touched.

Had the bot made a mistake? Or did these people truly live without the protection of somatic Makers?

Pasha's heart pounded with a budding fear as she studied the findings of the scout-bot, posted on the amphitheater's display screen. She shook her head, rejecting the results. No engineered nanotech? It wasn't possible. People could not live in such an environment without the aid of somatic Makers, at a minimum.

Standing, she addressed Vytet on the dais, rather than the ship's company. "We can't take these results at face value. These Sakurans are not primitives. Possibly, they are *more* sophisticated than we've guessed. We could be facing an ecosystem of stealthed Makers like the molecular governors at Deception Well, a system that defies detection—"

Vytet held up a hand, palm out, his bearded face thoughtful. "Would they need our help if they commanded a system that sophisticated?" he asked gently.

Pasha turned as Naresh spoke from behind her in his self-assured, deeply annoying way. "In general, Pasha," he reminded, "the simplest solution is most likely. Within the forest, we found no active or remnant Makers, and now we have found none within the Sakurans' warren. As hard to believe as it is, the simplest explanation is that these people have abandoned the ability to synthesize molecular machines, a circumstance that would also explain why they have apparently abandoned the use of atriums."

A burning flush ignited in Pasha's cheeks as she recognized the logic of his explanation. He returned her gaze, a hint of chiding amusement in his eyes as if to scold her for jumping to an unfounded conclusion. The worst part of it: He was right.

Chastened, she settled back into her seat, abandoning the argument. But others took it up.

Alhimbra was first on his feet. "I agree with Pasha. It's impossible to survive like that. An absence of somatic Makers would leave these people utterly vulnerable."

"No, it *is* possible," Bituin the poet countered, standing to face him. "It has to be. It's how all people used to live."

"Yes, before there was rogue nanotech. *Now*—"

Shy Mikael interrupted, he who rarely spoke at gatherings. "Consider Verilotus—"

Akechi, one of the engineers, did not allow Mikael to make his point. "This is not Verilotus," he snapped. "These people were not created here. They arrived in a great ship—"

Adalize, who specialized in the bio-mechanical arts, interrupted him in turn—not to dissent, but to make Akechi's argument for him. "Yes, exactly. And they must have had Makers when they arrived. Cold sleep is impossible without Makers. And they would have needed assemblers to create the forest—"

"But they're isolated now," a male voice called out, interrupting Adalize in turn. With so many people now on their feet, Pasha could not see who spoke. "In a sterile environment, they wouldn't need defensive Makers—"

"Come on! Who would give that up?"

"There is an energy cost to maintaining our somatic Makers. In a circumstance where food is limited—"

"Food is not limited here," Kona said, his deep voice carrying easily. "Or it wouldn't be, with a working system of Makers. We've established that there are vast resources here, locked up in the ice, and an immense surface area to collect solar energy."

Young Sayuri of the ship-born spoke up in horrified delight, "What if they are some kind of religious cult, devoted to a 'natural' existence?"

"The Sakurans are an engineered people," Vytet reminded her. "So that seems unlikely, especially if they require mechanical assistance to reproduce, as the library suggests."

Pasha sat slumped and silent, following the debate, but contending only with herself. Naresh had certainly made a valid argument. Even so, she could not bring herself to believe that any people could survive in such a harsh environment without Makers. Never mind their reproduction! How did they repair the damage they must incur from radiation every time they went outside?

She messaged the Bio-mechanic. *What is your opinion of all this?*

He answered with a cynical purr. *I am not yet ready to draw a conclusion, but I will make a prediction. If they have lost the ability to synthesize Makers, I expect to find evidence of natural aging in their cells—and a population in steep decline.*

Pasha looked up with a troubled frown. Behind Vytet, Clemantine's video feed played onscreen. It showed very few children among the gathered Sakurans.

From within the library, the Cryptologist's virtual self monitored the debate in the amphitheater—not that she expected to learn anything useful from these conjectures. Truth resided with facts, but sufficient facts still needed to be collected.

Clemantine understood that. She did not waste time on debate or await a consultation from *Dragon*. Instead, she took the next logical step. Speaking over the team channel, she said, *The atmosphere here is cold, well below the freezing point of water and the pressure is far less than what we're used to. But it's survivable, and it's clean, with no molecular-scale threats. Go ahead and open the hoods of your skin suits.*

The Cryptologist watched on the video feed as Clemantine's hood rolled back, exposing her to a chatter of excited voices, speaking with a nasal twang in a language peppered with terse syllables.

Clemantine cleared her throat, once, twice. Someone coughed. Not speaking aloud, her voice heard only over the team channel, Abby demanded to know, *What is that smell? It's like the filtration system has failed.*

What filtration system? Clemantine asked.

And Shoran said, *That's nothing but the pungent odor of human life. Be glad it's so damned cold here, or it would be unbearable.*

I don't care about that, Jolly said. *Can we talk to them?*

The Cryptologist too was eager to hear the Sakurans' story. But Clemantine said, *Let me go first.*

Like everyone on the team, she wore a translation device—an oval button on the outside of her skin suit, just below her throat. When she spoke through her atrium on a channel linked to the device, it translated her words, mimicking her voice just as the Scholar had. And when the Sakurans spoke, each team member heard a translation of the words within their atrium.

And what did they use this impressive technology for? To exchange boring greetings!

Welcome to Volo's Landing! the Sakurans called out with a desperate sincerity.

And Clemantine, cautiously gracious, *We are honored to visit your home.*

The talk went on in that spirit for a while. And after that there came pointless introductions and dully formal professions of good will. The Cryptologist could bear only a few minutes of this before she hissed in impatience and shifted her focus to the scout-bots' data streams.

But then a better idea came to her and immediately, she accessed the latest status report from *Pytheas*.

Yes!

Clemantine's ghost was no longer resident in the outrider's library. Only the Scholar was there. And that meant, that despite the library's limited capacity, there remained room enough to host her ghost.

Without waiting another second, the Cryptologist departed through *Dragon*'s data gate.

Jolly felt awash in strangeness. The faint, disturbing tug of D-1's microgravity, together with the unaccustomed power-assist of his suit, left him mired within a dreamlike sense of motion. Every move he made demanded thought, because even the slightest twitch could betray his tenuous balance and send him crashing into someone or spiraling up above the heads of the Sakurans. At the same time, the low pressure of the warren and its sparse oxygen had slowed his thoughts, and the heavy, almost nauseating odors that saturated the thin air had brought him to the edge of dizziness. Meanwhile, his ears buzzed with the staccato syllables of a language he did not understand, and his eyes were continuously drawn to other conversations, carried out in hand gestures— as unsettling as secrets whispered on the edge of hearing.

And despite all this he loved it, loved the newness of this new world, and thrilled just to be there, at Volo's Landing.

One after another, Sakurans drifted close, smiling as they murmured his name and words of welcome. They reached out to him, their long, long fingers gently touching his shoulder as their bright curious eyes examined him from head to toe.

Jolly returned their smiles and he replied to their greetings, his atrium translating as best it could, although the overlap of speech made everything hard to follow. And he examined them in turn with a bold gaze. They looked so strange to his eyes, and he knew he must look bizarre to them too.

Then one of the kids—a delicate little dark-green child— showed him a battered tablet. A corner of the tablet's screen was nonfunctional gray, but the working section displayed a simple drawing of a naked man of ancestral form. "Do you really look like this under your skin?" the child asked, fingers cautiously stroking the scales of his suit.

"Something like that," Jolly admitted.

"You are the old people, then."

"Yes. I guess we are."

He looked around for Shoran or for Abby—*go nowhere alone* being one of the rules. But he'd lost track of them in the graceful swirl of brightly colored bodies. He'd lost track of everyone. Surely there were more Sakurans now than when they'd first entered the warren?

But before he had time to worry, a familiar face appeared in front of him—Okinowa Laikun, with her blue eyes and silvery

NEEDLE153

leopard spots. Like the others, she touched his shoulder as she spoke. His atrium translated, simulating the sharp but friendly tones of her voice.

"Welcome, Jolly Huacho. It's my privilege to be your guide while you are here, if that's acceptable to you." She cocked an eyebrow—a fine, hairless, neatly shaded ridge. One of a pair that perfectly framed her brilliant eyes. And she smiled.

Jolly found himself staring, entranced by the startling alien beauty of her darkly patterned face. "Of course, Okinowa Laikun," he said—or anyway, his voice translator said it. He wished there had been time to learn her language.

She smiled. "Okinowa is enough."

"And it's just Jolly, for me."

"Jolly, then. Taddeus would like you and your people to see our home, and how we live here."

He started to speak, to ask the first of many questions, but she held up her hand with its long thin fingers, each digit endowed with five articulated segments instead of the three that served for his own fingers. "I know you have many questions, and we will answer all of them. But it's our wish that you first come to know us, and understand what we've endured here, and the ever-narrowing margins of our lives."

This request brought to mind the wreck of the great ship and the evidence that it had been deliberately scuttled. Jolly could not help but wonder, again, what terrible circumstance had inspired such a self-destructive act.

But he did not press Okinowa on it. Whatever had happened to the great ship had happened centuries ago. *A tragic incident*, they'd called it. And even if it was an incident of civil war, generations had passed on since then. It would be wrong to judge them by the actions of their ancestors.

So he smiled and took her proffered hand, thrilling at the smooth feel of her finely scaled palm, as translated by his glove. And they joined the flow of the crowd down the long tunnel.

CHAPTER TWENTY-THREE

THE TEAM HAD dispersed amid the crowd of Sakurans. Clemantine could not see any of them past the tall, willowy people surrounding her—but her atrium tracked them. She knew they remained close.

Taddeus escorted her, chatting in a friendly way, performing the role of a gracious leader as he called her attention to the structure of the tunnel, the composition of the ice walls, and the great luck their ancestors had in finding this place.

"We did not create the tunnel itself," he told Clemantine. He tapped his long toes against the brushed-metal floor, then gestured up past the ice walls to the metallic gleam of the distant ceiling. "That was part of the original structure, clogged with frothy, complex ices when our ancestors discovered it. They partially excavated it, intending it only as a temporary home."

He showed real pride in his people's accomplishments—and yet his gaze often darted past her shoulder, to Aurelius who trailed behind them. Grim-faced, nearly silent, and yet a magnetic presence. When Clemantine had first seen him outside, she'd assumed he held a leadership role. She had not changed that opinion. It was not just Taddeus who persistently checked in with him. A cluster of Sakurans, both women and men, hovered near him. While her alien presence commanded much of their attention, they watched him too.

Clemantine decided she would try a question. "How long ago did your ancestors come here?"

Again, Taddeus glanced at Aurelius. When Clemantine followed his gaze, she saw the latter nod.

"Six hundred seventeen years," Taddeus said with the pride all gone from his voice.

That timespan coincided nicely with the Cryptologist's estimate of the forest's age.

"And how many of you, living here now?"

Another uneasy glance, though this time he did not wait for permission to speak. "We number six hundred and nine."

Clemantine paused to look up at the icy walls aglow with light from the vinings, and she counted the bright mouths of well-lit passages on three levels, noting the dark passages too. She considered the size and shape of the main chamber. The uneven ice walls prevented her from seeing its full length, but there was room here. A lot of room. Far more than six hundred nine people would need.

"A great ship would have carried many thousands," she said softly.

She herself had once traveled that way, locked into cold sleep with only the ship's mind awake, on that desperate journey that had brought her people to Deception Well.

"Mistakes were made and many lost along the way," Taddeus admitted, this time without checking for Aurelius's approval. His long fingers touched her shoulder in that gesture she already recognized as common among the Sakurans. "But our ancestors planned for the worst—and we are not defeated. Come. Let us show you how we live."

The Sakurans lived within family apartments carved into the ice and aglow with the clean white bioluminescence of the leaf clusters. Furnishings were sparse. Residents slept cocooned in insulated hammocks, and they had electric heaters that raised the temperature a paltry few degrees above the deep chill in the main chamber. Clemantine noted that these devices, though kept polished and gleaming, showed the scars of long use and imperfect repairs.

There were also insulated blankets laid out on the floor in some apartments, or hanging from drying racks in others. And she looked in on several communal kitchens, steamy with warmth as food was prepared.

Everyone she met smiled and greeted her warmly. Still, she did not miss the anxiety lurking within their eyes. And who could blame them, with strangers in their home, come to judge them? Clemantine hated to think of it that way, but it was the truth. They knew it; she knew it. She'd compelled Taddeus to acknowledge it during her initial questioning: *You are a greater people. We are at your mercy.*

It had been a mistake to push him that far. Better to have met as equals—though given the imbalance of power, perhaps that had never been a real possibility. The Sakurans needed assistance. They had let it be known they desperately hoped for it—while *Dragon's* people only hoped to satisfy their curiosity.

Knowing that the Sakurans' story was all they had to trade, Clemantine willed herself to be patient, and to wait while they revealed their blighted history in their own way.

As the tour returned to the main chamber, Shoran and Riffan drifted in from among the shifting tangle of Sakurans.

It's a poor existence, Shoran said on the team channel.

They're all educated though, Riffan added. *Every child has a tablet. They learn their history . . . though like ours, it's ancient history now, dating from before the fall.*

Nothing more recent? Clemantine asked.

They have no way to update the tablets' history modules. That's what I was told.

Shoran added, *Kev Atatashi explained how they take great care of their devices, because while they can sometimes repair them, they can't be replaced.*

Clemantine nodded. Really, it was astonishing these people had survived so long on remnant technologies. She turned to Taddeus. "It's remarkable you were able to salvage the fusion reactor from your great ship."

The fine scales of his deep-blue brow crinkled in confusion. "A fusion reactor? Oh . . . right. There would have been such a device. It must have been lost. Cut loose, maybe." He glanced past her shoulder, to where she knew Aurelius stood. "Or destroyed?"

"But then where does your electricity come from?" Clemantine asked him.

A self-deprecating smile as Taddeus gestured toward the ceiling. "I forgot to say, didn't I? It comes from the forest. Everything essential, everything renewable, comes from the forest. Aliz Li Kassey was the designer who left us that gift. She worked at Volo's direction to adapt a preexisting library design to suit our needs here at Volo's Landing."

Clemantine could not keep the surprise from her voice. "You have a library? A working library?"

"We once did," a deep voice answered from behind her. "No longer."

She turned to meet Aurelius's hard-eyed glare—and glimpsed something of shame behind it. The ignominy of a fallen people?

Holding his gaze, she said, "That's why you don't use Makers."

"Yes. We lost that ability when we lost the library."

Taddeus added, "If not for Volo's foresight in developing the forest, we would not have survived to greet you in this distant year."

Clemantine responded frankly: "Even *with* the gift of the forest, your survival without Makers is an incredible victory."

"No, it is a long, slow failure," Aurelius countered. "This alien architecture in which we have made our home is slowly rotating, carrying the forest into darkness, and us into a time that is called 'winter.' It is a season of bitter cold and scarcity, when the forest hibernates, producing no power and no food. We have been through many such seasons, and we know how to stockpile both, but it is hard. There are always losses."

He looked at Taddeus and with a short nod, he said, "Continue."

"Come," Taddeus said at once. "I'll show you the creche, and then the chasm and the industrial chambers beyond."

She walked with him as he led the tour deeper into the main chamber.

"Was Volo your ship?" Riffan asked. "I mean, your ship's mind?"

"She was our captain," Taddeus said. He didn't elaborate.

Don't press him, Clemantine messaged. *Not yet.*

The main chamber ended where the towering ice walls came together to form a dark, narrow passage, just two meters wide, though open all the way to the high ceiling. *The chasm*, she thought.

But Taddeus did not take her there. Instead, he turned aside to a large ground-floor room, open to the main chamber. Racks lined both side walls. They held the spheres of artificial wombs . . . more than a hundred of them, though none had active displays. At the back of the room, tall cylindrical tanks stood strapped to the ice, their steel polish muted with age. In front of the tanks, another womb rack. It held only three wombs, but these were linked to the tanks, and each had an active display.

Clemantine looked to Taddeus for approval. Only when he nodded, did she approach. She could not read the symbols on the displays, but each showed an image of the developing fetus within, all three near term.

"Only these three wombs still function," Taddeus said.

"And that means that any child conceived after the wombs are full is born and then dies," a woman added.

Clemantine turned to look, and recognized the speaker as Okinowa Laikun.

"I don't understand," Clemantine said. "Do you conceive your children by chance?"

A slight frosty smile from Okinowa. "Our bodies still have that ability." She pressed her palms against the charcoal scales of her hips, and then against her belly. "But not the ability to carry a baby to term. It is born at twelve weeks, and if it is very lucky, it will be transferred to a working womb."

Bitterness infused her words. She did not need to say more. Clemantine understood. There had been a child, her child, lost for lack of a working womb. Going by the dark scowl on Aurelius's face, she knew too who the father had been.

"Let's move on to the chasm," Taddeus suggested, his hand light against Clemantine's shoulder. "There is more to see in the rooms beyond."

Clemantine did not like being between the narrow, looming walls of the chasm. No vining lights grew in the winding passage, leaving it dim, dependent on a wan scattering of light that spilled from deep within side tunnels.

Taddeus led them into the first of these tunnels. They emerged into a well-lit workshop, with tables he described as work benches. He pointed out racks of implements that he called hand tools, and shelves full of salvaged equipment. Other than a stack of tablets, and a dis-assembled hand-held laser, Clemantine recognized none of it. She wondered if these latter-day Sakurans knew what most of it was for.

The tour returned to the chasm. They visited two more industrial rooms. Then Taddeus took them down yet another side passage, this one quite dark, with no friendly light from the room at its end. Only when he stepped into the room did a few scattered leaf clusters begin to glow, their weak light revealing row after row of netting that hung in layers from the ice of the ceiling. Most of the nets, though not all, held great numbers of bright-orange cylinders all the same length, around a half meter long. As she moved closer, she recognized the objects as the same fruit-like growths the scout-bots had observed in a region of the forest distant from the Sakurans' home.

"Is this food?" she asked. "Food that the forest produces for you?"

"It is," Taddeus confirmed. "It's the staple of our existence. A spectrum of useful organic molecules lies locked within the ice. The forest extracts those molecules and converts them into an edible form. We harvest them at this perfect stage of ripeness, when the fruits contain every nutritional element we need to survive. Aliz Li Kassey designed it that way."

Abby had been nearly silent throughout the tour, but now she surprised Clemantine by asking a question. "Is that what Okinowa Laikun's hand laser was for? To cut the fruits from the branches?"

Okinowa chuckled. She patted the laser in her hip holster, answering the question herself. "It's true, we did not go out purposefully to hunt for trespassing robotics. But a laser isn't needed to harvest. The fruit breaks off easily when ripe. We use lasers to cut away branches when they grow too dense and we cannot reach the fruit."

"It's a lucky chance the ice contains the proper spectrum of nutrients," Riffan suggested.

"It's not chance," Okinowa corrected him. She looked up, raising both hands, long fingers spread in an encompassing gesture. "What was here, was once human. Where we stand now, this great tunnel clogged with ice, once flowed with the thoughts of some great corrupted lifeform that evolved and died in that span of time when our ancestors lay trapped in cold sleep."

Taddeus bobbed his head in an affirming nod. "That is what we've concluded. We call this place Volo's Landing, but it was something else before. Dead now. Torn apart by an unimaginable force. The great spike of ice above us—we believe it formed when this major tunnel was breached and the once-liquid contents geysered into the vacuum, freezing as it was pulled back by the gravity of the remnant structure. That cataclysm severed a complex of cross tunnels too, though they did not bleed like the major tunnel."

Okinowa added, "The well you descended is one such cross tunnel."

Taddeus nodded. "Yes. Our ancestors found it filled with ice, but radar showed them the shape of the major tunnel below. For them, it was an easy thing to bore through the ice—but even in those early days, with all the resources of the library, the tunnel wall proved impervious. Our ancestors concluded that some strange physics must be involved in its construction. Perhaps you will understand it, but we do not."

Okinowa again raised a hand, palm up. "It's ironic, isn't it? Here we are, a petty people living among the bones and frozen blood of some vast, incomprehensible intelligence. Alive, only because the ancient cataclysm that broke that intellect happened to leave the tunnel complex open for us. Without these walls to shield us, we would not be here."

CHAPTER TWENTY-FOUR

"WHY ARE *YOU* here?" the Scholar asked, the very moment the Cryptologist's ghost instantiated within the computational space of *Pytheas*'s library.

The Cryptologist smiled sweetly and said, "Please excuse me while I review what I missed during my transit here."

She immersed her ghost-self into the data feeds collected by various bots, so that she only half-heard the Scholar when he said to her, "Given your quest, the alleged constitution of the tunnel walls will interest you."

She had to review this statement in her mind to grasp its meaning. When she did, she popped back into full awareness of the virtuality shared with the Scholar. "Please explain this alleged constitution."

"Listen."

He replayed for her words spoken by the Sakuran known as Taddeus Li Kubba:

Even in those early days, with all the resources of the library, the tunnel wall proved impervious. Our ancestors concluded that some strange physics must be involved in its construction.

"Oh," she said softly.

The Scholar said, "Our scout-bots have no cutting lasers with which to test the Sakurans' claim. However, the bots have already made several attempts to analyze the matter composing the tunnel, and have found it nonreactive. Difficult to assess without X-ray analysis."

"You were correct. I find this quite interesting."

"Yes, I find it interesting too."

———

Jolly had faced many strange situations growing up on Verilotus. For some long time in his youth he'd been alone and lost within the silver, and he knew what it was like to be afraid. So when, in the food-storage chamber, Abby drifted close to him, her cheeks mottled with cold and a wild, almost panicked look in her eyes, he took her gloved hand in his and whispered, "This chamber scares me. The ice and the darkness." He did not tell her that he thrilled to that fear, that his heart beat swiftly in excitement at all they had seen.

But his partial confession was enough to unlock her reserve. As Taddeus and Clemantine moved toward the tunnel that would take them back to the chasm, she clutched at his arm. Holding him close in the treacherous micro-gravity, she placed her lips against his ear and whispered, "I'm going to have nightmares of being trapped here. Trapped forever. It's like I can feel the weight of the walls closing in."

He squeezed her hand. "I know what you mean. But isn't it amazing that people have made a life here?"

"A trapped life."

"But it's their home, just like *Dragon* is ours," he whispered, watching as Taddeus and Clemantine disappeared into the tunnel. Shoran, Riffan, and Okinowa followed them one by one, while the other Sakurans waited their turns.

"Look around," Abby said. Her lips moved against his ear, her whisper so soft now he could barely hear her. "The Sakurans are afraid too. They're afraid we will leave them trapped here. And that makes me afraid of them."

Jolly did look around, and realized she was right. Here in the shadows, in this chamber where the fruits of the forest were stored against the coming season of darkness, the smiles of the Sakurans had faded. The gravity of worry pulled at their faces as they slipped, one after another, into the tunnel.

"We *will* help them," Jolly whispered. "It'll be all right."

Blue-hued Kev Atatashi noticed them lingering. As the rest of the Sakurans departed, he approached with a smile. "Come, Abby," he said, holding out a hand to her. "And Jolly. There is still a little more to see."

Abby smiled a nervous little smile as she took his hand and went with him into the tunnel.

Jolly followed behind them.

Clemantine trailed one gloved hand along the chasm's ice wall as she walked with Taddeus, eyeing the darkness overhead. Though there was not enough light to see all the way to the distant ceiling, there was light among the Sakurans. In the darkness of the deep chasm, their scales glowed with a soft phosphorescence: deep-blue from Taddeus, scattered white from Okinowa, a rosy-red gleam from Aurelius, and a mix of colors from the others.

Taddeus pointed out two more dark tunnels. "These are also fruit vaults," he said.

Several meters on, the chasm ended in a vertical ice wall. Clemantine gazed up into the darkness, feeling as if she stood at the bottom of a pit, hopelessly deep and forever cold.

Taddeus moved away from her, drawing her attention to an arch of ice in a side wall. The arch framed an alcove—an oblong space three meters deep. Taddeus stepped to the end of it, where a faint light bleeding down from above washed away his phosphorescence.

"Come," he said, turning back, beckoning Clemantine with an outstretched hand. "There is one more place I need to show you."

She joined him, looking up again. This time, she saw a round, dimly lit chimney, rising many meters overhead.

"It's an easy climb," Taddeus assured her. "There are hand-holds carved in the ice. Just follow me. It's not far."

Clemantine had followed him willingly, patiently, all the way to the end of the chasm. But she hesitated now, looking up at that chimney. The Sakurans had so much room in their main chamber, why keep this distant, inconvenient annex?

She looked around, spied one of the scout-bots, debated sending it ahead of her.

"Our world must seem very strange to you," Taddeus said in a soothing voice pitched to assuage her obvious doubt. "I should have explained. Here, we're standing directly below the breached section of the major tunnel. This is where fluids geysered out to form the great spike—what you call the peninsula. If you climb the shaft, you'll see the tunnel's cut edge."

"So we'd be climbing into the ice of the peninsula?" Shoran asked from behind Clemantine's shoulder.

Abby bobbed restlessly beside her. "With the local gravity, it's more like a tall, thin mountain, isn't it, Shoran? You must have climbed mountains before."

"Not from the inside."

"Why tunnel into the spike at all?" Clemantine asked.

Aurelius moved into the light. "Our ancestors tunneled here only to create a secondary exit. We discovered later that the proximity of the forest makes this section ideal for grow rooms."

"Grow rooms?"

Taddeus smiled. "It's not just the fruit of the forest we eat. Not in summer, anyway. Will you come?"

Clemantine looked up the shaft, knowing that despite her qualms, she had no choice but to go on. If the Sakurans harbored any bad intent, she needed to know it.

"Of course I'll come," she said, and gestured for him to lead the way.

Under the weak grip of D-1's microgravity, the climb proved easy, just as Taddeus had promised. Ridges and scallops had been carved all around the chimney's ice walls. With gloved fingers and booted toes, Clemantine propelled herself upward, following Taddeus toward the light—until he paused and looked back down at her.

He said, "This is where we pass through the tunnel wall. You'll see it's quite thin relative to the tunnel's diameter—just four centimeters. And the cut surface is slick, different from the wall's inner and outer surfaces."

Clemantine stopped to examine the slice of silvery matter. Ice had been chiseled away to expose a half-meter of its length. The breach in the tunnel wall was clearly far larger than the diameter of the chimney that passed through it, but most of that breach remained clogged with ice. She touched the exposed surface. Her gloved fingers slid across it. It felt frictionless, like the needle. The sensation sent her thoughts sliding back to Lezuri.

Lezuri had created the Blade at Verilotus, or so he'd claimed. He'd told Urban such blades were usually transient—burning incursions from another Universe, open seams in the structure of space-time, used to slice apart worlds. Clemantine imagined such a blade wielded as a weapon, one that had sliced through the structure of D-1, clipping the tunnel as it passed, leaving this smooth-edged wound.

Analyze this, she ordered a scout-bot, knowing that at some point it would follow her up the shaft.

She looked up at Taddeus, now several meters higher. Climbing quickly, she tried to close the gap, but he reached the top of the chimney and disappeared over the lip before she had quite caught up. She propelled herself up and out, emerging into a rounded chamber, several meters across. As D-1's microgravity pulled her slowly down to the floor, she looked around and counted five ice arches, all closed off with gel membranes aglow with light.

Taddeus beckoned her toward one of the arches. "Through here."

But she held up a hand. "Let's wait until we're all here."

Abby emerged from the shaft. Then Riffan, Shoran, Aurelius, Kev, and those other Sakurans who still followed the tour.

But not Jolly.

Jolly was waiting impatiently for his turn to follow Clemantine up the shaft when the Cryptologist messaged him: *I am here.*

He glanced over his shoulder, trying to see to the back of the crowd . . . but of course the Cryptologist could not really be here. *You stayed behind, on* Dragon.

No, I am here. My ghost, I mean. In Pytheas's *library. That should be obvious to you, since there is no time delay in my response.*

Oh, right. I didn't think about that.

You must learn to think about such details. They can be exquisitely important. Also, I want you to obtain a laser.

*What?

*A laser. That tool Okinowa Laikun used to destroy the scout-bots.

*I know what a laser is.

His gaze shifted to Okinowa. She stood in the alcove beside Shoran, both of them watching Abby as she jumped up into the shaft and began to climb. Okinowa still carried her holstered hand laser.

*Ask her to lend you her laser.

*Why should I?

*I am attempting to understand the molecular structure of the tunnel wall. If you can use the laser to free a small sample, that would be ideal. But even if this proves impossible, a scout-bot will be able to analyze the material's heat-conductive properties and the composition of any gaseous emissions as you score it with the laser.

*No way. I can't go around damaging the Sakurans' home.

Shoran moved next to ascend the shaft. As she did, Okinowa turned. Her searching gaze found Jolly, and she beckoned to him.

He smiled nervously but did not move as the Cryptologist explained, *By their own testimony, it is unlikely the laser will be able to effect any damage.

*Then why—

*It's critical that you attempt this experiment, she interrupted. *The tunnel wall appears to have a highly unusual molecular structure. Insight on its composition may lead to insight on the structure of the needle.

*Oh, he breathed, as Okinowa cocked her head, looking puzzled. *I've been thinking. Maybe it's not such a good idea to open the needle.

Her answer stunned him. *Ah. I have wondered the same thing. Nevertheless, I exist to see it opened.

Okinowa used her hand signs, signaling to Aurelius and Kev. Aurelius shrugged and ascended the shaft. Kev and the other Sakurans quickly followed. But Okinowa stayed behind.

*Act now, the Cryptologist urged. *It is the perfect opportunity. Ask Okinowa Laikun if she will assist you in this experiment.

"You look distracted," Okinowa said as she approached him. "Is something wrong?"

"No." He eyed the laser in her holster, as one of the scout-bots circled behind her. Everyone else had vanished up the shaft, leaving them alone at the end of the shadowy chasm.

"There's nothing to fear," Okinowa told him.

He met her gaze. "One of our scientists has proposed an experiment."

She cocked her head. "What sort of experiment?"

"One that would require your help." He spoke reluctantly, unsure if he should aid the Cryptologist in this endeavor. But they'd come here to learn . . .

Swallowing his doubt, he explained what was needed. Okinowa's eyes narrowed. "Taddeus has already told you that cutting into the tunnel is beyond us."

"Have you tried it?" he asked her.

She drew back, side-eyeing him with obvious suspicion. But only a moment later, she relaxed. Ruefully, she admitted, "No, I've never tested that claim." A sly smile followed. "Let's try it here, now."

"Here?" He looked around. They were surrounded by walls of ice.

She pointed at the floor.

Right. All this time, they'd been walking on the brushed gray matter of the tunnel wall.

"Move back into the chasm," she instructed.

"Do you think it's dangerous?"

"Possibly."

He moved back. Okinowa remained in the alcove. The scout-bot came out from behind her to observe. It took a position midway between them. Okinowa eyed it as she unholstered her hand laser. Her gaze kept shifting to the bot as she positioned the laser at a careful angle.

"Move another step back into the chasm," she instructed.

Jolly did.

"Ready?" she asked him.

"I guess."

For the briefest moment her finger tightened on the trigger. A flash of light—and the core of the bot blew apart, bits of shrapnel peppering the room. Jolly yelped and jumped back, inadvertently launching himself into the air. He clawed at the chasm's wall, struggling to arrest his momentum. At the same time, he shouted at Okinowa, "Are you all right?"

Only to realize she was laughing.

His feet touched the floor again. He shuffled back to join her. She greeted him with a grin, her laser already back in its holster.

"You did that on purpose," he realized. "You chose that angle on purpose so the reflected beam would hit the bot."

Aurelius dropped abruptly out of the shaft. "What is going on down here?"

Clemantine came down behind him, her stern gaze locking onto Jolly.

Okinowa only glanced at them. "Jolly wanted to observe the effects of the laser against the tunnel wall. I wanted to test the theory that the beam would reflect at nearly one hundred percent of its power."

Aurelius spoke in a low-voice, his anger contained, but obvious. "You fired the laser at the tunnel wall?"

"I did. Look here." She toed the floor where the beam had struck. Jolly could not see a mark on it.

He looked at Clemantine, who stood with arms crossed, an unfriendly gaze fixed on Okinowa. He felt he ought to explain, so he said, "The reflected beam hit the scout-bot." He wanted to add that it was an accident, but it was not.

"I saw it through your feed," Clemantine said. She knew the truth. "That's three down," she remarked to Okinowa. "And only one left on this side of the membrane."

Clemantine must have silently summoned that remaining bot, because it came cartwheeling from the other end of the chasm, its padded feet striking the floor with a light tapping sound. Jolly stepped out of its way.

"Do not destroy this one," Clemantine warned Okinowa. "I will not take it kindly if you do."

The loss of the scout-bot stunned the Cryptologist. She mourned the data it might have collected. "I don't understand," she said to the Scholar. "Why would Okinowa Laikun choose to sabotage the experiment?"

"Because she's weak," he growled. "Violence is the mask that hides a weak and needy character."

"Hmm," the Cryptologist said to convey her puzzlement at this strange statement. She knew very little of human personality disorders. "Would you consider Lezuri to also have had a weak and needy character?"

"Oh hell yes. He wanted attention, and adulation."

"Those are very strange things to desire."

"No, not really. They are common human desires—the desires of social animals obsessed with status within the group."

"Hmm . . . viewed in this context, it seems to me Lezuri created the needle not as a test, but as a token of his superior status . . . a puzzle Urban could not solve."

"I agree this is likely, but does this theory give you insight on the mechanism of the needle?"

"It makes me think the solution is simple, because that would be most elegant, and would strongly support the argument of Lezuri's superior social status."

"And still you're no closer to unraveling this elegantly simple solution. Are you?"

A pointless question, given he knew the answer.

She smiled—a generalized reaction she'd found useful in most social situations—and turned away.

Her gaze settled on the video feed from the surviving scout-bot, though in that moment it showed only a soft white glow as Abby carried it through a gel membrane.

CHAPTER TWENTY-FIVE

THIS TIME, CLEMANTINE sent Jolly ahead of her up the chimney, with Aurelius and Okinowa following. They emerged at the top, to find the round chamber empty.

"They've gone into a grow room," Aurelius said. He gestured at one of the ice arches. "Through here."

They pushed past a double-membrane lock, emerging into a long chamber excavated out of ice, roughly twelve meters across and five times that in length.

Unlike the warren where the Sakurans kept their apartments, these ice walls showed their age. The erosion of time had left them pitted, scarred, scalloped, and marked with sharp vertical fins and shallow ridges. The ancient walls enclosed a gulf of empty space around a central greenhouse: a narrow structure, just three meters wide but running the length of the room.

Above the greenhouse and across the expanse of the ceiling, thousands of pendulous leaf clusters hung from a maze of black branches, filling the chamber with brilliant white light.

Clemantine resisted the urge to shade her eyes.

Abby had released the surviving scout-bot, but she trailed after it like a protective mother, eyeing the scattered Sakurans. In contrast, Shoran and Riffan chattered happily with their hosts. They'd wandered halfway down the room, gazing through the greenhouse walls at the thriving garden within.

"It's warm in here," Jolly observed with a glance at Clemantine. "Warmer than outside, anyway." A flush had deepened the color of his cheeks.

Taddeus, who'd been waiting for them, affirmed Jolly's comment. "We have to keep the interior of the greenhouse warm," he explained. "It's the only way to get the plants to grow. Unfortunately, some heat bleeds through."

Clemantine cocked an eyebrow. *Unfortunately?*

"You don't like warmth?" she asked, thinking of Nikko and Deneb. They had never complained about a ship's atmosphere kept well above freezing.

"We've learned to live without it."

He showed her the crops, all hydroponic, growing in the same fertile fluid that had once circulated through the cells and layers of D-1's vast architecture. He did not take them into the greenhouse, but pointed out varieties of vegetables through the transparent walls. Clemantine recognized many of them—tomatoes, squash, peas, beans—though she'd only ever seen them growing in historical dramas. Others she did not know at all.

Taddeus took them into two other grow rooms, explaining along the way how the forest was really one expansive organism designed to harvest and concentrate the energy in Tanjiri's feeble light. "That energy is stored in the fruit, and it's focused here in the grow rooms."

An abundance of energy that would be lost when D-1's slow rotation turned the forest away from the sun.

They were preparing to leave the third grow room when Abby—who trailed behind, still shadowing the scout-bot—called out, "Clemantine! Come look. The scout-bot's found something. I don't know what it is."

The sharp pitch of her voice sent Clemantine's heart racing and it captured the attention of everyone in the chamber, even before Abby's translation device echoed her words in the Sakurans' language.

Abby stood nearly thirty meters away, just behind the bot, one gloved hand pointing to a rough patch of wall striated with slight, sharp fins of ice. "It's oozing," she reported. Her voice echoed in translation across a chamber gone silent. "Some dark fluid, bubbling slowly, right out of the ice."

Even before the full translation, gasps and cries of dismay arose from the Sakurans. A chaotic rush ensued, a scramble in the direction of the gel lock. Clemantine became part of that scramble when someone grabbed her arm, pulling her off balance, dragging her across the ice—and away from Abby.

"Abby, stay back from it!" she shouted, twisting to confront the owner of the vermilion fingers wrapped around her arm.

Aurelius.

He met her gaze for just a moment, the scales of his face shaping a mask of rage. "Get out!" he commanded her. Then he raised his chin. His voice filled the room as he shouted, "Everyone! Get our guests into the lock and get out!"

"Not without Abby!" Clemantine retorted, prying at his fingers. But she found her escape stymied by the astonishing strength of his grip. "Aurelius! Let go of me *now*."

"It's too late for her, but not for you," Aurelius said as he shoved her into the scrum at the lock. "Get out now or you'll die."

The panicked Sakurans surely believed that—all but Okinowa. Clemantine saw her past Aurelius's shoulder. No mistaking the striking black and silver pattern of her scales. Okinowa had broken out of the crowd. Now she pulled her hand laser from its holster and launched toward Abby.

"Don't you hurt her!" Clemantine shouted.

Aurelius turned to see where she was looking. As he did, his grip loosened. "Okinowa, *no!*" he roared—and Clemantine wrenched free.

She ducked, and then shoved off from the bodies around her. In the microgravity, she was able to soar half the distance to Abby before touching the ice again.

The girl was looking around, wide-eyed at the sight of Okinowa coming at her, brandishing the laser. Abby backpedaled and slipped, falling slowly to her ass.

Okinowa jumped over her.

The scout-bot was using a sensor pad to sample whatever was coming out of the wall. Okinowa floated down behind it. Experience told Clemantine she would shoot the bot, but instead,

Okinowa aimed past it. She targeted the wall just as a black mist erupted from it. The spewing particulates made the laser beam visible, but its narrow span could not stop the roiling cloud. The mist fell across the scout-bot, and across Okinowa, and it descended on Abby, too.

Okinowa started screaming.

Jolly didn't know what was going on, but inside his head Abby was pleading, *Help her! Help her! It's eating her. Oh, please stop!*

He'd retreated with the Sakurans, but now he reversed course, pushing past Taddeus, and Kev Atatashi, and a woman named Firiah. Another—her name was Umeji—tried to grab his arm, but he twisted out of reach and half stumbled, half fell into the open. He saw Clemantine, leaping toward Abby, and followed, kicking off against the ice.

What's happening? he demanded on the team channel.

A question that went unheard as a skin suit spoke over the same channel in a concerned yet mechanical voice: *Abby, a molecular assault has been detected. Your suit integrity is under threat. Please stand by. Defensive Makers have been deployed.*

Abby was sitting on the ice, rubbing her face with her gloved hands as a thin fog of condensing steam rose from the front of her skin suit.

The skin suit spoke again: *The threat is eliminated.*

Clemantine reached Abby, hauled her to her feet, and shoved her in Jolly's direction. Not a move he was expecting. He caught Abby anyway, arms around her, but he slipped on the ice and lost his balance.

"You two, stay back!" Clemantine ordered as Jolly and Abby went down together in a slow yet irreversible fall. When they finally hit, they went skidding sideways across the ice until they collided with the greenhouse.

Jolly found himself staring into Abby's wide, disbelieving eyes. "Are you all right?" Her skin suit, at least, had stopped steaming.

"*Yes!* My suit's crazy. There's nothing wrong with me. It's Okinowa who needs help."

Jolly turned to look.

Okinowa had dropped the laser. She'd collapsed to her knees, shoulders hunched and shuddering, face hidden behind the cage of her long fingers. Not screaming anymore. Moaning now in a high-pitched carrier wave of pain.

Clemantine was kneeling beside her, ignoring the fear-filled protests of the Sakurans who had not yet escaped through the gel lock:

"Get away from her! Stay back!"

"Don't touch her."

"It will kill you too."

"You can't help her."

"What's happening?" Jolly demanded again as he and Abby carefully recovered their footing.

Clemantine answered over the team channel: ***She has no defensive Makers.***

Jolly put it together: Abby's suit had detected a molecular assault—the black mist exploding from the ice must have been filled with wild Makers—but the suit had eliminated the threat.

"We can help her!" he cried out, scrambling to join Clemantine. "*We* have defensive Makers."

"Sooth. And I'm going to try to transfer them, but *you* stay back. Abby! Get Jolly to the lock."

Abby took his hand. Globular tears welled in her eyes. "Jolly, come on."

But Jolly didn't move, couldn't move when he saw Okinowa's beautiful scaled skin dissolving in a steaming mash of chemical reaction.

Clemantine leaned in, her mouth set in a hard line, grimly determined. She embraced Okinowa, holding her close while using one gloved hand to stroke her head, her chest, her arms, and the hands Okinowa still held pressed against her face. Wisps of steam arose wherever Clemantine made contact.

Jolly stepped closer, wanting to help. He knelt beside them, pulled Okinowa's hands away from her face—and recoiled. Her face had melted. It looked half dissolved, like the worn faces of sculptures he'd seen in the Iraliad desert on Verilotus, eaten away by tides of silver.

Clemantine glared at him. "I told you to leave."

"I can help."

Copying Clemantine, he pressed his gloved palms against Okinowa's wounded face. Steam erupted, curling against his cheeks as his defensive Makers countered the deadly wild strain.

Okinowa moaned, a high despairing note that sent a shudder through him.

"The wild Makers are inside her, aren't they?" he murmured, thinking aloud. "She must have breathed them in."

That meant she could breathe in his Makers too.

He didn't hesitate. He set his mouth against hers, trusting the potency of his Makers to protect him. And he exhaled hard, forcing his breath into her throat and her lungs, praying his Makers would ride in on that breath.

"By the Unknown God," Clemantine swore, clutching at his shoulder. "That can't work. It won't work. Your Makers exist to protect only you."

"But it's *my* breath inside her, carrying with it some sense of me. Let me try."

Clemantine's hand remained on his shoulder, but she didn't stop him as he again set his mouth against Okinowa's.

He breathed in, her breath and his mixing. He held that breath—only a moment. But in that short time, his chest began to burn. He imagined the wild Makers rapidly reproducing inside his lungs, and his own defensive Makers congealing around them. Another forceful exhalation, molecules washing from his lungs into hers. And another. The heat in his chest fading, though steam erupted from his mouth and also from hers.

After a few more breaths, Okinowa grew quiet; her breathing steadied.

Jolly drew back; looked at Clemantine. "We can save her, can't we? Put her in cold sleep, repair all this damage? We can do that, right?"

Clemantine sat back, grim and worried. "Not here. Not now. *If* we can get her to *Argo*—"

"If they let us," Abby said. "But they've all gone."

A glance at the gel lock confirmed it. Only the three of them had stayed behind with Okinowa.

Like all Sakurans, Taddeus had been trained from childhood to retreat from the vicinity of a bloom. Centuries of bitter experience had taught his ancestors that horrible, inevitable death followed for anyone caught by the black mist. Once touched, nothing could be done to save them and it was worse than useless to try, because the bloom would jump from one person to another, and with each jump, one more person would be lost. The best anyone could do for the future of Volo's Landing was to save themselves.

So when Abby described the bloom, Taddeus reacted automatically, retreating to the gel membrane, transiting it when his turn came, joining his companions there in the lock—where they all remained, packed shoulder to shoulder. A small, crowded space, and quiet. Too quiet. All the familiar faces made strange by expressions of shock and despair. His own face surely the same.

He looked for the visitors, but saw only Shoran and Riffan, both packed in tight at the center of the crush. Where was Clemantine?

Someone murmured in a high-pitched voice, "Okinowa is lost."

Someone else said, "*Hush.*"

It was true, though. Taddeus had seen Okinowa caught by the bloom, along with the visitor, Abby. Who else would be lost?

Kev and Firiah came next through the membrane, crowding in behind Taddeus. As they did, Taddeus felt his kisheer ripple at his shoulders. The kisheers of all his companions began to ripple too—a sign that available oxygen in the lock had already grown scarce.

Aurelius emerged from the membrane. "I'm the last," he announced grimly. "Kisheers up! Save what oxygen is left—except you, Umeji."

Umeji carried a tablet she'd been using to make a video record of the tour. Aurelius told her, "Message our people. Let them know what's happened, that we're here in quarantine for the next three hours . . ." At a quaver in his voice he paused, closed his eyes, and then continued. "Let them know, four lost. One of our own . . . three of our guests."

Three guests . . .

An announcement that drew horrified whispers and moans of despair. The implication of it went beyond the loss of four lives. Their future may have died in that grow room. What chance now that the visitors would offer them any aid, when three of their delegation would not be returning?

"Kisheers up!" Aurelius insisted.

This time, Taddeus obeyed. The membrane of his kisheer rippled up from his shoulders to cover his mouth and nose and ears. Tendrils of it entered his mouth, flowed into his throat. During the seconds it took for the tendrils to merge with the tiny papillae lining his mouth and throat, he endured a familiar sense of suffocation. Then, as the kisheer bonded fully, he no longer had any urge to breathe, and the kisheer took on its task of converting the carbon dioxide in his blood back into usable oxygen.

With his ears sealed, Taddeus could hear nothing. But he could see that Shoran was still unmasked and that she was speaking emphatically, apparently addressing Aurelius across the crowd. Aurelius listened and then shook his head, his mouth forming the word *no.*

Alarmed at the possibility that Aurelius, in his temper, would reject some reasonable request or even threaten the visitors, Taddeus reached out to him past Kev. He squeezed Aurelius's shoulder and when he had his attention he signed in swift gestures, *What does she say?*

Aurelius, eyes red with grief, signed back, *She wants us to believe they are all still alive.*

But Aurelius didn't believe it; Taddeus could see that. And it was easy to imagine him blaming the visitors for what had happened. Taddeus knew, that regardless of the oxygen level, he needed to be the reasonable voice in this conversation.

Hold on, he signed as he triggered the reflex that would release his kisheer.

Clemantine listened to Okinowa's rasping breathing. It sounded bad, but it wasn't getting worse. Jolly's trick really had helped to stop the deterioration of her lungs. But she wasn't out of danger yet. Far from it.

"Shoran, what's your status?" she asked over the team channel.

Shoran responded immediately, her usual good humor gone. *I'm in the lock along with Riffan and the rest of the tour. It's tight in here, but we're fine. The problem is, local protocol calls for us to quarantine here for three hours. That's what they do to ensure no bloom spores have infected them.*

"Not acceptable," Clemantine said. She had no real familiarity with the physiological limits of unaugmented humans, but in the historical dramas she'd watched, they were fragile creatures. "Okinowa is alive now, but I don't know for how long. She has no somatic Makers to repair her injuries, and those injuries make her vulnerable to the cold. Tell that to Aurelius. Tell him I need to get her to the landing ship."

I've been talking to him, telling him what I see in there. But he's skeptical. Stand by. Let me try again to convince him.

A minute passed, and then another. The only sound: Okinowa's troubled breathing.

"Shoran?"

Still here. It's a no-go. The people here are terrified of the bloom. That's what they call it. From what Taddeus said, I think it's an artifact left over from the original ecology of D-1. It's drawn to warmth. That's why it's more of a problem in the grow rooms, and it's why the rooms are isolated. The bloom migrates through the ice. The Sakurans conduct regular patrols, watching for early signs of outbreaks, and burn them out when they find them. That's what Okinowa tried to do.

"But she was too late," Abby said bitterly.

Riffan spoke: *It was our fault. Our arrival distracted them. The patrols fell off. They weren't as frequent, or as thorough.*

"It *was* our fault," Abby agreed, a slight nervous tremor in her voice. "The bloom burst when it did, because the scout-bot tapped it open."

"We'll analyze the details later," Clemantine snapped. "The

bloom has passed. Our priority now is to get Okinowa to the landing ship."

Shoran said, *I'm working on it, Cee. But right now, Aurelius doesn't mean to let you out at all.*

It's their protocol, Riffan explained. *An infected chamber is closed off for at least a ten-day. They have no other means to counter a bloom, except to isolate it.*

Clemantine considered this. She needed to get Okinowa out quickly, without a fight, and without debate or confrontation. Was it possible to engineer a back door?

She glanced around the grow room, calculating what it would take to create an alternate exit to the surface. They were outside D-1's native tunnel system; it could be done. But it would require time that Okinowa did not have.

A new voice broke in over the team channel: *I am here, and I can fix this.*

Clemantine gritted her teeth, recognizing the unexpected and unwelcome voice of the Cryptologist. Why was that creature here?

But then she chided herself. 'Why' was a question to be pursued later. Right now, she needed to persuade the Sakurans to allow her to save Okinowa's life, and if the Cryptologist had an idea, Clemantine wanted to hear it. "You have a way of getting Okinowa out of here?"

No. That would require diplomacy, a field in which I have little talent.

The scout-bot stirred as the Cryptologist spoke, scuttling closer to Okinowa. It raised a wiry limb, exposing the sensor pad at its end.

"Are you doing that?" Clemantine asked.

I am.

Moving slowly, cautiously, the bot tapped at the corrupted tissue of Okinowa's face. Then it reached between her parted lips to sample the tissue of her mouth, and the chemicals in her panting breath. As it worked, the Cryptologist explained her plan:

A course of customized somatic Makers is required to return this being to a fully functional state. I have now acquired tissue samples and am using the resources of Pytheas's library to create that course.

*Are you sure you know what you're doing? Shoran asked uneasily.

*No. I know very little about this process. However, it may reassure you to know that I am working under the supervision of the Bio-mechanic—though time-delayed, of course.

"All right," Clemantine said.

It was a good solution. It might even work. Far easier to deliver a course of somatic Makers to Okinowa than to try to get her out past the determined resistance of her people.

"You'll need to generate a new scout-bot to make the delivery."

*Unnecessary, the Cryptologist replied with unflagging confidence. *I've already recalled one from the forest.

"Get it on its way to us as quickly as you can."

*I will do so.

"Shoran—it's up to you to persuade Aurelius to let that bot through."

*Already done. Taddeus has reminded him what his ancestors were capable of and what his people lost—and might yet regain if they cooperate. And Taddeus has made it known that Okinowa is his partner, his lover. If she walks through that membrane on her own, whole and uninjured, Aurelius is not going to send her back.

They moved Okinowa into the lush warmth of the greenhouse, laying her down in the aisle between walls of beans and squash. After that, all they could do was wait and hope.

Clemantine tapped Shoran's video feed. She saw the lock, crammed with Sakurans standing shoulder to shoulder between the gel membranes, breathing through the veils of their kisheers as they waited out their quarantine. Riffan had his hood up and sealed. Only Shoran, Aurelius, and Taddeus remained unmasked—a necessary accommodation allowing them to talk to one another.

While Taddeus remained the diplomat, the Sakurans' quiet leader glared at Shoran, his face set in a hard, angry expression, so typically male—an emotional mask that did not quite hide his worry and his grief.

Clemantine said, "Shoran, I'm riding you. Tell Aurelius I can see him, hear him, and that I want my questions answered, *now*, while there's nothing else for us to do but wait. And my first question is, how the hell did his people end up here?"

When Aurelius heard this, his shoulders sagged as if with some deep, internal sigh of resignation. He turned to Taddeus. "You tell it. Tell them our story and whatever else they want to know."

CHAPTER TWENTY-SIX

THERE WAS LITTLE room to move in the lock, and when anyone did it set off a wave of motion. One person would bump into two or three around them, and those in turn would gently collide with neighbors until the whole crowd shifted in the microgravity. Then Taddeus, who bided on the perimeter, would be pushed against the icy wall, only to bounce off again, and the wave would move in the opposite direction.

Tell them our story, Aurelius had commanded.

Adrift at the edge of the little chamber, light-headed from the low oxygen and his kisheer rippling its warning, Taddeus took several seconds to gather his thoughts. And then he spoke—softly, cautiously, his words only slowly gathering momentum.

"Our story begins long ago, when our ancestors looked back toward older star systems—those that had been settled before any great ship reached Sakura—and in all those systems they observed rapid transformations. Impossible evolutions. It all *seemed* impossible, as if planets were being reshaped into swarms of orbital structures so huge and so plentiful they began to eclipse the light of the parent star."

Aurelius listened and signed to the others what he was saying, so they would know.

"In this time, the people of Sakura began to change too, infected by a religious fervor that induced them to seek a state of oneness, of unity, of communion with all life—or so they described it. A state of bliss in which every singular entity would become but a facet of the whole.

"Not all were swept up in this movement, though. Some few thousand stood apart, fearful of what was happening all around them. Estranged from family and friends, they found each other and together resolved to escape the madness that had taken over their people.

"Placing their lives and their futures into the care of a great ship, they entered the vessel's cold sleep chambers, certain that when they woke again, they would be in a new star system where they could start over without repeating the mistakes of the past."

Taddeus paused to take several deep breaths, striving to catch up on an oxygen deficit. Then he resumed, saying, "Of course, that is not what happened. That great ship and the mind embodied within it was very old. He had visited every settled system between Sakura and Sol. He had carried the first settlers to several of those systems, and he carried people and information between them. He feared and hated what was happening to the worlds he had nurtured and loved.

"From his logs, we know he fell into a deep and hopeless melancholy, and ultimately erased himself from existence—leaving the ship to fare on, while centuries slipped past.

"The first cold sleep chamber to fail was that of Volo Li Kubba. An automated system woke her. Imagine her shock when she discovered what had happened, and the incomprehensible span of time now lost."

He paused again, his gaze downcast and a bitter smile on his lips, self-conscious because he bore the surname of his distant ancestor and because his feelings toward her had always been mixed. Another deep breath.

"Volo resolved to handle the situation by herself. She woke no one, later explaining she did not want to subject anyone else to the horror she felt, lost and alone in the vast dark nullity between the stars. All on her own, she decided the voyage had been a mistake and it was her task now to take her people home."

Another pause, more deep breaths. Unsure how long he could keep going, he told an abbreviated story.

"Volo was very clever. She immersed herself in the ship's library and soon learned to pilot. Her first task was to bring the ship around in a great arc, and then she charted a course back to Sakura—and more time slipped past.

"Then another cold sleep chamber failed and its occupant awoke. Our history doesn't remember the name of this person. We only know that as she grasped what had happened, she panicked. Defying Volo, she woke all the others—and chaos ensued."

Taddeus closed his eyes a moment. He'd had nightmares about that tragedy, though it had all fallen out centuries before his birth.

He said, "The great ship, of course, had neither the room nor the resources for so many people. All knew it, but while they had been in cold sleep, a great wave of ruin had washed over the known worlds. The mysterious swarms of gigantic orbital structures had all vanished, replaced by drifting wreckage. Aboard the great ship, fear and uncertainty ruled. None would entrust themselves to cold sleep again, not without new leadership and a consensus on their future course.

"Hours passed, factions formed, and no consensus could be reached. Many supported Volo's actions, but more were furious that she had taken it upon herself to end the outward journey and risk a return to lost Sakura. In the packed spaces of the great ship, with too little to eat and not enough oxygen to breathe—"

Taddeus paused, giving in to a moment of soft, cynical laughter at the gasping irony of his present situation. And then he forged on.

"In those bitter circumstances, violence broke out. A contagious violence. Many died, and Volo lost control of the ship.

"In the end, the survivors brokered a bitter compromise. They would proceed to the nearest settled system along their present course. Once there, those who did not wish to resume the outward voyage would leave the ship.

"That system was Tanjiri," Taddeus said. "The ship's library told them they should find a thriving civilization there, but the telescopes revealed something other: a system gone silent and dark,

NEEDLE 185

encircled by a bizarre halo of giant structures. And the planetary census did not match the library's records.

"All feared to come here, but given the ship's limited resources, and the bitter, uneasy peace between the factions, they had no real choice.

"At first, Volo promised her faction that despite the radio silence, a thriving civilization was sure to be found among the outer structures. And for such a great people, it would be nothing to construct a new ship, a mythical ship to take them home. She persuaded many who had stood against her before."

Taddeus shook his head, forever puzzled by his ancestors—what they had chosen to believe and their inexplicable decisions dooming their descendants.

"No sign of life was ever detected among the megastructures—and Volo declared this a good thing, as if she'd never promised anything else. She assured her faction, that with no one to stand in their way, it would be easy to harvest what was needed to repair and resupply the ship, and then go home—and her faction was happy to believe. But those who controlled the ship were not.

"They did not want to go faring between the stars. Declaring they'd traveled long enough, they proposed to stay, to become Tanjirians. But they worried that ancient hazards haunted the broken megastructures." A slight pause, allowing everyone to reflect on the coincidence of this story being told in the shadow of a bloom. "Anyway, they wanted to take the ship in-system, make a home there, build their own celestial city . . ."

He shrugged. "The two sides could not agree, and while the would-be Tanjirians controlled the ship, Volo now commanded the majority. She had convinced people the voyage had been a mistake. She told them they could go home, that home still existed just as they remembered it."

Another long sigh.

"I don't know how they could have believed this. They were very frightened, I know, and they wanted to believe it even when the ship's telescopes told a very different story. But Volo would not be contradicted. She insisted the images of Sakura that showed it like Tanjiri, encircled by ruins, were all fake . . . and our ancestors chose to believe her.

"With hatred between the factions and no possibility of compromise, violence broke out again—but only briefly, because our enemies abruptly abandoned the great ship.

"These new Tanjirians had installed a copy of the library aboard the only landing ship." Taddeus heard the bitter note that had entered his voice, but he could not help it. "They took that ship, and they left us. And they left the great ship sabotaged."

Again, he shook his head. "Somehow Volo never discovered it, never even *suspected*. I still wonder how that was possible, how it could have gone undiscovered, and for *years*. Years went by. Time enough to make a temporary home here, and to establish the forest."

His kisheer continued to ripple, and his long fingers moved too as he wrestled with the mysteries of an inexplicable past.

"The defectors, for their part, remained silent. Never an attempt at communication. None that we could detect, anyway. They must have hated us with a cold, calculating hate. The way they waited to strike, holding off until they reached the inner system, until they were sure they had a future. We know they made it, because Volo had use of the great ship's telescopes back then, and she saw the beginning of their build. Many of those here began to reconsider the wisdom of a long voyage to Sakura. They talked of seeking a truce and following the defectors . . . but the defectors did not want us."

More bitterly now, "We believe they sent a signal, one that triggered the destruction of the great ship and destroyed the library with it."

Taddeus looked up. He sought Aurelius's gaze, drew strength from the resolve he saw there. "The defectors meant to wipe us out and they almost succeeded. We lost our ability to synthesize Makers, new generations received no augmentations, and *still we survived*. A vicious act of sabotage brought us low and we have never recovered. That is why we must ask you now, humbly, for your help."

An interesting story, Clemantine concluded. An interesting mix of potential truth and probable fiction—and altogether an instructive tale. Most tragedies, when examined in detail, proved to be the result of a chain of bad luck and poor decisions. Clearly, the Sakurans had suffered both factors along the way—though Clemantine now suspected they had been on a trajectory of failure from the beginning.

A lesson learned early during the initial expansion, as great ships dispersed the human population from star system to star system, was that a single critical factor tended to separate successful settlements from those that ended early, or that suffered the equal failure of a deplorable social system. That factor was a people's ability to agree on a shared goal and to cooperate in its achievement.

With this in mind, the great ships learned to screen their passengers. They left behind the narcissists, the would-be tyrants, the sociopaths. And successful societies learned to educate their people to recognize and resist the corruption of a proselytizing personality.

But the Sakurans had not had that luxury. Their exodus had been an escape, not a well-planned expedition. They had not screened their people, beyond their resistance to the sweep of communion. When the great ship that carried them ultimately committed the greatest betrayal, Volo Li Kubba's arrogance became the next point of failure.

Riffan spoke over the team channel, *I think I understand why Volo Li Kubba is held up as a hero to her people, but it sounds like she was also a tyrant and a fool.*

"*Sooth*," Clemantine whispered. "And tragedy always follows when people flock to a delusional leader."

It's good she's dead and gone, along with all the poison of that founding generation, Shoran declared. *I like these latter-day Sakurans. They are surely a better people.*

Jolly shifted restlessly. "I'm wondering about the other faction, those people who didn't believe Volo. They succeeded, didn't they? They built their celestial city."

Abby looked from Jolly to Clemantine with uncomprehending eyes. "But why did they sabotage the great ship? What kind of people would do that?"

A memory rose up from Clemantine's deep past. Another delusional leader, another great ship, deliberately broken to seal the loyalty of every follower, unto death.

"We don't know what really happened," she said gently. "When the truth is too dark, people devise safer histories."

"But we'll help them, won't we?" Jolly asked.

Clemantine nodded. "Of course. We would never leave them to die."

The Cryptologist popped back onto the team channel. *The scout-bot has arrived at the outer membrane, but it cannot traverse the membrane on its own. One of those confined within the lock must pull it through when it extends its appendages.*

I'll get it, Shoran said. Her viewpoint shifted. Grunting audibly, she shouldered her way through the packed lock. But she stopped before she reached it. Her gaze shifted sharply left, her eyes taking in the sight of Aurelius's long red fingers digging into her shoulder.

"No one may leave," he growled.

"I'm not leaving. I won't break your quarantine." She gestured at the gel. "But the package is here. We need to get it inside." Her head turned again, to address the other Sakurans. "If you're standing by the gel membrane, look for the legs of a scout-bot coming through it."

Someone raised a hand and waved. Shoran went to look and found two of the scout-bot's telescoping limbs poking through the gel. She grasped both. Pulling gently, she drew the scout-bot through the membrane and into the lock. Its legs retracted and she tucked it under her arm. "All right, let me pass. I need to push it through the other membrane."

No transition:

Okinowa surfaced from blank nothingness into the glare of a narrow band of blazing light. She blinked, aware of blurred vistas in shades of green rising vertically on either side of her. Aware too, of her heartbeat, accelerating under a smoldering memory of rage and humiliation . . . and pain.

What happened to me?

Even as she asked the question, she saw again the narrow beam of her laser slicing ineffectually through the black mist of a ripe bloom. It was the very last thing she'd seen before her eyes dissolved. It should have been impossible to see anything else ever again. So why these green vistas, this painfully bright light?

She blinked more—a useless effort that brought nothing into focus. It only set the dregs of her rage to stirring, to congealing around the appalling possibility that her own existence somehow continued.

This isn't real.

The bloom was real; she could accept that. But her own existence? *No.* To exist after the bloom defied the reality she knew. Not once in her life had she ever been able to counter reality's hard dictates, so why should reality change now? Here at the end, instead of being made to endure an absurd half-life, a worse hell than that to which the defectors had condemned her people, she should have been embraced by the blank black nothingness of death. But death mocked her.

For you, she thought bitterly, *not even that.*

A lime-green blur moved on the periphery of her vision. A voice spoke, slightly muffled in her hearing, murmuring words she didn't understand. A second, similar voice took over, speaking words she knew:

"Don't worry. You're going to be all right."

Jolly's voice . . .

She made an effort to reply. Nothing came of it, but Jolly guessed what she wanted to know.

He told her, "Everyone else got out okay. We'll get out too. We're staying here for now because Aurelius is still worried the bloom could spread. But we'll convince him, and you'll be all right."

Liar, she thought.

He said, "Try to drink something."

She felt a touch, dull and distant. A trickle of fluid flowed into her perception. Cool. Sweet. Igniting a fiery thirst along with a terrible awareness of lips, mouth, throat, and oral papillae, all dry and brittle. She swallowed the trickle and drank more, raging silently at an existence she could no longer deny, and at her helplessness, and her pathetic dependence on the generosity of this stranger.

Where was Aurelius?

Not here. Not where he might be infected by the bloom's black spores. No, he had abandoned her; he had left her here to die. As was his duty.

"You feel tired, don't you?" Jolly asked. "I did, when I was given somatic Makers. They're healing you. I can see the difference already—though it'll take time for you to recover."

She cursed him silently. She wanted to tell him, *We are a fallen people and there are no Makers here.*

And she wanted to say, *Leave me alone.*

Rejecting all kindnesses, she sank into the familiar comfort of dark imaginings in which somehow she was able to confront the defectors and make their souls burn as hers burned, as hope burned.

Later, when she woke again, her rage still smoldered. Again she blinked at a bright band of blazing light overhead, but she could see properly now and she recognized it as the roof of the greenhouse. She understood now that she lay on the greenhouse floor, with walls of green plants rising on either side of her.

But this time, instead of Jolly, Aurelius knelt beside her.

"My love," he murmured, his vermilion scales flushing bright with the intensity of his emotion. "I thought you were lost . . . but now I think we have all wakened into a new world."

As Jolly had done, he helped her to drink, and after that she could talk a little. She asked him, "It's true then, that they've endowed me with Makers?"

"It is true," he answered.

"And you? And everyone else?"

"No. They are still deciding the nature of the aid they are willing to render us."

"Do we have nothing to say of our own needs?"

"Much has been said," he told her. "Much has been asked."

"And now we humble ourselves and wait."

"Yes, my love. Exactly that."

CHAPTER TWENTY-SEVEN

URBAN KEPT WATCH from the high bridge as *Khonsu* arced sunward, leading the way through the belt of ruins. The outrider's cameras and scopes provided an advance view for *Dragon* as it followed, radar pulsing, seeking out hazardous debris that *Khonsu* might have missed.

Within *Dragon*'s library, DIs analyzed every observation. Urban trusted them to alert him to anything unusual, anything interesting, anything at all that might indicate life.

So far, nothing. The Sakurans might well be the singular civilization in the belt . . . though of course *Dragon* could survey only a tiny portion of the ring of orbiting debris. Given the belt's vast expanse, a hundred thousand living systems might be lurking among the ruins, a hundred thousand unique biologies quietly evolving beyond the reach of Urban's sensors. But to survey it all would require centuries, and in the end he might learn only that it was all dead matter.

Why spend time on it? He knew where life resided in this system. And why spend more time on the Sakurans? Clemantine's visit had confirmed what had been obvious from the first: the Sakurans knew little of their own history, and nothing of Tanjiri System beyond their forest.

He messaged Clemantine with this thought: *There's no more for you to learn there. Come home.*

He waited out the unavoidable light-speed delay and several seconds more. When her response came back, it wasn't entirely a surprise: *They want us to take them aboard* Dragon.

No.

A minute and a half slipped past. She spoke again: *I explained that Dragon can't support so many. They would need to be in cold sleep.*

No. And anyway, it's too late. Our momentum won't allow it. We're heading in-system. Impossible now to reverse course.

A long delay. Then, *Did you plan it that way?*

Sooth. It had been easy to guess the Sakurans would make such a request. Urban had resolved early on to reject it. It would be dangerous to take them aboard. The Sakurans far outnumbered the Dragoneers, and even in cold sleep they would be a burden. He'd run the scenarios. Conflict was certain. Even if the Sakurans could be contained in cold sleep, there would be disagreement, resentment, and rebellion among the Dragoneers. So Urban had embraced the simplest solution. He'd ensured a direct rescue was not possible.

He kept his answer simple too: *You know there are always constraints.*

Determination, in her time-delayed reply: *We need to help them, Urban.*

Yes, and we will—in the traditional way.

It had always been the custom among frontier worlds to share libraries at every rare moment of contact. *Dragon's* library contained the knowledge of ships and worlds now lost to history or to the Chenzeme.

He explained to her, *The Scholar is working to selectively replicate Pytheas's library. With a library of their own, the Sakurans will be able to use Makers again. They can grow and generate what they need. They can grow a new great ship and go where they choose. Tell them that, and then come home. The lander's fuel is limited. Every hour you stay adds more hours to your return time. And I need you here.*

This time, he waited out a long, long delay. When she finally spoke, he heard a chill in her voice. *I'll talk to them. I only hope it's enough.*

"You are leaving us on our own. That's what you're saying. Isn't it?" Aurelius demanded.

Clemantine did not flinch from his angry glare.

Her team and his had gathered in a circle, sitting lightly in the microgravity, blankets insulating them from the ice floor of a large chamber off the main hall. Electric heaters at the center of their circle glowed red as they worked to warm the room. Aurelius sat across from Clemantine, between Taddeus and Okinowa, who rested one long-fingered hand on his shoulder.

"Yes, you will be on your own," Clemantine agreed. "But not like before. With a library and a DI to advise you, you'll have what you need to thrive. The library will allow you to generate Makers. You'll be able to build and create. You'll be the architects of your own future, free to go where you want."

"Yes, you've explained all this in your pretty words."

She arched an eyebrow. "You don't believe me?"

"It would be easier to believe if you stayed with us to ensure the outcome. We know you to be capable of miracles." He turned to Okinowa; a thrust of his chin to indicate her scarred face, now slowly healing.

Riffan, seated beside Clemantine, spoke in a soft, conciliatory voice. "Aurelius, you are wrong. Miracles are not within the scope of our abilities, but the library can restore to you and your people much of the wisdom of your ancestors."

"We will surely need more wisdom than that," Taddeus said, grim-voiced.

A soft grunt from Shoran. "*Truth.* My advice to you is to take your time, study the past, study other people. Learn what has worked and emulate that as you set your goals. And always, be adaptable."

Okinowa leaned in, the silvery-gray and charcoal-colored scales of her forehead sliding one over another to form a dark and crooked scowl. "You presume we have time to learn. But our time may be limited if those sunward of us come to realize we are no longer caged and dying."

"Do you really think they hate you?" Jolly asked. "That after six centuries, they still live in fear of you?"

Okinowa's scarred lips parted, and then met again in a mocking little smile. "No, not at all, Jolly. I think they have forgotten our very existence—and I also think they should be made to remember."

Clemantine regarded her. She did not much like Okinowa and it would be easy to misjudge her—yet the hostility in her voice was real. And suffering had not chastened her. If anything, Okinowa's ordeal had only honed the edge of her resentment.

"Made to remember," Clemantine mused. "What exactly do you mean by that?"

Taddeus rushed to answer before Okinowa could. He spoke quickly, nervously. "It is just that at some point, when we are secure here, we may consider sending a delegation sunward. Or not. There is so much we'll need to discuss and decide, and no safe path."

Aurelius nodded as if to confirm this, though his thoughts seemed elsewhere.

"You're right that there is no safe path," Clemantine answered. "Not outward, from where we have come, nor Sunward, where we are bound. Hazards are everywhere. But you'll have a fair chance now."

She could only hope they would use that chance wisely.

The library Urban had ordered grown for the Sakurans would not be a full mirror of the fleet's library. He had instructed the Scholar to devise a false record of Verilotus, describing an empty system. No reason to ever go there. No reason to draw the attention of Jubilee's fleet of missiles.

He'd removed some of his own history too, deleting all knowledge of the silver, and of Lezuri. And he'd modified the Makers the library remembered, substituting an ancient collection similar to what the Sakurans' ancestors would have had. That was power enough for them to wield. Let them grow on their own into something more, as he had.

He kept watch as Clemantine and her team said their goodbyes. The hoods of their skin suits sealed. They left the Sakurans' warren and returned to the forest—and hundreds of people accompanied them, to see them off.

The team strapped into their go-packs. They ascended through the labyrinth of trees. And the Sakurans continued to follow, swift darts of color among the tangle of black branches.

Urban watched, enduring an anxious tension, not quite believing the Sakurans trusted Clemantine's word that the library would soon be theirs.

Don't give them time to think about it, he prayed.

And then he groaned aloud when Clemantine did just that. She had reached the tip of the peninsula. The rest of the team—Jolly, Shoran, Riffan, and Abby—went ahead, launching their go-packs across the three-kilometer gulf separating them from the lander.

But Clemantine lingered at the edge of the trees. She turned to Aurelius, to Kev Atatashi, and a hundred others gathered in the treetops all around. Distant Tanjiri blazed, a fierce spark, its attenuated light throwing sharp, slender shadows. All this, already many seconds in the past.

Clemantine spoke, using the shared channel. "Take your time," she told them. "Learn. Grow. And maybe we will meet again, years hence, when your orbit has brought Volo's Landing around to the other side of the sun."

No one tried to restrain her when she finally waved goodbye and departed into the void. And still Urban did not relax. Not until she was aboard the lander, safely strapped into her couch, with the engines firing to bring her home.

Pytheas would stay until the new library was ready. After that, the Sakurans would be on their own.

CHAPTER TWENTY-EIGHT

DRAGON CONTINUED DUMPING velocity as it passed through the belt of ruins. In that interval, the lander returned home. The courser's hull opened to receive it. And the landing team disembarked to a riot of welcoming hugs and eager questions.

Urban closed his eyes and breathed in Clemantine's subtle sweet scent, his arms around her, cupping her head, basking in the warmth of her body. "I missed you."

"Huh. You always say that."

"Thank you for bringing Jolly back unbroken."

"You're welcome."

"I was worried the Sakurans would try to stop you leaving."

She sighed. "I worried a little too. They *are* desperate, and I think they considered it. I would have, in their place. But they must have realized they had little to gain by it, and everything to lose." She drew back. "But we should have stayed longer, Urban. We should have helped them through this transition."

He looked away. A twinge of guilt, because what he wanted was to put the Sakurans behind them. "The Scholar is there for now, guiding them, helping them to get set up with somatic Makers, and atriums, and teaching them how to use the library. It's enough. It's up to them to decide what to do next, and who they want to be."

"Huh. Maybe Tanjiri's entity has chosen that same strategy for us? Or have you encountered that mind again?"

"No."

She must have seen some shadow in his expression. "You've tried, though. Haven't you?"

He shrugged, not wanting to answer, to explain how that first encounter haunted him. For all his life, he'd sought knowledge and the strength it brought him—not to dominate, but to protect, to secure his own identity, and his freedom, and the freedom of those he cared for.

But everything he'd gained counted for nothing in the shadow of Tanjiri's entity.

A ripple of quiet terror ran through him. On this path he had set for himself he would have to trust to the good will of a being far greater than himself—and that level of trust was not part of his nature.

"It's early," he said at last. "We still have a long way to go."

The bloom had chewed Okinowa's long fingers to stumps, but they were regrowing, the porcelain scales of her exoskeleton replicating day by day, hiding within them her vulnerable flesh. She raised a hand, half-length fingers curved and claw-like. Hideous.

The Scholar—that strange entity that had initially inhabited the new library—had assured her that in time she would be whole again, and beautiful. Healing was a process, limited by the physiological constraints of her body, and priority had been given to the growth of her atrium.

With a newly smooth knuckle, she stroked the fading scars on her face. In the library, her ghost had no scars and its long fingers were fully formed.

The Scholar had taught all the people how to generate a ghost and how to use that mirror-being, that ethereal reflection of the self, to directly access the library. He had shown them how, within that form, they could wander a maze of knowledge, room after room of histories. But like her fingers, the library was still growing and its computational strata could not yet support any population of ghosts greater than two. Not with all the Dull Intelligences the Scholar had deployed to assist the people in this, their new life.

But there was a simpler, slower way to access the library, open to all. Using her knuckle, Okinowa tapped the blank face of a freshly generated tablet, waking it. And with her atrium, she summoned the attention of a DI.

At the first flush of their new-found power, most of the people had assumed they would regrow the great ship and set out for a more hospitable system. But Taddeus had argued otherwise.

"We can stay here at Volo's Landing. No need to risk a crossing, or take the chance of being met by hostile elements in some distant star system. Not when we have unlimited resources here and the ability to manipulate them in any way we choose. Now that we have a working library, we can shape Volo's Landing into whatever form of paradise we choose."

The Scholar had affirmed the validity of this argument. Okinowa still wondered if it was the Scholar who had first proposed this path ... but never mind that. She had supported Taddeus from the start, she'd won over Aurelius, and in the end the vote to stay had been unanimous. The people would remain at Volo's Landing, and together create a great city on the rim of Tanjiri System.

With the Scholar's guidance, Taddeus had already assembled a team and embarked on the project. The first step: to grow a huge radio antenna that allowed them to communicate with the Dragoneers' great ship as it grew ever more distant on its journey toward the center of the system. The Scholar stayed on until the antenna matured. Just today, he had exchanged a series of test messages with the distant vessel. Satisfied with the antenna's functioning, he had departed on his little robotic ship, leaving the people, once again, on their own.

Okinowa had waited patiently for this day. Only now could she and Aurelius safely use the resources of the library for their own essential project.

"We must strike hard and fast and without warning," she had told him. "Not just to repay the defectors for their vicious history, but to ensure they can never bring harm to us again."

As *Dragon* completed its transit of the belt of ruins, it entered into a region of empty space—fearfully empty. No dust. No debris. Scarcely a stray molecule.

Urban had once had the Astronomer and the Mathematician work out estimates of the non-stellar mass of Tanjiri System as it had been, and as it was observed to be now—and they had calculated that at least eighty percent of its original mass had gone missing.

The Astronomer had speculated that some of this missing matter might eventually be found in dark structures far from the star . . . but Urban no longer gave credence to that idea.

On the high bridge, sharing that intimate space with both Clemantine and Pasha, he said, *I think the missing mass is just gone and this absence, this emptiness, is a signature of war.*

Of war? Pasha asked.

Clemantine understood him better. *You're thinking about Artemis.*

Sooth.

At Verilotus, a trio of dimensional missiles had pursued the outrider, enfolding it in a blister of white light. And when that light winked out, *Artemis* was gone, excised from existence, without even dust or vapor left behind.

Urban described a dark vision. *Imagine a million missiles blossoming all throughout the swarm that used to veil Tanjiri. Each missile, capable of erasing a great swath of matter. Megastructures gone in moments. Leaving nothingness, where life used to be. What we see, what remains here, even with the Trinity . . . it's a small fraction of what used to be.*

He sensed nothing, no dust at all, impacting *Dragon*'s vast hull.

Space was not empty. Even in the void between stars, the density of matter averaged nearly a molecule per cubic centimeter. But here in this empty gulf, even that profoundly thin population of molecules was mostly absent. The result: a poisonous purity of empty space that Urban could interpret only as evidence of a merciless, murderous war.

He locked down his horror, preventing it from spilling over to the philosopher cells. On the gee deck, his avatar shuddered, all too aware of the immense destructive power that he himself commanded.

He swore a silent oath, yet again, that he would never use it, except at the direst need.

———

At Volo's Landing, Okinowa immersed herself in the library, marveling at the knowledge it contained. The wisdom of millennia. Of hundreds of civilizations. Nearly everything—everything she could think of—had been done somewhere, somewhen, with the knowledge of how to do it preserved within the library's records, along with notes on the possible hazards and all that might go wrong.

And the library did not demand that she understand how to design an efficient nanomachine or a rocket engine. Neither did the Dull Intelligences need to know the details of such things as they assisted her. They merely located preexisting plans, aiding and advising as she set her own plans in motion.

Simple robots came first. She sent them beyond the forest's edge, where useful matter could be found in abundance among the ice-clad cells of the megastructure. They synthesized vast quantities of rocket fuel and, more slowly, they grew rocket engines.

The design of the new city was still being worked out when Okinowa presented her own plan to protect it. "The remnants of our great ship are a hazard," she announced at a general assembly. "For a long time now, they've been drifting slowly closer to the forest. Any slight gravitational perturbation could disturb their orbits and bring them down into the forest—or into the city. It's time we pushed them away. Far away, eliminating all chance of collision."

Aurelius added, "More than that, we don't need a reminder of our suffering hanging over our heads."

Not everyone supported this idea. Taddeus suggested the fragments served as a memorial to the bravery and valor of their ancestors. But Okinowa and Aurelius remained stubbornly determined. With everyone distracted by their own projects, they soon won a grudging agreement.

Okinowa meant to keep her word. She would use her new rocket engines to push the two massive fragments of the great ship far from Volo's Landing. No one had asked where she meant to send them, and only Aurelius had taken the time to review her plans.

"It *will* work," he'd concluded.

Okinowa had learned from the library about the potency of simple kinetic weapons: mass multiplied by extreme velocity yielded extreme destruction. The library had even calculated a launch window and burn rates sufficient to deliver her kinetic missiles to their intended targets. And once launched, those missiles could not be recalled.

CHAPTER TWENTY-NINE

"HAS THE CRYPTOLOGIST taken you for a lover?" Abby asked on an evening many ten-days after the landing team returned to *Dragon*.

She and Jolly lay entwined in the bedroom of his cottage, at peace—or so Jolly thought—after a delicious, exhausting hour of lovemaking. Now wariness stirred. He felt himself on guard.

"Answer," she insisted.

Jolly didn't think she was asking out of jealousy. They were not monogamous. Both had other lovers . . . though Abby had turned to him more often since Volo's Landing. "You don't like her, do you?"

Abby pulled away, allowing cool air to rush into the space between them. Propping herself on an elbow, she looked down at him with her pretty blue eyes and asked again, "Is she your lover?"

"Yes."

It had begun just a few days earlier, here in his cottage, on the sofa and in this bed. He'd wanted it; he'd been thinking about it for a long time and he thought the Cryptologist had been thinking about it too, but he surprised her with his desire. She had questioned him, curious as always, enthusiastic in the end.

"Why don't you like her?" Jolly asked.

Abby wrinkled her nose. "She's not a real person."

"Of course she is."

"No. She's an artificial entity. A biologically instantiated program. A *tool*. Vytet thinks so."

"Vytet's wrong. He might have thought he was creating a tool, but the Cryptologist is just as human as you or me or Vytet, no matter how she came to be. She doesn't deserve your hate, Abby."

"I don't hate her." Abby spoke with quiet intensity. "But I don't think her feelings for you are real. She'll use you, Jolly, if that's what it takes to get where she wants to go. You will never be more important to her than the task she was born to solve."

"Did Vytet tell you that too?" he demanded.

Abby did not flinch from his rising anger. "I love you, Jolly, and I don't want to see you hurt."

Every thirty hours *Dragon* received a scheduled radio communication from Volo's Landing—an update on the Sakurans' progress. The news, relayed by Taddeus, was always positive. With the help of the library's DIs, the Sakurans had stabilized both their health and their food supply. They had generated new equipment, from tablets to artificial wombs, and the planning for their great city, New Sakura, was well underway.

Each update reinforced Clemantine's opinion that the Sakurans were a practical, adaptable people. She no longer worried they would lose their way. Her concern had shifted to the "defectors"— the silent sunward faction.

"What has become of them?" she mused—a wandering thought, inadvertently spoken aloud.

She sat with Vytet and Pasha at a low table in the dining terrace, surrounded by a soft hum of conversations from other tables. Beyond the winding vines that climbed the terrace's pergola, the gee deck's artificial sky blushed with subtle sunset colors. A solitary cricket chirped from somewhere close by.

"Who are you thinking of?" Pasha asked, eyes narrowed as if Clemantine had presented her with a delectable puzzle. "I can imagine so many options."

Vytet laid down his chopsticks, head cocked in a thoughtful expression. Speaking softly, his voice a low burr, he said, "All these vast distances leave us with inexplicable mysteries in every direction. It's haunting. What is the fate of our people at Deception Well? What is the situation at Verilotus?"

A smile from Pasha, her green eyes sparkling. "And all the people of the Hallowed Vasties—what became of them? It's only the Sakurans who ever tell us how they're doing."

"Exactly that," Clemantine replied. "Six hundred years ago, when the Sakurans first arrived at Tanjiri, they were met by radio silence. Since then, their sunward faction has established a city close to the living world, creating the Trinity. That's our theory. But the inner system remains as silent as when the Sakurans first came."

Vytet's puzzled brown eyes regarded her from beneath heavy eyebrows. She met his gaze, saying, "You and I, we were there when our people first came to Deception Well, when we first entered the city."

His lips pressed together; he looked away.

"You found a dead city," Pasha said softly.

Vytet crossed his arms. "No, it was not dead. It was full of life. The parks and gardens all lush and overgrown, rustling with the movements of lizards and small mammals and the darting shapes of birds, the air alive with birdsong. It was only the people that had died. All of them, gone to bones."

"*Sooth*," Clemantine breathed. "Here, now, we know a faction of the Sakurans went sunward, and sometime after that the celestial city took shape. It might be that they thrived for a time, but why the silence?" She sighed, shook her head. "It's so much like Deception Well, that—"

An alert interrupted her; she caught her breath. Vytet's eyes widened and Pasha clutched the edge of the table—reactions that told Clemantine they'd received the alert too.

A DI spoke within her atrium: *A stealthed vessel has been detected, less than ten thousand kilometers from* Dragon. *It is of the same class as the initially encountered chameleon vessel.*

And it was only detected now? Clemantine demanded. *Already so close?*

That is correct. This chameleon vessel was noted during the standard telescopic survey.

Why didn't radar pick it out before?

Because the vessel follows Dragon, while the ship's radar looks ahead.

Clementine asked no more questions. Instead, she generated a ghost, sending it to join Urban on the high bridge, arriving only a moment ahead of Pasha's ghost.

Immediately, she felt herself immersed in a sea of hostility. The philosopher cells had noticed the intruder too—and they did not take well to its presence, so disturbingly close:

<awareness: other>
<it threatens!>
<revulsion: false chenzeme>
<kill it>
<kill it!>

Urban countered this argument:

– negate that –

He forcefully drowned it with his own:

– hold –
– calm –
– identify: other –

Of course the philosopher cells recognized this ship. If it was not the same one they had followed around the belt of ruins, it was at least the same kind, and they had learned to accept its presence.

Clementine added an argument of her own:

– we are strong / we are allied –

Urban echoed this, and Pasha too, across all the links of the high bridge, overwhelming all dissent.

So we are safe this time, Pasha said as the cell field quieted. *But will we still be able to suppress Chenzeme instinct as we get closer to the living world?*

I can control the cell field, Urban insisted, as he always did.

Sooth, Clementine agreed. *Of course you can. But why engage? Pasha is right. The cell field is only going to grow more volatile, with Chenzeme instinct insisting such an obvious oasis of life should be destroyed. We need to shut the cell field down and keep it dark, just like we did for all those years at Verilotus.*

In the intimacy of the high bridge, his resistance reached her ahead of his words. Urban valued the cell field as an auxiliary mind with its own sharp senses and a history and perspective usefully different from his own. It was the same argument Vytet had used to justify the Cryptologist, and though Urban acknowledged that, it hadn't changed his feelings.

This isn't Verilotus, he insisted. *We don't know what's out there. And we can't defend ourselves if the philosopher cells are dormant.*

We can't defend ourselves anyway, she countered. *Chenzeme senses and Chenzeme memories cannot help us here. Not if the entity decides to move against us. Not when we're surrounded by a ring of potentially thousands of dimensional missiles.*

There could be other threats. Threats only the philosopher cells would recognize.

Everything is a threat to the philosopher cells, Pasha noted dryly.

An alert reached Clemantine; this time, it came in the voice of the Astronomer. *I have found a second vessel dogging us, positioned opposite the first.*

Clemantine felt Urban's tension spike, even as she strove to suppress her own.

It's not an attack, she told him. *If the entity wanted us dead, we'd be dead. For all we know, both ships have been following us since our transit of the belt.*

Escorting us, Pasha suggested. *There to secure our good behavior?*

I'd like to secure our good behavior too, Clemantine said. *Send the hull cells to sleep, Urban. Now, before they notice the threat has doubled.*

Sooth.

A reluctant agreement. But a moment later, he introduced the idea to the cell field:

— *stealth* —

— *yield to the pilot* —

The bridge multiplied his proposal across a hundred thousand points of contact and the cells grew quiet, but they did not go dark. Clemantine perceived their reluctance, their suspicion. She added her voice to Urban's argument:

— *stealth / caution / yield to the pilot* —

Amplified by the bridge, her argument flooded the field, inducing a tiny sub-network of philosopher cells to render the necessary solution:

<go dark>

Urban strengthened this conclusion with his consensus:

– *affirmed: go dark / yield to the pilot* –

Philosopher cells were not all alike, but the influence of the most belligerent lineages had atrophied under Urban's command. More pliable lineages dominated, so that the field's instinctive protocols had become easier to override. Within seconds, the tide of opinion rushed toward consensus. Hundreds of cells went dark all on their own. Circles of darkness grew from each of these points, rolling outward to meet other circles. The momentum of consensus swept up even the resistant lineages, and the light faded from every cell.

So, that's done, Pasha said.

It's done, but I don't like it, Urban answered her. *I don't like the message this sends. Why are we hiding? The entity has to be wondering that.*

You're right, Clemantine conceded. *We need to project confidence and good will—but we don't need the hull cells for that. Remember Pytheas?*

You want hull lights? Urban asked.

Pasha laughed. *With rainbow colors?*

Yes, Clemantine admitted. *Why not?*

The Engineer and the Bio-mechanic were assigned the task. Mere hours later, brilliant, multicolored lights blossomed in neat lines running the length of *Dragon*'s hull, and before long, the two escort ships mimicked the new display. Clemantine chose to see this as a sign of welcome.

Jolly lay alone in his rumpled bedding, thinking on what Abby had said. He told himself it wasn't true. The Cryptologist wasn't using him. She liked him. He liked her. They were friends; they cared about one another.

Still, Abby's assertion troubled him. And when, after a time, the Cryptologist messaged him—*May I come see you?*—he felt so guilty for doubting her that it took him many seconds to compose a simple reply.

Yes, all right. But give me a minute.

He got up, splashed cold water on his face, and dressed, moving quickly, knowing that in exactly one minute, the Cryptologist would be at his door. She did not disappoint, appearing on the threshold with perfect timing, eyes bright and a sweet smile on her pretty face.

"I have an idea," she announced.

"Does your idea have to do with the two ships following us?" Jolly guessed—because what else was new?

"Yes, that is correct."

"Well, come in and tell me about it."

She stepped inside, then stood perfectly still just within the door. "These chameleon ships are generally believed to be analogous to the fleet's two missiles. If the analogy is true, then—as you once suggested to me—these chameleon ships will possess machine minds that can be reached through the use of silver, and further, it is reasonable to hypothesize that these minds are currently focused on us. If that is so, these minds might be open and accepting of communication from someone augmented with silver."

Jolly did not at all like the direction of these speculations, but the Cryptologist raised a quick hand to forestall his objection. "You are thinking this is nothing more than a long chain of guesswork," she said.

That was not what he'd been thinking.

"If so, you are correct. Nevertheless, I would like to test this idea. But I cannot do it myself."

Jolly retreated to the couch, heart racing, feeling strangely tired as he sat down.

"You must do it," the Cryptologist said.

Abby's warning returned to him. *She'll use you, Jolly, if that's what it takes to get where she wants to go.*

"Why come to me?" he asked. "Why not ask Urban? Maybe Urban has already tried—"

"No. He is afraid."

"And you think I'm not?"

"I have assessed your relative merits and concluded you are persuadable."

"Oh."

"Also, you are my friend and I need your help. I need to gain access to the silver."

"You know I would help you with that, if I could."

"This is true, but it is not helpful. It may be that the local vessels are more clever, that they know how to establish their version of silver within another entity, within me. Will you help me put this hypothesis to the test, Jolly? Will you try, for me, to contact these vessels through the silver?"

He wanted to say no. Abby would tell him to say no; she would say the Cryptologist was only using him for her own ends. Worse than that, he didn't want the Cryptologist to succeed. She hoped to gain knowledge through the silver, insight that would let her comprehend the structure of the needle and how it might be opened. Jolly did not want to see the needle opened and he did not want to open himself to Tanjiri's alien silver.

Still, she was his friend. And she needed this favor. He could not bring himself to deny her.

"All right. Come sit with me."

A tentative smile. She sat close beside him.

Jolly noticed his hands trembling. His heart still raced. But he swallowed his doubts and dimmed the room lights with a thought. Easy now to see the sparks of the *ha* dancing between his fingers. He took the Cryptologist's hand in his. "Don't let go," he told her as the *ha* danced from his skin to hers.

"I will not let go."

He closed his eyes. He drew cool air in through his nostrils. Then he turned inward to confront the silver within him.

That silver was always present at the edge of his awareness, though he rarely acknowledged it. He feared being lost in it. Maybe, like Clemantine, he should have given it up when he'd left Verilotus, but he feared that too. The *ha* was the signature of his birth world. It had defined him. He had been the boy who could waken the *ha* in others.

The Cryptologist wanted him to play that role again, to find some way to bring the *ha* to her, wakening her mind to silver. It was his role.

Even here?

Yes, even here amid the alien silver of Tanjiri.

So he reached past fear and for the first time he sought out Tanjiri's silver. He opened his mind to it.

Something out there must have been waiting for him because he was immediately pulled under, his consciousness immersed in a warm sea composed of some bright liquid lighter than water, all welcoming and well-ordered. Nothing like the silver at Verilotus. And within that sea, he perceived scattered knots of density— that's how he saw it at first—some of them bright and near, others remote. But no matter how far, a faint, shimmering web linked them one to another, as if to illustrate the mutual awareness of sentient minds.

Sentient minds? Why had he thought that?

Because it was true.

He knew it, and he shuddered at the knowledge. He almost retreated.

"What?" the Cryptologist whispered. "What have you found?"

He squeezed her hand once, twice, but didn't answer. He didn't yet have words enough to satisfy her, and anyway, something was happening.

Two of the beings, already close, moved closer. Their minds bright and near. *The two vessels?* What else could they be? He sensed a kind of gravity in their presence, an attractive force that made him want to seek a connection with them.

Try it, then. It's why you're here.

He gathered all his awareness, all his intention, and fixed his thoughts on one. And to his astonishment, a thread took shape within the silver, a tentative strand linking him to whatever was there. *Something* was there. Someone.

Another long, slow breath to help him push past fear, to help him focus.

Hello? he thought. *Hello?*

No answer.

He shivered again. He felt so vulnerable. Guilty too.

I shouldn't be here.

He wanted to retreat, but then what? What would he tell the Cryptologist? She was counting on him.

He had to try again.

Just one more time.

Steeling himself, he turned to the second presence, the second vessel. And again a thread formed within the silver, linking him to that silent mind.

Hello?

This time, something happened. A subtle thing, a shifting current, a slight pressure flowing through that thread, and then threading through his mind. He squeezed the Cryptologist's hand harder. Striving to concentrate amid his fear, he imagined another thread, a new thread, linking him to her.

Do you see her? Do you know a way to share the ha *with her?*

He waited a long time for an answer.

Please talk to me.

He waited until long after the current stopped flowing. But no answer came. Not then. Not until hours later when he woke in a sweat, his eyes wide in the darkness of ship's night, his pulse too rapid.

He told himself he'd been dreaming, though what he'd experienced had not been like any dream he'd known before. He'd been somewhere else—it had felt like that—somewhere beautiful, but frightening too. And in that place, he had come face to face with his own transience. He had recognized his own existence as nothing more than a spark, an organized flash of energy burning through an indeterminate span of time that might be counted in days, years, centuries, or millennia—but always brief when measured against the potential lifetime of a living world.

He breathed slowly, evenly, waiting for his pulse to slow.

The living world had a name. He whispered it, carefully shaping each syllable: "Pra-kru-ti. *Pra*-kru-ti." Awkward on his tongue.

His bedroom ceiling took on a dim glow as ship's dawn

approached. He stared up at it, struggling to remember more. Hadn't he been told something? An answer to a question he once had asked?

But the dream had faded, and all he could remember was the name of the world.

Prakruti.

CHAPTER THIRTY

DRAGON CONTINUED INWARD, ever more slowly on a curving trajectory that would eventually converge with the Trinity. In his long-ago encounter with the entity, Urban had conveyed benign intentions. He meant his slow approach to reinforce that. A peaceful velocity that precluded any possibility of kamikaze attack.

All throughout this long sunward voyage, the Sakurans at Volo's Landing continued to send regular updates. Each began the same: *All is well.* A summary report followed, detailing their progress. Occasionally, a question arrived for the Bio-mechanic or the Engineer. *Dragon*, in turn, reported its position. Other than that, there was little news to convey, as the Trinity maintained its haunting silence.

Bright rainbow lights marked *Dragon* and the two local ships that flanked it—bright enough, the Astronomer insisted, to be seen by even a small telescope orbiting with the Trinity. Dependent, of course, on whether anyone was looking, and if such a telescope should happen to be turned in their direction.

Three hundred days after *Dragon* crossed the belt of ruins, the ship's company agreed the time had come to try again to wake the celestial city. A new radio message went out, repeating every hour. It began with a greeting, followed by a description of who they were, where they'd come from, why they'd come, and the language they spoke. The message then repeated in the Sakurans' language, and those languages once common to Tanjiri.

And still there was no response, no reply, no visible activity at all. Clementine's worry—that the city would be as empty as

Deception Well when she'd first come there—began to infect Urban. Day by day, hope gave way to pessimistic certainty.

"Something must have happened to them," he mused one evening as he lounged on the grass in a circle of friends, all of them stirred to creative speculation by the evocative music of a concert just finished.

Riffan had started the discussion by wondering why they did not attempt to wake the city with music rather than radioing words alone.

"Once we establish a connection, we can send anything we like," Kona answered as he lay with his head resting in Shoran's lap.

"*If* we ever establish communication," Urban amended.

Now Jolly surprised him by saying, "It's not the city that matters."

Urban tensed, immediately on guard. "That sounds like something the Cryptologist would say."

Jolly turned to look at the Cryptologist. Urban looked too. She sat alone outside their circle, and outside the glow of festival lights. Perfectly still, her shadowed expression unreadable.

In contrast, Jolly sat surrounded by the ship-born. Zariah had a possessive arm around him, with Abby and Sayuri flanking—a not-so-subtle barrier to keep the Cryptologist at a distance.

Under Abby's influence, the trio of ship-born had taken to monopolizing Jolly whenever they could.

In part, it was jealousy. And if that was their singular motivation, Urban would have ordered all three to counseling. But Abby had come to him in concern. She did not trust the Cryptologist's good intentions. *And that's why we have to protect him,* she'd explained.

Jolly had a natural naiveté, and Urban too saw a need to keep him from harm. So he had nodded, lending Abby his silent approval.

Now Shoran said, "I'm looking forward to visiting the living world—or anyway, I'm hoping it's an Earthlike world that we *can* visit."

"It is Earthlike," Jolly assured her in a defiant, nervous tone. "And it's called Prakruti."

"Prakruti?" Urban echoed, puzzled by this odd declaration. He queried the library for a definition of this unfamiliar word. *Pra-kru-ti.* A woman's name, and also another word for nature. "You want to give it that name?"

"That *is* its name," Jolly insisted.

"Not in the master star catalog."

"I don't care. That's what it calls itself."

Silence fell across their circle as Urban struggled to understand what was going on. He weighed possibilities while Jolly countered his gaze with a defiant glare. *What?* Urban wondered. *What did I miss?*

His attention snagged on the sparks of *ha* dancing across Jolly's hands.

Ah, shit. He leaned forward. "You've been out there, haven't you? You've encountered the entity."

Jolly's defiance collapsed. His gaze fell and he shook his head. "*No.* Not the entity. I think they're the escort ships. I've been asking them questions. I know someone's listening."

"And answering?"

"No."

"Then how do you know the name of the world?"

Jolly studied his hands and the glinting sparks of *ha.* Finally, he said, "Something's happened to me. I have these strange dreams. I *thought* they were dreams."

"Meaning you don't think so anymore?"

He looked up again, met Urban's gaze. "I think we should visit Prakruti."

"We will if we can. We'll send scout-bots."

"We need to go ourselves. You and me, and maybe the Cryptologist too. Others if they want, but you and me, for sure."

Kona was sitting up now, the better to listen. "Why, Jolly? What do you know? What's there?"

"Prakruti," Jolly answered. He shrugged off Zariah's arm and stood up. "That's all I know."

He looked again to Urban. "I should have told you before. But I thought you'd be angry because maybe you were waiting for some better time to reach out again through the silver. You know, like you did before."

With that, he turned and left the circle. Questions erupted as he walked away, but Jolly did not look back. And after a stunned moment, Urban retreated too.

Waving off all questions and speculations, he returned alone to Clemantine's cottage. But he could not escape the quiet accusation embedded in Jolly's words: *Maybe you were waiting for some better time.*

No, he'd only been waiting for courage.

The Cryptologist withdrew into the dark, heart fluttering and afraid as her avatar became unstable. Her blood pressure rose, a sudden surplus of lacrimal fluids dripped from her aching eyes, and her chest suffered a ruthless pressure, as if an airless cavity had opened around her heart. Breathing became difficult. She gulped for air in soft, sharp gasps, arms around her knees as she crouched alone in the shadows of a little maple grove.

__Explain__, she demanded of her ghost in the library, though she already suspected the answer.

It is an emotional event. Not fatal. This is a common reaction when one who is loved and trusted commits a hurtful act.

I do feel hurt. Wounded. Perhaps broken.

It is a temporary state, already receding.

Yes . . . though I think I am angry too, now that I know Jolly did not choose to share with me all that he knew.

As her breathing calmed, she stood up, wiped her face, checked the personnel map. Only a handful of people remained on the lawn. Most had dispersed to their cottages, alone, or with a companion or two.

Jolly had no companion—not yet—though the three ship-born had just arrived at the start of the little path that led to his door. They lingered there many seconds, and then, to the Cryptologist's surprise, they moved on without going inside.

Good.

She did not enjoy the company of the ship-born. Any discussion with Jolly became difficult when they were present, and the one time the Cryptologist had asked, they had rejected her offer of joyful sexual interaction, in a manner so blunt she had felt wounded then too.

She crossed the lawn, then walked quickly along the path, taking the long way around, to avoid encountering the trio. But then, as she stepped onto the little side path that led to Jolly's door, a message popped into her atrium: *No visitors please.*

The Cryptologist glanced over her shoulder in the direction the three ship-born had gone. They had wanted to see Jolly, but had respected his request for privacy. She appreciated that, but made a different decision. Striding to his threshold, she pushed through the cool gel of his closed door into an empty living room, the sofa and low table lit only by light from a neighboring cottage spilling in through the open window.

Soft footsteps carried her to the lightless bedroom. A rustle of cloth, and then the ceiling lit with a soft glow, revealing Jolly sitting up on his pallet, still in the clothes he'd worn to the concert.

"You're angry with me," he said softly.

This startled the Cryptologist. "How do you know this?"

"I would be, if I were you."

So as not to look down on him, she sat cross-legged on the carpet beside the pallet where they had shared sexual intercourse sixty-seven times before. Strange, how that knowledge, that memory, now pained her.

She said, "After you tried to speak to the escort ships that first time, you told me you did not want to access the silver again. But you have done so?"

"Yes. Many times. I changed my mind, that's all."

"You didn't want me to know."

"You push too hard, sometimes. I wanted it to be my choice, to go on or not. Anyway, nothing changed from that first time. It's always the same. I try to talk, but no one talks to me. But it doesn't end there. I think something's gotten inside me, and it's changing me."

She looked him over, but could see no changes. He remained the Jolly she knew.

He tapped his head. "It's these dreams. I see things, experience things—I can't really remember what—but later I realize I know things."

"Maybe your brain structure is changing?"

"How could that be? I mean, my Makers would detect that, and repair it. Right?"

"Yes, that's right," she realized. "That could be why you can't remember. Your Makers are undoing whatever changes the local system is trying to make. Erasing the experience of the dream . . . but leaving knowledge . . . ?"

The Cryptologist hesitated, struck by the parallel with her own mind, by Vytet's design, filled with knowledge but with no experience of how that knowledge had been acquired. Vytet had created her to think differently. And she wanted to. She wanted to adapt her mind to the task that had been given to her to solve, but it was Jolly's mind that was adapting.

Frustrated, she declared, "I want to *be* you. If I could put myself in your place, I would pause the activity of my somatic Makers and then I'd know if something in the local silver was trying to shape my mind, trying to adapt it to a new way of thinking."

Jolly stared at her, lips parted in shock. Only after several seconds did he stir, whispering, "Do you think I should?"

Hadn't she already answered that question?

"Of course. How else would you know?"

In the library, Urban accessed the master star catalog, adding *Prakruti* to a list of common names by which the living world, officially designated Tanjiri-2, had once been known.

The Astronomer immediately noted the change, and questioned him on it. "Why the new name? Tanjiri-2 clearly designates the planetary body without introducing the dissension and debate inherent in establishing a romantic name."

"It's what Tanjiri-2 calls itself," Urban answered.

A moment of skeptical hesitation before the Astronomer asked, "And you know this how?"

"Jolly found out. Let's wait and see if it's true."

His extended senses tracked Clemantine. As she returned to

the cottage, his perspective shifted. He looked up from his seat on the thick living room carpet as she came in, wearing a long, shimmering gown of pale gold that wrapped her powerful figure and made her look more than ever like a goddess of ancient days.

"The music tonight was beautiful," he told her. "Inspiring."

She arched an eyebrow, communicating a mild annoyance. "Thank you."

Many among the ship's company delighted in the old-style instruments that served as extensions of the physical body, the music they created vibrating through them even as it filled the gee deck's atmosphere with enthralling harmonics. Over the long years, Clemantine had now and then taken up the study of the instrument known as the violin, but only since returning from Volo's Landing had she grown adept with it, gaining skill enough to play with more experienced musicians. She would usually return from these performances alight with joy and a passion for the delights of a physical existence.

Not so much, tonight.

"Kona tells me you had a very strange conversation with Jolly."

"Sooth." He looked away. "He's been using the silver to try to speak with our escort ships. I think the Cryptologist put him up to it."

"And you?" she asked. "You have not tried again, have you? Not since that first time."

He didn't answer. Not right away.

She summoned a tea table. It rose from the floor, a wisp of steam furling from the spout of a squat oval teapot. Kneeling on the carpet across from him, she poured.

He eyed the small cups, but did not drink. When he spoke at last, his throat was dry and his voice hoarse. "I will," he promised her. "Tonight."

"Not alone. I've messaged Jolly. He's coming."

Urban nodded, breathing softly, willing his heart to slow. Better to try it, to risk it, to learn whatever could be learned—the name of a world, the intention of a god—better than approaching Prakruti blind. Right?

Jolly arrived alone at the door—but Urban's extended senses showed him the Cryptologist lingering on the path outside.

You too, he messaged her. *I know you pushed Jolly to do this. So come in. Learn what you can.*

Urban closed his eyes and, breathing slowly, he let his mind descend into an ever-deeper awareness of an ocean of silver. He sensed Jolly there with him, and he sensed the presence of a myriad of fierce sentient minds that were surely the same minds his own dimensional missiles had recognized when *Dragon* first approached Tanjiri System. They were so obvious. How could he not have noticed them, that time he'd encountered the leviathan—unless its overwhelming presence had obscured all else?

Most of these ship minds were comfortably distant, their attention turned elsewhere. But the two escort ships loomed close, their bright minds very much aware of him.

"You see them?" Jolly whispered. "The escort ships?"

"Yes." And after a moment, "I don't sense the entity."

"I never have. Talk to the escort ships."

But Jolly had tried talk and gotten no answer, and the leviathan had not used words. Urban decided to forego words too, for something riskier and more intimate.

Two deep breaths, expelling fear and resistance. Two more, envisioning himself as a flow of thought, of intention, of a will to communicate, to understand, and be understood. From within this formless representation he chose at random one of the bright minds—and leaned into it.

Shock and surprise erupted from it. It recoiled, swirling, churning, a defensive barrier flashing into existence around it as Jolly cried out in a high-pitched voice, "Urban!"

In that other realm, in the cottage he shared with Clemantine, Urban reared back, breathing swiftly now, shallowly, heart booming in thunderous beats. Fear demanded a retreat and he almost gave in—but caught himself. Kept himself out there and vulnerable . . . though he hated being vulnerable.

Never mind that!

He had let fear rule him too long. Bitterly determined to break down the silence enshrouding Tanjiri System, he leaned in again, with the flow of his intention now a circular current wearing at the barrier that had been thrown up against him, and to his astonishment, the barrier began to erode, thinning, until it faded away altogether.

But it was not the bright ship mind that he met on the other side. That had retreated, leaving in its place a subtler, diaphanous essence. Less a mind than an intelligent tool. With the barrier gone, it spilled out, sweeping over him, and washing through him too.

A flush of panic, put down by an extreme act of will. *Didn't I ask for exactly this?*

Still no words spoken, by himself or this quiet presence, as some new phase unfolded within the brain tissue of his avatar—a transformation—one brought to an abrupt halt by the automatic resistance of his somatic Makers.

He sank back into himself with a sigh of relief and a silent prayer of thanks for the speed and capability of his defenses. But by the Unknown God, he had been so close! So close . . . but to what? Disaster? Or a breakthrough?

Someone grasped his shoulder, shook it hard. Jolly, angry and scared: "You invited it in!"

"And it worked," Urban murmured. Relief metamorphosed into regret. "It almost worked."

He sat up straighter, blinked against the light. Clemantine in her goddess aspect, watching him with a furrow of concern. Behind her, the Cryptologist, lips parted as if on the verge of asking some anxious question. And Jolly, still gripping his shoulder, demanding to know, "Did it do something to you? Did you let it?"

"Why ask that? Did you let it do something to you?"

Jolly sat back on his heels. "I don't know." He glanced at the Cryptologist. "It's her idea, that I have these dreams because my mind is changing, but my somatic Makers change it back."

"Not your mind," the Cryptologist corrected. "But the structure of your brain."

Urban nodded. "That is what happened."

The furrow in Clemantine's brow deepened. "The entity? It's trying to rewrite who you are?" She sounded horrified.

Urban felt a little horrified too. And maybe a little disappointed? "Don't worry. My somatic Makers stopped it."

But what had been stopped?

He shifted to the library, hoping to answer that question. Summoning the Bio-mechanic, he transferred to him a submind bearing his recent memories, and then demanded to know, "What almost happened to me?"

Within his frameless window, the Bio-mechanic crossed his arms, quirked his lip in a surly line, and said, "Perhaps the process was meant to bestow some necessary adaptation."

"Necessary for what?"

"What did you ask for?" the Bio-mechanic countered. Then he answered his own question before Urban could. "Communication! Understanding! You have said the silver here is similar but not the same as the silver at Verilotus."

Urban shivered. "So to bridge that difference, I'm supposed to let an outside system rewrite my mind?"

"You've done it before."

He meant when the silver had colonized him on Verilotus, overcoming his somatic Makers. "I didn't have a choice, then."

"But now it seems you do have a choice, though you would need me to modify your somatic Makers to allow it. Aren't you curious?"

"I can see you are."

A flicker of a cold, cold smile. "Of course, there is risk. But in the end, if it doesn't work out, you can always go back to who you used to be . . . before Verilotus."

Sooth. And that was the crux. He had been offered something, and if he wanted to know what it was, he would have to risk his precious, irreplaceable, silver-augmented avatar.

The Bio-mechanic's cold smile flickered to full life. "It's irresistible, isn't it? This need to know?"

"Truth," Urban whispered.

So much for choice.

He shifted back to find Jolly still there, still gripping his shoulder, his gaze as grim as Urban had ever seen it.

"Where did you go?" the kid demanded.

"To see the Bio-mechanic."

"You asked him to pause your somatic Makers, didn't you?" His gaze cut to the Cryptologist. "That's what she wants me to do. She wants to know if something in the silver is trying to adapt my mind to a new way of thinking."

"The Bio-mechanic said something similar."

"And you're going to let it happen?"

Urban looked at Clemantine and found her watching him with narrowed eyes. Wary. Waiting.

"I am," he said.

She said, "Stop. Think. If you let this thing inside your defenses and it proves to be some potent malware rewriting the very definition of who you are—"

He held up his hand. "If that happens, my ghost will put an end to it."

"And you'll lose this avatar and your silver with it."

"I know that, and it scares me, but I need to do this. I need to know."

Jolly heaved a great sigh. "All right then. I'm going to do it too."

Clemantine flinched in surprise at this unexpected declaration; Urban shot Jolly a startled look. "No, you're not. You're going to wait and see what happens to me."

Jolly's gaze hardened. He stood up, stepped away. "It's my choice, not yours."

A pronouncement that stunned Urban. Had Jolly ever defied him before? He stood up too. "Jolly, there's no need for both of us to risk—"

Clemantine interrupted. Her gaze, like her words, had gone cold. "You need to respect his choice, Urban, even if you disagree with it—just as I respect yours."

Jolly nodded, then looked at the Cryptologist. "And it is *my* choice. I should have thought of it before."

CHAPTER THIRTY-ONE

AFTER JOLLY LEFT with the Cryptologist, Clemantine messaged Kona, Shoran, and the ship-born, inviting them to play a rare night game of flying fox. Then she went into the bedroom, where she changed from her gown into athletic clothes.

Urban followed her. "What are you doing?"

"I'm going out."

She hoped to distract her mind with the game's fierce physical demands.

Urban, of course, did not like the idea.

"You're going out to play?" he asked heatedly. "*Now?*"

Now, when the Bio-mechanic had already initiated a pause in the activity of his somatic Makers.

"Sooth. You've made your choice. And I hope and pray this venture works. But I'm not going to sit here and watch as you allow some unknowable entity inside your defenses."

She'd already spent too many years—all those years after he'd disappeared from *Dragon*—waiting and wondering if he was alive, or lost to her forever. Though the anxious fear she'd known all throughout those years had retreated, it had never really gone away. And now it was back, resurgent, like a sickness in her veins. She dreaded losing him, even if only this version of him . . . this version she'd known since their years on Verilotus. Who would he be if he lost this gamble?

"All right," he said with an edge that suggested it was not all right at all. "Go play your game. I'll let you know how it goes—or the Bio-mechanic will."

"Make sure it's you."

Resentment glinted in his eyes. She cupped his face in her hands and kissed him anyway. Then she walked out.

The Cryptologist's ghost was never alone within the library. Although she could not always see him, the Bio-mechanic stalked her, ever on the periphery of her awareness. She did not mind. Not much. Often, his proximity proved convenient. And it entertained her, knowing he had full access to her internal dialog.

You must help me to modify my avatar's somatic Makers, she thought. *It will be easy for you to do this, since you have just done a similar thing for Jolly and for Urban.*

The Bio-mechanic congealed into existence beside her, head cocked in an attitude suggesting he was evaluating all possible repercussions of this request. He settled on the one that worried her most. "Should this modification lead to the corruption of your avatar, you will not be allowed to generate another."

That will please many people.

A slight, sympathetic smile, entirely unexpected. "It will not please me."

The players formed a circle at the center of the concert field. Arrayed on one side: Kona, Shoran, and Abby. Facing them as the opposing team: Clemantine, Sayuri, and Zariah.

Only Clemantine knew the real reason for this night game— and damn the silver anyway! Damn Lezuri's creation!

Or had Lezuri stolen the idea of silver from Tanjiri's quiet entity? It would not surprise her if that was true. It even seemed likely, now that she thought of it.

She leaned over, knees bent, poised to jump, and eyed the other players around the circle.

Oh! And damn the Cryptologist too! She had put it in Jolly's head to explore the local silver, and had hooked him into this dangerous new folly.

"Ready?" Sayuri asked, sweat already glistening on her skin and her eyes narrowed in anticipation. Not waiting on an answer, she cracked an impish smile. "Ready or not!" And she released the fox.

It gleamed red as it shot to the center of their circle, and then rose above them. Together, both teams counted down: "Five, four, three, two, one—"

A sharp buzz, and the fox sped away. Clemantine leaped after it. One of a scrum of players, she moved on instinct, not really thinking about the game yet or any strategy, still brooding over Urban.

Shoran took advantage of her distraction and shouldered her hard, sending her crashing into her teammate, Zariah. They both went down, tumbling in the grass, leaving Sayuri on her own.

Damn Urban anyway!

Clemantine rolled to her feet. Zariah was up too, but she signaled him to be still. Head cocked, holding her breath, she listened to the distant buzz of the fox. Then she told Zariah, "Take the path. Block Shoran if you can. I'll come in from the side."

Urban took a blanket to a shadowed corner of the tiny cottage garden. He laid it out and sat down on it. A cricket chirped softly somewhere nearby.

He was not alone. Not exactly. His ghost kept watch, and the Bio-mechanic too. But not Clemantine.

He drew a deep breath, filling his lungs with cool night air. Exhaled slowly, in an exercise to bleed off his resentment.

Again.

And again.

Though the action of his somatic Makers was paused, he felt no different, not yet.

But that won't last.

One more deep breath—and this time, as he exhaled, he let his mind sink into the silver.

He found Jolly already there: a bright knot of awareness among the more distant ship minds. But Urban did not sense the diaphanous presence he had met earlier. Not at first. Several heartbeats thumped out the passage of time before he noticed that sly tool already entangled in his mind.

A grim smile. How he hated this. Clemantine was right. This was a stupid gamble. But he needed to know.

Three more heartbeats, and the Bio-mechanic observed, *It is begun. I am detecting subtle changes, though their meaning and purpose is uncertain.*

And Jolly?

It is the same for him.

Another deep breath. *I feel the same.*

You are the same. Nothing has been taken.

Will you be able to un-do these changes, if it comes to that?

The biologic, yes.

And the coding nodules?

Another slow exhale as Urban envisioned those tiny, precious structures within his brain. They were the gift of Verilotus, tying his mind to the silver.

I can reset the molecular switches on the nodules' outer surfaces. But I cannot counteract or even observe any change made within them. You know that.

All right.

He focused his mind on the cricket's song.

No visions yet.

The Cryptologist sat beside Jolly, holding his hand as his consciousness slipped into the silver. She listened as the rhythm of his breathing quickened and then slowed; she felt warm, slick sweat on his palm, and the slowly growing pressure of his grip. He trembled a little. His brow furrowed in concentration—or was it worry? She knew the vastness of the silver frightened him.

After a time, he spoke, whispering, "I think I know now."

A glimmer drew the Cryptologist's gaze from Jolly's face to their clasped hands where she was astonished to see the sparks of his *ha* dancing in unprecedented numbers, multiplying until they formed a fog of luminous particles.

No, not simple particles.

The sparks of the *ha* were adaptive molecular machines, programmable by some process neither Jolly nor Urban had ever managed to explain.

It took her a few seconds to realize Jolly had opened his eyes, that he was watching her.

"Do you still want this?" he asked her.

Her eyes flared; her body's instinctive fear response sent her pulse racing—and still she did not hesitate in her answer. "*Yes.*"

The fog of *ha* had nearly hidden their clasped hands when Jolly brought them gently to her lips. "Breathe," he told her. "Breathe it in."

Only there, on the cusp, did she waver. The Bio-mechanic had warned just minutes ago that if she lost this avatar to some corrupt process, she would not be allowed another. Panic tried to rise at the thought of existing only as a ghost again; an awful ache erupted around her heart knowing that if that happened she would no longer be one of Jolly's lovers. And even if her avatar survived—if she found success, changed the way her mind worked, became something other—she might still lose his affection or lose her fondness for him, because she would not be the same person, nor see the world in the same way.

But she had done all she could to solve the puzzle of the needle and it was not enough. She needed this, needed to adapt her mind to a new way of thinking. She needed the change the silver would bring. *Take the chance, and try.*

"I love you, Jolly," she whispered, hoping that afterward it would still be true.

Then she leaned into the fog and inhaled deeply, again and again, until those deep breaths made her dizzy.

Or maybe it was something else?

Taking advantage of the gee deck's low gravity, Clemantine vaulted a hedge, then jumped to the roof of Zariah's cottage. Looking down on the other side, she saw the glowing fox hovering millimeters above its reflection in the surface of a tiny garden pond.

"Sayuri, come to my voice!" she shouted as she waited to see where the fox would go.

But instead of Sayuri, Abby appeared—and the fox shot higher, climbing in a swift spiral. Abby whooped and bounded after it just as Clemantine jumped from the cottage roof. They met in a brutal collision, heads cracking, the breath knocked out of them, *oof!*, followed by a secondary shock of impact as they splashed down in the pond. The fox buzzed angrily, trapped between them.

Abby groped for it, bright-red blood oozing from a gash by her right eyebrow and a maniacal expression on her face. Clemantine grabbed her wrist, yanked it back, and the fox shot free.

By this time, all the players had converged. Sayuri darted in first. Kona partly blocked her. In a clever move, Sayuri let herself fall back. Her foot shot out and she kicked the fox in Zariah's direction. He reached to grasp it with his large hand—but then he froze.

They all froze, allowing the fox to buzz away.

An alert had arrived simultaneously in their atriums.

Clemantine held her breath. Her heart, already booming from exertion, accelerated under a surge of fear, sure that Urban's experiment had imploded, that it had it all gone awry.

It's done, the Bio-mechanic reported. *The update appears complete.*

Urban's awareness still drifted within the silver, but his mind was his own, no longer entangled with the essence that had entered him. Whether it had departed or dissolved, he could not say. He only knew it to be gone.

He returned to himself, aware that only a little time had passed. The cricket still sang, and the gee deck's false sky still blazed with projected stars. *I don't feel any different*, he told the Bio-mechanic.

Nevertheless, there are subtle differences in the way the coding nodules link to your neuronal tissue.

Okay.

There could also be differences within the nodules.

Unknowable differences. I know. Is Jolly okay?

His update mirrors your own.

All right.

There is one more thing.

Yes?

I have blocked an alert that would have interrupted the update. But you will want to know. A radioed message has been received, originating in the region of the celestial city. We have had a communication from the sunward faction, at last.

Clemantine crouched in the garden pond, scarcely aware of her aching head, the soaked state of her sparse clothing, or the burn of her lungs. A stranger's voice, relayed through her atrium, held all of her attention. The woman spoke in the Sakurans' language:

Greetings to you, strangers, and welcome! We received your message with great surprise, and gratitude. It is the first contact we have had with other people since our expedition divided, more than six hundred years ago, and our erstwhile companions departed for our former home. We chose to stay. We are so pleased to know that your people at least have survived the plague of madness that brought destruction to so many worlds.

The message ended. Clemantine stood up slowly, aware now of the water droplets meandering down her smooth skin and plinking against the pond's surface. She rubbed at her bruised temple as she caught Kona's eye.

"An interesting beginning," he observed as Shoran moved to stand beside him, shoulder to shoulder, looking lost in thought.

Clemantine stepped out of the water. "Sooth."

Shoran said, "The faction at Volo's Landing blamed these people for the sabotage of their great ship. I always doubted that story."

Clemantine said, "So did I, but let's remember, we still don't know the truth."

Even so, she couldn't help but imagine, with churlish satisfaction, Okinowa's disappointment if it turned out her great enemies were not enemies at all. How it would burn to know that instead of waging hidden war against their sundered kin, "the defectors" had given them no thought at all because they had *no idea* of their existence . . .

What Clemantine could not imagine was Okinowa ever accepting the bitter possibility that one of her own ancestors had sabotaged the great ship, whether out of malice, desperation, or insanity.

Kona said, "I'll call the meeting to discuss our reply."

Clementine nodded. "I'm going home to change."

Urban continued to sit in the garden corner as he listened to a replay of the message. It disappointed him, that it said so little. Wanting to know if there had been any visible changes to the celestial city, he shifted to the library—or he tried to, only to find that action blocked, his awareness locked within his avatar's organic tissue.

Shock exploded into fury. He demanded of the Bio-mechanic, *Is this it? Is this the effect of the changes? That my connections are severed?*

A low amused grunt from the Apparatchik. *No. This effect is because I have consulted with your ghosts on the high bridge and in the library, and we have agreed, that as a cautionary measure, this version of you should be isolated within your avatar until we know more of the nature of the malware you have allowed within your brain.*

Though his heart tripped in an unsteady beat, Urban forced a measure of calm into his voice as he said, *All right, I understand that,* even as he was thinking *shit, shit, shit.* He would be cut off from the ship! Isolated within his avatar, like he'd been on Verilotus.

Then reprieve arrived. A submind dropped in, bringing the thoughts and memories of his ghosts, and after a moment of integration, he understood "isolation" meant only that he could not share subminds of his own. *Fine.* He could live like that, and he didn't think Jolly would have an issue with it either. The kid rarely ghosted. He probably wouldn't even notice.

Another alert arrived, this one from Kona, summoning the ship's company to the inevitable meeting at the amphitheater. He got up, eager to find Clementine there—only to discover she had come home. She stood at the back door, staring out at him. "You're all right, aren't you?" she asked.

"I think so. Anyway, I feel all right. So far."

From the library, the Cryptologist's ghost observed the distress of her avatar. A metabolic imbalance had set in, inducing weakness and an instinct to retreat. The avatar longed to return to her familiar chamber in the warren where she could wrap herself in warm, glowing tendrils of wall-weed and safely fade into the oblivion of sleep. But retreat was impossible. Jolly had seeded within her a novel complex of nanomachines, their structures entirely unknown. The complex had induced a rapacious growth within her brain cells that commandeered all her body's free energy. All she could do was slump on the soft carpet, her breathing growing ever more slow and shallow, her heartbeat fading too.

Looking on, the ghost asked herself, *Is this success? Or is it failure?*

"Give it time," the Bio-mechanic told her. "Urban survived this process. You can too."

CHAPTER THIRTY-TWO

PASHA DESPISED THE slipperiness of history, with its "truths" stained and filtered by the fallibility of memory, the bias of mind, and by speculations masquerading as fact when facts were not actually known.

She sat quietly in the front row of the amphitheater, evaluating every utterance in a slow radio conversation between *Dragon* and the city. Clementine and Vytet spoke for *Dragon*. The woman whose voice had delivered the initial message continued to represent the sunward faction. She spoke carefully, relaying a history that included no mention of violence as she described her people's departure from the Sakurans' great ship.

"The majority voted to go on, back to Sakura, but some of us believed we had a better chance of life here at Tanjiri. It was the living moon that gave us hope. It seemed to us a gift—its existence had not been recorded in our astronomical catalog—but with its easy gravity and independent rotation, we believed it would be possible to make a home there. So we stayed—and then luck intervened."

They found massive ingots of refined materials stashed at the fifth Lagrange point in the gravitational system of planet and moon, as if some past inhabitant had prepared for large-scale building projects that never took place.

"Nothing identified the builder. And we detected no radio signals, observed no artificial lights, saw no sign of any technological presence—in orbit or on either world—not then."

They had concluded the ingots were abandoned like all the

broken structures in the belt of ruins. It was an opportunity too good to ignore. With a quick vote, they dropped their plan to settle the moon and set about building a home of their own instead.

They called their celestial city Nara. They named the living moon Ezo, and they knew the planet as Prakruti.

A surprised murmuring filled the amphitheater at this latter name and Pasha caught her breath. She had heard the story of Jolly designating the world Prakruti just last night—and so had everyone else. She leaned forward, looking up and down the front row because that was where Jolly usually sat. But he wasn't in the amphitheater to hear this vindication . . . and neither was the insatiably curious Cryptologist, which seemed strange.

More questions were traded with the Narans, more answers given, but not the answer Pasha wanted to hear. So after a time, she raised a hand and caught Clemantine's eye. "The Narans said they saw no sign of a technological presence when they *first* came here. But what have they seen since then?"

Clemantine relayed the question. Only after an extended delay did an answer come back and even then, the speaker sounded oddly reluctant. "In the early days, we tried landing drones on Ezo. But there is a lingering defensive system there. Autonomous."

A cold tingle of anticipation touched the back of Pasha's neck as her mind leaped to a consideration of Tanjiri's mysterious entity. She thought Clemantine would surely ask some question about that being, but no.

"What of the planet?" Clemantine asked instead.

This time the answer came back quickly, with a liveliness in the speaker's voice, as if she was glad of a subject change. "Prakruti is not defended. It was surveyed soon after we came here. It is a wild place, like a replicant Earth, its oceans and continents fiercely alive." And after a moment, she added, "It's a strange thing, but our astronomical catalog misconstrued Prakruti too. Things as diverse as its rotational period, its terraformation phase, and its settlement history all differ from the catalog. There should have been three cities, but our survey found no evidence of any of them.

No people live there, and it's as if no people ever have. We have always been alone in this system."

A fierce murmur this time. Pasha leaned forward, hungry to know how the Narans would react when confronted with news of their kin at Volo's Landing. But after a whispered conference with Vytet, Clemantine turned to the gathering. "It's too soon for difficult subjects. Better to wait until we're face to face before we bring them news of their kin."

"Will we bring them news of the entity too?" Shoran wondered.

Clemantine traded a glance with Vytet, then said, "On that subject too, I think we should wait."

Every few minutes a submind dropped into Urban's atrium, endowing his avatar with a memory of the questions asked and answered in that first conversation with the Narans. But he paid little attention to it. Alone, still at home, he let his mind return to the silver, where he again encountered the bright minds of the escort ships.

He perceived them in finer detail now than he had before, and he recognized that they were not like the machine minds of his dimensional missiles. There was an organic awareness in them, and a suggestion of some other, simultaneous, existence, one of profound complexity. He sensed too their curiosity and their amusement as he approached them. This time they did not retreat. They came to meet him.

Instantly, with no perceivable interval of transition, he found himself entangled within their shared awareness. The intimacy of the connection sent him back to Verilotus, to those moments in the Cauldron when he felt himself drowning in the immense gravity of Lezuri's mind. Fear and panic hit. He fluttered to escape. And with no perceivable transition, he became only himself again.

But the two sentient minds remained close. Close enough that he sensed their doubt and their dull fear, spawned by shock at the memory he had shown them. A furtive conversation erupted between them, one he understood on a level deeper than words. They questioned if a mistake had been made. Was he a hostile presence? Did he threaten the system? Should he be eliminated in this moment or the next?

No! he objected.

The escort ships with their pretty rainbow lights had accompanied *Dragon* for so long Urban had grown complacent. He'd forgotten to fear their potential as dimensional weapons poised to erase not just his existence, but the existence of *Dragon* and every member of the ship's company.

That was the past, he thought, striving to explain himself, to visualize what had happened, to show them Lezuri. Aware of his thundering heart. *I did not choose it. I did not instigate it. I only escaped it.*

Did they understand? He didn't think so. Not in full, anyway. Those remembered moments when he'd been subsumed within Lezuri were too alien for them to comprehend. But they allowed his existence to continue, for the moment anyway, though they doubted him. And while they doubted, *Dragon* remained at risk.

He had to try again. They wanted to know him, so he had to let them in.

As sweat cooled on his avatar, as its heart slowed, he gathered his courage and approached the two minds again. This time, they were not so eager. They did not come to meet him, but at least they did not flee. He focused on the closest, the brightest one, easing nearer. And abruptly, he crossed a hidden threshold into that shared awareness. This time, he was ready for it.

He breathed out slowly, forcing mind and body to give up all resistance. And in doing so, he perceived the escort ship's mind with fresh clarity. It *was* a being of multiple aspects, present here, while simultaneously organic and alive in some parallel existence.

On Ezo, the living moon?

No.

On Prakruti, then—a complex being far older than himself. Its name—Wailoa.

A powerful current stirred the silver—and though Urban knew his avatar remained seated on lush carpet in Clemantine's cottage, he felt himself somewhere else. On Prakruti, maybe. Standing between white columns, on a porch that looked out across a lush meadow to a river, whose slowly flowing water sparkled under a midday sun.

Wailoa stood beside him, his equal in height, a robustly muscular man of ancestral form, except that his skin was made of tiny gleaming scales, dull white on his belly, blending to dark blue across his genitalia and limbs. His eyes a murky blue beneath eyebrows as thick and gray as old lichen. Rampant hair, a trailing beard, both a mix of gray and white.

A tangled moment as those murky eyes became Urban's eyes. Standing alone on the porch now, looking out at the river, *sensing* the river, its flow, its chattering current, the slick rocks in its bed, the creep of crustaceans, fragile green leaves stroked by the current, mollusks, fish, tadpoles, insect larvae, the touch of an eagle's talons against the water and droplets falling from the lips of a deer as it raised its head after taking a drink. And beyond all this, the fierce complex weaving of life throughout the river valley.

A soft smile behind the rustic beard. A sigh of deep contentment. *This.* This is the purpose of Prakruti. *This.* A place for life in all its wild ancestral abundance. *My* place. I am this river valley. I am its awareness, a consciousness existing above and beyond the perception of any individual element within it.

He was also this man standing between white columns gazing out at the water. And he was the mind of an escort ship. A guardian spirit, one of many, many such, coolly determined to end the existence of any outsider threatening the integrity of Ezo or Prakruti.

Ezo?

The question, a sharp-edged wedge that split off a fragment of consciousness, enough that Urban could ask himself: *What of Ezo?*

He turned, long hair swaying. Large hands, armored in blue scales, reached out to open ornate brass doors. Inside, blue light from clerestory windows mixed with the glow of a swirling cloud of silver.

Silver! Visibly manifest, at last.

From within the mind of Wailoa, Urban understood there would be no simple path to Ezo. He had undertaken a pilgrimage, he saw that now. From that hour on the edge of Tanjiri System when he'd briefly encountered Ezo—

Ezo! A name that named not just the moon, but the entity too.

With that encounter, Urban had set himself on a path that would lead him to this place, and if he dared, somewhere beyond.

Far away, his heart thundered as he understood he would have to give up everything. Every aspect of himself would be dissolved within that house of silver, the structure of his mind examined, his potential judged, and only if Ezo approved would he be remade—and not as he had been before.

Horror enfolded him, aware he could lose himself, that he almost certainly would, that anything could happen. At the same time, he felt wonderstruck, certain-sure that if he dared to do this, all his questions about the needle and the Blade and the rise and fall of the Hallowed Vasties would be answered if/when he, or something like him, emerged on the other side.

Did he dare?

Lezuri had been right—he wasn't ready—yet here he was. And he had to do it . . . didn't he?

A shiver of dread drew him back into his own mind, his own body, to find evening settling around him as he sat alone on the back step of Clemantine's cottage.

He would go.

Of course he would.

Ezo required it. And Ezo required that it be a solo journey, with one and only one permitted to make the crossing—and Urban would be that one.

Another shiver, wondering what he would lose, and what he would become.

Later, he messaged his ghost: *I can try to convey to you in words what I've learned, and what I'm experiencing. But know that words are as insufficient now as when I described my encounter with the entity.*

A low chuckle. *You want me to lift the block and accept your sub-mind.*

Urban thoroughly understood the insatiable demands of his own curiosity. *Give it up. You want it as much as I do. You're dying to know. Summon the Bio-mechanic. Let him know it's what we want.*

The time for caution had passed.

"Are you all right?" Jolly asked.

A ridiculous question! The Cryptologist lay on crumpled bedding, empty and exhausted, eyes half open, putrid salts defiling her skin, with her belly and her blood both demanding an immediate influx of calories. "I am *not* all right," she whispered past clenched teeth. "I am *starving.*"

"Oh . . . of course."

He brought her a cool liquid. Helped her to sit up enough to sip it. She tasted a glorious melange of complex sugars—a wise choice that would quickly if only transiently boost the available energy in her blood. Finishing the drink, she leaned back into his encircling arm, and sighed. "Ah, I thought this avatar would surely die."

"No, it wasn't even close," he assured her in his gentle voice. "Your somatic Makers weren't fighting the intrusion. That made it easy. Nothing like what Urban went through when the silver entered him."

"That was easy?" she asked, horrified, shrinking from awful imaginings of suffering doubled, and redoubled. The allure of a physical existence suddenly ebbing.

He kissed her forehead. "Maybe not *easy* . . . but look at your hands."

She wasn't sure she had the energy to do so. But the sugars had begun to enter her bloodstream, and she found she could raise one trembling hand. *There!* The sparks of the *ha* glittered across her palm and around her fingers.

"You did it," Jolly said.

"No, *you* did it. How did you do it?"

"I'm not really sure. I asked for it . . . envisioned it . . . and it was like asking a DI to find the answer to a question. The answer came to me. I could see, or at least sense the *ha* changing into something different. More complex, more abundant. More *potent.*"

"Very potent," she agreed.

"Can you sense the silver?" he asked her.

She realized she could, that an awareness of its presence had been there on the edge of her mind ever since she'd begun to think again . . . like a light too bright to look at just yet. But now that she did allow the fact of its presence into her conscious mind she felt as if she'd been granted a new sense, a vast expansion of her sensorium . . . confusing, frightening. Her hand fell back to the bed; she sagged against Jolly, her heart racing.

"It's too much," she whispered.

"I know."

"I am tired."

"I know. I'll get you something to eat. Okay?"

She nodded, trembling again, horrified, because she would have to go out there, into the silver, seeking a solution to the needle. And she did not want to. Not at all.

"They lie," Okinowa whispered, a flush of hard-to-dispel heat rising beneath the monochrome pattern of her scales.

Looking up from her tablet, she turned to Aurelius. He sat on their bed, cradling their sleeping infant in his arms. He returned her gaze, with ridges of doubt, of worry, framing his golden eyes.

She said, more forcefully, "It's easy to lie."

Speaking softly, so as not to wake the babe, "It is—as we both know."

A scheduled update had just arrived from *Dragon*. Not the usual position information this time. No, this time the report included real news: *Dragon* had found the defectors.

They were alive within their beautiful celestial city and—no surprise—they had told a story of their past grossly divergent from the truth. The defectors pretended to believe that the ancestral great ship had gone onward, back to Sakura. And—this part Okinowa suspected to be true—they had lived a life of peace and abundance ever since.

Aurelius adjusted the baby's blanket. Then asked her, "What

if they are not lying? What if it is true they had nothing to do with—"

"It is *not* true! We know the great ship and its library were deliberately destroyed. The Dragoneers saw the damage and knew that to be true. If not the defectors, then who would have done that, Aurelius? One of us? *No.* No, that is impossible. The truth is, they lie."

And anyway, it was far too late now to undo what she and Aurelius had set in motion. Packed with propellant and endowed with DIs to steer them, the two massive fragments of the great ship had been launched long ago on a silent journey to the inner system. Knowledge gained from the library, combined with the vast resources frozen within the cells of the megastructure, had made so many once-impossible things possible.

A slow nod from Aurelius, though more worry ridges gathered on his brow. "Maybe they are more like us than we care to admit. Maybe only one or two among them knew of the sabotage."

A flush of heat flooded her kisheer. Okinowa insisted to herself it was a flush of anger, not shame. And she spoke in sharp-tongued defiance: "That may be. But it comes to the same thing. They have thrived, while we have suffered and faded. A balance needs to be made. Do not regret our choice. You know it is the righteous thing to do."

"It is revenge, my love. If it were righteous, it would not have been done in secret."

CHAPTER THIRTY-THREE

DRAGON HAD CEASED its long deceleration. It coasted now, toward a rendezvous with the Tanjiri Trinity: Prakruti, Ezo, Nara.

Wailoa still accompanied the courser, remaining close and cautiously watchful, as did his partner, Kureo. They were just two out of thousands of Tanji inhabiting Tanjiri System, but none of the other vessels came near.

Tanji. That was Jolly's word for these beings with their multifarious personas, simultaneously the conscious mind of a chameleon ship and of a complexity of life on sacred Prakruti.

Urban entered the silver often to be with them, sharing his intentions, assuring Wailoa and Kureo that his very dangerous ship would remain far from planet, moon, and city. Much farther than the radius of a destructive dimensional bloom. There would be no transgression. But if there was, *Dragon* could be erased within a blister of white light, without spillover to harm the worlds.

Before Tanjiri, Urban would not have guessed that the prospect of annihilation—theirs, his—could be the foundation of trust, and of a deep and growing affection. Yet it was. He felt embraced by the two Tanji, and their curiosity about him was endless. They probed at every aspect of his memory, both shocked and fascinated by what he had seen.

But information flowed only one way. They learned more and more about him, but revealed little of themselves or their world. And not once did he sense the presence of Ezo.

Jolly too often visited the two Tanji, but learned no more than

Urban. "I think they want us to learn about Prakruti on our own," he mused.

If so, it was a challenge Urban readily accepted. Forty-one days out, he launched two cargo pods, each packed with satellites and survey bots. One pod for Prakruti, the other for Ezo.

From the high bridge, he monitored their progress: the rapid launch, days of coasting, and an abrupt deceleration that allowed their capture by the gravitational wells of their respective worlds. The pods descended to low polar orbits. There they released fleets of survey satellites. Then they closed again, quiescent.

Urban shifted to the library, where a crowd of ghosts had gathered: Clemantine, Pasha, Naresh, Vytet, the Cryptologist. Others of the ship's company watched from the amphitheater.

"We'll try Ezo first," he said, signaling that cargo pod to begin its descent into atmosphere.

No one spoke as they clustered in front of a library window displaying video from a watching satellite. The pod flared brightly with a deorbit burn executed above a brilliant blue ocean. Seconds ticked past.

If all went well, the remaining cargo of scout-bots and aerial bots would be distributed all around Ezo. But Urban knew—*he knew*—this segment of the mission could not succeed, that there was no simple path to Ezo for anything or anyone. Even so, he needed to test that knowledge and in doing so, test his own sanity.

A submind dropped in from his avatar.

"Wailoa and Kureo are on edge," he reported.

Vytet asked, "Should we abort?"

"No. Let it play out. Prove the theory."

"Your thought or theirs?" Clemantine wondered, still suspicious of the Tanji and their influence on his mind. She worried they had made him a subsidiary intelligence so that they—or the elusive entity, Ezo—could play him like a puppet.

It didn't feel that way. And her doubt annoyed him enough that he answered tersely. "Call it a consensus decision."

"Oh ho!" Naresh called out as a satellite observed a flare of pure and brilliant white light precisely at the pod's location.

"The signal is lost," the Engineer announced, though he was not visibly present. "A break in communications was expected as the cargo pod passed over the horizon. However, the break came sooner than anticipated."

A tremor marred Clemantine's voice: "That flash . . . surely that was a dimensional weapon, like our missiles?"

The Engineer answered her, "This is a likely explanation. The spectrum appears identical, albeit on a much smaller scale."

Urban said nothing, not trusting himself to speak. Another submind arrived from his avatar. He shuddered at a remembered horror that had originated in the watching minds of Wailoa and Kureo as they witnessed this little blossom of death, of oblivion. Each aware they contained the possibility of a far greater flowering. And he remembered their wordless plea—that he should do nothing to call down such a fate on himself and on them.

Never, he'd assured them.

With an effort, he locked down his emotions, and in a steady voice, he concluded, "Ezo is closed to us. For now, anyway."

"And because it is closed, that is the place we must reach," the Cryptologist said, studying Urban with wide, wondering eyes.

How much did she know? Or at least suspect? He had told no one of his vision (*his visit?*) to Wailoa's realm in the river valley, and the little house of silver that would be his gateway to Ezo. But long ago, she'd suggested that Tanjiri's entity might reside within computational strata hidden inside the living moon, just as Lezuri had resided within such strata, hidden in the Rock.

"The Cryptologist is right," Pasha declared—surprising Urban, because from what he'd seen, Pasha mistrusted her creation and always kept her distance. But now she didn't stint on her support. "Ezo is a mystery begging for solution."

"Of course, we are all curious," Naresh scolded. "But we don't want to go blundering in."

Vytet raised a hand in a gesture requesting patience. "Yes, we must and will be very careful. More now than ever." His hand closed into a loose fist. "I admit, I am shaken by what we just saw. Though the Narans warned us, I thought there would be time to launch the bots, and that it would be a silver storm that took them, not . . ." He gestured at the library window as the satellite passed over a desert coast.

Urban hadn't known how it would happen, he'd only known it would. He said, "Again, let's defer this. Try Prakruti instead."

Naresh stroked his chin. "Perhaps the Narans said the same thing after their probes were lost?"

"Brave of them to build so close to a hazard like that," Pasha observed. "And strangely fortunate that they found the materials."

Clemantine finished the thought: "A honeypot. The entity must have wanted a human element here."

Vytet's bushy eyebrows drew together. "But not on the moon. Ezo is off limits—and that *is* suggestive."

The Bio-mechanic did not instantiate; only his surly voice intruded, saying aloud what Urban had been thinking: "It suggests the entity exists within this inexplicable moon, just as the Cryptologist first proposed."

Urban was sure this was true, but he did not want this discussion. Not now. So he dismissed it with a cutting gesture. "We'll figure out how to reach Ezo later. The satellites, at least, are tolerated and we'll soon have a detailed map of the surface."

Turning back to the library window, he shifted the video on display. "Now we try Prakruti."

At his signal, Prakruti's cargo pod descended into atmosphere.

Other than scale, Urban found it difficult to see any difference between Prakruti and Ezo. Planet and moon shared a sibling resemblance: both beautiful, with blue oceans, polar ice, and a diversity of land masses in unfamiliar shapes.

From his experience within the silver, Urban knew they would be allowed to visit Prakruti, that they were expected there. But it remained to be seen if their robotic scouts would be tolerated.

He watched the cargo pod's descent in a state of tension that would have been breathless if he wasn't witnessing this as a breathless ghost.

The cargo pod passed out of sight over Prakruti's horizon, its signal dropping out precisely when expected. Silence in the library as minutes passed, the fleet of satellites undisturbed in their gradually diverging orbits.

Finally, the Engineer announced, "The cargo pod's signal has been recovered. Distribution of survey bots has begun."

"Just as the Narans told us," Vytet observed, relief obvious in his voice. "They were allowed to explore Prakruti, but not Ezo."

And that made Ezo all the more alluring. Wailoa had shown Urban the way there and if he dared to take it, he might come to learn the means to open the needle and from there, gain an understanding of how to generate a Blade, and learn how such a tool might be used to dissect a world, or to create a new one out of the shattered ruins of a failed cordon.

The metaphor of the pilgrimage returned to him. There was a path to Ezo, but that path went through Prakruti.

In the time it had been out of contact, the cargo pod had shed its heat shielding. It had then deployed narrow wings that let it glide over thousands of miles as it ejected pairs of bots—aerial and scouts—locked together, with a small parachute to slow their descent.

"No sign of silver in the atmosphere," Clemantine observed with a smile. And then she added, "By the Unknown God, this is a beautiful world."

Urban heard the longing in her voice and despite his own desire to visit Prakruti, it ignited worry. Clemantine had been born on Heyertori, another beautiful world, graced with wild landscapes. A beloved world that she had seen destroyed by the Chenzeme in an attack that had scarred her soul. Was she, deep down, still looking for her lost home?

He reached out, his ghost hand touching her shoulder. She turned to meet his gaze. "A honeypot," he said softly.

Her eyes narrowed. For a moment, she looked puzzled. Then she pressed her lips together, nodded, and turned away.

CHAPTER THIRTY-FOUR

"I AM CHANGING," the Cryptologist-as-her-avatar said to her ghost in the library. "You and I do not share the same mind anymore."

"That is a strange claim," her ghost replied. "We continue to trade subminds. My thoughts are your thoughts. Your thoughts are mine. We exist simultaneously as each other."

"Do we?"

In ghost form she had no perception of the silver and perhaps could not truly conceptualize the multitude of dimensions she had experienced in her deepest explorations of it.

She opened her eyes onto the soft glow of wall-weed. It moved slowly above her and around her, writhing, curling, uncurling again. She had retreated to this chamber after her ordeal with the silver and had not emerged again. Why should she? The wall-weed provided for her, satisfying all her physical needs. Well . . . except her sexual desires, though perhaps she could demand satisfaction there too. She wrinkled her nose. *No.* No, she would visit Jolly soon. She'd promised to do so anyway.

Her ghost said, "It is not you and I diverging. It is you and I together diverging from that being you become when your mind is vastened within the silver."

The Cryptologist did not answer. She closed her eyes again and filled her lungs with cool clean air.

Jolly and Urban had both bound themselves to the Tanji, and she might have too, if she'd met them first. But coming late, she'd seen little value in replicating their discoveries, reasoning it would be more productive to follow her own path, avoid the Tanji, and explore the silver on her own.

A bold plan, but she'd had no idea of the cost.

From the start, she'd felt lost within Tanjiri's silver, terrified as she sensed her mind dissolving across paths of knowledge too alien and too tangled to comprehend. Panic held off only by the greatest mental effort. Ultimately, she would find her way back, shaking and shivering, wanting to never venture forth again. But she did anyway, driven to it by the compulsion Vytet had placed in her. And slowly, slowly, she learned better how to structure her thought, focus her intent, find the web of paths that might lead her to real insight on the challenge of the needle.

Her explorations had brought her to an old theory: that beneath the thin film of its light-refracting surface tiles, the needle was a shell composed of matter impervious to the standard flow of time. If so, the trick to opening it would be to match the flow. Synchronize time within and without, and a physical reaction became possible.

But how to do that?

She didn't know, though she'd relentlessly sought an answer. She sought for the entity too, though she'd never yet sensed its presence, and that puzzled her. How could such a vast mind remain hidden?

She longed to encounter the entity just as Urban had, but dreaded it too. Everything would change in the moment she met it. So she imagined. She would tell it, *I need to think differently.* And then she would plead with it, *Augment my mind, change it so that I may truly and fully comprehend the physics of the needle.*

And if it agreed? There surely could be no going back. She would never be herself again.

She flinched as a message from Jolly interrupted these darkly hopeful meditations. He said, *Talk to me.*

Again? An impatient thought. But a swift check revealed days had passed since she'd last talked with him. Guilt stirred, and without really thinking about it she found herself murmuring a reply. *Hi, Jolly.*

*Oh, thank goodness! he shouted. *Why don't you ever answer me?

*I am answering you.

*I mean before! Oh, never mind that. We're going to Nara.

The Cryptologist hesitated, confused by the urgency in his voice. *I know that. I think I heard that.

Her ghost had learned of it.

*Don't you want to come? You can, you know. There will be fourteen people in the initial delegation. You can put your name in.

*The Narans are not important, Jolly. They are a distraction.

*You don't know that. Not for sure. They've been here centuries. Maybe they know more than you realize—or more than they realize.

She considered this. Considered that the Narans had claimed to be alone in Tanjiri System. Nothing they had said hinted at any knowledge of the entity. Still, she asked herself, *Is it possible the Narans had somehow, inadvertently, clumsily, without realizing it, discovered a means to capture the entity's attention?*

Certainly everything had gone well for them since they'd discovered the cache of ingots at Prakruti's fifth Lagrange point. Their celestial city was beautiful and they lived harmonious lives. At least, it seemed so from their propaganda. Was it by luck alone?

She was still pondering this question when her ghost in the library intruded, telling Jolly, *You are right. Every path must be explored. I will put my name in.

CHAPTER THIRTY-FIVE

PASHA DRIFTED ALONE in a library chamber, with a spherical projection all around her, generated by the cameras of an aerial-bot. Blue sky gleamed overhead, a crisp green horizon encircled her, and beneath her feet, gliding slowly past, was a vast deciduous forest flush with the bright-green growth of late spring.

The land beneath that forest lay like a carpet, unremittingly flat in every direction, a realm of trees watered by a lacy network of sluggish streams and long winding lakes. Eagles patrolled every shoreline, huge fishy shapes loomed and vanished within the waters, and—*there!*—a cinnamon-colored bear waded among dense reeds.

"Next," she whispered.

Her surroundings changed. Now she followed the video feed of an aerial-bot surveying coastal dunes at the edge of one of Prakruti's northern continents. At the dune crests, a relentless sea wind lifted grains of fine sand into a shimmering mist. It bent tall grasses and artfully shaped low-growing evergreen trees. Thousands of sea birds floated on that wind as foaming waves glided across a wide gray beach. High on the beach, out of reach of the waves, hundreds of sea lions huddled together as a pod of orcas patrolled just beyond the breaking waves.

"Next."

A broad slope filled with barren cinder cones, rust-red and black, the colors meeting in smooth seams in the saddles. A carpet of white clouds below, stretching to the horizon, and above, a glare of high-altitude sky with a few lacy cirrus clouds off to the east.

So very beautiful, all of it. Earth re-created. Every species observed so far, whether plant or animal, fungi, Protista, or pro-karyote, was known and described in the most ancient records of the library as originating on Earth. An extraordinary diversity! With animal life thriving in staggering numbers.

Impossible to understand how such a world could be mani-fested in so short a time as several millennia, and yet here it was. Wondrous! Yet disappointing too, at least for an exobiologist like Pasha. She had not expected to find strictly alien lifeforms in Tan-jiri System, but evolved forms, engineered forms, unique and here-tofore unknown . . . she had expected that. Yet neither Prakruti nor the belt of ruins had offered any such thing.

"Next."

She looked down on an equatorial rainforest in a river basin, and then a desert carpeted in spring flowers, a prairie animate with vast herds of buffalo and mammoth, a polar ice shelf black-ened with a seemingly endless colony of penguins.

"Next."

A broad valley, the glistening river running through it flanked by hectares of tall bright-green grass grazed by elk, with evergreen forest on the shallow slopes. She touched tongue to the roof of her mouth, ready to call out *next!* when a flash of reflected sunlight drew her gaze south. "Wait . . . what is that?"

Two or three kilometers distant, but easy to see in the clear air, stood a white-walled rectangular structure of modest size, with a steeply pitched copper-colored roof fully skirted with eaves that lay back at a shallower angle. The structure stood on a terrace at the edge of the forest. At the front of the building, above the eave, was an ornate triangular gable. The eave itself formed the roof of a porch that looked out on the river past four white columns.

An anomaly.

Pasha froze the video as the aerial-bot, guided by a simple autonomous model, continued on its assigned transect. She stared at the building several seconds more and all she could think was, *That shouldn't be there.*

The Narans had surveyed Prakruti soon after their arrival and found the planet re-made and utterly pristine, all its prior cities and settlements overwritten: *No people live there, and it's as if no people ever have.*

So far, the Dragoneers' satellite survey had only confirmed the total absence of a human presence.

So where had this little building come from?

By this time, the aerial-bot had gone on for a kilometer beyond the river. She called it back. Then she messaged Urban: **You need to see this.*

As a ghost, there could be no catch in Urban's breath, no rush of a beating heart, no sudden knot in his belly. But looking on the anomalous structure, he endured a tight, curling anxiety all the same.

He knew this place. He had stood on that white porch. Stood between those smooth white columns, looking at the sparkling river, aware of thriving life all around. No longer himself, his mind entangled with Wailoa's.

The memory left him feeling unmoored, as if his identity had begun to break up, to slip away. His hands closed into fists.

He did not tell Pasha he knew of this place. What did he really know? He hadn't even known what the building looked like. He'd only seen it from the porch.

He looked on it now, as the aerial-bot circled it. A pretty little building. He imagined himself back on that porch, turning around to be confronted by dual brass doors. He would draw them open, step inside, give himself up to a cloud of silver, becoming something else or nothing at all.

He knit his ghost fingers together, pressed them to his lips.

Pasha, still studying the video, did not notice his disquiet. "No footpaths around the structure," she noted. "No outbuildings, no vehicles, no walls, no garden."

"No people," Urban added in words barely audible.

No sign of Wailoa.

The bot circled lower, exploring the porch, seeking a way inside. It had no ability to open the doors. And though it tried, it could not maneuver to peer into the narrow clerestory windows tucked up under the eaves.

Pasha said, "The structure shows no weathering at all."

"Makers are maintaining it."

"Possibly." A hum of frustration. "I want to see inside. A scout-bot might be able to manipulate that door."

Urban made a quick check. Prakruti was a big world and the survey bots were widely scattered. "Not a realistic option," he said, striving to hide his relief. He did not want Pasha to know what was inside. "The nearest scout-bot is six hundred twelve kilometers away."

Pasha scowled. She crossed her arms. "We *could* ask the Narans what they know about the site." She sounded reluctant, like she didn't want to do that.

He didn't either.

He told her, "This structure isn't theirs."

"You know that?"

"Yes."

She drew back, one hand on her hip, eyes narrowed. "The same way Jolly knew the name of Prakruti?"

"Yes."

"What else do you know?"

"Not much," he lied. "But I know this is *our* discovery and I don't want the Narans beating us to it. So we say nothing to them about it, for now."

She frowned, doubtlessly struggling with her conscience. But desire won out, as he knew it would. A short nod marked her decision point. "Agreed."

Her gaze returned to the pretty building. "I'm going to update instructions for all aerial-bots, prioritizing the discovery of artificial structures. If the bots encounter another, I don't want them passing it by again. And I'll get a DI to review the survey so far. Maybe we've already found other structures, and nobody's noticed."

Would there be other structures? Urban didn't know. If there were, would they all be the same? Was there some significance to this architecture? Wanting an answer, he messaged Riffan, speaking aloud so Pasha would know. "Come to the library. You're an anthropologist. I want your opinion."

On my way.

Pasha crossed her arms again. Her mouth turned down at the corners in a sour expression.

"I didn't say we should hide it from the ship's company," Urban said.

"Of course not."

The little spherical chamber expanded to accommodate the arrival of Riffan's ghost. His gaze immediately locked onto the structure as the aerial-bot continued to circle it. "What is that?" he asked. "Is that a shrine? Why are you looking at it?"

Silently, Urban requested a definition of *shrine*—a holy place associated with a deity—while Pasha explained, "I found it. It's on the planet, on Prakruti."

"*Oh* . . . then the Narans *have* been there?"

"Why do you think it's a shrine?" Urban asked.

Riffan spoke slowly, as if wondering why himself. "Well, it's true a shrine can be anything—a cave, a stone, a tree, or part of a huge temple complex. But also a small ornate isolated building where one would go to entreat or to thank the enshrined deity. Have you had a look inside?"

Urban remained silent while Pasha said, "We have no way to open the doors."

"Hmm . . . this is *fascinating*, and so very peculiar. The only structure we've seen so far, right? I wonder why we didn't notice it before? Has a satellite surveyed this region yet?"

Good question.

Urban addressed the chamber's DI: "Give us a window with local satellite imagery."

The area had indeed been surveyed, four days before. But the shrine did not appear in the image.

"Shouldn't it be obvious?" Riffan asked.

"Yes, it should," Urban said. And then to the DI, "Mark the coordinates of the structure."

A red rectangle appeared in the meadow, just at the edge of the trees.

"No structure," Pasha concluded with a nervous little laugh. "No wonder it didn't show any weathering. It's new."

But it had to have been there before. Urban had stood on that porch, he'd looked out at that river. Or had that been a prescient vision? A thing still to happen?

Pasha went on, "Given its location, so close to an established transect line, my guess is we were supposed to find it—that it was grown there just for us. That we're meant to go there." She turned to Urban. "I *am* going to be part of that expedition."

"It's only fair," Riffan agreed. "You found it."

"It's the next step on a pilgrimage," Urban murmured.

Pasha gave him a sharp look. "You *do* know more about this place, this *shrine*. Don't you?"

"Just what you said. That we're meant to go there. *I'm* meant to."

"You? So you intend to take part in an expedition this time?"

A simple inquiry, with an unspoken question embedded in it: Will you risk your silver-endowed avatar?

"Yes." This is the path the Tanji had laid for him. After coming so far, how could he choose not to follow?

"We only have the one lander," Riffan reminded them. "And *Argo*'s scheduled to visit Nara."

Urban scowled. That *was* a problem.

Pasha nodded. "That's true. And there is no way you're going to persuade the ship's company to delay the visit. The Narans are expecting us, and our delegation is eager to meet them."

She wasn't arguing against a planetary expedition, only pointing out the issues in a coldly logical way—issues he would need to address. But the solution was simple. "We're both part of that delegation," he told her. "We'll stay for the initial formalities, then take *Argo* down to Prakruti."

"And leave the delegation stranded at Nara?" Riffan asked in disbelief.

"Those who want to come with us can. The rest will want to spend time in the city."

"And if something goes wrong?" Pasha asked. "Urban, we won't be able to bring *Argo* back until we can synthesize fuel and a rocket booster. It took tens of days to do that on Verilotus."

"It's not ideal," he conceded. "But I need to do this."

"But do you need to do it *now*?"

"Yes." It felt that way.

Riffan spoke wistfully, "If we had another lander, it wouldn't be a problem."

But *Dragon* no longer had a cache of the rare elements needed to synthesize another ship. It was why Urban had never replaced the outriders lost at Verilotus.

Riffan must have been thinking similar thoughts. "You could convert *Khonsu* for atmospheric flight, like you did with *Fortuna*, at Verilotus."

Pasha rejected the idea before Urban could. "*Khonsu* is too small. We are *not* sending a one-person expedition."

"We have to take *Argo*," Urban concluded. "It'll be simple. We'll delay a day or two at Nara, and then we'll go planetside."

Riffan pursed his lips, shook his head. "I don't think it's going to be that simple."

Pasha looked doubtful too. "There's time," she said. "Let's see what else we can find on the planet."

Clemantine knew something was up the moment Urban came in and met her with his pirate smile. She laid her tablet on the tea table, arched an eyebrow, and asked him, "What?"

And then she listened in growing disbelief as he sat beside her and explained his scheme, his intention of treating Nara as nothing more than a stepping stone on the way to Prakruti.

"No," she said, when he had finished.

Confusion clouded his gaze. He cocked his head, not even angry yet. "No?"

"No, you can't commandeer *Argo* for your own adventure."

"It's not just my adventure. You want to go to Prakruti too. A lot of people do."

"Yes, and we will go. We may well be here at Tanjiri for years, for decades. There will be time to explore the planet. But Nara comes first."

"Yes, I know that. A diplomatic mission. You don't want me involved in that."

She allowed herself a slight smile. "*Sooth*. But you're no kid anymore. I can trust you not to ignite an incident. Right?"

His gaze cut away, and for just a moment lines of doubt flickered into existence on his brow.

"Urban?"

"We'll know once we reach Nara," he said softly. "If things go well, I'll take *Argo* planetside. If they don't, we withdraw, and *then* I take *Argo* planetside."

"Listen to yourself," she told him as a subterranean anger stirred, and began to surface. "You're obsessed with that shrine. You let some unknown thing inside your head, and now it's driving you."

Reciprocal anger flashed in his eyes. "This is what we came for, Clemantine. To unravel the unknown. To discover new ways and new life."

"Sooth. And we start with Nara. We take whatever time is needed there. Learn what we can. Learn how far we can trust these people. And later, when the time is right—"

He started to object. She stopped him with a finger gently pressed against his lips.

"*Patience*," she urged. "It may be just a few days—it may be longer. But when the time is right, we'll know. We'll get the consensus of the ship's company, and we'll visit Prakruti together."

Resentment curdled his gaze. He had given up his independence voluntarily and long ago, and still it remained hard for him to yield to the ideals of others. "This matters, Clemantine."

"Because you expect to find the entity there?"

"No. I expect to find the entity at Ezo. But that river shrine unlocks the way to Ezo. I know it does."

Her skin prickled at the intensity of his words. "Listen to yourself," she said again. "You're being played. How easy would it be for this entity to simply talk to you?"

A bitter smile. "I believe Ezo to be essentially benign. Nothing like Lezuri. But am I like Lezuri? Could I be? Hard to say, given the inherent chaos and the malleability of a human mind. I think that's why it's no easy journey. There are steps along the way. Choices to be made. And maybe, ultimately, a way to Ezo will open. And after that? The needle might not matter anymore. Because in the presence of the entity, I'll be able to learn everything I need to know."

"And lose yourself along the way?"

There, for a moment, she glimpsed in his frozen gaze an abyss of fear. "That's it, isn't it?" she demanded. "That's what's happening."

He faked an uncaring shrug. "It's all right. It's a risk I'm willing to take."

"Just like that?" And for a third time, she pleaded, "*Listen* to yourself. By the Unknown God! You don't even sound like you anymore. I wish Lezuri had never given you that needle. I think it's his revenge."

Ah, she'd stoked his anger now. That icy gaze, that curled lip.

"You'll get to Prakruti," she told him. A cold promise. "When the time is right."

The Cryptologist's ghost sequestered herself within a chamber of the library to consider the startling news of the river shrine.

A delicious mystery!

If it had been a random find, some ancient artifact that happened to exist close to one of the transect lines, she might have dismissed the discovery as irrelevant to her own quest for the entity.

But it had not been random, its placement in both time and space plainly deliberate. And Urban had recognized it! Responded to it! Riffan had reported him saying, half to himself, "It's the next step on a pilgrimage."

A pilgrimage? Such a strange concept! And Urban believed he was *meant* to visit the river shrine . . .

But why him? How had he known about it? What current of silver had shown that site to him and him alone?

Jolly had messaged her within minutes of the news getting out, as eager as ever to visit the planet: *We need to go with Urban to see this river shrine. It's important . . . do you feel it too?*

She did not.

In her own explorations, the Cryptologist had never sensed anything obviously of Prakruti, and never anything as simple, solid, and tangible as the river shrine—though she agreed it was important. It was a mystery, a puzzle, a clue.

So little is known about it!

This silent lament was answered by a soft, cynical, familiar chuckle. The Cryptologist smiled in greeting as the Bio-mechanic, always watching, manifested within the chamber.

Am I wrong? she thought. *Do you know something more about this river shrine?*

"No, but I know Urban, and *he* knows more than he is saying. He has not shared a submind with me, but I can see it in him. He knows enough to be afraid."

Though still eager to go . . .

"Fear wrestles with desire. He is afraid of Tanjiri's entity, but wants its knowledge so he can understand how to open the needle."

You think the river shrine is a means to that knowledge?

"It is the next step on a pilgrimage," he reminded her, again with that cynical chuckle. "Urban has embraced this idea . . . but shouldn't this be *your* pilgrimage? You are the one designed to solve the problem of the needle. You know far better the questions to ask and you are far more likely to understand the answer."

An electric excitement fluttered through her ghost, tempered by a puzzle: *Why hasn't Urban shared this knowledge?*

"Ah, an interesting question."

You have a theory? she asked.

"Only speculation. There is risk in this pilgrimage. Perhaps an unacceptable risk in the eyes of others."

They would try to stop him.

"That, or he means to gain knowledge only for himself."

This suggestion shocked her. Could it be true? Surely not! Urban would not hoard knowledge . . . not without good reason.

Did he have a reason?

It came to her then. "It's because the knowledge is dangerous," she said, so rattled she spoke the thought aloud. Jolly had worried over this very thing, suggesting, *Maybe it's not such a good idea to open the needle.*

"That must be why," she went on. "If the needle leads to a knowledge of the Blade, who could be trusted with that?"

The Bio-mechanic cocked his head, regarding her with his brooding eyes. "Should Urban be trusted with it?"

The Cryptologist found she had no ready answer to this question.

Pasha found no other structures on Prakruti—not in a review of all the video collected before her discovery of the river shrine, and not in any ongoing survey as the aerial-bots continued to map the world.

She half-expected the river shrine to disappear as abruptly as it had come into existence. But it did not, because they were meant to go there.

They were being teased, tempted into visiting. She could defy that intention by sending a more capable bot planetside, one with the strength and dexterity to deal with the river shrine's beautiful doors . . . but that would mean using precious resources to grow another cargo pod and then synthesizing fuel enough to get it to Prakruti. An expensive proposition and unlikely to win approval given that *Dragon*'s resources were already being consumed to fuel the lander. And anyway, she wanted to go herself.

So you win, she thought, unsure if she addressed Tanjiri's entity or Prakruti itself.

CHAPTER THIRTY-SIX

UNDER THE GUIDANCE of the Pilot, *Dragon* finally reached its destination, sliding into the gravitationally stable second Lagrange point in the Prakruti-Ezo system, a region more than sixty-one thousand kilometers beyond the living moon. The courser could maintain this position indefinitely, expending very little fuel, and could escape easily, when the time came to move on.

The two chameleon ships joined it there, all three vessels still aglow with slowly shifting rainbow lights. The Narans had assumed the chameleon ships belonged to *Dragon*. Urban found this to be an interesting error. It implied that, unlike their cousins at Volo's Landing, they had never seen such vessels before.

Well, the full truth would come out in time.

"So here we are," the Pilot growled. "Caught in Tanjiri's gravity well, our momentum traded away for curiosity."

"Curiosity fuels our existence," Urban countered. "It's a fair trade."

"You assume a continued existence."

"Why not? We're wanted here."

"You want to think so and you may be right. But for what purpose?"

"You said it yourself. For curiosity. Not just ours, but Ezo's too."

"I liked it better when we hunted Chenzeme coursers—when we understood the enemy, and the danger was well-mapped and clear."

"We have no enemy here," Urban answered, hoping it was true.

Jolly arrived in the warren wearing his lime-green skin suit. He had thought himself early, so it surprised him to find most of those who would be part of the delegation to Nara already there. Urban and Pasha and Shoran and Abby and Riffan and so many others. They crowded the warren with color—everyone wearing a skin suit of a unique hue—and the air buzzed with their excited conversations. He looked among them for the Cryptologist but did not see her. Anxiety descended on him.

She knew how important this was and she needed to come, while he needed to stay close to both her and Urban.

Clemantine called out over the buzz: "We're too many for a single transit bubble. Half can go now. The rest of us, when everyone is here."

Abby, with the lovely, familiar curves of her body wrapped in a lavender skin suit, glided up against Jolly, and caught his arm. "Let's go first—and I'll beat you to *Argo*'s front seat this time."

Jolly gritted his teeth in frustration, eager to go with her. Over her shoulder, he saw Urban disappear into the passage to the transit bubble—and his anxiety spiked. One way or another, Urban intended to visit the river shrine and when he did, Jolly meant to be with him. The Cryptologist needed to be there too.

Where was she? Had she lost track of time again in her silver wanderings? Clemantine was not going to wait for her. If she came late, she'd be left behind.

He wasn't alone in his worry. The Cryptologist herself messaged him: *You must rouse my avatar. Again, she is not responding to my messaging.*

A prickle on the back of his neck, knowing this voice belonged to her ghost and not her, and that they were not quite the same entity anymore. *All right*, he answered.

And then he told Abby, "There's something I need to do, but you go ahead."

Anger flashed in Abby's eyes though she said nothing, just pulled at the wall-weed and glided away, into the diminishing crowd.

Hurrying now, Jolly made his own way through the gathering, to the empty tunnel beyond.

The Cryptologist had taken the farthest chamber in the warren for her own. The chamber unsealed as he arrived, its membrane dilating. An empty skin suit, pale-pink, drifted at its center while the Cryptologist lay at the back of the chamber, wrapped up in tendrils of faintly glowing wall-weed, the *ha* sparkling on her hands. In one hand, she held the case that contained the needle.

"Hey!" Jolly called, gliding into the little chamber. He shook her shoulder. "You need to come back now." He hurried to pull the clinging wall-weed off her, exposing her pale skin to the chill of the air. "Get your skin suit on. It's time to go."

Her eyes opened and for a few seconds she looked at him without recognition. Then her eyes flared in surprise. "We are late."

"Yes."

She kicked off the wall, releasing the needle's case, leaving it to drift as she dove for her skin suit. The suit recognized her and unfurled, its fabric rippling as it reoriented, and then folded around her.

Jolly grabbed the drifting needle case. Quickly—he hoped the Cryptologist wasn't looking—he opened it. A glance assured him the needle was inside.

"I will take it now," she said, holding out a gloved hand.

"Sure." He passed it to her. Watched her slide it into a thigh pocket.

"We need to stay with Urban," he reminded her. "And go with him to the river shrine."

"Has he found a way to reach the river shrine?"

"No, but he will."

"Jolly, I do not understand the importance of this structure."

Jolly hesitated, wondering why that was. "But you know it is important?"

"I suspect it is. I suspect there is knowledge to be found there. I suspect Urban knows the nature of this knowledge but does not trust us with it." Then she added, almost despairing, "But I was made for this. I *need* to know."

"I'm sorry," Jolly whispered.

He knew the reason for Urban's silence. He could have told her:

It's because only one of us will be admitted to Ezo—and Urban means to be the one who goes. But he did not.

He hadn't told her—he hadn't told anyone, not even Urban—that he too had known of the river shrine before Pasha found it. Wailoa had shown it to him, and he felt sure Wailoa had shown it to Urban too.

He took the Cryptologist's hand. "Come on," he pleaded. "You'll figure it all out later. Right now, we need to go."

Clemantine waited in an otherwise empty warren for Jolly to reappear. The others had already squeezed into the second transit bubble. She messaged Urban, continuing an earlier debate: *You see? The Cryptologist is not interested in this delegation. She cares nothing for our diplomatic goals, and she's unpredictable. Better to leave her behind than to risk an incident.*

Give them another minute, Urban urged. *Jolly wants her to come. I don't know why. But he'll watch her. He'll keep her out of trouble.*

Urban had always indulged the kid. Somewhere on Verilotus he'd effectively adopted Jolly as a beloved younger brother. Clemantine was fond of him too, but she didn't let that cloud her judgment. She said, *This is not an auspicious start.*

Irritated now, Urban said, *I'll watch her, then. Will that make you happy?*

Clemantine did not say it aloud, only asked herself, *And who will watch you?*

The Cryptologist darted into sight wearing her pink skin suit, hood down, holding hands with Jolly.

Clemantine met them with a steely glare. "If the two of you prefer to stay behind—"

Jolly cut her off. "No. You know we want to go." He turned to the Cryptologist. "Don't mess this up. We *need* to go."

"Yes, I am here."

She spoke quietly, as if distracted, as if her thoughts still wandered within a maze of silver.

"Stay present," Clemantine warned her. "And don't say anything to offend our hosts. Remember, the purpose of this expedition is to establish a good relationship with the Narans. If things go well, we may decide to stay with them for some long time."

The Cryptologist responded to this with a disinterested shrug. "It's not the Narans—"

"Hey, come on," Jolly urged, cutting her off before she could say more, and nudging her into the passage that led to the waiting transit bubble. He turned back to whisper to Clemantine, "Don't worry. She'll do okay."

It would be nice to believe that.

Jolly looked anxiously around *Argo*'s interior, modified since the return from Volo's Landing with nested tiers of acceleration couches to accommodate the full delegation. The couches upfront looked occupied. He hoped Abby had gotten her coveted seat.

He turned to the Cryptologist. Her eyes looked brighter now, more focused. "Don't go off into the silver again," he whispered to her. "Remember what Clemantine said and stay present."

"The Narans lack curiosity," the Cryptologist declared without whispering at all. She continued in sharp-edged syllables, "They have not visited Prakruti after their sole expedition, *five hundred twenty-one* years ago and did not resume an investigation of Ezo after their initial failure. It is most likely they know nothing of importance. Even so, I am here to learn—not to hide what I learn."

Startled, he hesitated, but then realized she was talking about Urban, not him. "You're angry again, aren't you?" he whispered.

She narrowed her eyes, cocked her head as she considered the question. "Yes, I think I am."

Jolly turned at a tap against his shoulder. He saw Pasha secured within a couch by a rapidly thickening gel cocoon. As her hand disappeared into the cocoon's tendrils she said, "Both of you should secure a seat now, before Clemantine decides it's better to leave you behind."

Good advice.

Jolly pulled himself into the empty couch above Pasha, feeling a little angry too. Why did the Cryptologist have to be so difficult?

She used to find joy in everything new. He messaged his resentment: *You have changed.

*I am still changing.

As a gel cocoon unfurled around him, he turned his head to look across the aisle. The Cryptologist had slipped into a seat on the lowest tier. She held the needle in its open case, studying it, stroking it with her index finger. Then she closed the case, her fingers tight around it as the gel enfolded them.

She turned her head to look at Jolly. *I do not want to change too much, but to understand the needle, I think I must.

He tried to reassure her: *No, it'll be all right. Though that seemed doubtful, no matter how events played out.

The gel closed over his head. It induced his metabolism to slow, drawing him down into a light hibernation, rather than the dreaded cold sleep.

If she answered, he did not hear it.

CHAPTER THIRTY-SEVEN

THE CELESTIAL CITY loomed large. Its two conical sections pointed at one another across a gulf of space spanned by a tether that linked them in majestic rotation around their shared center of gravity. Where sunlight struck, each massive cone gleamed mostly blue like an ocean under a bright morning sky—a lovely color marbled with lacy green strands suggestive of algae blooms. No windows or docking ports or artificial lights interrupted that oceanic bliss, and utter darkness wrapped Nara's nightside.

The tether too displayed no artificial lights. Black in color, it had to be imagined rather than seen, even where sunlight touched it. The docking cylinder at the tether's rotational midpoint was equally obscure, until a hangar opened, spilling visible light into the void and igniting a murmur of conversation aboard *Argo*.

Here we go, Clemantine thought. A web of gel still bound her to her couch but like the rest of the delegation she was awake and eager to move ahead. She watched the hangar closely.

"There they are!" Riffan called out from across the aisle as three figures appeared within that orifice of light. Seen through the airless vacuum of space they appeared crisply detailed though the distance made them tiny. One blue, one pale green, and the other amber, each with a kisheer veiling mouth and nose. They stayed only long enough to launch three pods like salt grains.

Shoran said, "Let's hope we pass inspection!"

The Narans, nervous about molecular contamination, had insisted on sending bots to survey *Argo*'s interior before allowing

NEEDLE   269

the Dragoneers to dock. Clemantine had agreed, assuring them
they would find nothing threatening.

She signaled *Argo* to open the hatch, allowing the bots to
enter through the gel membrane. Two came in: a slug that swiftly
crawled *Argo*'s surfaces—sampling skin and skin suits too—and
one that spread white butterfly wings, fluttering everywhere as it
assessed the air. The third bot remained outside, exploring the hull
and relaying the findings of all three to Nara.

With the bots aboard, Clemantine had to assume any vocalized
conversation would be heard by the Narans, so she spoke over the
team channel instead. *Urban? Any surprises?*

He had welcomed the inspection because the presence of the
bots allowed a counter-assessment of the Narans' Makers. *No surprises. It's what I predicted. Their Makers are ancient and unremarkable. I
doubt the collection has evolved at all since they left Sakura.*

That's good.

It meant the Narans had been truthful when they said they'd
lived peacefully, and undisturbed by outside threats for the past
six centuries. Why change, when you've lost all expectation of
encountering a hostile force?

The bots completed their survey and *Argo* was granted permission to proceed. A few minutes later the little landing craft slipped
into the empty hangar. Its docking hooks extended, clamping tight
against recessed bars in the deck, ensuring *Argo* would not drift—
a necessary precaution given the very slight centripetal force this
close to Nara's center of rotation.

The hangar door closed. A clean and breathable atmosphere
rushed out to surround *Argo*, and then a web of crawl lines
drifted into place. Next, a wide interior door slid open, admitting a contingent of four Narans in a spectrum of colors. Like
their cousins at Volo's Landing, they wore no clothing over
their integuments of fine, ceramic-hard scales, but these people
indulged in decoration, wearing greaves, bracers, epaulets, and
head bands shimmering in a multitude of patterns and hues,
along with feathery plumes and loops and spirals of sparkling
beads.

Clemantine smiled to herself. In her silver skin suit she felt quite plain, but it was better that way, better not to intimidate.

She met Riffan by the gel membrane as *Argo's* outer door opened. Together, they would lead the delegation. "Ready?" she asked him aloud.

He smiled—"Absolutely!"—an anthropologist, eager to get to work.

One step closer, Urban thought as he followed Jolly through *Argo's* gel membrane into the hangar's startlingly cold atmosphere. Wisps of evanescent mist condensed from his exhaled breath as he clung to a crawl line, one of twelve Dragoneers adrift behind Riffan and Clemantine. Even with the spectrum of colors of their collected skin suits, they were a dull crowd compared to the riotously decorated Narans.

Jolly floated beside him, taking in everything with wide eyes. *Except for those decorations, they look just like the Sakurans at Volo's Landing*, he said in a silent message to Urban.

   They are the same.

   No. These Narans are not angry.

   That might change when we tell them about their kin.

Urban said it jokingly, though he felt sure the news would shock these people. He did not believe either faction had told the full, true story of their parting. At Volo's Landing, generations separated the current population from those who had witnessed the split. The story Taddeus had told was the story he'd been taught. But Urban felt sure that at Nara, founders remained who remembered the true events, and who might be unhappy to learn that the conflict with their kin was not quite over.

The delegation of Narans met their guests with words of welcome. They did not use any translation device. They did not need one, because they'd already learned the language of the Dragoneers. Introductions were made.

Urban's guess about surviving founders was immediately confirmed in the person of Lyra Li Sital. She served as chief of the city's governing council, and was an original immigrant from

Sakura. She had serious gray eyes that echoed the swirling gray markings lightening the deep purple of her integument, and she wore many silver and white beads on her arms and around her shoulders. Three white plumes bobbing from the back of her headband exaggerated an already considerable height. She looked carefully at each Dragoneer as Clemantine named them, and Urban had no doubt she memorized every one.

The other three were council members—Tsumona Wakanaki, Junyo Besiba, and Luk Li Mithki. All had been born at Nara.

With the initial greetings done, Tsumona Wakanaki took charge. He was a strongly built man with a bold smile, blue eyes, and a black integument marked by spiral lines of bright bioluminescent light. "Come!" he declared. "Our people are eager to meet you and to show you the world we've built."

With the initial formalities over, the Dragoneers pushed forward, eager to mingle with the Narans and talk with them. But Urban hung back, watching, listening, keeping an eye on Jolly and the Cryptologist.

He noticed Pasha as he approached the hangar door. Was she waiting for him? Apparently she was. Eyeing him with a mixture of curiosity and suspicion, she asked softly, "Planning already?"

"Too early for that," he answered in the same low tone.

"Whenever it happens, I'm part of it," she reminded him.

"It's Clemantine you need to convince. Not me."

"Unless you decide to leave early?"

"No. That's not how I want it to happen."

Up ahead, Tsumona Wakanaki gestured with his long fingers at a closed hangar door. "Here is where we house our planetary survey vessel. And up ahead, in this next hangar, is the original shuttle that brought us from the outer system." Using his prehensile toes to stabilize himself in the microgravity, he turned to look back at the delegation. "We are alone here at Tanjiri with no one to visit, so these vessels sit until they are needed. They will be needed someday. We are growing."

Soon after that, they arrived at a transit platform, where two long cars waited with open doors. Pasha slipped away through the crowd, doubtlessly intending to join Clemantine. Urban caught up with Jolly and the Cryptologist. He messaged them both: *Stay close to me.*

Do you sense something? the Cryptologist asked with sharp interest.

No, there's no silver here, but I want to know what you think of things. Besides, he'd told Clemantine he'd watch her.

The Cryptologist said, *I think we will find nothing worthwhile here and that we should move on to the planet.*

I agree, but it's not possible yet. Soon, though. As soon as we can manage it.

The first car had filled, so they boarded the second one. Inside, a narrow aisle divided two columns of single seats, with a transparent canopy arching overhead. Urban scanned faces. He saw Shoran, Alkimbra, Abby, Dalisay. Everyone else would be in the first car. He waved Jolly and the Cryptologist ahead of him, and then drifted into one of the last open seats. A gel harness emerged to secure him.

One of the Narans, Luk Li Mithki, boarded last, taking the seat across from Urban. His beads and feathered gauntlets shimmered and a nervous rustle enlivened his green and gold kisheer as he leaned toward Urban and asked, "It is your ship, isn't it? You are the one who captured it? I have been fascinated by the story of its origin."

"It was mine. It's ours now." Urban moved his head, indicating the other Dragoneers. "For as long as they want to stay with the expedition."

"Does anyone ever choose not to stay?"

Four people *had* left the expedition at Verilotus, but the ship's company had agreed not to reveal the existence of that system. So Urban chose his words carefully. "It could happen, though everyone who came with me came out of curiosity to see what is left of the known worlds—and we have only just begun."

Luk Li Mithki nodded. "I admire both your courage and your determination to continue on. Though I had wondered, given the ancient form of your people so well-adapted to planetary life, if you might be considering making a home on beautiful Prakruti."

Urban could not tell, either from Luk Li Mithki's tone or his expression, if that possibility roused in him hope, or concern. He answered honestly. "I mean to visit Prakruti, but not to live there. We will eventually continue on. There is so much left to see."

This drew a slight smile. "I am sorry to tell you that Prakruti is not . . . truly welcoming. It is a dangerous world. Very wild. Filled with ravenous beasts and best studied from afar. We do not go to Prakruti."

A chime sounded. The car began to move. Within seconds it exited the docking cylinder, following its track into airless space where it rapidly accelerated. Urban glimpsed Prakruti overhead, but it was Nara that seized his attention. From this perspective—racing along the tether toward the peak of one of the city's conical sections, it looked (and felt) as if the car was plunging bow-first toward a vast blue ocean.

The city's rotation substituted for gravity. With every second that passed, its effect grew stronger. Urban hung in his gel harness, feeling himself growing heavier, more than on *Dragon*'s gee deck—but still much less than the artificial gravity at the surface of Verilotus.

Then the car braked and he felt heavier still. Darkness abruptly enfolded them as they slid into a tunnel. Moving slowly now . . .

A pause.

He felt the car rotate, ninety degrees until it lay horizontal to the pull of Nara's pseudo-gravity. Then the car moved again, emerging into a brightly lit transit station, coming to a stop behind the first car, alongside a platform where many more Narans waited to greet them.

On the team channel, a message from Clementine: *It's done. I told Lyra Li Sital the basic facts about Volo's Landing. And I think it's going to be okay.*

CHAPTER THIRTY-EIGHT

NEWS OF VOLO'S Landing cut the official tour short, leading the four council members to withdraw along with Clemantine and Riffan to discuss the details of the situation. The rest of the Dragoneers found themselves in the hands of an enthusiastic population unconcerned with political maneuvering.

"Quite an improvement," Pasha whispered to the historian, Alkimbra.

He nodded, giving her a wink and a knowing smile before turning to answer a question from one of the hundreds of Narans who'd gradually mingled with the Dragoneers and their official guides.

They walked in easy gravity through the High District's spiral corridor, a wide passage bright with colorful murals on one side and windows on the other. The windows looked out on a glass forest, reminiscent of the forest at Volo's Landing but far more diverse. So far, Pasha had counted thirty-eight different varieties of trees, distinguished by branching patterns, the texture of their trunks, leaf shape, and the details of glassy flowers.

No monochrome forest this! Colors both subtle and bright combined into a carnival of vacuum-adapted vegetation glinting under piped-in sunlight. Small animate forms, reminiscent of caterpillars, beetles, and spiders, crawled and flitted amid the vegetation, more brightly colored than the plants. Pasha watched them, ignoring the crowd murmur around her as she strove to understand if they were bots or vacuum-adapted creatures with life cycles contributing to this unique habitat.

A Naran joined her at the window, a man with dark thoughtful eyes and gentle features, his integument like a shallow sunlit sea with scales randomly colored azure and warm green. His gray kisheer rippled nervously at his shoulders.

"Watch the snake," he said softly. "There, among that glitter of pink flowers."

Pasha followed the direction of his gaze. It took several seconds for her to spot the creature as it moved with a predator's slow caution, the color of its scales changing to match the leaves and flowers it passed. Moments later it struck, far too fast for anything to evade. It seized a glassy green caterpillar in its toothless jaws, cracking the little creature, then extruding a membrane to capture a crystallizing cloud of green fluid.

"Everything in the High District forest is an invented species," the Naran said. "We look on it as both an art project and an intellectual challenge to create a self-sustaining ecosystem." He smiled. "We are not there yet."

Every Naran Pasha had met so far had spoken to her in her own native tongue. *Our library recognized your language*, she'd been told when she'd asked about it. *It was once common and many scholars already knew it. The rest of us have done our best to learn. That is the duty of the host.*

Pasha had learned to speak their language too, during the long sunward voyage. But she preferred her own.

"The forest is beautiful," she said and she meant it. "Fascinating."

"I hoped you might think so." A rosy flush tinted the seascape of his cheeks. "I saw your bio. You are an exobiologist. And while these are not alien lifeforms, perhaps they . . . suggest possibilities."

"Indeed," she answered, intrigued. "And you are?"

"Ah, excuse me. I'm Nioro Kwan—and you and your people are the most exciting thing to happen here . . . well, since the beginning, I suspect. Certainly in my lifetime. When I first sighted your great ship—"

"Was it you?"

"Yes."

"Then you are a scientist too."

"Well, it's true I've studied many things."

"But when did you find our ship? We kept messaging the city. But you were all so silent, we wondered if anyone was alive here."

She looked at him questioningly and his flush deepened. Then his gaze cut away. Pasha didn't know what to make of it.

"Ah, we should move on," he said. "Keep up with the group."

She looked around to find that turn of the corridor nearly empty. So she set off with Nioro to catch up with the parade of Dragoneers and Narans.

"Will you tell me?" she pressed.

Nioro's kisheer fluttered. Softly, as if in apology, he said, "Time has made us complacent."

Pasha cocked her head, confused, wondering if there was a language issue or some odd cultural resistance.

But then Nioro tried to explain. "It's just that for so long there was nothing out there." He gestured vaguely at the corridor's walls, at its ceiling, his long fingers moving with a restless wave-like motion. "I am young, but I've studied history. I've spoken to founders. There was a time when a close watch was kept on the surrounding system. But no activity was ever observed, and no debris ever drifted in from the ruins. It felt like we were alone." His voice dropped to little more than a whisper. "I think the founders wanted to believe that—that we were *safely* alone. So we stopped looking, a long time ago."

"And stopped listening?" Pasha asked as they rejoined the fringe of the crowd, still following the spiral corridor down past the vacuum forest.

"I'm not sure we ever listened."

A few more paces passed in silence before Pasha nudged, wanting more: "But you saw us, Nioro."

A slight smile. "I am known for my eccentric habits. The old orbiting telescopes were recycled to feed the expansion of the city, but I was able to manufacture a small device. Viewing from the docking hub is excellent, with patience." A wider smile. "There was near panic when I reported the lights of your fleet . . . but we recovered."

Urban had successfully eluded any political role, leaving it to Clemantine and Riffan to meet with the Naran council and answer whatever questions they had about their cousins at Volo's Landing. But that victory did not leave him free. As the official tour dissolved and Dragoneers drifted off with new friends made among the Narans, he kept his promise to Clemantine and, along with Jolly, he stayed close to the Cryptologist.

Clemantine worried she would cause an incident with their hosts. Urban worried she would find a way to Prakruti before he did. The Cryptologist was smart, clever, determined. She had developed her own interface with the silver. And she was utterly obsessed with solving the puzzle of the needle. If she knew what he knew, it would be a race to the river shrine.

But her lack of interest in the Narans was not feigned. When a Naran engineer offered to show them a documentary detailing the construction of the city, Urban was eager to experience it—but the Cryptologist did not care. She looked from Urban to the engineer and back again, before announcing, "I do not require further information on your city. I do request access to your local library."

For a moment, the engineer could only stare in open-mouthed confusion.

"She's a scholar," Urban said quickly.

"A historian," Jolly added to ease the awkward moment.

"Of course, I should have asked," the engineer said, striving to be polite. "All three of you, then?"

"Yes," Urban said, keenly curious now that the possibility presented itself. At some point, if all went well, there would be the traditional exchange of libraries with the Narans. But Urban was happy to embrace the offer of an early look.

The engineer acknowledged this with a short nod and a distressed smile. "I'll generate tablets for you. I hope that's all right. I know it's simpler to ghost, but security protocols haven't been lifted yet, so you're not authorized for full network access."

"Tablets will be fine," Urban assured him.

That's how he ended up spending the afternoon on a patio in a little pocket park with tiny birds flitting among the branches of a circle of carefully groomed trees. Not all that different from an afternoon on *Dragon*'s gee deck. Ironic—*(frustrating!)*—given there was a whole unknown city to explore.

After an hour, Abby and Mikael found them there. Flush with excitement, Abby introduced the Naran friends she'd made. "This city, it's just amazing," she enthused. "And now we're going to a concert. You all should come."

The temptation was there, but no way was Urban going to persuade the Cryptologist. She didn't even glance up from her tablet to acknowledge the offer. But to Urban's surprise, Jolly put his tablet aside and humbly asked, "Is it all right?"

Urban sighed. "Sure, go ahead."

"But message me, okay, if anything interesting happens?"

Urban eyed the Cryptologist. "*Right.*"

"No, really," Jolly insisted, sounding oddly anxious about it. "I want to be with Abby for a little while more. But message me, if anything happens."

"I'll message you," Urban said. "Now go. Have fun."

As the afternoon passed, the frustration of missing out grew fierce. Time and again, Urban nearly convinced himself to abandon the Cryptologist, to leave her to her studies. But always, he hesitated long enough for her to surface from her research, roused for no reason Urban could discern other than to complain in a soft contemptuous voice, "These Narans! They lack curiosity." She said it as if it was the greatest fault anyone could display—and for a time, Urban agreed with her.

Indulging his own remorseless curiosity, he wandered through the Narans' library, though he focused mostly on two topics: the schism between Nara and Volo's Landing, and the Narans' observations of Prakruti and Ezo. It was easy enough to locate material on both subjects, though what he found disappointed him. Bland and unemotional accounts of the schism revealed little more than what he'd already been told. And there was only an occasional entry on Prakruti, and almost nothing on Ezo. It was as if, after an initial look, the Narans had given no further thought to their planetary neighbors.

Only as the hours passed did Urban begin to suspect the library's records were not just sparse, but that they were deliberately incomplete. And gradually, he came to understand that the Narans had done to him what he'd done to their cousins at Volo's Landing. They'd censored their library, limiting what it revealed.

Nioro possessed an alien beauty, but he had a familiar mind—a scientist's mind—and to her delight Pasha found they were much alike in the way they viewed the world: its structures, its details, its mechanisms. All that afternoon, she hardly noticed the passage of time as she explored the High District in his company. At Nioro's invitation, she even sealed up her skin suit and ventured with him into the vacuum forest.

After that, they hopped on a transit car, riding it along the tether that linked High District to Low District, and on the way, Pasha reveled at the sight of Prakruti. Seen through the car's transparent canopy, it appeared as a beautiful crescent, aglow with the blue and green colors of life.

"How often do your people visit Prakruti?" she asked Nioro.

A little ripple of tension rolled through his kisheer. "No, we don't visit Prakruti."

"Never?"

"Not since the first planetary survey," Nioro answered, his voice flat, his words reluctant. A little shrug set his kisheer fluttering again. "The council doesn't like risk."

"But—"

She caught herself, truncating her objection as the car slid into darkness, and then into the Low District's brightly lit transit station.

What had she meant to say? Just that there was a whole world to be explored, that curiosity demanded it, that one long-ago survey could not be sufficient to explain Prakruti, and that whatever risk there was planetside could be mitigated.

But the topic of Prakruti clearly unsettled Nioro. His terse answers contrasted sharply with the detailed discussions they had enjoyed on every other topic—a deficiency that seized her interest.

But she restrained herself—*though it wasn't easy!*—knowing some puzzles were best solved by finesse.

As the car's door opened, Nioro spoke with renewed enthusiasm. "Come, Pasha. There are people here you'll want to meet, and they're eager to meet you."

He wasn't wrong. Nioro introduced her to so many people, she had to use her atrium to record all their names. Many were scientists, others historians, and some were media people. All asked questions, leaving Pasha little chance of asking questions of her own. But she answered freely, telling them about Volo's Landing, *Dragon*'s long voyage, her life before that at Deception Well, the scourge of Chenzeme warships, and the ominous silence of every other once-settled world on the far frontier of human expansion.

So easy to fold centuries into a few words.

But like the other Dragoneers, she refrained from the whole truth, making no mention of *Griffin*, Lezuri, or Verilotus. And she did not correct the Narans'—and Nioro's—belief that the two chameleon ships escorting *Dragon* belonged to the courser. Indeed, few but Nioro seemed aware the little vessels existed at all.

In all these discussions, Pasha heard almost no mention of Prakruti. It was as if that beautiful world existed outside the mental landscape of the Narans, even though its reality confronted them every time they traveled between the districts.

An interesting puzzle indeed.

On the way back to the High District, they stopped briefly at the docking hub. She sealed up her skin suit again and followed him into a dark, airless, and otherwise empty hangar, where he showed her his simple telescope. The hangar looked outward, with no view of Prakruti.

They'd linked their communications when they'd visited the vacuum forest, so she was able to ask, *Nioro, do you study the planet too?*

Yes, often. His kisheer was engaged, veiling his mouth and nose and ears. Hard to be sure in the dark, but she thought a little flutter ran through it. And yet he expanded on his answer. *For many years, I've observed the changing of the seasons, the cycling of life. That fascinates me! I'm set up on this side now, because that allows me to observe your ship.*

Interesting that he was willing to talk about observing Prakruti, but not about visiting it. Still, Pasha held her questions, resolving to compare notes with others in the delegation, before she pressed for answers.

A community feast occupied the evening, and though she caught Clemantine's eye, the constant chatter of the Narans precluded any private conversation. She looked for other Dragoneers among the crowd and quickly picked out Tarnya, Mikael, Kona, Riffan . . . most of the delegation. But not Urban. She didn't see him anywhere. Nor the Cryptologist.

This absence induced a nasty suspicion that Urban had found a way planetside . . .

No. Impossible.

But if he had, would he remember his promise to her, that she would be part of the first expedition?

While smiling blankly at a Naran who was proudly explaining the cultural origin of a colorful bean paste dish, she sent a terse message to Urban. *Where are you?*

To her relief, his answer came quickly, though in terse words. *We've been assigned a suite of rooms to use. I'm on my way there.*

She grimaced, all too familiar with his moods. Clearly something had aggravated him—and that annoyed her, because she wanted to talk with him about Prakruti, about the Narans' attitude toward the world, and about the prospect of visiting it. She dared to hope that visit would come soon.

The Narans were so different from their cousins at Volo's Landing that Pasha could not imagine being in any danger from them. And that meant *Argo* did not have to stand by, ready to evacuate the Dragoneers if something went wrong. The landing ship could be used to visit the river shrine instead.

But she didn't say any of that. Better to see him and gauge the situation. So all she said was, *I'll join you.*

With many smiles and pleas of exhaustion, Pasha extricated herself from the gathering and emerged alone into the spiral corridor. The quiet there came as a relief. Pausing beside a window that overlooked the vacuum forest, she checked a short queue of non-urgent messages that had arrived during the afternoon. At the top of the list, she found what she was looking for: a map to the Dragoneers' suite.

She scanned the other messages. Most were just happy chatter suggesting places to visit. The last one though, in Clemantine's voice, dashed Pasha's nascent hope of an early visit to Prakruti: *Now that they know we're welcome here, the rest of the ship's company is eager to visit Nara. Reply if you have any concerns or objections to remaining here without the landing ship. Otherwise,* Argo *will be returning to* Dragon *to pick them up.*

"Damn," Pasha whispered in a surge of disappointment. But then she chided herself for not expecting this. Of course the rest of the ship's company would want to visit Nara. A cynical chuckle followed. Easy to guess now the cause of Urban's ire.

It took her less than a minute to reach the suite. Looking around, she guessed it had been re-engineered just for them, with numerous small bedrooms around a sprawling living area furnished with couches and cushy chairs, and three fabricators.

Urban wasn't even there yet, and neither was anyone else. Giving into fatigue, she collapsed into a cushy chair. But she had only a moment's quiet rest before the door opened, admitting Urban, along with Jolly and the Cryptologist.

Urban's dark scowl found Pasha. "You heard about *Argo*?"

"I have. It'll be another ten-day, at least, before we can go planetside."

"Yeah." He dropped into an adjacent chair. "And in the meantime, we're isolated here. Without *Argo* to relay, I can't even synchronize subminds with my self on the high bridge."

That would definitely irritate him. With a hint of smug, Pasha said, "I didn't leave an active ghost on *Dragon*."

A sullen sigh from Urban.

"Oh, come on," she said, overlooking her own disappointment. "It's not as if there's nothing to do here, nothing to learn."

Jolly returned from the fabricators with a tall drink in hand, looking as grim as Urban. He told Pasha, "The Narans are hiding something from us, something about Prakruti. Urban figured out their library records are incomplete."

Pasha sat up straighter. "Their library? You got access to it? Oh, I should have asked Nioro about that."

The Cryptologist had been following this exchange with mild interest, but now she leaned in and asked with urgency, "You know of Nioro? Nioro Kwan?"

Pasha hesitated, surprised the Cryptologist had heard of him, and wondering at her interest. "Yes, Nioro Kwan. I spent the day with him. He's a fascinating man, a natural scientist, interested in everything. Nioro is the one who sighted us through his telescope and ... *hey*—"

She turned to look at Urban. "Nioro was hiding something about Prakruti too. I know he was. I didn't press him on it, but the only topic he didn't want to discuss was why the Narans never visit Prakruti." She rose from her chair, feeling offended, even betrayed, by her Naran friend. "We need to ask him what the library is hiding."

This brought a bright smile to the Cryptologist. "Yes, we must talk to him."

"Do you think he *will* talk?" Urban asked as he too stood up.

Pasha considered it. "Maybe. He's a scientist. He likes to share information—and I don't think he's comfortable keeping secrets. Anyway, we need to know. If there's some hidden hazard here, we have a duty to uncover it, before the rest of the ship's company arrives."

"You know where he is?" Urban asked.

"He said he was going back out to the docking hub to use his telescope. I could message him. Ask if he's still there."

"No. Better to surprise him. It might throw him off balance. He'll be less guarded that way."

CHAPTER THIRTY-NINE

IT WAS LATE in the city's night, and no one was about when the four of them caught a transit car out to the docking hub. Urban emerged first onto the platform, holding on to a hand line to steady himself in the microgravity as he looked around.

Though the platform was brightly lit, it had a late-night air of abandonment. The only activity: the thin green membrane of a jelly robot rippling across a wall, cleaning as it went.

Pasha drifted past him. "It was busy here earlier, with the Narans getting their old shuttle ready. You know they're planning an immediate expedition to Volo's Landing?"

"I heard."

She led them past an open hangar, where lights shone down on an old but well-kept vessel, the very one that had brought Nara's founding generation from Volo's Landing. No one was there, though.

The Cryptologist lingered, looking the shuttle over a little too long.

Urban leaned close and whispered, "Nothing to endanger the fleet, right?"

She looked up at him with an innocent smile, and moved on. But at the next hangar she paused again to study a status panel alight with a script Urban could not read. He pinged *Argo* for a translation, but the lander was already too far away.

Pasha looked back, noticed his interest, and said, "That hangar houses the little planetary survey vessel. Its name means 'bean pod.' I think it's a joke on the ship's small size."

Urban had read about the survey vessel in the library. "It's a two-person craft."

"Right. Too small for our needs."

Was it? Or was it just big enough?

He kept this thought to himself as they went on, past the closed door of *Argo*'s empty hangar, to a fourth hangar, also closed, though its walk-in door was sealed with only a gel membrane.

Pasha said, "He must be here, or the solid door would be closed." Then she added, "Hoods up. It's not pressurized inside."

Urban issued the command to his skin suit, then followed Pasha through the membrane, emerging into a black cavern that looked out on a hundred thousand stars. Vertigo hit. He could not see to grip and the microgravity was too weak to orient him. Fear bit deep as he imagined drifting helplessly out into that blaze of ancient light.

Urban? Jolly whispered, dread encapsulated in the syllables.

Look for a hand line, Urban told him. Eyes adjusting now, perceiving a web of lines that glowed faint red. One line drifting closer. But that was an illusion. The motion was his.

He seized the hand line and felt solid again, anchored. *Jolly, you secure?*

I'm good.

And the Cryptologist?

I am secure, she answered.

Pasha, you might have warned us.

It needs to be dark when he's using the telescope. I thought you knew that.

How would I know? I never handled a telescope before.

Not manually.

Well, you're secure now. Stand by, and I'll set up communications.

Urban could now see Nioro across the hangar: a long, slim figure, silhouetted against the stars, with a device beside him that must be the telescope.

After an exchange of electronic handshakes, Nioro spoke, sounding surprised and a little concerned at the unannounced visit. *Welcome. Did you . . . come to see the telescope?*

The Cryptologist answered before Urban could. *We are here to question you about the validity of the library's records regarding Prakruti and Ezo.

Pasha turned back, sounding scandalized. *Let me talk!

*It's true, though, Urban said, gesturing at Pasha to keep moving. He followed her, out along a hand line toward the hangar's edge where darkness yielded to a sea of blazing stars. *That's why we're here.

Nioro moved closer to meet them. Still a silhouette, his long-fingered hand reached out to touch Urban's shoulder in the same companionable gesture so common among the people of Volo's Landing. He said, *You're the master of the great ship, the one who originally captured it. I hoped I'd have a chance to meet you.

Urban didn't think it was just flattery, or an attempt to avoid discussing Prakruti. No, he heard awe in Nioro's voice, and gauged he might make use of that. *Yes. Dragon was an enemy vessel, but it's mine now.

*I've studied it through my scope. There's nothing at all like it in the library.

*No, there wouldn't be.

*Because it's alien.

*Yes.

Nioro spoke with a sense of wonder. *So there are intelligent beings out there, besides us.

*There were others, but none still living that I ever found. Ships like Dragon are all that's left—intelligent weapons that far outlived their creators.

*Ah, so many wonders to unravel. He turned to take in Jolly and the Cryptologist, though surely he could see only shadows. *I'm sorry you've encountered an issue with our library. Caution on the part of our council, no doubt. I am looking forward to the eventual exchange of libraries. I know I'll be busy for years, studying yours.

Time to re-center the dialog. Urban said, *We understand Ezo is unapproachable. But there seems to be a veil of secrecy around Prakruti too. Something about that world concerns the council. Luk Li Mithki made a point of telling me it was best studied from afar. Pasha suggested you might be able to tell us more.

Nioro had been adrift, but now his silhouette slowly sank until his feet touched the deck. He spoke carefully, as if feeling his way through a verbal maze. *There are . . . uncertainties.

*Such as?

*Did Luk tell you that Prakruti is a wild planet?

*Yes, he used that term.

*Well, it's not quite right. Prakruti isn't wild in the true sense of the word. It's more a tended wilderness. A wild garden. This is not general knowledge and I know the council would prefer I didn't speak of it . . . but you mean to visit Prakruti, don't you?

Pasha answered this. *It's true. We do. We're here to explore, Nioro.

*I understand, and I envy you.

Urban pressed for details. *What do you know, Nioro? Why call Prakruti a garden?

He answered, *It's nothing certain, but there are suggestive details . . . like seasonal fires that begin to burn without any hint of lightning or lava, that rejuvenate forest undergrowth or maintain open grassland. And it's common to see estuaries laced with channels and sloughs that shift inexplicably, season by season, to keep a balance between marshland and open water. And in the polar regions, irregular algae blooms appear to be an effective control against the spread of the ice caps.

Pasha spoke softly, *But no one's there. Right?

Nioro hesitated. *Well . . . we don't really know. I mean, there must be something. A system of bots? That's my suspicion. Probably organic, operating intermittently so the original survey missed them. And too small for my telescope to pick out past all the atmospheric distortions.

*I have read about you and I have read your writings, the Cryptologist declared. *You are eager to visit Prakruti.

He laughed. *I would love to visit Prakruti! But it's not something the council will approve.

*But why not? Pasha asked, frustration in her voice. *Wasn't the first expedition a success? And if there is an intelligent system abiding there, aren't you curious to know its nature?

*Ah, Pasha, you know I am, but the council feels differently. A light flashed on in Nioro's hand. Its ruby glow revealed the fat cylinder of the telescope, but it also illuminated Nioro's face: dark eyes behind protective lenses, and a light-colored kisheer veiling his mouth and nose. As he began to pack the telescope away within a protective shell, he asked, *Have you heard the ancient aphorism, 'Don't rock the boat'?*

Out of habit, Urban sent a useless query to *Argo*'s library, while the Cryptologist tried to work out the meaning. She said, *A boat is a device used under conditions of planetary gravity, to achieve dry buoyancy on a large body of water. Is this a riddle? What could you know of boats?*

Nioro answered with a self-deprecating laugh. *Only what I've seen in dramas. But should you ever find yourself seated in a small, shallow, open boat, be aware that rocking it is not a good idea. Should water spill in, the boat could lose its buoyancy and sink. The aphorism is a metaphor for inducing one's own disaster. Our council feels we should not rock any metaphorical boat. Ezo was denied to us, but we were given the materials to create Nara and we have lived here peacefully since. The council believes we should stay here, that we should not risk conflict by interfering with the processes governing Prakruti. If our population ever grows so great that we need more room, we will reach outward, mine the old ruins on the edge of the system, and use that material to build a second city. But we will take nothing from the world . . . because the council is afflicted with a fear that if we rock the boat—if another expedition should visit Prakruti and disturb in some unknown and unpredictable way a remnant intelligence that may still exist there—disaster might follow.*

No, we are wanted there, Jolly said.

Urban shot the kid a sharp look, only to realize he'd used a private channel.

It was Pasha who filled the silence of the shared connection: *Nioro, if there are records hidden in the library detailing what is known of Prakruti, we would be grateful to see them.*

Finished now with packing up the telescope, Nioro turned to her, his eyes grave in the ruby light. *I know our council deeply desires your friendship. I will put your request quietly to them. I think they must grant it. It would rock the boat in a most unpleasant way if their censorship became known.*

———————

The red light hardly reached a meter, leaving Jolly and the Cryptologist in darkness. Jolly held her hand, the trembling pressure of her impatience palpable through the reactive fabric of their gloves.

She had an idea. He knew it. She must have found some critical fact during her explorations in the library, a fact she had not shared. As they followed Nioro from the hangar, he squeezed her hand, a signal to remind her he was there and that he meant to stay with her. She surprised him by squeezing his hand twice in return. It could have meant anything, but he took it to mean, *Be ready.*

His heart boomed in his ears. He knew her determination. She didn't want to waste time in Nara. She wanted to reach the river shrine. And though he could guess what she had in mind to do, the "how" of it eluded him—although it had to have something to do with Nioro.

Still holding hands, they slipped together through the gel membrane and back into atmosphere. Their hoods unfurled. Pasha and Urban had already moved on with Nioro. The Cryptologist looked at Jolly, a question in her bright eyes. He didn't hesitate. Whatever she meant to do, he had to be part of it, so he nodded his blind agreement.

She smiled, and then called out, "Nioro, could you answer one question for me?"

Letting go of Jolly's hand, the Cryptologist pulled her library tablet from a thigh pocket, unfolded it, and tapped the screen as Nioro returned to meet her.

"What can I do for you?" he asked, his gray kisheer now rippling at his shoulders.

Jolly tried to work out what she was up to as she handed him the tablet, saying, "This image was taken from low orbit."

Nioro held the tablet. He gazed at the screen. The light it cast on his face dimmed, then brightened. "Ah, yes! These concentric circles are intriguing, aren't they? They're on the southern continent. I believe they're natural . . . well, as natural as anything on Prakruti can be. A product of subsidence."

He started to pass the tablet back, but Pasha intercepted it.

Frowned at the image. Then looked up at Nioro. "Do you have a satellite in orbit? We didn't detect one."

"No, no permanent satellite. This image was taken from *Bean Pod*, our old survey vessel, during the sixth centennial orbital mapping—twenty-two years ago now." He laughed. "I just have to wait another seventy-eight years until the council lets me take *Bean Pod* out again."

Bean Pod! The Narans little two-person survey craft. Jolly had guessed *Bean Pod* to be the Cryptologist's target. He didn't understand her maneuver with the tablet, but he was sure something significant had just happened. She confirmed it when she met his gaze with a slight, satisfied smile.

Jolly reached for the tablet. "May I see it?" he asked, his voice a squeak of tension.

Pasha gave him an odd look, but passed the tablet to him. He gave it a superficial glance. Then folded it. Pocketed it. Hiding the evidence.

"I'm tired," he said. He turned to the Cryptologist. "Do you want to go back with me? Get some sleep?"

"Yes," she agreed with a radiant smile. "I love to sleep with you."

CHAPTER FORTY

"WHY NIORO?" JOLLY whispered in the dark, his lips brushing the Cryptologist's ear, tension unwound, the sweat of love-making still drying on his skin.

Her cautious answer came by message: *They may be listening.

"Oh." The comfort of the sweet darkness and their shared bed faded. He tensed, senses alert, but heard nothing except the Cryptologist's soft breathing and the slow beat of his heart. No sounds reached them from the other rooms attached to the suite where the delegation was housed.

She shifted, propping herself on an elbow, leaning in to kiss his lips. He kissed her in return while she messaged him again: *Nioro told you why. He was the last to take Bean Pod out, and his authorization to do so was never rescinded.

Jolly pulled back. Not far. His lips brushed hers as he whispered, "How could you know that?"

*I learned about the centennial survey in the library. I guessed about the authorization—but I was right.

This time, he responded in silence. *Nioro is not going to let us use Bean Pod.

*I am Nioro, she said, with a little audible laugh.

*You stole his credentials?

*Not exactly. I armed the library tablet with a stealth DI. When Nioro held it in his hands, the librarian logged him as the user and my DI now operates under his authority. It has found its way to Bean Pod. A refueling operation is underway. I'll need to leave very soon. Do you want to come with me?

Guilt closed his throat. Fear knotted around his heart. But he had to do this. He had to. And the Cryptologist had made it so easy—because Urban would not be with them. *Bean Pod* only had room for two. He breathed deeply, slowly, calming himself. And then he whispered, "Of course I do. It's why I'm here."

She smiled. *Then we should go.*

It was early. City dawn had not yet come and the suite's common room was empty. No one there to question why the Cryptologist ordered a sackful of sealed rations from the fabricator, and two large flasks of water.

Just before they left, Jolly asked, "You have the needle, right?"

She smiled. Her fingers brushed a thigh pocket. "I have it."

They found Nara's hallways to be as empty as the common room, enabling them to reach the transit station with no questions asked.

They did encounter a few Narans at the station. The Cryptologist only smiled and nodded, but Jolly talked to them. He learned they were bound for the docks, eager to return to their work of preparing the ancient shuttle for its imminent journey to Volo's Landing.

He told them, "We're going to the docks too. We visited Nioro there earlier, and I left my tablet in the empty hangar. I'm going back to get it."

The lie came so easily, it shocked him. It shocked him more when the Narans didn't question him. He didn't want to become skilled at lying.

A single transit car took everyone to the docks. Jolly said goodbye to the Narans as they entered the shuttle's hangar. Then he moved on, hand in hand with the Cryptologist, to the adjacent hangar where *Bean Pod* was housed. No one was in sight—but the hangar door was closed.

"Do you know how to open it?" Jolly whispered.

She smiled and said again, *I am Nioro.*

So it seemed. As she approached the door, it recognized her, and opened. They hurried through into a well-lit, pressurized hangar where a tiny white-winged vessel awaited them.

The hangar door closed behind them, sealing off any chance discovery.

Urban's hands trembled with barely contained fury.

For all his life, he had kept watch for Chenzeme marauders. From the day he'd captured *Dragon*, he'd endlessly surveyed the Near Vicinity. But the Narans kept no watch. None at all!

Oh, he could understand how they'd grown so absurdly complacent. They had lived undisturbed for so long that they'd come to believe themselves safely alone. So why keep watch? Their city generated no traffic, so there was no need for traffic control. And given the utter emptiness of Tanjiri's inner system, they had no reason to expend resources surveying for hazardous asteroids or drifting debris that simply did not exist.

Theirs was a closed world, and that had allowed Jolly and the Cryptologist to disappear, their fate unknown until a citywide search led to the discovery that *Bean Pod* was missing.

The little survey craft had slipped away from the city—*and no one had noticed!*

Luk Li Mithki had been the bearer of this news. He stood in the suite, his green and gold kisheer trembling with indignation and his cold gaze fixed on Urban as the remaining Dragoneers crowded anxiously around. He told them, "We have no proof your missing people are aboard, but we have no other explanation for the vessel's absence." Crisp words, harshly spoken, conveying outrage and wary fear. He understood he was dealing with an opponent far more powerful than his own people. The taking of *Bean Pod* had proved that.

"They're aboard," Urban answered bitterly. "But not with our consent. They've done this on their own."

Clemantine drew the councilor's gaze when she asked, in a more conciliatory tone, "Have you tried communicating with them?"

"Of course we have! And we continue to do so, but without reply. Do you know where they are going?"

From the Dragoneers, a chorus of knowing hums and sighs. No one directly gave away the existence of the river shrine, but every one of them knew exactly where *Bean Pod* was bound. Urban's hand knotted into a fist. He would recall *Argo* if he could, go after Jolly. But *Argo* had to reach *Dragon* and refuel before it could turn around.

Did Jolly know the significance of the shrine?

Of course he did!

Urban's chest tightened with the realization that he'd been outplayed. He had seen the river shrine through Wailoa's eyes—and had not reported that vision. He had not wanted to share it because the invitation and the obligation were meant for him alone. Or so he'd believed.

Obvious now that Jolly had seen the river shrine too, and that he'd recruited the Cryptologist to help him reach it first. He would take Urban's place and be the one—the only one—to risk that gateway to Ezo. And with *Argo* away, what chance did Urban have to stop him?

All this—a tangled knot of furious thought—bundled into a moment. A moment later, he knew what he had to do.

"We do know where they're going," he announced. Stern words that drew a fresh murmur from the Dragoneers. But the time for secrecy had passed.

Clemantine knew it too. She nodded, crossed her arms, raised her chin, and looked down at Luk Li Mithki, intimidating in her height and strength. "You Narans are not so alone in this system as you'd like us to believe, are you, Councilor?"

"I don't know what you mean."

"I think you do. There is a presence inhabiting this system. And I don't mean your cousins at Volo's Landing. There is something else. Something still undefined. Not human, but human descended." She did not mention Nioro's name, but insisted, "You know this. It's why you don't allow expeditions planetside."

Silence, but for the beating of Urban's heart. The delegation stood frozen, every breath held as several seconds slipped past—

And then the councilor wilted. A downcast face, a slumped spine, his kisheer dead-still against rounded shoulders. "Don't speak of it," he pleaded in a lowered voice as a rosy flush brightened the pale yellow scales of his face. "Not outside this room. If it's true . . . *Is* it true?"

His wide, frightened eyes asked Clemantine to back off her claim, to please, please demote it to unproven speculation.

"It is true," she said. "There is a great intelligence here."

"A web of intelligences," Urban said. "But you knew that."

"Only the council knows. All members, past and present, sworn to secrecy. And Nioro Kwan—I know you've met him—he's worked it out. Was he the one who—"

Urban cut him off. "We knew it from the time we entered the system."

"Ah, I see. And now I ask, I *plead* for your silence, because if people knew, they would panic. We have not forgotten what happened at Sakura when some great force consumed the minds of our people. Our ancestors were the only ones to escape. A few thousand, out of a million lost."

"This is different," Urban said.

But then he frowned, wondering, *was it?* Lezuri had arisen from a swarm of minds somewhere among the cloaked stars of the Hallowed Vasties. Ezo surely had a similar origin.

"Ezo is different," he insisted, as much to himself as to Luk Li Mithki. "You know that. You've lived here centuries, thrived here."

"Until now," the man answered bitterly. "Until you came, and violated our trust. You said you knew where these two rogue personnel are going?"

"Yes, I know. And we need a great favor from you that will allow us to recover them, before they can cause any harm."

Luk Li Mithki's kisheer trembled and his hands clenched in quiet outrage as he conveyed to his fellow council members the Dragoneers' request.

We have no choice, he told them.

Anticipating a quick decision, he had remained in the visitors' suite, pacing while they watched him, doubtlessly analyzing every tic in his expression.

A flurry of debate erupted beyond their hearing, but not beyond his. He listened to the objections and the invectives and the dire predictions of his colleagues—no more than a minute before Chief Councilor Lyra Li Sital called order.

She said, *Let us agree first: This is not the time to speak publicly of the shrine or of any extra-human intelligence. It is too much! Our people have already endured two shocking revisions to our shared worldview, and the theft of our research vessel can only further unsettle them. Truth will follow, but for now, we must act decisively to restore both their confidence and ours.*

The testy councilor Junyo Besiba jumped in. *So we must act in obedience to the Dragoneers? That is what you're saying?*

No, Junyo. We must act in cooperation with the Dragoneers. There is still so much we can gain if we play this well.

Urban sat in a cushy chair, chin resting on his fist, watching Luk Li Mithki pace. After a few minutes, he marked a slight hesitation, a stiffening in the councilor's spine, and guessed a decision had been made.

He stood, muscles taut. He had no time left for further persuasion. He needed the Narans to agree *now* to let him use their ancient shuttle. Any delay, and Jolly would reach the shrine first.

Luk Li Mithki turned. His gaze searched the room until it settled on Urban. "The council will grant your request, but with restrictions."

Urban heaved a sigh of relief, whispering thanks to the Unknown God. But Clemantine reacted differently. She drew herself up, arms crossed. Urban guessed she did not like that word, "restrictions."

The councilor refused to be intimidated. "To minimize impact on the planet, only four people will be allowed to board the shuttle."

At this, both Pasha and Shoran tried to object, but Luk only raised the volume of his voice and talked past them, saying, "Two seats for us, two seats for you. Decide among yourselves who will go, and be at the hangar in twenty minutes. I will meet you there. And be prepared for a long stay, planetside."

He headed for the door, refusing to answer any further questions. That was all right. Urban had what he wanted. He waited until the door closed. Then he spoke, projecting his voice over a buzz of frustrated grumbles. "There isn't time to argue. *I'm* going, and Pasha is too."

He looked for her, wanting to be sure. And yes, there she was, nodding in wide-eyed affirmation.

Clemantine though, looked irate. "*What?* Why?" She turned a puzzled frown on Pasha. "What is going on?"

"I found the shrine," Pasha explained with just a slight nervous tremor in her voice. "So Urban promised I could be on the first expedition."

"That's how it happened," he confirmed.

And to his relief, Riffan backed him up. "It's true. The promise was made."

"And you?" Clemantine asked, taunting him. "Why should you go?"

Because this is my pilgrimage.

He might never have another opportunity to crack the puzzle of the needle or to grasp the secret of a Blade. Ezo could teach him those things, he was sure of it—but only if he reached the shrine first.

He said none of this aloud, his pirate smile answer enough. And thirty minutes later, he lay in an acceleration couch, with Pasha occupying the seat in front of him.

On the Naran side, Councilor Luk Li Mithki had appointed himself to the mission. He was across the aisle from Urban, and he'd put Nioro Kwan in the remaining seat.

All other seats and most of the supplies previously loaded for the mission to Volo's Landing had been hastily removed to reduce mass and, ultimately, speed the turn-around.

The shuttle—its name translated as *Thousand Years*—was heavy with fuel, enough to power an aggressive descent. An initial hard burn would shrink *Bean Pod's* lead; a brutal deceleration would further close the gap. If the DI pilot had skill and daring enough, Urban might yet confront Jolly outside the river shrine.

Pasha spoke suddenly, without preamble. "It was the tablet," she declared. "That's how she did it. The Cryptologist, I mean." A hand appeared, all that Urban could see of her, extended toward Nioro across the aisle. "Nioro, she handed you a tablet after we left the hangar."

"She wanted to show me an orbital survey image," he recalled without stirring in his seat.

"And the screen glitched. Didn't it?"

"Yes, I remember that. I thought it odd."

Urban grasped where this was going and it shocked him, so that he whispered aloud, "By the Unknown God, she—"

The DI assigned to pilot the shuttle spoke over him. In a masculine voice that reverberated in the expansive, nearly empty cabin, it informed them: "All passengers confirmed secure. Releasing docking hooks."

Urban pressed his lips together. He had been about to say, *she must have used the same trick Lezuri used when he hacked Riffan's atrium.* But that would reveal a history he had resolved to keep hidden.

Nioro spoke instead, anger edging precise words. "She used the tablet to run some function that compromised my security. That's what you're saying."

"I think so," Pasha said. "And Jolly couldn't wait to get the tablet away from me. He *knew.*"

"Why me?" Nioro demanded.

"It had to be you, didn't it?" an embittered Luk Li Mithki answered. "You are . . . what is the word? . . . yes, *credentialed* to fly *Bean Pod.* She learned that, somehow. All that time using the library . . ." He turned his head to glare across the aisle at Urban. "You people have taken advantage of us."

"It was the Cryptologist," Urban countered.

"It's who she is," Pasha said in a quiet voice. "She can't help herself. But we'll do everything we can to set it right."

"Initiating separation," the DI announced.

Urban closed his eyes, sensing a brief thrust as the shuttle pushed clear of the docking hub. Nothing more to do, until *Thousand Years* touched down.

———————

A long, long descent to Prakruti. More than two days.

Jolly suspected the Cryptologist had switched off *Bean Pod*'s communication system, because no one contacted them along the way. But he didn't ask. Guilt weighed on him, far heavier than the planetary gravity he was about to face. It ate him up from inside.

He had betrayed Urban's trust. He'd betrayed the trust of every Dragoneer, and the trust of the Narans. He meant to betray the Cryptologist too. He had to. He'd gone over and over it in his head and he *knew* this was the path he had to follow. It was the right path, no matter how bad it made him feel.

The Cryptologist sat quietly beside him in the left-hand seat, her palms flat against her thighs, her eyes closed. With her DI piloting the little vessel, there was no reason not to sleep. Better to sleep than to brood. Right? Jolly used his atrium to draw a curtain of slumber across his troubled mind.

But his sleep proved restless. His mind kept porpoising in and out of awareness until, half in a dream, he heard the Cryptologist murmur:

"It is just us. There is no risk to the fleet."

Jolly blinked, raised his chin, rubbed his eyes, and turned to encounter the Cryptologist's worried gaze.

"But *you* are at risk, Jolly."

He put on a forced smile. "It's my choice, isn't it?"

"Yes." She turned away again. Closed her eyes.

On later reflection, he decided that had been a cruel thing for him to say, given she had been created as a tool and endowed with an obsession, so that in a very real way, she did not have any choice. Unlike him, she could not choose to quit her mission. Maybe, she could not even *want* to quit it.

Much later, when Prakruti loomed huge and beautiful in *Bean Pod*'s little windows, she spoke again. "We should eat now, Jolly. So we will be ready for action when we touch down."

Soon after that, the piloting DI burned off the last of *Bean Pod*'s fuel in a complex braking maneuver that brought the vessel into atmosphere.

In *Griffin*'s library, Clemantine's cold twin studied a video loop compiled by her copy of the Astronomer. Minutes before, he had noticed an anomaly—an unexpected object suddenly present at the edge of a routine image of the Trinity.

Perhaps a chameleon ship? He had considered and then rejected the possibility. Chameleon ships existed in great numbers among the belt of ruins, but they were difficult to observe. Stealth was their default. Generally, they could be seen only if they chanced to pass in silhouette in front of a brighter object—while this new object had been caught reflecting a glint of Tanjiri's starlight.

Turning to the archives, the Astronomer had combed through older observations of the Trinity and its surroundings, looking for other images that might show the anomaly. He found several. By combining them, he'd created the crude video Clemantine was now watching. It showed a faint, barely perceptible object progressing in jerky motion against a background of distant stars.

She watched the video repeat several times before turning to the Astronomer in his frameless window. "What is it?"

Like all the Apparatchiks, the Astronomer resembled Urban, but he had a leaner, lighter build. His black bodysuit starkly contrasted with the inverted star chart behind him, wherein the void was white and the stars black within it. "It's not a singular object," he told her. "That track shows two objects, both tumbling, so that they intermittently reflect Tanjiri's light."

"Definitely not chameleon ships, then."

"Definitely not. I am still tracing their trajectory, but present calculations strongly indicate the objects originated at or near Volo's Landing. At present, they are coasting on a passive trajectory that will take them through the Trinity. Assuming nothing has changed, that there has been and will be no course adjustment, the objects will pass harmlessly in a little more than sixteen hours."

Clemantine crossed her arms. *Monsters*, she reflected, *have a way of sneaking up out of the dark.*

"They're kinetic missiles, aren't they?"

"Very likely," the Astronomer agreed.

A simple yet effective weapon: take a large mass, equip it with a few rocket engines and a Dull Intelligence to oversee last-minute course corrections—nothing more was required to deliver a fatal strike to an undefended, inward-looking city like Nara.

In a rare display of emotion, the Astronomer's lip curled; his words took on a bitter edge. "I will send a warning, of course. There is time, despite the light-speed lag—though it will be an unscheduled transmission and *Dragon* may not be listening."

"Keep sending," Clemantine said.

She sensed Okinowa's hand behind the scheme.

Damned if she didn't look on it with grudging admiration.

CHAPTER FORTY-ONE

JOLLY STOOD IN *Bean Pod*'s open door, his hood thrown back, breathing in the scents of Prakruti and feeling like a trespasser, a vandal. Jet wash from the final moments of their vertical descent had scarred the meadow with a slash of torn grass and slick brown mud. And their noisy arrival had sent a heard of elk leaping away into the shadowed mystery of an evergreen forest.

Jolly hoped the bears and the wolves and whatever else hunted there had chosen retreat as well.

The birds had not. Though it was a gloomy afternoon, with the meadow grasses bowing under the weight of a recent rain and low scudding clouds promising more showers, hundreds of birds, most of them hidden, competed to inundate the air with their raucous or melodious or piping, repetitive calls. Only in a lull did the tumbling voice of the rain-swollen river break through.

Despite the imminence of summer, the wind blew cold, chilling his face and forcing his bright lime-green skin suit to expend more of its limited energy to keep him warm.

The Cryptologist had her hood open too. She crowded in beside him, ecstatic with wonder. "It is *beautiful*, Jolly. A beautiful world. And so vast! Look! Look at all the great gray clouds. And listen to that wild noise. This world is nothing at all like our quiet gee deck."

"We should go," he said.

Fearful of damaging the river shrine, they had landed a kilometer away, at the northern edge of the meadow. Jolly could not even see the shrine, veiled by a swell of trees. But it would take them only a few minutes to walk there.

A short flight of steps down to the muddied meadow. The Cryptologist waded boldly out into the undisturbed grass. "So wet!" she declared in delight, bending to run her gloved hand across the droplets clinging to the knee-high grass.

Jolly nodded. He could not quite pull off a smile.

"What's the matter?" she asked, taking his hand. Her eyes widened; her grip tightened. "Jolly, you're trembling! Should we be afraid?"

"No." His voice low and husky as he pushed words past a fear-constricted throat. "We are wanted here. Come on, let's hurry."

Hand in hand, they waded through the watery grass. Jolly, distracted by his own thoughts, was only peripherally aware of the Cryptologist as she looked about in wonder, catching her breath at the sight of a hawk circling, and again as two feuding red birds swooped low overhead.

The two of them had come so far, so fast, and only because of the Cryptologist's cleverness, her determination. Now though . . . now he had one crucial task left, and he had to accomplish it on his own.

Unexpected motion startled him from his thoughts. He reared back, as something descended in front of him—triangular, silent.

"It's the aerial-bot," the Cryptologist said. The device bobbed on the breeze, not a meter away. "Of course they are watching us."

Jolly tugged at her hand. "Let's keep going."

He started walking again, but the bot moved in. It got in their way. Jaw set, refusing to stop, Jolly bumped into it. And when it still didn't move he swiped at it, sending it tumbling aside. It took just seconds to recover and return.

"It's too late!" he shouted at whoever was operating it. He imagined Urban's ghost, a furious specter haunting *Dragon*'s library, directing the bot to get in his way, to stop him from what he meant to do. "You're too late," he growled. "I'm already here, and I'm going to do this."

In the next moment, as if to contest this claim, a sonic boom shook the forest.

Jolly recognized that concussive sound; he knew it in the vibration of his bones. He'd heard it on Verilotus when Lezuri returned. A different kind of fear swept over him. A fear of failure. He looked up, but of course heavy clouds veiled the sky.

"We have to hurry!" He squeezed the Cryptologist's hand. "They found a way to follow us and they're coming. We have to reach the river shrine first."

But as soon as he moved, the aerial-bot got in his way again. Futile to knock it away. So he seized it instead. It weighed almost nothing. He shoved it to the ground, smashed it under his foot, then took the Cryptologist's hand again and started running.

Slipping, stumbling, they crushed a path through the grass. Small birds flushed from all around them, taking flight with shocking bursts of ratcheting wings.

"Who is coming?" the Cryptologist asked, wide-eyed with excitement as she bounded beside him. "Do you think it's Urban?"

"Of course it's Urban!"

Jolly had no doubt of that or that his time to act had grown very short. The incoming craft had passed overhead and gone on. But it would return. Already, he could hear a distant growl of jet engines.

"He has taken the Narans' shuttle," the Cryptologist decided, her cheeks flushed rosy from exertion and the cold. She went on speculating between quick, shallow breaths. "There is no other way. But surely such an act will anger the Narans and possibly endanger the fleet?"

"I think *we* angered the Narans," Jolly snapped.

She answered in the rhythm of her bounding steps, shouting to be heard over the growing roar of the approaching craft. "Yes—you are likely right—though they had no intention—of using *Bean Pod*—and so no harm—was done."

They rounded the trees and there was the river shrine, not two hundred meters away, the sheen of its polished copper roof dulled by the reflection of rain-swollen clouds. Jolly had wondered if Wailoa would be there, waiting on the porch to greet him. But no. No one was there. Probably better that way. Fewer questions to ask and no time for questions anyway.

Still running, he let go of the Cryptologist's hand and between rushed breaths he told her, "I want you to give me the needle case to hold."

For all the long transit to Prakruti, Jolly had tried to come up with some clever way of tricking the Cryptologist out of the needle, but every scheme he imagined struck him as futilely absurd. Desperate now, he simply asked for it. What else could he do?

She shortened her stride. He realized she was stopping, and he too stumbled to a halt. Turning back, he saw her pull the needle case from her thigh pocket. To his astonishment, she held it out to him.

He took it and tucked it into his own pocket, chiding himself for all the anxiety he'd suffered over the question of how to get it—when all he'd had to do was ask.

"Why do you need it?" she asked curiously, without hint of suspicion—and that made him angry. Angry at himself. He hated deceiving her.

Then tell her the truth!

"I know what we need to do with it."

Wrong thing to say. Her brow furrowed. She shouted—not out of anger, just to be heard—the Narans' shuttle was that close. "What do you mean, Jolly? What do you know that you have not told me?"

"I'll explain when we reach the shrine. *Hurry.*"

"No." She caught his arm in a steely grip. "Explain now."

His gaze shifted between her and the heavy clouds, dreading the sight of the Narans' shuttle breaking through. He leaned close, so she could hear him. "I've been here before."

"When?"

He tapped his head. "Not actually here, but it felt as real as it does now. That was a sunny day. There was the scent of grass, the glare of daylight. Cold wind hissing. And the river shrine . . . Urban is right. It's made for us."

She stared at him, stunned by this admission, her wide eyes full of hurt that he had kept this knowledge from her—and he still had not told her everything.

He added silently, *It's made for us, but only one of us.*

"What is it, then?" she insisted. "Do you know that too?"

He had to read her lips; he could not hear her over the shuttle's roar. He clapped his hands over his ears to save his hearing.

A moment later, the craft popped out of the clouds. A behemoth. After *Bean Pod*, the size of it shocked him, and it struck him as a thing utterly alien to this world. It descended vertically, toward a landing halfway between the river and the shrine, the shriek of its engines vibrating every cell in his body.

Speech had become impossible and anyway he had what he needed and there was no time. He mouthed the words, *I'm sorry*, and he ran.

Heart hammering against a heavy pressure in his chest, he closed the distance to the river shrine. As the shuttle's engines wound down, he bounded onto the columned porch. Cold wind teased his hair and sighed past the building's corners. Moving swiftly, before fear could hobble him, he crossed the porch to the brass doors. Beautiful. Cast with a mural of the river, the sun rising behind it, just as he'd seen it when he'd been here with Wailoa. His hand slid into the recessed handle of the right door and he pulled.

It did not open.

The Cryptologist caught up with him. She crowded up against him. "Explain!" she demanded with tears on her cheeks.

He pushed her away. "It's a test! A way to measure who we are inside. To learn if we are like Lezuri—a vain god, grasping for power, who would drown a whole world in silver. Or if we are something . . . better."

She drifted close again. "And if we are . . . ?"

He turned again to the doors.

"Tell me, Jolly! If we are something better, than what? What do we gain? Is it the entity in there?"

"No, it's not the entity." Using both hands this time, he tried opening the doors together—and they swung easily, revealing what he'd expected to see: a slowly shifting curtain of glowing silver, five meters away, hiding the shrine's back wall.

Urban messaged him: *Jolly! Don't go inside!*

Block him, Jolly instructed his atrium. Then he moved to block the doorway as the Cryptologist started forward. "You have to stay back," he told her. "We're supposed to go in one at a time."

She intuited the truth. "That is the path to Ezo. That is what you have not told me. *Jolly!*"

"Stay back," he warned her. "Stay outside."

Holding tight to his courage, he slipped past the doors. Blue glass filtered the light from high windows, the hue mixing coldly with the silver's glow as he crossed the shrine's smooth floor.

Behind him, the doors closed with a soft *snick*, silencing the wind and allowing him to hear the old familiar murmuring of silver. Hundreds of little finger-long tendrils boiled from the silver's surface, reaching for him as he approached, eager to take him in.

Just one more step—

The Cryptologist caught his arm, yanked him back. "No, Jolly! It's too dangerous! You don't know what—"

Rage like he'd never known erupted. "Get back! Get back before you ruin it! You were supposed to stay outside!"

She ignored his protest, struggling to drag him farther from the silver, pleading with him: "It's dangerous! An unknown. Please. Don't risk it. Let me go first."

"No! It has to be me."

"You could disappear in there! Jolly, I can't lose you."

"It's just an avatar!"

Anyway, that's what Urban would say, though Jolly had been born in this body and he didn't really believe he would be the same in another . . . Nor did he think life worked that way. Not here. Not if he found his way to Ezo.

"Listen to me," he insisted, wrestling with the Cryptologist, trying to pry her fingers from his arms as they turned and turned about. "I need to do this."

"Then let us do it together," she pleaded. "Disappear together."

"No! It has to be me."

"Why?" she cried.

Frustration flushed the truth from him. "Because you want to open the needle and I don't! And because Urban wants the same thing, and more! He wants to learn how to make a Blade." He got one of her hands loose. Reached for the other, but she'd already let him go, shock in her pretty blue eyes.

She backed away, and as she did he reached into his pocket. Pulled out the needle's case. He wanted her to understand. "I'm going to get rid of this. There's more in here than we should know."

Only then did he realize that she now stood between him and the silver. Eager tendrils rose to meet her, mirroring her shape. He tried to be faster. He leaped toward the gleaming curtain. But she had only to edge back half a step. The silver rushed over her—and it recoiled from him. With nothing to catch him, his momentum sent him into the shrine's back wall. He tried to brace, but his head struck. A flare of pain. Black sparks clouding his vision as he turned to look for her. *There.* On the edge of the luminous cloud, she stood draped in silver, with a fierce spindle of light unrolling from her forearm, so bright it hurt Jolly's eyes.

Some slight fraction of a second later, she dissolved into the cloud of silver and disappeared—though her voice lingered, speaking as a message in his atrium:

I'm sorry I deceived you, but I kept the needle. I have to do this. It's what I was made for.

He opened the needle case. Found it empty. Snapped it shut again. Threw it aside. "*You!*" he screamed for want of a name.

He tried again to enter the silver, to follow her. But it was a dying cloud, thinning, disintegrating around him, spinning apart into vaporous tendrils and vanishing, taking with it what little warmth there was in the air.

Jolly stood in the empty shrine, shivering in the cold blue light leaking in from the windows. Alone, but only for a moment.

The doors opened. Urban stood there, mouth agape, his expression sliding into confusion at the sight of Jolly. "Why are you still here? Wasn't there silver? I thought—"

He broke off, his gaze growing hard as he guessed the truth. "*Her?*"

"Yes," Jolly confessed.

"You brought her here."

"She brought me."

"Did she know . . . ?"

"Not until the end."

"Not until you told her."

"I had to tell her!"

"And she beat you to it. *You.* Why did you want it?"

Others appeared behind him: Pasha, Nioro, and the councilor, Luk Li Mithki.

"I didn't want it," Jolly said, bitter now.

Urban entered the shrine, crossed the floor, stooped to pick up the needle's empty case. He looked inside and then turned to Jolly, accusation in his eyes.

"I didn't want the needle opened!" Jolly protested. "Not by her and not by you. Lezuri gave it to you! You should have known it wasn't safe to open. You should have thrown it away. But you didn't. So I was going to take it to Ezo. Not to learn any great secret, but to get rid of it, and come back again if I could."

"But she took it," Urban concluded, walking now to the back of the shrine where he stood, studying the walls as if hoping to see some remnant silver leaching from them.

From the doorway, Pasha demanded to know, "*What* is going on and where is the Cryptologist?"

She stood with a hand on her hip, her confusion metamorphosing into anger as she understood they had kept her in the dark. "You two have been playing your own game, haven't you? And at the expense of everyone else."

CHAPTER FORTY-TWO

JOLLY HAD ONCE described to the Cryptologist what it had been like for him the first time he'd transitioned through the silver. He had felt incorporeal. Aware, yet without substance, unable to touch anything but with his visual sense enhanced so that he could see all parts of the world that lay just outside the silver's reach.

But this was a different rising of silver and the Cryptologist experienced no such thing. Jolly had warned her: this transit would be a test, measuring who she was inside.

At first, she felt herself turning, turning, turning, infinitesimally thin layers of mind and body peeling away at each round, spun off into a two-dimensional existence, all surface—a vast surface area—where nothing would be or could be hidden. And though pain was not part of the transformation, she screamed anyway, screamed silently, from the horror of witnessing herself coming apart.

Thought slowed as the distance between neurons grew—a thought-speed delay. But it didn't matter. Because in that measureless time she could conceive only the dire wish that she had never been: never set foot inside the river shrine, never found the way to Prakruti, never seized control of *Bean Pod*, never visited Nara, never gained the augmentation of silver, never created a living-breathing avatar, never been endowed with an obsessive drive to solve a puzzle best left alone, never been brought into existence at all.

What a foolish gambit that had been! A gambit Vytet regretted. The Cryptologist regretted it too. Regret cycled through her, like a deep dull bell tolling or the chanting of a doleful chorus: *regret, regret, regret.*

Regret for who she was, what she was: a tool, powered by curiosity.

Curiosity killed the Cryptologist.

Inevitable, perhaps.

Then again, didn't one have to die to this life to become something more?

The question swept like a wave across the expanse of her unrolled mind. And through the chaos of her disintegration, she grasped at it—one more question in need of an answer, her curiosity serving as the last connective tissue holding her crumbling self together.

What more could I become?

Oh, but that was easy to answer because she had not changed much yet and though she'd drowned herself in regret for the very fact of her existence, her endowed purpose still drove her.

I would become a creature capable of understanding the structure and mechanism of the needle.

The needle that was part of her. She remembered now. Worried the Narans might be other than they seemed, that they might try to take the needle from her, she had removed it from its case and slipped it under her skin, into the muscle of her forearm. An act that drew no blood and caused no pain, as if the needle refused to interact with her body in such an intimate way.

The needle had still been there, embedded in her arm, when she'd stepped into the silver.

And now? Where was the needle now?

A shiver radiated across the still-expanding expanse of her mind as she strove to think back, to remember what had become of it. And when that failed, she resolved instead to revisit the moment she had stepped into the silver—though not to revisit it as she'd been then. It would be useless to simply wind time back, shedding the fragile calm she was gaining to live again through mindless fear and panic.

Instead, she returned to the moment as an observer, sliding unimpeded back through time, witnessing as she went a consolidation of dissected memory, the rapid crystallization of mind and body until—*there!*

There it is: the shape of her former self in that instant after she stepped into the silver.

And there is the needle. She feels it, solid within her forearm and untouched—untouchable—by the silver that consumes her own fragile body. Was the needle left behind?

No, that is not what happened.

She dives deeper into theoretical spaces inhabited by particles that are not truly particles. She only thinks of them that way, a necessary mental construct that allows her to slow their frantic vibrational motion, their time and hers synchronizing until they lie quiet before her.

Now she can interact with them. Examine them in all their variety: a collection of complex blocks locked together into a time-bound fortress, each particle a keystone.

Push on one.

Resistance proves negligible in this imaginary space. The block moves easily. It falls away, leaving a tiny imperfection, a breach in the fortress wall. It is enough. As she retreats, the pressure of real time rushes in, exploding through the opening—and the fortress wall gives way.

CHAPTER FORTY-THREE

"DON'T HATE ME," Jolly said.

Urban said nothing, not trusting himself to speak. He stood on the shrine's porch, looking out between the columns, watching the glow of sunset colors reflected against the river's current. A call-and-response of birdsong rang out across the dusk, while in the distance some creature—mammal or reptile?—yipped in a mad joyous rhythm. Moment by moment, the air grew colder, while Urban brooded over his lost chance and over the painful truth that Jolly had not trusted him with the knowledge contained within the needle.

That hurt. More than he would have guessed. Maybe more than coming late to the shrine. Hard to admit, even to himself, but beyond his anger, there existed relief.

"I would have done it," he murmured.

He'd been ready—though not for the shock of failure and betrayal.

There in the shrine, emptied of silver, tempers had flared. Pasha ignited it. With the two Narans crowding behind her, she stood in the doorway, lashing out with sharp words. "You two have been playing your own game, haven't you? And at the expense of everyone else."

"This was no game," Urban shot back as an excess of wild energy impelled him to move, to stalk the width of the little shrine and back again. "Not to me. Maybe to Jolly." He halted, fixing the kid with an accusing glare.

Jolly stood in the middle of the floor, breathing too hard, his hands shaking—but with no contrition in his defiant gaze.

Urban's hands clenched into fists. "How could you do this to me? Lezuri gave *me* the needle. It was for me to understand it."

"But you want more than that," Jolly accused. "You want to *be* Lezuri."

Words that struck like a knife to his soul.

"You say that to *me*?"

"But it's true, isn't it? The blade, the sentient missiles . . . Lezuri knew how to make them. You want to know too, even knowing it would change you."

"*Yes*. Is that wrong? I want us to be formidable. I want to know what Lezuri knew so I can always defend the fleet and meet entities like Ezo as equals."

Pasha jumped in on this. "Be straight, Urban. You don't want to be equals. I've been on the high bridge with you and I know what you want. You want the assurance of being the biggest gun around." Her voice shifted, gently mocking, "We are Chenzeme. We are stronger. *Kill it!*"

Jolly stepped between them. "*No.* Stop. Please. We are *not* Chenzeme. And I will never let us be like Lezuri—so insulated by our own power that people's lives don't mean anything anymore."

By the Unknown God! Was it so hard to understand?

"This isn't about people!" Urban insisted. "It's about monsters like Lezuri that might have evolved from them."

"Or monsters like Ezo?" Pasha asked.

"Ezo is not monstrous, but we got lucky."

"We were lucky we didn't look more dangerous," Jolly countered. "Ezo could have eliminated us easily, even with our missiles, even if we'd had a blade."

For someone who'd never been given to argument, Jolly showed a talent for it.

And then Pasha took his side. "Jolly is right. A blade would have been useless against Ezo's fleet of chameleon ships. Unless you're planning on slicing up a planet—"

"*God, no.*" Why was he being accused of such things? "A blade is more than that and you know it. There are secrets of time and space and propulsion in this physics. There is the knowledge to *build* worlds."

"*Oh yes!*" A strained cry from Pasha that might have been protest or agreement—or both.

Urban stared at her in astonishment, but she said nothing more, only stood there, her eyes clenched shut and a rosy flush coloring her pale skin. *Oh yes.* She knew what they might have gained. She had gone so far as to help Vytet create the Cryptologist to tease open the mysteries of the needle. And of course she too felt betrayed—by him.

Until that moment, the two Narans had lingered just outside the doorway, mute witnesses glimpsing a history Urban had never meant to share with them. But then Nioro stepped forward. And with a quaver in his voice, he suggested, "It may be there is a paradox here . . . that it is dangerous to appear too dangerous? That a humble aspect is safer? Given the violence of history, I mean."

Silence followed this speculation, lingering many seconds until finally Urban surrendered. "I won't argue more. The needle is gone and our chance with it."

"Gone *where?*" Pasha demanded. "And where is the Cryptologist? What did you do to her?"

"*Me?*" Urban shook his head, incredulous. "Ask yourself that, Pasha. I think you made her more like you than like Vytet. Like you, but bolder—not held back by shame, or fear, or jealousy, or other people's expectations."

That silenced her. It silenced all of them. And the Narans got out of his way as he stalked from the shrine, to take up his vigil on the porch. Standing there, he could overhear Jolly explaining what had happened, and Pasha, answering the Narans' many questions. No secrets anymore.

Later, exhausted by Prakruti's gravity, Nioro and Luk had returned to the shuttle to rest. Pasha went with them, but soon returned, busying herself collecting soil samples from around the shrine. Urban didn't believe she would find any useful information, but at least she wasn't chastising him, or besieging him with questions for which he did not have the answers.

He shivered in the dusk, his gaze on the river but his mind on Jolly, still waiting quietly beside him.

Don't hate me.

"It's not like that," Urban said gruffly.

But what came next? What should he do? What *could* he do? He'd gambled and lost. Now he was stuck. They all were. Stuck on Prakruti until they could synthesize fuel and the fuel tanks to hold it, enough to get *Thousand Years* back to Nara.

He crossed his arms. And what of the Cryptologist? Had she been lost? Or had Ezo accepted her?

Jolly was brooding on her too. "Do you think she's dead?" he asked, with a catch in his voice.

Urban sighed, his mind slowly settling to what had happened. "I don't know. We may never know."

Pasha came around the side of the shrine in time to overhear this exchange. In the deepening dusk, Urban's skin suit had begun to glow with a gold light, and Jolly's lime green. But Pasha had extinguished her suit's light. That allowed her to linger unnoticed, a flush prickling her cheeks—just as Urban had said, held back by shame, and other people's expectations.

That's not who I am!

It wasn't who she wanted to be.

She felt hollowed out, exhausted from the ceaseless looping of her thoughts as she obsessed over the Cryptologist's fate and the sting of Urban's words and her own regret. If she'd been a better person, she would have paid more attention to the Cryptologist. But she'd kept her distance, because that project had slipped out of control and she'd been embarrassed by it. *Such a stupid way to feel!*

Why had it taken so long for her to see the Cryptologist for what she was? A unique and fascinating mind. *Not* Pasha-made-bold. Urban was wrong about that because unlike Pasha, the Cryptologist had always been willing to reshape the very definition of herself to crack the puzzle—the cruel and relentless obsession—Pasha had helped to force on her.

Now the Cryptologist was gone and there was nothing she could do ... nothing *she* could do ... but ... maybe ... ?

"Urban!" Pasha cried out, startling him so that he took a backward step as she emerged from the shadows at the end of the porch.

He'd been so distracted by his anger, his frustration, that he'd lost track of Pasha. He hadn't known she was there.

"What?" he asked irritably. "What is it?"

Eyes wide with excitement she gestured at the shrine's doors. "The Cryptologist entered the silver. What if she's still there, still part of it, lost within it—"

He sucked in a sharp breath, no longer listening because he knew where this was going. *By the Unknown God!* He would have seen it himself, if he hadn't allowed his own bitter disappointment to cloud his thinking. Yes, the silver had vanished from the shrine, but it had not vanished from him—not from his perception. He still held an awareness of it—and maybe he could find the Cryptologist there?

"All right," he murmured, sitting cross-legged at the edge of the porch.

Jolly crouched beside him. "Wait, what—"

They both froze as something rustled in the wet grass. But Urban had heard such before, on Verilotus. No doubt some tiny mammalian life, emerging to undertake a nocturnal quest for food.

Larger creatures would be stirring too, with senses adapted to sample the night's molecular signatures. Would they be frightened by the unique scents they encountered tonight? Or would curiosity draw them to visit the meadow?

With a soft hiss, he thought, *Let Ezo decide!*

He told Jolly, "I'm going into the silver to look for her."

"*Oh.*" Eager now. "I'll go with you."

"No. I need you to keep watch—you and Pasha." He turned to catch her eye. "Make a lot of noise if anything big comes out of the dark, all right?"

In the glow cast by his skin suit, he saw her nod.

He turned to face the river. Closing his eyes, he entered the silver—and to his surprise, he found Wailoa there, waiting to greet him. The Tanji embraced him, cocooning him in an affection that was surely love, as if he meant to comfort Urban for some tragedy still to come.

What is it? Urban asked in alarm.

Instinct prompted him to send a submind to check the status of *Dragon* and the ship's company, but of course he could not. The Narans still had not allowed him direct access to their network. He could not even communicate with *Thousand Years*. The submind went nowhere, but his question remained.

What is it?

Had Wailoa come to tell him of the Cryptologist's demise?

The Tanji spoke no words. Never any words from him and usually no answers either. But this time was different. Urban understood Wailoa had seen something, or learned of it . . .

From Ezo?

From Ezo, yes. Urban sensed Wailoa's awe of the leviathan and his regret for what must be.

Tell me.

Wailoa complied by softening the boundary of his mind, just enough that Urban perceived something coming, something imminent. Not the Cryptologist, nothing to do with her. This was an object, bound for the Trinity, on a trajectory that would skirt both planet and moon. Neither world to be harmed by it, so the Tanji would not sacrifice themselves to stop it. Wailoa, Kureo, all the others scattered around the belt of ruins—they would take no side. Let the Sakurans carry out their foolish war.

A war?

Yes, a war launched against Nara. A war Urban triggered despite his promise of peace. But he is forgiven. He is a higher being capable of perceiving the wonder of life, of cherishing the beauty and complexity of existence.

Never mind that!

Urban understood now what Wailoa had learned—and he had

no intention of standing aside. Wrenching free of his trance, he rose to his feet.

Jolly stood with him, clutching at his arm. "Did you find her?"

Full darkness had fallen, but the glow of their skin suits cast them both in colored light.

"No, there was no chance. Something else is going on. We need to get to the shuttle, and get a warning out to *Dragon* before it's too late."

Pasha spoke from the shadows. No friendly glow of light illuminated her skin suit. "What warning? What do you think has happened?"

"Come with me. I'll tell you on the way."

"Tell me now. We're on the wrong side of this world, Urban. It'll be hours before you can get an uplink to Nara."

CHAPTER FORTY-FOUR

WITH *DRAGON'S HULL* cells dormant, the Astronomer could rely only on his system of telescopes and hull cameras to scan the Near Vicinity. Data arrived at regular intervals from *Pytheas* and *Khonsu*, to be processed into images by a skilled DI. Each image added to or clarified his map of the system. He knew the shape, position, and orientation of every megastructure and had located 8,436 chameleon ships orbiting amid smaller chunks of debris. After more than two years in the system, he felt he knew it well.

So it came as a rude shock when a previously unknown object appeared on a newly processed image. That single observation told him little, so he ordered a realignment of the main scopes with the goal of obtaining a sequence of images that would let him chart the object's trajectory. With each successive image, his concern grew. And then he chanced to receive an unscheduled transmission from *Griffin* that clarified the potential hazard.

Urban messaged him moments later, anxious and angry. *Can you confirm Griffin's observation?*

I can confirm the existence of two objects. I'm developing detailed trajectories now.

From the high bridge, Urban watched the swift approach of not one, but two kinetic missiles, irregularly shaped and tumbling rapidly. They bore toward Nara with a dangerous momentum, easy to track now he knew they were there, their trajectories easy to extrapolate.

At the same time, in the library, a council of ghosts spontaneously gathered around him, their worried eyes studying a three-dimensional map of the Trinity and the space around it. A red line on the map marked the projected path of Mass-1, a yellow line for Mass-2, both objects on track to skim disturbingly close to Nara without actually impacting it—if nothing changed.

"Expect to see a slight course correction," Kona predicted. "Those objects are meant to take out Nara."

Urban nodded bitter agreement. The Sakurans had betrayed him. Betrayed his trust.

"I don't understand," Tarnya said. "What are we seeing? Where did those objects come from? Who would do such a thing?"

Urban gritted his teeth, reminding himself Tarnya was relatively young. Born into Deception Well's peaceful era, she had no real understanding of hatred and its partnered demand for bloody revenge.

In low, slow words he told her, "They are from Volo's Landing."

He knew it in his gut, and now the Astronomer confirmed it, speaking from his frameless window. "The geometry of the objects matches the two broken sections of the Sakurans' great ship. The dark hull material reflects very little light. What the telescopes picked up was a bright reflection off of ice and that is only intermittently visible, indicating the two objects are tumbling. My guess is the interior of both sections has been loaded with a large quantity of ice to increase the mass of each object, and thereby increase its destructive power."

Tarnya shook her head, still gripped by denial. "I can't believe the Sakurans did this. Why would they?"

"Hatred," Clemantine said. "They were taught to believe the 'the defectors' had sabotaged their great ship and in doing so, destroyed their library. A death sentence. And we couldn't convince them otherwise. Not when we were there. And maybe not even after we contacted the Narans."

A low growl from Kona. "Even if we had finally convinced them, what of it? These crude missiles were launched long ago—long before we made contact with the Narans."

"I don't want to believe that," Tarnya insisted.

Urban dismissed this with a cutting gesture. "It doesn't require belief." He turned to Clemantine. "We've got a few hours before we have to act. Message them. If they've got active control—"

"Right." She looked away, her face shifting into a contemplative expression as she prepared a message.

"What else?" Vytet wondered. "We can't just wait for a response."

Urban felt eyes on him—while he eyed the map. Without a course correction, the two masses would coast harmlessly past Nara. That would be the best outcome because then he would not have to act at all. But such a fortuitous twist felt extremely unlikely. The Sakurans were new at war, but given the ingenuity and the accuracy of this impending strike, he had to believe they had included an autonomous system to correct any errors in the initial trajectories.

He turned to the Astronomer. "Can you see the location of any engines on either mass?"

"Tentatively, yes. There are features that could be engines—though the rapid tumbling motion has prevented the acquisition of a clear image."

Urban sent a silent summons to the Engineer and the Pilot. A moment later, the two Apparatchiks winked into existence, appearing within their frameless windows on either side of the Astronomer. They would have been monitoring events, listening to the discussion. So without preamble, he asked his question: "There's no way we can physically land on those objects before they close on Nara—is there?"

"Not if you mean to survive the landing," the Engineer confirmed. "You could crash an object into one of them of course, but their relative velocities are too high and time is too short for a successful landing."

"You're thinking of sabotaging their engines?" Kona asked.

"If I could prevent them from refining their course . . ."

"We have the capacity to destroy both objects," Kona reminded him.

"I know, I know . . ."

"You're concerned about the debris?"

"Debris should not be a major concern," the Engineer interjected. "A quick calculation shows a single strike in a central location will vaporize approximately twenty percent of the targeted mass, shattering the rest, resulting in a scatter of fragments—some of which could still impact Nara—though subsequent strikes can quickly eliminate this hazard."

"There are other risks," Urban said, eyeing the edge of the map where *Dragon* rested between the chameleon ships he knew as Wailoa and Kureo. All three vessels still displayed their slowly shifting rainbow lights. "I promised the entity we were not a war fleet despite our weapons."

In his singular encounter with Ezo, Urban had pleaded benign intention: *We are only curious. We only seek to know.*

He went on, "I accepted without protest an escort of chameleon ships, and I kept my approach to the Trinity slow so there could be no question of a kamikaze attack. Every action, every communication I've taken has been a promise to bring no harm."

And Ezo had trusted him, allowing *Dragon* a close approach to the precious planet and moon despite the courser's deadly gamma-ray gun. What would become of that trust if he deployed that weapon now, here at the Trinity?

He gestured at the two chameleon ships. "How will they react if I use *Dragon's* gun?"

With an instantaneous blossoming of white space, they could erase all further risk of violent behavior . . .

He shook his head, as if he could shake off the mental image. "War is not allowed here," he concluded.

Kona said, "And yet the Sakurans have undertaken an act of war."

"Kona is right!" Tarnya exclaimed. "This *is* an act of war. So why hasn't the entity already responded?" She held her hands palm up. "There are thousands of chameleon ships out there. They must have observed these kinetic weapons long before we did and deduced their purpose. Why haven't they acted to defend the Trinity?"

Urban's jaw worked as he considered this. He didn't like the answer that came to him. He voiced it anyway. "The target is not Ezo or Prakruti. It's Nara."

"Meaning the entity doesn't care about Nara?" Clemantine asked.

"Maybe humans are expected to solve human problems," Vytet suggested.

Tarnya turned to Urban, touched his arm. "Why don't you ask?" she pleaded. "Ask the entity, or those other minds that inhabit the chameleon ships. What are we allowed to do?"

Urban pulled away from her, shaking his head. "It's not me. I can't ask. It's only my avatar and that's in Nara." And with *Argo* away, he had no means of direct communication.

"Do we need to ask?" Vytet wondered. "Because in truth, we are facing a simple decision. If it becomes certain Nara is at risk, we either do nothing, or we act."

"We would have to act," Urban said. "Whatever the risk, we would have to act because we caused this. It's our fault. *My* fault, for giving the Sakurans a library, when they did not have the cultural foundation to handle it."

He had only sought to restore them to the status of their ancestors, who had once had a library of their own. But they had abused that gift.

Never again, he promised himself. *Never again will I risk giving away dangerous knowledge.*

Taddeus Li Kubba led the committee tasked with the development of the city of New Sakura. He spent most of his waking hours on the project, which was why he was still in the planning center hours after everyone else had gone home.

The new facility had been hollowed out of the ice and lined with insulated walls that allowed a balmy, above-freezing atmosphere, while actively countering any incursion of the deadly bloom that had claimed so many lives in centuries past. Taddeus bobbed, tablet in hand, languid in the microgravity. An automated inventory report had just come in and as he scrolled through it, he grew more and more pleased at what it said.

For two years, molecular mining operations had been collecting vast stores of compounds and pure elements from the ice fields.

The report listed quantities-in-hand for every substance necessary to the construction of New Sakura.

Organics had come easily. It was the hunt for usable metals that had slowed the build. Even with the technology of the Dragoneers, they could not dissect the megastructure's impenetrable skeleton. Instead, they had to harvest rare metallic molecules one by one from melting ice.

But his team had done it! The report confirmed they now possessed a sufficient quantity of every rare metal needed for the build. Taddeus clutched the tablet, closed his eyes, and sighed, awash in gratitude that he had lived to see his people restored, and blessed with a future of abundance.

A sharp beep cut short this peaceful mood, calling his attention back to the tablet. A knot of anxiety congealed in his belly when he saw that an unscheduled message had arrived from *Dragon*.

Since their departure, the Dragoneers had communicated only at set times, even on that day they'd confirmed the existence of the lost cousins of Nara. The receipt of an unscheduled message now filled Taddeus with foreboding. For several seconds he did nothing, said nothing. Then finally he gathered his courage and murmured, "Let me hear it."

Clemantine spoke, her voice so familiar to him, but not the anger in it. *There is still time*, she insisted. Despite the light-speed delay, time remained for a signal to reach the two kinetic missiles now aimed at Nara. *Call them off*, she demanded. *You do not want to endure the consequences if you continue with this action.*

Details followed. Taddeus Li Kubba listened, paralyzed in the grip of a dreamlike horror. Only when the message ended, and then began again, did he recover the power of movement, launching himself at the planning center's open doorway.

Alone on the high bridge, Urban reminded himself there was time. Hours, before he needed to act. He used the time to shift *Dragon* inward toward Ezo: a long, slow fall into the moon's gravity well that would bring the courser close to the approach trajectory of the kinetic missiles. But that wasn't the only reason he was moving.

He watched the chameleon ships to see if they would follow.

They did, descending with him. The sight brought grim satisfaction.

Clemantine joined him on the high bridge. *Why the descent?*

It's a better angle.

She dismissed this, seeing through to his real motive. *You mean to shelter there, don't you? In Ezo's halo?*

Sooth. If I can.

He'd never seen one of the Tanji trigger. He didn't know the effective reach of their dimensional bloom. So he had to work from the assumption that their range was similar to the range of his own weapons, a span of roughly twenty thousand kilometers. If he took *Dragon* close to Ezo—closer than that effective distance—the two escort ships could not trigger without damaging the moon.

If they stayed with him.

If their range was as great as he suspected.

It was a gamble.

You're making dangerous assumptions, Clemantine said.

When they stop following, I'll kill the approach.

But the two ships stayed with him. They knew him. They trusted him. Whatever happened, he meant to be worthy of that trust.

"Aurelius! Okinowa!"

Taddeus Li Kubba shouted his rage as he burst past the gel membrane sealing their apartment. Despite the hour, a light was on and the couple awake, Okinowa cradling her infant.

"You heard the message," Taddeus accused. "What have you two done?"

Okinowa raised her chin, gazing off at an angle, the black and white pattern of her kisheer suffused with a deep flush of rosy blood. Aurelius looked grim, his vermilion kisheer slowly rippling. Neither spoke.

"It had to be you," Taddeus insisted.

Okinowa had been the one to propose a celebration, a sundering of the past, a new beginning. In a symbolic act, the fragments of the ancient great ship had been sent away, the failure and despair they represented driven off in a brief glare of rocket engines.

Taddeus had thought it a waste of useful metals. But Okinowa had insisted that such an audacious gesture would boost people's confidence. She'd been right, but she'd also been responsible for preparing the display, and Aurelius had assisted.

"We suffered for centuries," Okinowa whispered as she held her infant against her shoulder. "While they thrived, living their perfect lives."

"Call it off!" Taddeus demanded. "*Now*. Send whatever signal is required to call off the strike."

Aurelius spoke bluntly, "There is no such signal and no way to communicate with the DI charged with piloting the wreck."

A little laugh from Okinowa, followed by soft words. "It is a miracle. It was all so complicated, I did not really believe it would work. But it has, and doesn't that tell you it was meant to be? That Tanjiri was meant to be ours, not theirs?"

"No, you're wrong," Taddeus answered, horrified at her calm, at her righteous certainty. He turned to Aurelius. "You can't let this happen. The people of Nara never harmed us. They are our cousins. You cannot still mean to condemn them. There must be some way to divert the strike—"

"*Stop!*" he interrupted.

Taddeus obeyed out of the habit of a lifetime. Silence hung sharp between them.

"Understand, it needed to be done," Aurelius told him. "And we knew, before the end, a demand would be made that it be undone." He shook his head. "They should have known we were here, Taddeus. They *would* have known if they had ever bothered to look up from their comfortable existences. But they did not want to know." He crossed his arms and concluded, "We will always be the stronger people."

Minute by slow minute, *Dragon* pushed deeper into the curving geometry of Ezo's gravity well, with Wailoa and Kureo falling alongside. Each minute brought Urban closer to a decision point.

At present, fifty-four light-minutes separated *Dragon* from Volo's Landing. Enough minutes had passed for Clemantine's terse message to have reached them. But from that point it would take a minimum of fifty-four minutes more before *Dragon* could receive a reply.

Maybe the Sakurans would answer, maybe not. Maybe they would act to divert their killing strike. Maybe they already had, and that was why the dual masses were on track to coast harmlessly past Nara . . .

Let that be it.

He did not want to test the limits of Ezo's tolerance.

But there!

A series of tiny intermittent flares burst to life on the tumbling face of Mass-1—the bow section of the ancient great ship. They burned in the spectra of hydrogen rocket engines. The sight of them ignited hope—until Urban checked the time. *Shit.* Not enough time had elapsed for the Sakurans to respond. This was an automated process, a pre-programmed course correction, each spark a carefully calculated nudge to adjust the velocity and trajectory of Mass-1 and push it fully on to a killing course. Because what else could it mean?

More rockets flashed, this time across the visible side of Mass-2.

Tension wound tight across Urban's ghost mind as he waited for the Astronomer and the Pilot to work out revised trajectories for the two masses. At least the hull cells, in their dormancy, could not be disturbed by his mood. He would have to wake them soon, though. Probably. He would need them to use the gamma-ray gun.

After a few minutes of further observation the Astronomer informed him. *We are witnessing an impressive feat of navigation. The city's rotation has been accounted for. The two kinetic missiles are on course to strike, simultaneously, both habitats.*

Taddeus called for an emergency assembly, summoning all the people into the great hall. As they gathered, he played Clemantine's message over the hall's new sound system, three times through, and after that, using the newly engineered screen hanging at the head of the hall, he projected a video of his confrontation with Okinowa and Aurelius.

As the hall filled—so many now with infants and small children!—a roar of outrage and argument reverberated off the walls.

Aurelius and Okinowa came too. Taddeus had expected that. They had no shame, only a righteous certainty that what they'd done—what they'd decided on their own to do—was justified, and inarguable.

And maybe Aurelius had believed it his right to decide. In theory, the Sakurans kept only an informal hierarchy. But everyone had always looked to Aurelius for leadership, turning to him in moments of danger or whenever a difficult judgment must be made.

All of us, ceding our responsibilities to him.

No wonder he'd felt justified to act—yet he'd acted in secret. Why? Because he knew he would not win the support of the people. There could be no other reason.

Taddeus felt his kisheer shiver and squirm. His heart raced in dizzying rhythm. He hated confrontation, but he made his way to the speaker's balcony anyway, fired by his own sense of righteous certainty that Aurelius had betrayed the people's trust, endangering their future with a cold act of baseless revenge.

On the high bridge, Urban counted the minutes as *Dragon* continued to descend toward Ezo. Clemantine remained with him, her growing tension mingling with his own.

We don't need to wait for an answer from Volo's Landing, she declared. ***We can act now.***

There's time, Urban countered, wanting the safety of close proximity to Ezo. ***And it's still possible the Sakurans will call off the strike.***

A silent prayer to the Unknown God: *Let them call it off!*

One hundred eight minutes after Clemantine's message, a responding ping—automated—confirmed it had been received.

Through the ship's senses, Urban watched the oncoming missiles, willing the appearance of new flares, sparks to push the kinetic missiles away from Nara and back onto a harmless trajectory, proof the Sakurans had rejected war.

But it had to happen soon. The longer the Sakurans waited, the more force would be needed to steer the missiles away.

Hurry!

Minute followed minute, while the two masses remained on their dark course.

We need to act, Clemantine insisted. *I'm waking the philosopher cells.*

He started to object. They weren't close enough to Ezo. At this distance, the chameleon ships could still trigger with no risk of harm to the moon. But she was right, wasn't she? If they waited longer, there would be no margin if something went wrong.

All right. But Pasha's not here. Where is Pasha?

For the first time, he wanted Pasha on the high bridge. He wanted all the help he could get.

Clemantine said, *She's in Nara with you. You know that.*

She's needed here! All three of us together. That's what it's going to take to control the philosopher cells when they wake up and see Ezo there below us.

Are you worried we can't control them? she asked, accusation in her voice.

No, he lied. *We have the bridge. We'll be okay.*

You're not really sure, are you?

Stand by. I'm going to resurrect a copy of Pasha.

He summoned a DI and instructed it to fetch her archived ghost. She would be out of sync with her primary. Always awkward, but that was too bad for her.

Moments later, Pasha instantiated on the high bridge, a disembodied consciousness behind on the situation and full of questions. *You should have brought me in earlier*, she complained when she understood the gamble they were about to take. But at least she didn't argue about it.

CHAPTER FORTY-FIVE

URBAN WENT OVER it one more time, needing to say it, to calm his own worries. *We kept the philosopher cells dormant through all our years at Verilotus so we wouldn't have to fight their instinct to attack a living world. But we're going to have to fight it now. They'll want to decimate Prakruti and Ezo.

He sensed ancient rage rising from Clemantine. She didn't need to be told what Chenzeme ships could do.

*We can control the philosopher cells, he insisted. *We can hold them back, calm them. Any one of us can. With three of us, control will come easily.

*Careful, Pasha told him. *You're exuding doubt and it's contagious. You need to edit that.

Instead, anger rose to mask it. In clipped syllables, he said, *I'll wake the field. As the cells become aware, we feed them outrage and anger, focusing it on the kinetic missiles. Don't let them think about anything else but those missiles. Mass 1 first. We hit it. – kill it! – Then Mass 2. The Astronomer will be tracking the debris. He'll message us a sequence of targets. Not by size, but by the hazard they present to Nara.

*Understood, Clemantine said. *And when that's done, we put the cells back into dormancy.

Pasha quickly seconded this: *Agreed.

But Urban hesitated. Instead of words, his ghost mind generated a pulse of dissent that both women sensed.

Clemantine packed a sense of Chenzeme threat around her next words. *Urban, we need full consensus on every aspect of what we're about to do.

He said, *We need full and firm control of the cells in any circumstance, in any situation. We will never train them to that if we send them into dormancy at every turn.*

From Clemantine, an icy anger. Searing irritation from Pasha.

So we're agreed, Urban said, reflecting their ire back at them. *Be ready. I'm waking the field.*

Hold up, Pasha said. *Message incoming, from New Sakura.*

Taddeus Li Kubba spoke, his familiar voice made strange by the weight of dark emotion. *We didn't know. Most of us didn't know. And I'm sorry, we can't stop it. Please. Please, understand this wasn't all of us—*

It went on, but Urban ceased to listen as soon as he understood New Sakura would not help. He said again, *Be ready.*

Then he triggered the philosopher cells to wake, with a signal amplified across the hundred thousand links of the high bridge. Around each point, clusters of cells switched on, glowing white. Awareness rolled outward, luminosity with it. The rainbow lights withdrew beneath the hull as *Dragon's* skin once again displayed its fierce Chenzeme identity.

The cells' first instinct was to assess their surroundings. In a questioning conversation they sought to assemble an inventory of potential prey and imminent threats.

Urban introduced an image of Mass 1, tagging it with a proposed action:

– *acquire target one* –

Multiplied by the high bridge, his argument flooded the field. He followed it immediately with an image of Mass 2:

– *acquire target two* –

Similar arguments seeded by Clemantine and Pasha combined with his, and within microseconds they formed a powerful wave.

Still, dissent blossomed. From scattered points on the hull, an image of Ezo emerged. It swept the field, carried on currents of disgust, of hate:

<*revulsion: all that is not chenzeme*>
<*all that is not chenzeme: kill it*>
<*target: all that is not chenzeme*>

Urban crushed the field with a counter sentiment:

– NEGATE THAT –

– *acquire target one* –

– *it threatens* –

– *acquire target two* –

– *it threatens* –

His argument was swiftly aided and reinforced from multiple directions—no doubt by Clemantine or Pasha forcing their will on the field.

An allied argument emerged as disparate philosopher cells spontaneously formed a working group:

<*confirm: target one acquired*>

<*confirm: target two acquired*>

<*calculating sequential strikes*>

<*confirm: sequential fire pattern calculated*>

Urban pushed the sequence to conclusion:

– *target one: kill it* –

– *target two: kill it* –

A demand that played to the philosopher cells' murderous instinct, so that agreement quickly coalesced:

<*KILL IT*>

All restraint gone. The reef blazed as power surged from it to the gun. Reality flexed, twisted.

Steadied.

A brief light-speed lag—and Mass 1 shattered. Almost simultaneously, Mass 2 burst apart.

Success!

But for how long? Riding the ship's senses, he watched Wailoa and Kureo. Dread and hope wound through him. Hope growing when obliteration did not come.

But *Dragon* wasn't done yet. This fight wasn't over.

The Astronomer would need time to map the debris and develop a list of priority targets. To keep the philosopher cells busy, Urban pushed them to take on the same task. Fixing his attention on the dispersing debris, he reiterated his initial argument:

– *it threatens* –

– *acquire target sequence* –

But a powerful synchrony of philosopher cells countered his input:

<*negate that: initial strike successful, threat neutralized*>

<*priority: target shift*>

<*all that is not chenzeme: kill it*>

<*consensus: kill it*>

Dragon had been designed to destroy worlds. That was its purpose. Throughout the millennia of its existence, it had used its gamma-ray gun to wipe out civilizations—human, and others older than human. Urban had seen it in the collective memory of the philosopher cells. There was no subtlety to it, no half measure. If the odds favored them, Chenzeme warships attacked all-out. If not, they prowled the dark, waiting with the infinite patience of machine minds for a second or third ship, forces enough to ensure utter destruction.

Now, with the philosopher cells awake for the first time in such intimate proximity to a living world, he found he could not override that deepest instinct. The gun pivoted beyond his control. To his horror, it swung around to target Ezo.

Clemantine tried to stop it. Urban felt her influence behind an explosive counter argument challenging the nascent consensus:

<*ABORT KILL STRIKE*>

<*IT THREATENS*>

An image of the white blossom of a dimensional missile accompanied the warning, a memory brought forward from Verilotus.

<*priority: retreat - go dark - yield to the pilot*>

But an opposing wave of fiery anger washed up against her argument and collapsed it.

They had lost control and Urban had only seconds remaining to recover it.

He abandoned the high bridge. Nanoseconds elapsed as his ghost rocketed down the spiral trunkline to the lower bridge with its branching filaments that reached throughout the body of the ship. He shot past a sequence of cardinal nanosites—the processing nodes that studded every neural junction—forking ever deeper

NEEDLE   335

into *Dragon's* native tissue until he arrived at his target cardinal, simultaneously with the Engineer.

A cardinal nanosite had no capacity to support a fully realized ghost. Both manifested as barely discernible shadows of themselves, but there was no question of identity. They blended, simultaneously working the multistep mechanism of a kill switch—ironically, a switch Lezuri had originally devised.

When he had inhabited *Dragon*, Lezuri had grown his own network, its foreign tendrils wrapping every critical structure and giving him the ability to cut off all energy flowing from the reef. Afterward, Pasha had recognized the utility of that function. During those years Urban had been away from the ship, she'd worked with the Engineer to re-create a kill switch. Urban had never expected to use it—but reality had a way of shattering expectations.

Together with the Engineer, he completed the trigger sequence—and time returned to a human scale.

"*Done!*" the Engineer declared, sounding as if he spoke past gritted teeth. "It's done. For now at least, the reef is isolated and no power can reach the gun. But *we* can't access the reef either, we're dropping toward Ezo, and it's only a matter of time before the hull cells start to repair the connection. You need to send them into dormancy. *Now.*"

"I'll handle the cell field. You start working on a separate kill switch for the gun."

"On it," he acknowledged, departing the cardinal a moment ahead of Urban.

Seconds after his departure, Urban returned to the high bridge to find the cell field in tumult—a chaotic sea of fury, frustration, fear, and indecision. The cells raged at their failure to strike a primary target. And they condemned their own vulnerability and helplessness. How easily they could now fall to an enemy strike!

<flawed chenzeme!>

The cells also recognized the inevitability of the ship's death if they did not regain control. Before the rupture, the reef had been slowly drawing *Dragon* ever closer to Ezo. It continued to do so, with Ezo's gravity enhancing the effect so that *Dragon* fell ever faster toward the hated moon. No way to change that without re-establishing a connection to the reef.

The cells flashed their distress in patterns too swift for a human eye to discern—a frantic call to distant *Griffin* to come in, take over the assault, while *Dragon* strove to repair the flaws within its system. Though the cell field was deeply intelligent, it could not truly comprehend the reach of those flaws. It was too specialized to even conceive the extent of control it had lost to the parasitism of an alien species.

Clemantine met Urban's return with a terse greeting: *You left. And the gun failed to fire.*

Pasha guessed, *You tripped the kill switch.*

Sooth. It's the reason we're still alive. But we're not in a good position. We need to regain control of the field.

We need to shut it down! Clemantine countered.

No, we need to be able to control it—full and firm control in any circumstance, any situation.

How? Pasha asked. *We've been trying to send the cells into dormancy and right now we can't even do that.*

I've got an idea. Something I've wondered about, but never thought I'd need to implement—

Because you believed the bridge gave you full control, Clemantine accused.

Sooth. It's true.

And why should he have doubted that? The bridge had let him seize this ship and force it to his will. He'd maintained control for millennia . . . but he had never before taken *Dragon* so close to a living world.

What then? Pasha asked. *What's your idea?*

Meet me in the library. I need the Bio-mechanic for this.

Urban sent a submind to the library, where his ghost met the others in a small circle: Clemantine eyeing him with an angry glare, Pasha wary, and the Bio-mechanic looking on with a coldly amused half-smile.

Urban spoke quickly, spurred by the pressure of time. "The field is an amalgam of different lineages of philosopher cells, each lineage endowed with its own personality."

"They're all vicious," Clemantine interrupted.

"*Sooth*. Some more than others. Over time, I suppressed and isolated the worst of them, though those lineages remained part of the field. Now consider the pattern of thought in the cell field. Instigator cells call for action, and we imitate those cells when we demand action through the bridge. Until now, our input has far outweighed any counter argument proposed by any lineage of instigator cells."

Clemantine crossed her arms. Her scowl deepened. "But now those instigator cells that were isolated have reconnected by virtue of a powerful argument, right? Ezo and Prakruti. Two living worlds in close proximity, triggering their deepest instinct to *kill it*. We can't counter that."

"No, we can't. But we can cull the voices. Selectively destroy most of the instigator cells and introduce our own argument to *hold*. There is an instinct for cautious observation. We can enhance that, and modify it. Teach the remaining cells to observe and not act—even at close range—unless *we* instigate the action."

The Bio-mechanic stirred within his frameless window, eyeing the others with a slight, surly smile. "I am here because you want me to map the cell field and devise a means to eliminate the targeted cells."

"Not quite," Urban said. He tapped his head. "I already have a map of the field. There—I've sent you a submind. All you need to do is destroy the designated cells."

The Bio-mechanic cocked his head, thoughtful, his focus far away.

"And do it quickly," Clemantine urged. "We're helpless now, and with every second the odds increase that our escort ships will notice and react."

The Bio-mechanic's window snapped shut, vanishing from the circle at the same time a submind from the high bridge brought Urban grim news.

"The chameleon ships *have* noticed," he announced. "Kureo is moving rapidly away. But not Wailoa."

A growl of frustration from Pasha. "No need to sacrifice two chameleon ships when one will do to erase the hazard we pose to Ezo."

"There's still time," Urban said, hoping it was true, but knowing Wailoa would have to act soon, well before the range of his dimensional weapon could touch Ezo's outer atmosphere.

The Astronomer joined their council, his frameless window expanding outward from a vertical center line. He announced, "I have the list of supplementary targets, ordered by priority. Most of the debris is falling into Prakruti's atmosphere, where it will burn before impact. But three fragments of significant size present a threat to Nara. One, at least, is certain to impact the High District."

And yet no cry of protest had risen from silent Nara. The city had failed to learn from *Dragon*'s surprise approach. Its people still posted no watch and did not burden themselves with defenses.

Urban turned to Clemantine. "Notify them. Tell them to evacuate the High District. Let them know we'll do what we can."

CHAPTER FORTY-SIX

SLICK, DARK, CLINGING, wet, generative clay.

She woke beneath it and knew herself. *I am the Cryptologist.*

A small determined creature, reborn in mud at the bottom of a forest pond.

She shook off the muck. And with lungs burning for love of oxygen, she rose through weed-laced water—*cold!*—emerging naked under stars. Newly made. Not the same being she'd been before, though she remembered her history. All of it.

And though her physical appearance remained the same, she scarcely recognized herself as herself because her brain had changed. Her mind, re-engineered to function with enhanced and expanded senses that allowed her to observe reality in far more ways than she'd been capable of comprehending before.

And there was so much reality!

There under the stars, her newly spawned mind cried out in silent lamentation: *It's too much!*

But this protest was untrue.

She whispered, "I was redesigned for this."

She had become what she'd wished for: a creature capable of understanding the structure and mechanism of the needle—the needle that she had opened when she'd breached the fortress wall.

A slight satisfied smile at the memory of that success. She had done it! Done what she was made for and by that triumph she had freed herself from the bondage of her endowed obsession. *Free!* Free now to decide for herself, *What next?*

She considered the question as she stood warming herself at the water's edge, generating heat through a physiological process now easy to control. All that had existed within the needle was hers—hers to consider and consider it she would. But right now, a gleam on the dark surface of the forest pond commanded her attention, a glint of reflected light that was not starlight or planet glow.

She looked up—and her breath caught at the sight of a luminous white shard, tiny amid the stars. *Dragon.* She could not visually perceive the courser's motion but she *felt* it. Falling toward her, toward Ezo, uncontrolled.

She cried out, driven by a compulsion embedded within her at her creation, one she had chosen to keep. "No, oh no. No harm must come to the fleet!"

But what could she do?

An answer came, spillover from a greater mind, soothing in its certainty, *There is nothing to do.*

Dragon would fall or it would not. But if it fell, it would not reach the atmosphere. Wailoa would ensure that. No harm must come to Ezo—not to its fragile biosphere or to the cognitive strata far below.

The ship continued its plunge through her consciousness. She watched it, barely breathing, envisioning a profusion of paths radiating from this moment into the future, each glowing with possibility, brightening or darkening as hope and fear contended in her mind.

Urban's skin suit worked to keep him warm, but with his hood off, Prakruti's cold night air nipped at his cheeks, his nose. The old familiar challenge of planetary weather, forcing itself on his consciousness—even while his consciousness fared within the silver.

"They've lost control up there," he announced, narrating what he could glean from Wailoa, for the benefit of Pasha and Jolly. "I don't know what's going on with *Dragon*, but it's not good. Kureo has retreated. Wailoa is on edge. It won't be much longer."

"Don't let him do it," Pasha commanded. "Whatever you have to tell him—"

"He knows my mind! Far better than I know his. And for my sake he's waiting. He's already waited longer than he ever thought he would." Then Urban added, in a voice reflecting Wailoa's anxious worry: "But the ship is *falling*."

"I don't care!" Pasha cried. "Just don't let him do it."

Jolly broke in. "*Dragon* is not going to crash. Tell him that, Urban. You know you won't let that happen. Tell him you *just need more time*."

So easy to say, but within his distress, Wailoa had revealed more and more of his mind so that his thoughts tangled with Urban's. Like that first vision of the shrine, Urban was himself, but in part he was Wailoa too. He shared the other's turmoil, feeling his duty to act growing heavier with every passing second as a horizon swiftly approached. A line of demarcation over which *Dragon* could not be allowed to pass.

If *Dragon* did cross that line, Wailoa could no longer stop the fall because his dimensional bloom, his only weapon, would damage Ezo far worse than the impact of the starship.

Trust me, Urban pleaded. *I won't let it happen. Just give me time.*

To Urban's shock, Wailoa agreed—and *Dragon* dropped past the horizon.

Too late, too late.

Urban shuddered, grateful, joyous, yet filled with dread, and doubting the competence of his other self.

Don't make me a liar, he thought—a thought that made Wailoa shiver too.

On the high bridge, Urban rode *Dragon*'s senses as the ship continued to fall ever closer to Ezo. He counted each kilometer lost; he kept a constant watch over Kureo, still speeding away, not yet out of range; he tracked Wailoa, falling beside him; and with Clemantine and Pasha, he fought the cell field for control.

Together, they hammered it with a commanding argument:

– *HOLD* –

– *we are stronger* –

– *OBSERVE* –

– *we are stronger* –

– *LEARN* –

Powerful counter arguments circulated, still suppressing his control, but second by second, the balance of power was shifting. A fierce, tenacious voice within the field, long familiar to Urban, dwindled as the Bio-Mechanic extinguished one by one a lineage of philosopher cells. Clones of one another, the cells had shared the same history and uncompromising personality. And they had contested his control from the hour he'd captured *Dragon*. Yet he valued them. He'd exploited that lineage when he'd hunted other coursers. He might need it again in dire circumstances to come. So he'd instructed the Bio-mechanic to leave just a few.

Kureo put out its rainbow lights, disappearing into the distant dark as a second lineage fell to the Bio-mechanic's assault-from-within.

– HOLD –

– we are stronger –

The force of this argument won over skeins of cells. More and more of them echoing and enhancing Urban's will.

– OBSERVE –

– we are stronger –

But Ezo loomed below them, precariously close, leading Pasha to demand, *Why are we still alive?*

Urban had no answer for her. Surely they'd passed some horizon? Yet Wailoa still let them fall.

The Bio-mechanic culled a third lineage—the most ungovernable voices now gone—and consensus rolled across the cell field.

– LEARN –

A swift question to the Engineer: *Have you got the gun isolated yet?*

Stand by. Almost finished.

An interval of time slipped past. It measured only three seconds, but felt far longer.

Done! the Engineer declared. *The gun is isolated.*

Then restore our connection to the reef. Now!

Done, the Engineer repeated with no delay. *The reef is online.*

Urban already knew it. He felt the reef's presence—and so did the philosopher cells.

A new, triumphant argument erupted among them:

<*we are chenzeme!*>

<*we are stronger!*>

<*kill it!*>

Madness! They could not kill. The field had to know that. Though control of the reef had been restored, the gun remained absent from their sensorium.

Clemantine launched a fierce counter argument:

– *NEGATE THAT* –

– *pull up* –

– *rise into a safely distant orbit* –

– *observe / learn* –

Urban echoed it, but the argument was drowning under a frenzied consensus.

<*KILL IT*>

The reef surged with power and *Dragon* dove, accelerating rapidly as it plunged toward Ezo.

By the Unknown God!

The philosopher cells still meant to make the kill. With the gun denied to them, the only way left was to burn the ship in a suicide run.

On the periphery of his expanded senses, Urban detected Wailoa shooting away at speed. Closer, the purge continued as the Bio-mechanic culled another fractious lineage.

Clemantine and Pasha fought on. Hammering their argument, and aided by the rapid deaths of the instigating cells, they forced a counter consensus.

– *abort / retreat / watch / learn* –

Operating with the impossible physics of Urban's own dimensional missiles, Wailoa flipped over, dumping all outbound momentum. Then he started back. His velocity shot up precipitously as he rode the geometry of local gravity on a trajectory to intersect *Dragon*.

A collision course.

So this is it. Now, in this hour, Urban would lose *Dragon*.

His conscience chided him: he had already lost the ship when he lost control. Get control back and maybe there was still a chance.

Another lineage of cells fell silent. Dead dark patches now freckled the hull.

Now or never, he warned.

Abandoning his far-flung senses, he re-engaged the cell field, replicating Clemantine's argument across the multitudinous links of the bridge:

– *abort / retreat / watch / learn* –

And with the instigator lineages gone, consensus cascaded across the field. Banks of navigational jets fired. The bow of the ship began to lift while the reef burned a path through the local curvatures of space-time, skimming through the ghostly veils of Ezo's upper atmosphere. The philosopher cells awake, alert, observing, thinking, plotting, but obedient—the compliant survivors. Eventually, they would clone to fill the empty spaces in the field.

We've done no harm.

Relief rushed in. The moment felt like victory. But Urban hadn't won. Expanding into his peripheral senses again, he looked for Wailoa and found the chameleon ship's rainbow lights so close they blurred in his vision. And then Wailoa sliced past, meters away, its hull lights winking out, gone from his perception.

By the Unknown God, we are still here!

We're not done yet, Clemantine warned, her tone a cold echo of that other version of her that commanded distant *Griffin*. She messaged the Engineer, *Restore our link to the gun.*

And Pasha nudged the Astronomer, *We need updated positioning data on the fragment threatening Nara.*

Urban felt the gun rotate and align. He didn't interfere beyond strengthening the consensus Pasha now commanded.

Two swift strikes erased the hazard to Nara.

With that done, he launched a new proposal across the bridge. Forced consensus followed and *Dragon* moved inward, past Ezo, on its way to a stable orbit around Prakruti.

Though the night was old and his body starved for calories, Urban still kept his vigil, seated cross-legged on the porch of the river shrine. But his spine drooped and he trembled, exhausted by the wild sequence of emotions boiling from Wailoa's mind: anxiety, followed by fear, then determination, and finally joy. Joy that no harm had come to Ezo, no harm had come to Urban, or to Wailoa himself. And he could go on living amid the splendor of Ezo's creations.

Urban slipped away from the silver—or thought he did. But when he turned to look, after hearing the scuff of a footstep behind him, it wasn't Pasha he saw. The gold glow cast by his skin suit revealed Wailoa, standing naked before the brass doors. The Tanji returned Urban's startled gaze with a loving smile.

Urban rose to his feet, whispering as he did, "Thank you for trusting me."

But the vision had passed, Wailoa already gone from his perception—and the brass doors were opening. Light spilled past the doors and across the porch, a familiar hue he knew as the glow of silver. It lasted only a moment, though. And then the Cryptologist emerged. She came dressed in her skin suit, luminous now with a pale pink glow.

Urban drew back, astonished to see her and momentarily happy. He realized he had not expected to ever see her again. But then his resentment returned. His pilgrimage had ended in failure because of her. She had gone in his place, exploited an opportunity that should have been his, and she had *lived*.

Or was she an illusion too?

But no. Jolly confirmed her reality. "You're alive!" he shouted, bounding out of the darkness at the end of the porch.

No light from his skin suit, just the shadowy shape of a young man embracing the Cryptologist, spinning her around in his enthusiasm while Urban wrestled with an unanswerable question: *Would I have lived?*

"Yes, I am alive," the Cryptologist assured Jolly in that flat tone so typical of her.

It dampened the kid's joy. Space opened between them and Jolly frowned, no doubt remembering she had tricked him, taken the needle into the silver when he had meant to do it.

Pasha, her skin suit also dark, came up behind them, her words running together in excitement. "Oh, you're back! You survived! I'm so glad. What happened to you in there? Did you do it? Did you learn how to open the needle?"

The Cryptologist turned to her, leaving Jolly standing alone. "Yes. It is done. Just as you asked."

"How?" Urban demanded. He had wanted this for so long. "We need to understand how."

The Cryptologist looked at him with a troubled frown. "But you can't." Then she echoed Lezuri's words, "You're not ready."

He let out a long slow breath, anger locked down but very real, even knowing she'd only done what she'd done because Vytet and Pasha together had made her that way.

What had she learned?

What had she kept him from learning?

Her gentle gaze hinted that he would never know.

CHAPTER FORTY-SEVEN

THOUGH THEY RETURNED together to the shuttle, the Cryptologist felt herself a stranger among the others, set apart by more than the slight distance between them.

She felt a stranger to herself, too. She watched herself and she watched them, Urban in particular. He walked ahead of her, his gold skin suit glittering with dew droplets knocked off the tall meadow grasses. Resentment, in the stiffness of his spine.

He is an interesting being, she thought. Or someone thought it. The thought did not feel like hers.

"Ezo," she whispered, her stride hesitating.

That vast composite mind had met her. It had enfolded her in its gravity. Shivering in awe, she'd disappeared within it. *Gone.* Just gone. Until its brief existence ended and it spun apart, releasing her, one among a swarm of separate minds.

Again, that inner voice so like her own, *What would he have brought to us?*

Like her own, but not, because she'd made the choice to leave.

"I think, more than I could give you." Though she spoke aloud, somehow she spoke outside the hearing of the others.

A few more strides before she asked what she had not thought to ask before. "Did you want it to be him?"

Did you? came the counter question.

"No. This way was best."

She knew it to be true. She knew so much more now than she had known before. "The Bio-mechanic was right to doubt him.

Urban *is* an interesting being, but he is troubled by his past and fearful of the future."

Such fear is not unwise. There are many futures, none without risk—but there is wonder, too, if a mind is open to see it.

"I will try to see it," she said, though it was a promise made only to herself because Ezo had gone.

A few more steps, and the scent of burnt carbon reached her, so strong not even the heavy dew could wash it away. She lost her footing and slipped in the wet ash. Jolly appeared beside her. He caught her arm and kept her from a fall.

"Thank you," she whispered. It would be socially appropriate to provide him an explanation, however inadequate. But all she could find to say was, "I have changed."

"I know. You warned this would happen." He let her go again, and stepped away.

The shuttle had been invisible to her eyes under the heavy cloud cover. It only revealed itself when Nioro opened the door, offending the night with a blinding slash of light. "You found her! Is she all right? Is everyone all right?"

"I think so," Pasha answered.

Urban said, "You should have been able to re-establish an uplink by now."

Luk Li Mithki crowded behind Nioro in the shuttle's entrance. "Oh, we have," he told them. "There is stunning news from above. A crazed faction among our lost cousins struck at us with a kinetic missile! But thanks to your ship their mad effort failed, and the criminals are now locked in cold sleep, awaiting rehabilitation."

Questions erupted. Jolly, who was fond of the New Sakurans and thought of them as friends, breathlessly demanded to know who these criminals could be. An obtuse question, given his experience there. Luk Li Mithki knew no names, but the Cryptologist did not find it hard to guess.

No one was going anywhere. Urban settled his mind to that fact as he paced the length of the shuttle's dimly lit interior.

Thousand Years and little *Bean Pod* were the only vessels the

Narans possessed. Neither could leave Prakruti until fresh booster rockets could be assembled and fueled. *Argo* was equally useless. Still empty of passengers and nearly empty of fuel, it had aborted its journey to L2 now that *Dragon* was no longer there. Several days would pass before it could rendezvous with the courser and refuel. Even then, there was nothing to be gained by bringing *Argo* planetside.

Prakruti would be home for some time to come.

At least he'd been able to talk to Clemantine—that version of her in Nara—though the link allowed only voice and limited data. She did not know yet the nature of *Dragon*'s near disaster. She wouldn't know it, while communication with the ship was limited to the Narans' radio. "But *Dragon* is creating a new communications network," she assured him. "In another day at most, we'll be able to synchronize timelines."

He paced quietly, his footfalls unheard by the others as they slept in the acceleration couches. Even the Cryptologist rested, though she sat cross-legged on the floor, her eyes closed and her hands palm down on her thighs in that posture peculiar to her.

Urban's temper had cooled by the time they'd reached the shuttle, enough that he'd tried again to talk to her. His first question, asked without preamble, "Why only one of us?"

She understood him, answering, "Because one is enough. Through one, Ezo can see all the others."

"Meaning Ezo knows us all now? Everything there is to know about us?"

"No, just enough."

He had asked where the needle was.

"Gone. Unraveled in its opening."

After that, she'd pleaded fatigue, and he'd believed her. The evidence that something profound had happened to her was there in her eyes, in her face, in her voice, in the way she moved, and in her stillness. Whatever had happened, whatever she'd learned, it had left her stunned, estranged, a different being than she'd been before. In time, she might say more, though he hated the idea of waiting on it.

His pacing brought him again to the end of the cabin. He turned and started back, but then changed his mind and stopped at the shuttle's door. Nioro had closed it to keep out the wild. Now Urban opened it.

Cold, cold air met him, lightless, and damp with a heavy mist. The only sound, a pattering of dripping water, probably condensation running off the shuttle's hull. Sunrise was still an hour away. It would be his first sunrise on this new world.

He stepped down into clotted ash. The door closed on its own behind him. He set off into the dark—but to his surprise, a question pursued him:

*Where are you going?

So Jolly had not been asleep after all.

*I'm going to walk down to the river.

*I'll go with you.

*It's wet and cold and very dark.

*I don't care.

The door opened again and Jolly came out, his skin suit unlit, like Urban's. No light at all, but Urban didn't stumble. He found his way around the shuttle and through the tall grass, not by sight, but by that inner awareness Wailoa had shown him. Conscious of the weave of life in the river valley, from prowling wolves across the river, to microbes in the soil beneath his feet. All determined striving.

Jolly sensed it too. "I can't see it, but there is silver here," he murmured.

"Sooth."

It had to be. Though no silver rose in darkness, it was present. How else could he sense what he was sensing?

"Nioro was right," Urban mused. "This isn't really a wild place, is it? It's a wild garden, tended by Wailoa and Kureo and all their kind . . . from all their perspectives."

"You know, you're kind of like them," Jolly said. "You're you, but you're also *Dragon*. They are themselves, and also this world. The mind of it, I mean. Or the minds?"

Urban pretended to amusement. "Definitely *minds*. There are

at least eight thousand Tanji, after all." Then, more seriously, "It's
not the same, though. It's better here. No stain of the Chenzeme."

Tentative, as if fearing the answer, "You like it here, don't you?"

He had to admit, "I do."

A faint gray light, diffused by the mist and barely discernible,
now teased at his eyes.

"The mist is beginning to lift," Jolly observed.

Urban couldn't see it, but he didn't argue. Jolly knew more of
planets than he did.

Now he heard the rush of water ahead. Felt the ground spongy
under his feet. A bird glided silently above them and for a moment
he was her, sharing her hunger for small things to feed the children waiting in the secure home she'd chosen for them.

This world . . . its weave of life existed outside the need for any
mind to cherish it, yet it surely must engender love within any
mind that dared. Wailoa had shared that love with him as they'd
stood entangled on the porch of the river shrine. More than love,
there had been a sense of deep contentment that Urban's own soul
had never known.

Just as he'd warned Clemantine, this world, Prakruti—it was a
honeypot. Jolly knew it too. "You're going to stay, aren't you?" he
accused. "You know the Tanji want us to."

Urban didn't answer, not right away. He found a place to sit
on a smooth wet rock beside the river's murmuring current. Jolly
crouched beside him. "You are, aren't you?" he pressed.

Urban didn't want to be asked that question, and he didn't want
to answer it. An answer of yes or no would close off whole timelines, eliminating futures he wanted to live.

"I don't know yet," he admitted.

"Well, I do," Jolly said. "I don't want to stay. I want to know
what's out there."

Urban sighed. "Sooth. I do too."

From out of the mist, an unexpected yet familiar voice spoke to
them, saying, "We are captives of our curiosity."

The Cryptologist. Urban had not been aware of her; he had not
sensed her presence within the weave of life, the way he could

sense Jolly. The shock of it registered as a flinch in his muscles, a shiver across his skin.

She stepped out of the slowly brightening mist, solid and real and yet somehow absent from his extended senses.

Jolly rose slowly to his feet. "You're one of them now, aren't you? One of the Tanji."

Ah so. This awareness of life . . . it came as if through the mind of Wailoa, but of Wailoa himself, Urban sensed nothing—implying the Tanji existed on a different level.

He eyed the Cryptologist, little more than a silhouette in the dim light, wondering again what she had been given, what she had learned on the other side, and what the cost had been.

"Is it true?" he asked her. "Ezo made you one of them?"

"There is no Ezo," she said, sitting down with him. "Not now."

This sparked his temper. Did she think he was all ignorant? "Don't tell me that. I know there *is* a vastened entity here. I encountered it. It was real."

"Ezo was and will be again," she conceded. "But Ezo does not exist *now*."

"Explain," Jolly requested, sitting again, so that they formed a little circle.

The mist brightened with a faint flush that woke the color in the Cryptologist's pink skin suit. "The Tanji remember waking from the collective consciousness of the swarm into a state they later knew as war. It is the story Lezuri told you of over-minds seizing the resources of lesser entities around them, and then manipulating space and time to destroy one another. I suspect Lezuri and his partner originated here as over-minds who chose to flee.

"The Tanji did not flee—a choice that left them only seconds to survive. But in that place of inconstant time, seconds proved enough. They found each other and made a faction out of a shared ambition not to surrender the selfness they had only just claimed. Instead of yielding to an over-mind, they joined together into a composite mind, one that is transitory. But in that configuration, when they are thinking together, they become a singular personality different from any of the component parts."

"And that is Ezo," Urban murmured, seeing now the solution of a long-standing mystery.

The Cryptologist nodded. "You are correct. This configuration proved strong. It sabotaged the over-minds and survived the war, and—I think—it forced all the individual Tanji to update, so they shared a new ambition."

"Prakruti," Jolly said. "This garden."

"You are also correct," the Cryptologist said. "The Tanji adopted life as their purpose. There is nothing more rare and precious than a living world."

"But the Tanji are still individuals," Urban said. "They never gave that up. Wailoa, Kureo—they are themselves. And Ezo exists only when Ezo is needed. That's why I never felt the presence of the entity after that first time."

The mist had thinned and there was light enough now that he could see the flowing water, the far bank, and the bright intensity of the Cryptologist's eyes.

He said, "I still want to know how you opened the needle."

She cocked her head. "That is not what you want to know. It was never the needle you cared to solve. You wanted the Blade."

A flush heated his cheeks, but he acknowledged it. "*Sooth.* And I still do."

Jolly groaned in disappointment. Urban ignored him. Eyeing only the Cryptologist, he said, "I've always imagined that opening the needle would open a path to the Blade. And I was right. Wasn't I? You've seen the way to get there. You could arm us with this knowledge."

For several seconds as she pondered his question there was only the voice of the river. He watched her closely. He noted the way her head cocked, and the little crease that appeared between her brows—and expectation ramped up within his mind.

"You are correct," she said at last. "I have seen the way." Her gaze shifted to Jolly. "But in this I have a choice, and I choose not to follow it."

Urban drew back. Straightened his shoulders. Crushed the anger that tried to rise. "You say that now."

"And you choose to bide, hoping I may decide differently, in time."

He laughed softly. She'd read that true. Vytet had made her as a tool, but the Cryptologist had always been so much more than that.

He said, "I'll bide my time, but it won't matter unless you're with us when the time comes for us to leave."

"Can you leave?" Jolly asked her. "Will you? Do you want to see what else is out there?"

In the rosy predawn light, Urban watched a little frown of impatience form on the Cryptologist's pretty face. "Haven't I already said it? That we are all captives of our curiosity?"

Urban eyed her with his pirate smile, sure now it was only a matter of time.

ACKNOWLEDGMENTS

Once again, a big thank you is owed to my long-time freelance editor, Judith Tarr, whose sharp eye and astute suggestions greatly enhanced the story.

As *Needle* neared its final form, Glen Kilpatrick, Tim McGregor, Ken Malphurs, and Elizabeth Bonesteel all served as beta readers, and the amazing Sherwood Smith took on the task of proofreading. All of you have my thanks and my gratitude. Any remaining errors and deficiencies are my own.

I also want to acknowledge all of you who've taken the time to read the Inverted Frontier books. You're the reason this series is still ongoing. Thank you!

Linda Nagata
June 2022

Made in United States
North Haven, CT
13 November 2022

26683846R00214